The

DIABOLICAL
MISS HYDE

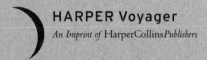
HARPER Voyager

An Imprint of HarperCollins*Publishers*

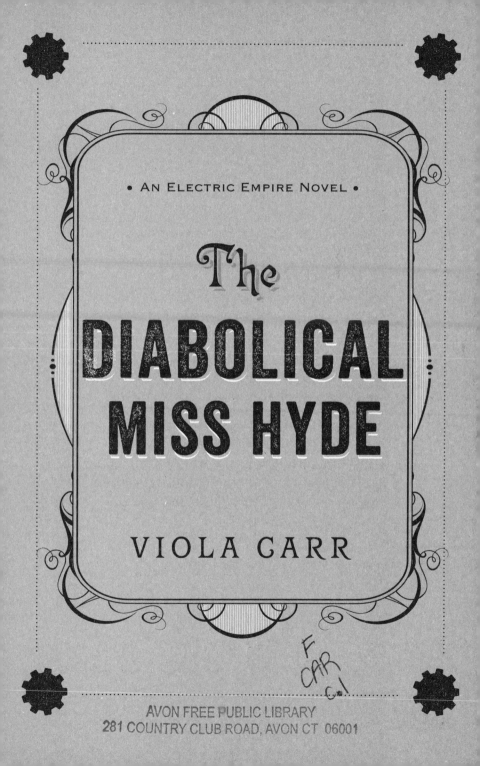

• An Electric Empire Novel •

The
DIABOLICAL
MISS HYDE

VIOLA CARR

Harper Voyager and design is a trademark of HCP LLC.

THE DIABOLICAL MISS HYDE. Copyright © 2015 by Viola Carr. All rights reserved. Printed in the United States of America. No part of this book may be used or reproduced in any manner whatsoever without written permission except in the case of brief quotations embodied in critical articles and reviews. For information address HarperCollins Publishers, 195 Broadway, New York, NY 10007.

HarperCollins books may be purchased for educational, business, or sales promotional use. For information please e-mail the Special Markets Department at SPsales@harpercollins.com.

FIRST EDITION

Designed by Janet M. Evans

Library of Congress Cataloging-in-Publication Data has been applied for.

ISBN 978-0-06-236308-4

15 16 17 18 19   OV/RRD   10 9 8 7 6 5 4 3 2 1

I do not like thee, Doctor Fell,

The reason why I cannot tell;

But this I know, and know full well,

I do not like thee, Doctor Fell.

—MOTHER GOOSE NURSERY RHYME

The

DIABOLICAL
MISS HYDE

A SHUDDER IN THE BLOOD

•●•

IN LONDON, WE'VE GOT MURDERERS BY THE DOZEN. Rampsmen, garroters, wife beaters and baby farmers, poisoners and pie makers and folk who'll crack you over the noddle with a ha'penny cosh for the sake of your flashy watch chain and leave your meat for the rats. Never mind what you read in them penny dreadfuls: there ain't no romance in murder.

But every now and again, we gets us an artist.

See here, now. A woman lies dead, in a bleak slum alley just yards from the glittering theaters and smoking purple arc-lights of Haymarket. He's bunched her petticoats around her thighs, a black mess of blood. And above the knee, smart as a slice o' bacon, he's hacked her legs clean off.

Her face is twisted, shock and terror and *sweet-baby-Jesus-just-let-me-die*. Takes his precious time, this cove. What a charmer.

A ragged crowd has gathered—naught more invigorating than someone else who's dead when you ain't—and the coppers have put up a screen of bedsheets to keep 'em back. But no one can see me, not where I'm hiding, and I get meself a real good look. It's mid-morning—I've spent a fitful night in here, let me tell you, trapped in my bleak nightmare of chains—and the watery sun's already blotted out by the city's pall of filth. Here in the slums, where the *weird* lurks, the gutters run with shit and the air chokes me, thick with cholera and black lung and the forbidden stink of spellwork. Rats the size of tomcats snigger glint-eyed in the shadows, coveting that tasty corpse. The rotting alley walls lurch inwards, threatening to crush us all.

And here's Eliza, examining the dead meat for evidence. Sweet Eliza, so desperately middle class in those drab dove-gray skirts, with her police doctor's satchel over her shoulder. She's a picture, ain't she? Gaffing around with her gadgets and colored alchemy phials, those wire-rimmed spectacles pinched on her nose. Her shiny brass goggles, with their electro-spectrical this and telescopic that and ion-charged the other, perch on the brim of her tiny hat. Her little clockwork pet scuttles beside her, four spindly brass legs splashed with muck.

Here's Eliza. And here's me, the canker in her rose. The restless shadow in her heart.

"As I thought!" exclaims Eliza, poking at the dead woman's severed thighs with a pair of iron tweezers. "A bayonet, Inspector. Or some other blade shaped thus. And a saw for the bones. Our killer came prepared."

"Wonderful. Another lunatic. Must be something in the water." The plain-clothes copper with the mustaches—yes, he, the pompous prat—strides over. Detective Inspector Hoity-Toity, in his tall hat and fine black morning coat. *What's the color of a tuppence piece? Copper, copper . . .* Blue-uniformed constables—coppers, crushers, bobbies, peelers, whatever, they're corrupt scumbags all, and I'd give 'em a sprightly chase, so I would—the crushers mill around, parroting their fool questions, chasing away nosy broadsheet scribblers, and kicking at dirty urchins with rat's tails or cloven feet who try to sneak in.

"Any sign of the missing limbs?" says Eliza.

"None." The detective strokes his mustaches. "But I don't imagine they walked away by themselves."

"Amazing. Your deductive powers are truly uncanny."

He grins. "One does one's best."

I itch to spit in his face. Detectives are London's new golden demigods, with eyes and ears everywhere, guardians of the shady line between *them* and *us*. What with coppers plus government spies and the god-rotting witch-burners of the Royal Society, it seems these days everyone's a snout, and we weird-city folk don't take kindly to being lorded over.

Still, to be fair, they're dab hands at catching bad men, this copper and my Eliza—more than one bloke gone kicking to the hangman who'd testify to that, not to mention the ones moldering in Bedlam or starving their skinny arses off in electrified dungeons at Coldbath Fields—and I for one won't shed no tears if the charming cove who sliced up this poor dolly swings on a chilly morning to sate the bloodthirsty Newgate mob.

My blood boils, alive with all the rage Eliza don't dare to feel. I want to throttle the bastard who did this. I want to grab that copper by his immaculate throat and squeeze until the lights in his eyes wink out.

Eliza's fist crushes tight . . . but then she blinks, and shivers, and shoves me away. And like a mad wife locked in the attic, I'm helpless.

God's poisoned innards. I scream and fight, clawing for her eyes, but she ignores me. Me, Lizzie Hyde. Her own blood. Her own SOUL.

I hate this. I want to get out. To roam where I choose, feel skin under my fingers, harsh winter wind on my face. To put a match to this ugly world and dance while it burns.

But I can't escape. Not without her help.

If I could, d'you think I'd be pissfarting around here, flapping my gums with the likes of you?

———◈◉◈———

"Dr. Jekyll?"

"Eh?" Eliza blinked, dizzy, and the world shimmered back into focus.

Beside her gaped the dark hole of the theater's stage door. Bills plastered on the walls advertised GISELLE and THE ETHEREAL MISS IRINA PAVLOVA and THE IMPERIAL RUSSIAN BALLET! alongside painted slogans that announced THE QUEEN IS DEAD and KILL ALL THE CRUSHERS and BREAD BEFORE PROFIT. Her little clockwork assistant, Hippocrates, twittered self-importantly at her skirt hem, his square brass body gleaming on long hinged legs.

At the alley's end, on Pall Mall, electric carriages rattled by, their glowing blue coils spitting sparks. Prostitutes prowled, a riot of feathers and colored gowns. Clockwork servants in frock coats clicked and whirred, striding to and fro on brass legs as they ran their errands, their painted plaster faces impassive. The ground rumbled as the Electric Underground hurtled by, and from an iron vent in the street, black smoke and sparks billowed in the stink of hot copper wire.

And the corpse, at Eliza's feet. Another murdered girl, in a city haunted by murdered girls. Another killer, to be brought to justice with careful detective work and the miracles of science.

But faintness rinsed her thin, a fevered warning. A dark specter shifted inside, a restless shadow yearning to be free . . .

Unwilled, an image hovered: the elixir in its black glass flask, locked up safe in Eliza's secret cabinet. Crouching in the dark, a sniggering demon. Whispering to her. Waiting . . .

Her mouth watered. Rage, ecstasy, sweet oblivion. The dark pleasure of doing whatever she pleased, saying what she felt. Not the impotent mutterings of lawyers and judges, but the keen slice of a blade . . .

"Are you quite all right?" Harley Griffin steadied Eliza's elbow. The dark-haired inspector wore plain clothes—smart black coat, tall hat, neatly knotted necktie. Even the dirt of this greasy theater-side alley didn't seem to rub off on him.

"Perfectly well, thank you. Shall we proceed?" Briskly, Eliza smoothed her skirts and adjusted the heavy brass optical atop her head. Thick metal rims, with a set of glass lenses of differing colors and properties. The latest scientific equipment. She'd designed it herself. Not strictly orthodox, but what useful gadget was?

Griffin flipped the pages of his notebook. "Victim's name is Irina Pavlova—"

"The ballerina?" Eliza's fists clenched. Not a poor woman of the street, then, savaged by some evil predator, all too replaceable in the eyes of polite society. The Imperial Russian Ballet's veteran principal dancer, famed for her beauty and grace. No less an outrage. No more a tragedy. Truly, no woman, celebrated or forgotten, was safe.

"The very same. It was to be her swan-song tour, I'm informed." Griffin looked mildly pained. "It certainly is now."

"A ballerina with no legs," mused Eliza. "Can that be random? Seems . . . lurid, wouldn't you say, for a typical recreational murderer?"

"No legs," muttered Hippocrates, his little electric voice sullen. "Recreation. Does not compute. Re-examine reasoning."

Griffin shrugged. "Hardly a fit target for radicals, either. Still, these Muscovites are known to be rash and hot-headed. Perhaps a family feud, an act of vengeance. Teaching the enemy a lesson."

"Evil Russian slayers? You do enjoy your wild-flung theories, Harley. Have you considered a crazed rival ballerina wielding a hatchet?"

Griffin grinned, and made a note in his book. "Rival ballerina, hatchet. You mentioned it first. And my wild-flung theories have paid dividends before, as you well know."

Oh, aye. That warm, secret murmur tickled her spine. *Razor Jack and his glittering steel princess. You can't forget Jack, Eliza, his fingers in your hair, warm metal whispering against your cheek. Do you even want to?*

Eliza shivered, sweating. "Indeed. What I can tell you is that the blood on Miss Pavlova's dress is still rich. A large quantity has pooled without disturbance on the cobbles, and there's one bright splash on the wall. Which points to syncope as the mode of death."

"The Queen's English would be adequate."

She rolled her eyes. "Exsanguination, Harley. Miss Pavlova

bled to death. Also, the lividity—that's the post-mortem bruising, as the blood pools in the corpse, you can see there, beneath the petticoats—that indicates she died where she lies. Our man knelt here." She pointed to a pair of smears in the blood beside the body, the imprints of trouser-clad knees. "And worked undisturbed. For at least four or five minutes, I'd say, to get this done."

"You're saying he amputated while this poor woman was still alive? God's blood." Griffin stroked his impeccable mustaches. Since the sensational trial of Razor Jack, he'd been the Metropolitan Police Commissioner's darling. Which was why he was permitted to employ a lady legal medicine specialist with dubious antecedents, when his Scotland Yard colleagues regarded her with suspicion and scorn, at worst outright mirth.

"Yes. A professional could do it faster, but it doesn't take an expert to sever a limb in this fashion. Any able man with these tools could have done it."

"But why didn't she struggle, for heaven's sake? She's within earshot of the busiest street in Haymarket. No, there must be something more."

Eliza crouched and sniffed the dead woman's lips. "Aha!" She dug in her satchel for a swab, wiped it carefully over the woman's tongue, and applied solution from a glass bottle. Drip, drop. The golden liquid spread and soaked in, and the swab turned bright green.

"Just as I thought," she exclaimed happily. "Our victim was drugged. A narcotic, or . . ."

She tipped her optical down over her spectacles and flicked a few spectroscopic filters, frowning. How strange. Perhaps an alchemist's concoction . . . "Ah, I see," she covered briskly. "How delightfully mysterious. I shall require further tests—"

"The short version?" Griffin interrupted, with a long-suffering smile.

"For shame," she scolded, but her skin prickled. If it was alchemy, she'd have to find a way to cover it. To keep the evidence and omit its origins. "Don't you know one ought to avoid conjecture in the absence of basic facts?"

"Flirt with disaster, then, and give me your best guess."

"If I *must* speculate so irresponsibly? A substance that rendered her insensible, unable to complain. Though it might not have deadened the pain."

"Ether, then," suggested Griffin. "Or chloroform?"

"Chloroform," echoed Hippocrates hopefully. His blue glass *happy* globe flashed atop his head. Even Her Majesty had breathed chloroform while giving birth, to ease the pain. Chloroform was respectable. It didn't get you burned at the stake.

"No," said Eliza, taking another swab of the substance and storing it carefully away for analysis. "That stupefies slowly, over a period of minutes. Our man had a few seconds, at most, to subdue her . . . that is, I venture no screams were heard?"

Griffin snorted. "How did you guess? Dozens of noble citizens strolling by and no one noticed a thing. Not even a man covered in blood, carrying a woman's legs. My astonishment knows no bounds . . . here, get that fellow away at once!"

Crack! A magnesium flashlamp erupted in a puff of white smoke. The constables dived on a skinny man wearing a ruby-red waistcoat and dragged him away, knocking over the camera he'd somehow managed to erect just beyond the linen barrier.

Griffin shrugged. "Damn fool writers. They encourage more crime than they expose. As I was saying: our killer seems to have escaped rather easily."

"Perhaps the murderer lives or works nearby," offered Eliza, secretly satisfied. She was acquainted with that particular damn fool writer, and good riddance to him. "Or, he brought a change of clothes. Such an elaborate scenario isn't enacted on the spur of the moment."

"Agreed." He flipped through his notebook again. "Two . . . no, three different witnesses say they heard an arc-pistol going off, around two o'clock."

Eliza frowned. "But I see no gunshot wounds. Strange, that the killer should give himself away, after going to such effort to quieten this poor woman. Assuming it was he who fired."

"So why remove the legs? Is he making a point? A warning?"

"Perhaps. If you still favor your vengeful Russians."

"Or a souvenir," suggested Griffin grimly. "A trophy from the hunt. Perhaps we have another collector on our hands. Like the Lincoln's Inn Toe Merchant . . ."

"Or the Mad Dentist of Fleet Street. The world is alive with strangeness, Inspector."

"Most of it in my division, apparently," he grumbled. "Always with the lunatics. Why don't we ever get a good honest bludgeoning anymore?"

"Indeed. This decline in boring murders is most distressing. But . . . hmm." Eliza flicked on a buzzing electric light, a tiny filament set into a small half-globe of brass, clipped to her waist on a short chain. She slotted the correct filter into her optical. A violet glow blossomed, and she scanned the body swiftly before the filament burned out with a bright metallic flash. The blood glared, a black accusation. But no smears, no creeping gleams.

"As I suspected." She stood, skirts swishing. "The absence of fluids on her clothing suggests there was probably no intimacy. Miss Pavlova was not assaulted."

"Absence of evidence . . ."

". . . isn't evidence of absence, no. But such *interesting* killers are not often so meticulous, nor so restrained. It does rather tend to rule out a purposeless crime of passion."

Griffin cleared his throat and fingered his necktie.

Eliza glanced at her gadget, the goggles still boggling her eyes, and grinned. "Oh. Yes. Fascinating, isn't it? It is called 'ultra-violet.' A gift to my father, many years ago, from Mr. Faraday."

"The Royal Society burned Faraday," reminded Griffin gruffly. "You should be more careful."

Eliza tucked the ultra-violet coil back into her belt purse, uneasy. Griffin had a point. In the past twenty years, while bloody revolution swept the Continent at the behest of sorcerers and charlatans, the Royal Society had become sole arbiters of what was science and what was witchcraft. Anyone found disputing the Philosopher's Laws—or deliberately defying them by dabbling in classically unexplained phenomena—was mercilessly re-educated . . . or worse.

"Yes, well," she commented dryly, "if given free rein, the Royal's Enforcers would burn everyone who dared study any science published since Newton's *Principia*—"

"Do you take argument with the *Principia,* madam?"

Eliza's heart somersaulted. At this new voice, the crowd shuffled and muttered, and the constables suddenly grew deeply fascinated with the contents of their notebooks.

"Oops," muttered Hippocrates, and jigged on jittery feet.

Inwardly, she groaned. *Oh, bother.*

NULLIUS IN VERBA

...

GRIFFIN SHOT ELIZA A DARK *TOLD-YOU-SO* GLANCE and arranged his polite, professional face. "Not at all, Captain. The doctor was merely being amusing."

With what she hoped was a primly confident air, Eliza turned to squint up at her accuser. "And you are, sir?"

"Captain Remy Lafayette, Royal Society." The fellow bowed, but his grin was insolent. His hair was flaming orange, his eyes dazzling azure. He wore a glaring purple tailcoat with flashing epaulets.

Eliza frowned. How peculiar . . . Ah. She tugged off the optical, leaving just her spectacles. Better. Immaculate red-and-gold officer's uniform, white trousers, tall black boots, and a jaunty black hat. Some infantry regiment? Saber—cavalry, then—sheathed at one hip on a black sash, a polished electric-coil pistol holstered at the other. He looked about her age—not old, but no longer especially young—and his rainbow of campaign jewels indicated far-flung theaters of war: India, Calais, Samarkand.

A career officer. How mind-numbingly tedious.

But unruly brown curls spilled carelessly close to his collar, suggesting a disregard for authority that she rather enjoyed. His open, attractive face was permanently suntanned, his hands scarred with gunflash burns. He'd seen some combat.

And his eyes, *sans* optical, hadn't dimmed. Dazzling, electric sky blue.

Her corset suddenly seemed to be laced too tightly. How inconvenient.

She lifted her chin. He was alone, no team of clockwork Enforcers behind him. It didn't make him any less threatening. "Well, Captain Lafayette, I trust you've good reason for interrupting our investigation. Last I heard, murder was still a police matter."

"Police matter," repeated Hippocrates smugly. Eliza swiftly shoved him behind her skirts, eliciting a buzz and an indignant whir of cogs.

"Just a routine check. I trust you'll all cooperate." Lafayette studied her boldly, sizing her up. Examining her simple gray gown, her tightly wound hair, her wire spectacles, and the doctor's satchel slung over her shoulder.

Plain, clumsy, middle-class Eliza, twenty-six years old and unmarried. Police physician and alienist, with a world of dark secrets to hide.

Old resentment frothed in her breast. No wedding ring— nothing so radical—no fraying on his uniform or wear on his boots to tell of the interwar poverty many officers suffered. And a cavalry officer's life was notoriously expensive. No doubt he'd purchased his commission, in the army or the late and sincerely unlamented East India Company, using some indecently vast family fortune—and spent his half-pay leisure time killing foxes on his country estate, lounging in his private box at the opera, and romancing dashing *equestriennes* on Rotten Row.

That didn't explain his commission with the Royal. Or his attendance at her crime scene.

Her mind spun in circles. Did the Royal suspect her? Had they tracked her from Finch's Pharmacy? God forbid, was Mr. Finch in danger? Or had she simply made some trivial slip at a crime scene, conducted some test that wasn't strictly orthodox? Uttered some careless remark that smacked of sorcery, within earshot of the Royal's numberless spies?

Heaven knew, she was more conspicuous these days than she liked. Her name and likeness had made not only the garish penny pamphlets, but the daily newspapers too—notoriety, that horror of all middle-class horrors—in the sensational reports of Razor Jack's trial at the Old Bailey. But the trial was months ago, the murderer long since locked away at Her Majesty's pleasure. And purely by chance, the Royal chose *today* to review her crime scene?

No. This wasn't because of Razor Jack. It was something else. Something more.

Captain Lafayette cocked a single eyebrow, still expecting some reply.

Hungry shadows tugged inside her, a dark undertow. *Ooh, I say. The very devil in scarlet. Sparks'll fly there, let me tell you.*

Eliza sniffed dismissively. Such romantic fascination with danger was for fools who read too many novels. She preferred a more mathematical approach. But the Royal's witch hunts were anything but mathematical. The sooner she got rid of this Lafayette—with his scandalous French name and impeccable British self-importance—the better.

She straightened her satchel with a sharp tug. "Very well. I will cooperate. Now kindly move aside and cease trampling my crime scene."

"Trampling," squeaked Hipp, muffled beneath her skirts. "Move aside."

Lafayette rested a cocky hand on his sword. The iron badge pinned to his lapel was engraved with the Royal's motto, fine silver letters glinting in pale sun: NULLIUS IN VERBA. "You didn't answer my question, Miss . . . ?"

"Doctor," she corrected coolly. "Doctor Eliza Jekyll. And since you ask, Captain, I've no argument with the Philosopher's science. Just with the mis-educated apes who interpret him. Do excuse me." And she stepped neatly around him and crouched again by the murdered body.

Ha ha! Mis-educated apes, eh? That'll tell him. Jesus, you can't even insult the man properly, let alone make a decent effort at flirting . . .

Fuming, she kept her gaze down and yanked out another swab to check for matter under the fingernails. Offending this Captain Lafayette was probably not the wisest course. The Royal had burned poor Mr. Faraday. They'd not think twice about doing the same to her, Eliza Jekyll, medical practitioner of dubious orthodoxy, daughter of an infamous dabbler in arcane diabolicals.

God help her if they ever discovered the rest of it.

Griffin was already covering. He had his career to think about. "I do apologize, Captain. If there's anything you require—"

"Naturally." Captain Lafayette cut him off breezily. "Witness statements, drawings, that sort of thing. I'll have my people examine your findings. You know the drill. It's all just routine."

"Naturally." Griffin bristled like an angry badger, but, with ill grace, he handed over his notebook.

Lafayette digested the inspector's careful handwriting in a few seconds and tossed the book back to Griffin. Then he squatted beside Eliza, his shiny black boots creaking. "What do you make of this?"

She eyed him coolly, slipping her sample into a glass tube and jamming in the cork. "Are you addressing me, Captain?"

Brr. Chilly in here, ain't it? Royal or not, he's a man like any other. Lift them prim-and-prissy skirts o' yours, and orthodoxy will be the last doxy on his mind . . .

"You're the police physician, aren't you?" He prodded the corpse's lips, exposing the small white teeth. He wore a silver chain around his wrist, locked with a seal of some kind. How odd.

Eliza swatted his big hand away. "Kindly cease contaminating my crime scene, sir."

"Contaminating? What do you mean, pray?"

She sighed. Crime scene science was new and mysterious. Few understood it. "Every contact leaves a trace. Our villain, however careful, has unwittingly sprinkled the scene with clues. Clues I am unlikely to unravel once you've smeared your clumsy paws all over them."

He flashed her his smile, a half-sheathed weapon. "Clumsy? Ouch. And I've such a reputation for elegance."

She held up her slim hands, which she'd encased in white cotton gloves.

"Ah! I see. My apologies, Doctor." He peered at the wounds

on the body, this time careful not to touch. "What would you say about the time of death?"

She'd already opened her mouth to retort to some snide remark of his about lady doctors and their hysterical fancies, and her cheeks warmed. "I'm sorry, did you just ask for my opinion?"

He grinned, full force this time, charming as any swell ruffian. "I'm a Royal Society investigator, madam, not an ignorant. Show me science, not detectives' guesswork."

She glared over her spectacles. "Your flattery is wasted on me, sir."

"Is it?" His blue eyes sparkled. "What a shame. It's the part I'm so good at."

His good humor was infectious. She refused to contract it. "Then kindly flatter yourself with an explanation. What, pray, is the Royal's interest in this case?"

"That remains to be seen, doesn't it? Time of death?"

She looked around for Griffin, but he was studiously keeping his distance. "Ah . . . well, the body temperature in these outdoor cases is notoriously unreliable. But from the clotting and lividity? Not before two o'clock this morning."

"The very hour of our famous arc-pistol shot."

"Legal medicine is not an exact science, Captain—"

"*Science* is an exact science, Dr. Jekyll. Material results must have material causes. For an arc-pistol shot to sound, someone must fire an arc-pistol." He inspected the corpse, tugging the bodice's fabric with one finger. "Yet we have no wound. Ergo—"

"The killer must have missed," she suggested. "Or someone else fired the pistol."

"Well? You're a doctor, madam, not an ornament."

A back-handed compliment, if she'd ever received such. Chastened, she rummaged in her bag for a test for gunflash. An arc-pistol would leave a tiny charged carbon residue on the wielder's palm. She adjusted her optical and swabbed the corpse's hands. "Nothing," she reported. "She was almost certainly not the shooter. Which means . . ."

"Do you smell that?" Abruptly, Lafayette strode to the stone wall, three feet behind the corpse, and glared about in the shadows, lifting his nose to the stagnant air.

How peculiar. She rose and followed, Hippocrates trotting in her wake. "Smell what?"

"That." Lafayette's nose twitched, and he bent to the ground, sniffing. "Like a storm. Or . . ."

"Electrical discharge," she finished eagerly. "Yes! I smell it, too. But where . . . ?"

He pointed to a patch of ground, close beside the alley wall. "What's this?" he demanded. "Can you identify?"

She crouched. A small pile of black particles, like coarse dirt. Luminiferous aether, burned by electrical voltage. A large quantity. Too large for a pistol.

She traced a fingertip up the wall, where the stone was . . . melted. In a jagged line, dripping down like glass. As if extreme heat had been applied. She'd never seen anything like it outside a raging house fire.

Inside her, shadows stirred. An alchemical drug. And now this strange heat. How dangerously fascinating.

"Gunflash," she reported, trying to cover her excitement. "Or something similar. Your pistol, sir, if you please."

"I'm sorry, are we under attack?"

She stepped back. "One shot, there, beside that mark. Medium range." He cocked that arrogant eyebrow again, and she smiled sweetly. "*Nullius in verba,* Captain. 'Take nobody's word for it.' You're an investigator, not an ornament."

"*Touché,*" he murmured, and fast as a wild-frontier gunslinger, he drew his pistol and *crack!*

Eliza gasped, her hand flying to her chest. Jagged blue voltage sliced into the stone. Static crackled in her hair. Steam hissed, a swirl of blue-burning aether and the sharp scent of thunder. Hippocrates yelped and scuttled away.

The burning purple coil in Lafayette's pistol glimmered and died. Neatly, he holstered the weapon. Not exactly a flourish, but he didn't need one. Everyone was already staring at him.

She caught her breath, indignant. He'd done that on purpose. But my, he was fast. Accurate. Dangerous. She'd barely seen him move.

He grinned. "Impressed yet?"

Apparently, also an insufferable show-off. Behind Lafayette's back, Griffin rolled his eyes. She could almost hear the inspector grumbling. *Bloody Royal show ponies, all flash and no fire . . .*

"Entertaining as well as decorative," she remarked coolly. "Perhaps you should consider joining the circus. Shall we take a look?" She slotted her magnifying lens and peered at the resulting scar on the wall. Just a faint charcoal smear. Certainly no melted stone. She pointed to show Lafayette. "As you see."

"Hmm. Then what could have carved this furrow? Is it a new kind of weapon?"

A trick question? Uneasily, she thought of nice Mr. Faraday, burned in the shadow of St. Paul's for his insistence that luminiferous aether was a fallacy, that light required no medium, that unseen lines of force held the universe together. He'd never been able to prove it, and the creaking ancients at the Royal sniffed dismissively at his experiments and dragged him away to the Tower.

The Royal didn't use burning as their execution method for religious reasons, as in days gone by. They cared nothing for cleansing the soul. It was merely a horrible death. A warning. Defying their authority was treason, and traitors burned.

Distantly, she recalled her father's secret laboratory, the smell of hot metal, electrical coils glowing in glass globes. His chemical apparatus, bubbling and smoking: retorts; pipettes; flasks of gleaming liquids, green and blue and violet. And little Eliza, just a tiny girl in dusty skirts, blinking short-sightedly under the table. A lonely child, left to her own devices in the big old house with its secret passages, dusty clerestories, and concealed rooms.

She'd listened wide-eyed to his clandestine midnight meetings, arguments, cursing in German and French as well as English, the rapid squeak of chalked equations on a blackboard. She'd understood little of it, of course. Faraday was young, then, barely educated but brilliant, his plain face shining with ideas. Magnetism, electricity, the secrets of the stars, the radical experiments of Volta and Lavoisier, Lamarckian evolution, alchemy and mesmerism and the search for eternal life.

All scientific and political suicide, naturally. Faraday was burned, her father nearly twenty years dead and disgraced.

She'd not discovered the elixir until later, in her adolescent years, when the shifting longings drove her to desperation, and a mysterious man hid behind the curtain at midnight in her flickering firelit parlor and offered her a strangely warm, bitter drink . . .

All of which was no concern of Captain Remy Lafayette, IRS. No matter how charming his address or skilled his handiwork.

"Doctor?" Lafayette's question hung.

"I've no idea," she replied shortly. "What a fascinating conundrum." She peeled off her cotton gloves, heedless of baring her fingertips in public. "Sergeant? I'm finished here. Kindly transport the remains to the morgue."

"Very good, Doctor." Griffin's plain-clothes sergeant signaled to his constables, and two men began to wrap the body in linen.

She tugged on her plain gray day gloves and adjusted them with a snap. "Come along, Hippocrates. Captain Lafayette, I'm due in court. How nice to make your acquaintance. Goodbye."

And she jammed her optical into its leather case on her hip and swept away.

A FOOL FOR A PATIENT

•••

ON NEW OXFORD STREET, THE TRAFFIC CLOSED IN around her. Clanking metal and whirring gears, brass wheels turning and blue sparks showering. Hansom cabs pulled like rickshaws by frantic two-legged clockwork runners careered madly between top-hatted gents and ladies in crinolines and corsets. Black was the predominant color. Mad Queen Victoria had put on mourning for her beloved Prince Consort (murdered by sorcerers, indeed; more likely the poor man died of typhoid fever, but hunt for witches and witches are what you'll find), and fashionable ladies liked to follow suit.

Real horses, too, and donkeys plodded along, pulling carriages or sellers' carts, ears twitching at the noise. Wheels squelched in their refuse, and beneath the carriages scuttled crossing-sweepers, tiny ragged children who scraped up the dung and darted away before they could be flattened.

Eliza was late, and hurried along, clutching her bag to her hip. She was used to traveling unescorted—good gracious, how scandalous—but no need to take chances on being robbed. Amongst the well-dressed gentlemen and ladies lurked the swell mob: professional thieves in disguise, with elaborate ruses and fingers deft enough to rob tie-pins, brooches, even earrings without the wearer knowing.

Hippocrates trotted beside her, clucking, his tiny brass head at the level of her thigh. Cogs whirred inside his boxy body, and his hinged legs pistoned up and down. "Time," he grated in his electric voice. "Old Bailey, one o'clock. Make greater speed."

"Thank you, Hipp, you're a great help." She dodged a young dandy on a speeding two-wheeled scooter and tripped over her skirts, barely keeping her feet. The dandy's umbrella twirled above his head on a tall stick as he swerved along.

"You're welcome." Hipp's *happy* light twinkled. Blue for happy, red for sad. She should install one for smug. No doubt it would flash constantly.

As if to remind her, a distant clock tower chimed a quarter to one. She'd never make it in time along the crush of Holborn to the Old Bailey, not on foot.

"Dr. Jekyll!" A hand tugged at her elbow, that familiar, hyper-energetic voice. "Just the lady I wish to speak to. Quite a mess, wasn't it? What's your opinion of the victim's condition? What kind of madman do you think the killer is? Is it the Moorfields Monster?"

She sighed and turned to see the young writer in the red waistcoat, whom Griffin had unceremoniously ejected from the crime scene. "Mr. Temple," she said pleasantly, "truly, you are the worst kind of pest. Whoever said the murderer was a madman?"

"Isn't he? How many people must one kill and dismember in this town before one qualifies?" Matthew Temple grinned, and it split his pointy face in half like a puppet's. Ragged autumn-leaf hair stuck out from beneath his cap. Under one arm he clutched a sketch pad and a boxy brass clockwork recorder. "I'll have to think of a name for him. The Ballet Beast, perhaps. The Footlights Fiend. Or . . . The Chopper!" He sucked in a theatrical gasp of horror. "What do you think?"

"Matchless. Verily, we have a new Shakespeare in our midst."

"Walpole, surely. King of the gruesome Gothic! And such wonderful material you provide, Doctor. Razor Jack killed seventeen. The Monster has dispatched five so far. Do you think this killer will match that?"

"First, Mr. Temple, we have only circumstantial evidence that there *is* a 'Moorfields Monster.' A few slashings do not a rampant beastly killer make. And second—" She cut him off with a raised finger as he started to interrupt. "Second, sir, I find your enthusiasm for multiple murderers disturbing. The only answer I have for your bloodthirsty questions is 'clear off.' Print *that* in your sordid dreadfuls."

"Clear off," echoed Hipp, and danced a saucy jig, his blue light flashing.

"Oh, come, madam." Temple winked, cheerful, her insults washing off like dust. "You're one of my most popular characters! The pretty lady doctor who caught Razor Jack, both intrepid crime-fighter and damsel in distress—"

"I am not a 'lady doctor,'" she interrupted coldly. "I am a doctor, no more and no less. And if you persist in pestering me, you'll be the one in distress. Good day, sir."

She hailed an electric omnibus, and it squealed to a halt, sparks spitting from the engine's purple-glowing coils. She clambered on, squeezing in amongst black-frocked serving maids and clerks in threadbare suits. A mustached fellow at the end smoked a cigar, and the fug clogged the small cabin.

Hippocrates sprang onto her lap, folding his legs, and she absently petted him as the omnibus lurched onwards. He clicked like a cricket, contented, his lights twinkling, and she felt a small twinge of envy.

If only *she* could be made content so easily. Fatigue tugged at her limbs, and her breath felt too warm in her throat. Her pulse was elevated, the beginnings of an all-too-familiar fever. The air in the omnibus was stifling, smoke and hot breath and sweaty skin. She pulled the window sash down a few inches, but it didn't help.

Temple's idiotic questions, his cheerful disregard for the victims' dignity, only irritated her more. And Captain Lafayette's sly insinuations—his very *presence* in her world, with his smug Royal Society attitude and poorly veiled threats—still itched under her skin like a parasite.

Were the Royal onto her? Or was it just an unhappy coincidence? And why had they sent a flesh-and-blood investigator when an impassive mechanical Enforcer would do?

She thought back to the last time she'd visited Mr. Finch, several days ago now, at his utterly respectable Mayfair pharmacist's shop. Naturally, alchemy was forbidden by the Royal. The Philosopher himself had long ago concluded its aims to be futile. There was no *aqua vitae,* no vital force that held the universe together and sparked life into lifeless matter. Alkahest, the so-called universal solvent, did not exist. You could not make gold from lead, and eternal life was an impossible dream.

But Mr. Finch was a crafty veteran, with a convincing line in "doddery old man" and the mildest, most innocent blue eyes. No one who hadn't seen firsthand his dark, smoking laboratory, with its furnaces, bubbling phials, strange symbols, and crucibles of mercury and molten gold, would ever believe him a criminal. Little chance he'd let something slip to a stranger.

Eliza squirmed in her cramped seat as the omnibus rattled past the ornate turrets of Lincoln's Inn. Perhaps she should warn Mr. Finch. Perhaps she'd been followed to his shop . . . and besides, she was running low on her remedy.

Not her *elixir*. No, she still had some of that, locked away in her secret cabinet like an embarrassing relative. But Finch also brewed her a prophylactic against the addiction, a tranquil balm that—temporarily at least—banished the need that chewed in her veins, ever hungrier the longer she let it fester. The remedy let her sleep, reduced her fever, kept the gibbering nightmares at bay.

Theoretically.

She hadn't sampled the elixir for weeks now. Hadn't slept properly in days. And the famine in her blood was getting nasty. She needed to see Mr. Finch. But if Lafayette was following her . . .

Her heart sank. He didn't need to. She'd stupidly told him where she was going. Such a fool she was.

"Hipp, I want you to wire Mr. Finch." She wound the little creature up with a few brisk turns of his ornate brass key. "In cipher, if you please. Tell him I won't be calling for my prescriptions until tomorrow morning. Oh, and ask him what he knows about a Captain Lafayette, IRS, cavalry officer."

"Yes, Doctor." Cogs and springs clicked as he recorded the message. He could use the telegraph at the courthouse to transmit.

The omnibus pulled up, with a *bang!* and a blue crackle of voltage, on the corner of Old Bailey, where Newgate Prison's blackened stone walls loomed out of the grimy pall, topped with electrified wire. She paid the conductor threepence, hopped out into blessedly cool air, and lifted Hippocrates down.

Distant wails drifted from the prison's dark depths, and a fetid stink hung like fog, a vile gray miasma thick with disease. Typhus was so common and deadly within that they called it "prison fever"—and during particularly bad seasons, they even moved the courtrooms outdoors in search of clean air.

Prison warders and thief-takers in dirty suits mingled with the street mob, those attending trials or visiting inmates or simply raising mischief for its own sake. Most of the visitors were women, dirty sleeves pulled down at the shoulder, hair falling loose from pins as if suggesting the condition of its wearer's virtue.

Everything was for sale to prisoners awaiting trial (or execution) in Newgate, from better food and rum to fresh air to whores and conjugal visits, so long as you knew someone who was willing to pay. Half the inmates had been put there by the Queen's spies—political *agents provocateurs* who fanned the flames of working-class discontent and then exposed the ringleaders for traitors and revolutionaries—or by corrupt thief-takers, who arranged elaborate criminal plans specifically in order to entrap the perpetrators. Those same officials were only too happy to accept bribes now. Even the Metropolitan

Police weren't immune to payoffs and sly dealings. Not all officers of the Detective Branch possessed Harley Griffin's moral courage.

Eliza shouldered through the crowd, Hipp clunking at her heels. The system was crooked. Everyone knew that. But she, Eliza Jekyll, would do her part for justice. Honor demanded it—and if she didn't, who would?

Who, indeed?

At the big studded doors of the Central Criminal Court, a huge clockwork sentry frisked her impassively, its magnetic hands fanning her skirts, ready to buzz and flash warning lights should it detect iron. Judges were fair game for radicals and criminal types with a grudge, and civilians weren't permitted to carry weapons into the Old Bailey.

The sentry clicked in satisfaction and waved her inside. Hippocrates scuttled off importantly to dispatch his telegraph, and Eliza trotted down the wide stone corridor and slid into a seat in courtroom two, just in time.

———◈———

Eliza jams her padded behind on the long wooden bench in the witnesses' gallery, catching her breath, and not a moment too soon, because here's Billy Beane climbing into the dock, in the moldy green frock coat and jaunty top hat that's his habit. His scrawny wrists are shackled in front of him, his lice-ridden hair clipped ragged from the Newgate cells, and he's grinning like a penny-gaff clown. Billy "the Bastard" Beane, pimp, defiler of little girls, and all-round stinker.

Now I'm all for justice, me. Innocent until it's proven he done it, and all that. Don't want no dirty copper fitting me up for some lay I had naught to do with. But in Billy's case? March in the guilty scumbag, my friends, because you gotta be twelve to say "yes" to a man, and mothers and daughters all over Seven Dials know this dirty child-raper for what he is.

If Billy the Bastard's innocent? I'm his friggin' maiden aunt.

The prosecutors make their case. The crusher what arrested Billy, the little girl's mother, some ratty-haired snout says he seen Billy lurking nearby, on-the-night-in-question-guvnor-sure-as-I'm-standing-straight.

And then they call Doctor Eliza Jekyll, who tells 'em some fine palaver about scratches and bloodstains and fluids on Billy's clothes that sure sounds a whole lot like he's guilty as Cain. I cheer loudly in her ear. You tell 'em, Eliza, my love. Can't argue with bloodstains, can they?

But the beak is a patronizing prick—ain't they all?—and puts air to some tosh about hysterical lady doctors that makes me want to grab him by those dusty black robes and smash his pudgy nose flat with my forehead. Eliza protests, but he cuts her off. Billy's grinning. The coppers don't say nothing. And now I know what's going on here.

Prison screws, coppers, jurymen, snouts. Everyone's for sale. And it seems His Honor is too.

Not guilty.

It ain't right. The little girl's mother is crying. The Bastard is laughing and joking with the crushers as they let him go. A woman in a green dress yells and throws old fruit from the gallery. Eliza just stares, her prim little throat aching with unshed tears.

And inside her, I rage and scream and tear my hair, and yearn with all my heart for a jagged blade.

Darkness had swallowed the sun by the time Eliza trudged up to her town house in Russell Square. Moonlight glared red through smoky clouds, spreading on the cobbles like a bloodstain, filtering eerily over the shadowy park. Electric streetlights glimmered, blue filaments buzzing. A walking carriage lolloped along, its six insectoid feet clattering over the stones. Mist drifted, wrapping wisplike along the fences and wrought-iron gates, settling over her smart brick town house. The smells and sounds of the foundling hospital along Guildford Street—waste, vomit, the wails of sick children—made a ghastly backdrop.

Normally, Eliza didn't mind. She was used to it. But tonight, it only made her think of Billy Beane, the horrid things he'd done, his depraved giggles, his damp fingers on that little girl's skin, his smug grin in the courtroom as they let him go. And when she thought of Billy, her unladylike anger swelled like a monster . . . and the dark shadow inside her growled to be free.

Eliza's own mother had died in a senseless accident, with those responsible never held to account. Would the man who'd killed Irina Pavlova escape justice, too? Vanish into the night like an evil dream, a habitual monster drifting from victim to victim, unable to understand or stop? Or had it been an aberration, the only blot on a blameless character, a horrible secret that some guilty gentleman would take to his grave?

Unlikely. In Eliza's experience, most murderers didn't feel guilty. At best, they were angry and careless and sorry they'd been caught. At worst, they were beasts in human disguise.

Mostly. Some—an unfathomable, frightening few—defied diagnosis.

The polished brass shingle nailed to the doorpost read ELIZA JEKYLL M.D. Wearily, she stumped up the steps and let herself in, Hippocrates trotting after her.

Dim quiet greeted her, the comforting scents of herbs and medicines, a faint whiff of some tasty supper on the boil. A warm yellow arc-light gleamed in a brass wall sconce, and to the right, the doorway of her consulting room lay dark. The walls were papered in cream, the pressed-metal ceiling white. An Indian rug lay soft under her aching feet. A gilt-framed mirror adorned the hall, above an expensive inlaid mahogany hall table.

Her house was fine. More expensive than she could have afforded on her own, with the meager income from her police work and the part-time position at Bethlem. Female doctors were few and didn't attract many patients, and by the time she qualified, first in general practice as an apothecary, then as M.D. against the wishes of a hostile, all-male College of Physicians, her late father's practice had long since disbanded. Henry Jekyll had been a society doctor, with considerable fortune and prestige in his day—but he'd squandered both on his strange experiments, and now they were gone. Eliza lived prudently, without show or extravagance, but everything cost money.

No, she could never have afforded this address, the servants, the fine furniture. This house was paid for by her guardian, the man into whose care Father had left her in his will. She was a legal adult now, in charge of her own allowance, and she'd barely heard from her guardian since she turned twenty-one, but the house still belonged to *him*.

An odd fellow, to be sure. For a man she'd never actually seen face-to-face, his rough, infrequent letters could be strangely affectionate. But he'd spared no expense and no trouble. And an absent guardian better suited her purposes than an ever-present one. Better by far than a husband, meddling and disapproving, taking up her time with trivia such as housekeeping and mealtimes and children. "Wife" was a busy full-time job, for certain, and not to be sneered at. Just not her career of choice.

"Welcome home, Doctor." Hippocrates squatted by the hallstand, a spindly brass frog.

"Thank you, Hipp. Have a nap, there's a good boy." Gratefully, she closed the heavy door. Her head was pounding. Dizziness lurked, threatening. Her pulse was dangerously elevated. She needed her remedy.

But she had none. Only the elixir. And inside her, angry shadows roiled, thirsting to be free . . .

Someone was talking. She shook herself, trying to focus. "I'm sorry?"

Her housekeeper bustled from the passage, dusting rough old hands on her apron. Mrs. Poole was only five feet tall, the bonnet pinned over her graying hair barely reaching Eliza's shoulder, but she was built like a grande-dame bulldog, fierce and muscular in body and affection. "Supper's ready, Doctor. Lay the table, shall I?"

"Good evening, Mrs. Poole. I'll take a tray in my room, please. I'm feeling a little unwell."

"You do look a sight," teased Mrs. Poole dryly. "You work too hard, young lady. Just like your father, and look how he ended up, God rest him. No wonder no respectable man will have you."

"I say, do you think not? Shocking. I shall mend my unladylike ways immediately."

A twinkle of faded green eyes. "Make a difference, would it, the way you pull your hair back like a schoolmarm, and never wear nice shoes?"

"Mrs. Poole, as always, you are the very soul of comfort."

"Always here to help. You look positively peaky. Shall I break out the leeches and bloodletting myself, or send for one of your charlatan physicians?"

"I am a physician, last I looked. The shingle on the door seems to think so."

"Aye, well," said the imperturbable Mrs. Poole, "a fool for a patient, and all."

Eliza suppressed a laugh. "The saying is 'a fool for a client.' Referring to lawyers who represent themselves, not doctors who self-medicate. A small but important distinction."

"If you say so. Go on upstairs, I'll send for Molly." Mrs. Poole ushered Eliza towards the big mahogany staircase. "Bless me," she added slyly, fishing a sealed letter from her apron pocket. "I almost forgot. This came for you. Hand delivered."

The folded paper was smooth and warm. Expensive stationery, no postage stamp, her address smudged in crude black handwriting, and a red wax seal stamped with a shape that looked like a crooked crown, or maybe a court jester's belled hat.

Eliza's heart clenched, dread and fascination in equal measure. "Forgot," indeed. She knew that seal. What did he want, after so many months of ignoring her? Sometimes his letters were aimless, strange, the wanderings of a lost soul. Other letters were terse missives regarding the dispersal of funds, the house, her yearly allowance. Yet others . . . well, he had the soul of a poet, if an ill-mannered one.

Toss it away. He's a dirty old lecher. Probably hides behind the bed curtains and fiddles with himself while you sleep. . .

Clasping the letter to her bodice, Eliza hurried up two flights of stairs, past her darkened study to her bedroom.

The fire was already lit. Twin candles gleamed in brass sconces on the elaborate marble mantel. Her ruffled bed was neatly made, pale covers beneath a gossamer canopy. Her wardrobe—Eliza's wardrobe—stood in the corner.

Above the dressing table hung her mother's portrait, framed in gilt. Madeleine Jekyll wore an old-fashioned, high-waisted cream silk ball gown. Her lips turned up in a secret smile. A diamond necklace adorned her slender throat, a wedding gift from her bridegroom. She looked young, happy, uncommonly pretty.

Eliza hadn't inherited Madeleine's looks. She'd barely known her mother. Just another scandal that people whispered about. No, Eliza took after her father: gray-eyed, sharp-chinned, compelled to meddle in dangerous secrets.

She sat at the inlaid writing desk, warming her booted feet by the fire. She turned up the electric lamp, and in greenish light cracked the letter's seal.

Snap! Too loud in the silence. Her heart skipped. She unfolded the paper, pushing her spectacles up.

As always, his handwriting was rough, untidy with crossings-out, as if he scribbled in a hurry and didn't care too much for his spelling. The paper was smudged with grime or coal dust, as if his hands were dirty, like a laborer's. An odd sort of gentleman.

> *My Dear Eliza*
> *Tomorrow midnight in your Study.*
> *You know the Rules. Don't look*
> *behind You.*
>
> > *your Servant*
> > *A.R.*

And beneath his initials—what did they stand for?—a little sketch of that same jester's crown. Wicked, unhinged, the sly wink of a madman.

She swallowed, excited yet fearful. A little dizzy. Was it the fever? Why did he want to see her? Their meetings were scarce, and always shrouded in darkness, shadows, secrecy. As a girl, she'd been afraid of him, his strange rough voice behind the curtain, his masculine scent of tobacco and leather, once a hesitant hand on her hair that made her whirl, only to see no one. Now, as a woman grown . . .

Rap-a-rap! A knock at the door. Swiftly, she tucked the letter away in one of the desk's many secret drawers. "Come."

Molly, pretty and blond, carrying a dinner tray. "Shall I set it down here, Doctor?"

"Thank you, Molly." The plate held hot pork pie, potatoes, warm bread, a steaming pot of tea. Her stomach swam, as if she'd swallowed seawater. Mrs. Poole's pie was invariably excellent. But Eliza had lost her appetite.

For food, that was. For anything except the elixir, bitter and delicious, stinging her throat like salt, that glorious fireburst in her belly . . .

Molly busied herself turning down the bed and fluffing the pillows. "Everything all right, Doctor? Mam says you weren't feeling well."

"Nothing a cup of tea and a good night's sleep won't remedy."

"You know," Molly remarked, "when I was just a scullery maid, I broke a cup in the kitchen, and I was too scared to tell anyone." Her skirts billowed as she worked. "Ate away at me, it did. Never got a wink of sleep, until at last I owned up. As if a load of bricks tumbled off my back. Ever since then, if something's bothering me, I find it's best to talk about it."

"I'll take that on board." Eliza tried a smile, but it stung false. Mrs. Poole had kept house for Henry Jekyll, and though she made a point of pretending ignorance, her sharp wits missed nothing. Molly was Molly Poole, Mrs. Poole's daughter—or granddaughter?—and cut from the same practical cloth. Molly and Eliza were of an age, and though Eliza's secrets were never spoken, such a clever maid had surely heard enough strange happenings late at night in the Jekyll household to realize something bizarre was going on.

But Eliza could not make a confidante of Molly, no matter how tempting. She could have no friends. If she were discovered—if that intolerable Captain Lafayette of the Royal had his way—her servants would suffer along with her.

"Shall I help you undress?"

"That won't be necessary . . ." She sighed at Molly's expression. Keeping up appearances was important. But so very tiresome. "Very well. Thank you."

She unlaced her boots and eased them off with a sigh, wriggling her pinched toes in the fire's warmth. She fidgeted as Molly helped her with her gown, unclipping the dove-gray fabric and stiffened corset, and soon she stood in only her linen chemise, pale hair tumbling around her face.

She peered at herself in the polished dressing table mirror. Her cheeks flushed pink, her hair hung damp. Shadows gleamed sickly beneath eyes aglow with fever. Her stomach ached as if she'd not eaten for days. And an ugly pressure swelled in her blood, beneath her skin, in the secret places between her legs. She wanted, hungered, thirsted for . . . satisfaction. Completion. A bold kind of . . . release, something urgent she didn't fully understand.

Escape. . .

Molly reached for the hairbrush, but Eliza tossed her head impatiently. "I can do it meself," she snapped, and flushed. "I mean, that's all for tonight, Molly," she amended hastily. "I shan't need you again. Good night."

The girl's eyes narrowed, but she nodded. "Good night, Doctor."

As soon as the door clicked shut, Eliza sprang to her feet. Turned the key in the lock, *click-clack!* and tossed it onto the bed, out of reach of prying fingers. Ran to the fireplace, grabbed the left-hand sconce, and yanked it downwards on its secret hinge.

Clunk! Hot wax spilled over the back of her hand. She didn't care. Thirst tore into her belly. The sharp-clawed beast had to be sated. *Come on, come on . . .*

Agonizingly slowly, the section of wall beside the wardrobe swung outwards. Silently, without a whisper or a creak. She kept it oiled for that purpose. A dark passageway loomed. Her secret cabinet.

Before the door had even fully opened, she dived in. On her knees, shaking, fumbling the little cupboard door aside. Yearning, sweating, trembling with anticipation yet gripped by terrible fear that she'd miscalculated, there'd be nothing inside . . .

There it sat. Mr. Finch's black glass flask, gleaming evilly in firelight. Bulbous at the bottom, narrow neck, flaring at the mouth. It seemed to snigger like a living creature, hungry for mischief.

Yes. Her mouth watered, and her eyes drifted closed. She gripped the flask's warm neck—always warm, this bubbling hellbrew, a vile heat of its own—and flicked off the cork. *Pop!* Tiny drops spattered, and *that* smell drifted out, intoxicating like opium, delicious like bitter chocolate, velvety and delectable and oh, so alluring . . .

A desperate feather of reason tickled the back of her neck. Startled, she opened her eyes.

The long mirror on the cabinet wall reflected her, stark and pale in her white chemise. Her reddened eyes were demented. She breathed deep, shuddering, sweating, the fever sprinting madly under her skin, a dread curse she couldn't escape.

She shouldn't. She mustn't.

But she had to.

She squeezed her eyes shut against the fire's glare and tipped the flask to her lips.

Molten gold, rolling down her throat. Thick salt stung her tongue, coated the inside of her mouth, sickening yet delicious. Thirst ripped her raw, and she gulped, mouthful on mouthful . . .

Fire erupted in her guts, sweeter than any caress. She groaned in pure abandon. Spreading outwards through her belly, tingling along her limbs, a shivering shock wave of delight . . .

Agony, hacking every nerve ragged. Muscles contorting, bones twisting, red mist descending like poison, it's torture, it's being dragged apart on the rack in some rat-infested Tower chamber, beyond endurance, no one can take this, no one. A scream crawls up her throat, she's yelling, *I'm* yelling, she's clawing at her face but it's *my* face, *my* hands, *my* nails catching in her hair. We throw our head back, arching our spine, joints grating, our muscles shudder and squeal and thrash one final time . . .

Suddenly, the pain falls silent. The red mist dissolves . . . and in the mirror, dark eyes flash, wicked and alive with intent.

Sharp intelligent face, crooked seducer's smile, a body with lush, dangerous curves. Long curly hair tumbles over the white chemise, no longer fine and blond but dark, lustrous mahogany.

And here I stand.

THE ART AND SCIENCE OF EVIL

• •

I LET OUT A LAUGH, RICH AND RAUCOUS, AND I HAVE TO cover my mouth or they'll hear me. Wouldn't do to make a fuss.

Then again? To hell with it. My blood's up. The rage burns like venom in my belly. My muscles are strong, my body's alive and hungry and full of fire.

Lizzie's out, my friends. And she intends to make the most of it.

I unhook Eliza's spectacles—my eyes is just fine, thank you—and toss 'em away. The empty flask is still in my hand, and I fling it aside. It hits the floor and smashes, but no matter. Eliza can clean it up later. This elixir lasts only a few hours. No time to lose. I flick the cabinet lamp on—fancy electric lights, this house of ours—and head for the wardrobe.

My wardrobe, that is.

I hang my clothes in here, behind the locked secret door where the servants won't see. Eliza can keep her drab gray doctor's frocks, her high collars and chest-flattening stays. Me? I like to stand out. I flick through my dresses, frowning.

The red, the scarlet, the crimson, the ruby, the cherry, the claret, or the rose?

I settle on the cherry, a flounced satin thing with a deep lacy neckline, and pull on *my* corset, the one that hooks in front and shows off my womanly advantages. Oop, suck it in, shove 'em up there, yep, that's it. I snap the last hook, pull on the dress, petticoats 'n' all—I don't go for no stupid crinolines, that's one thing Eliza and me has in common—and button it up.

That's better. I wiggle my toes into silky black stockings and tie them at the top with a lacy pair of garters. Some boots—shiny dancing ones, that is, with pointy toes and buckles and proper heels that make me tall, not the clunky sensible things she wears—and I'm done.

I check myself in the mirror and grin my saucy grin, tilting my half-bared shoulders. I say, Miss Lizzie, you're a fine-looking woman. I clip on my favorite necklace, a beaded jet choker, and pin my hair up loose under a little red hat. None o' that actress face paint for me. Just ask the flash gents down at Seven Dials, and they'll tell you, so they will. I'm far too classy for that.

Sweet. I shove a fistful of coins in the secret pocket deep in my skirt and toss a long black cloak around me. Wouldn't do to be seen around here, after all, not in Eliza's snotty neighborhood where the crushers strut by every hour and chase away anyone who don't look rich enough to breathe their air.

Last of all—best of all—I slide open a drawer and pull out my little darling.

She sparkles in the firelight, four inches of shiny stiletto steel on a blackwood handle. Hello, sweet sister. I give her a kiss, and she's cold on my lips. My breath frosts on the metal for a moment, then vanishes like a ghost.

I hike my skirt above one knee and snap her into my garter. Sleep now, sister. Won't be long.

And down the dusty back stairs like the red satin harpy of vengeance I prowl.

———◦◦———

It's cold outside, the late winter night closing in, and I wrap the cloak tighter and walk on. Down the back alley, where rats lurk in the nightman's wagon tracks, and out onto Southampton Row. Moonlight drenches the smoky sky with blood, and mist drifts, a yellowing specter that haunts the blue-glowing electric lampposts and iron fences.

A cold finger trails down my spine. I whirl, in case anyone's following me . . . but ain't no one there. Just shadows.

It takes me a good quarter hour to walk to New Oxford Street. Carriages and hansoms rattle by, electrics flickering purple and green in the night with the stink of thunder and hot iron. Costermongers yell their wares—*sweet strawberries, ripe!*—and expensive whores strut like duchesses in fine gowns and feathered hats. Beggars of all ages weep, bleed, shake with faked palsy. Children ramble and scatter, selling matches, picking pockets, dancing like hurdy-gurdy monkeys under spinning carriage wheels.

Square-rigged gents in fine coats and gloves stroll in pairs and threes, flicking their canes and tipping their lids to ladies. Unless you're like me and have an eye for these things? Ain't no telling who's quality and who's the swell mob, stalking through the crowd to relieve 'em of their purses and jewels and fancy tie-pins.

On a corner, an Irish ballad-chanter sells his latest tale of woe, scraps of paper with the words printed on jabbed onto his pointed stick. *"Gold watch, she picked from his po-cket, and shyly placed into my hand . . ."* He tips his hat to me as he sings. *"The hair hung down on her shou-l-der . . . tied up with a black velvet band . . ."*

Aye. You fell for a pair of pretty diamond eyes, and got yourself transported to the colonies for seven years. Such is life.

I duck along a narrow street beside a broken churchyard wall, where crumbling gravestones loom and the shadows reek and thicken with *weird*. Down a twisting alley, beneath an overhanging doorway, and suddenly I've left civilization behind and I'm deep in the Holy Land.

People teem, filthy dresses and torn coats, feet bare on the freezing cobbles. Blank eyes slide over me and away. In a shitty gutter, two dirty children gnaw on the same bone. A skinny girl soaked in gin burps loudly in my ear and hitches up ankle-cut skirts to show me her goat's feet.

Yells and drunken laughter chime through the night. All kinds of accents; Irishmen, to be sure—it's where the name *Holy Land* came from—and these days they can hang your sorry carcass for an Ave Maria but it still ain't no crime to be Irish. Scots accents, too, Welshmen and Geordies and guttural Rom, Chinamen and Turks and the dense dialects of navvies and coal diggers.

Everyone comes to London, desperate for a better life, and when they get here there's no work and no food and cruel monstrous winter is always on its way, the hungry chill that never quite leaves your bones again, no matter how much rot-gut gin you choke down your throat.

I walk on, and the streets get darker. Shadows and flame flicker, a single taper in a window. Guttering blue and yellow lights, glimmering from some drunken Romany conjurer's fire tricks. The stink is grotesque, crawling under my clothes to lick me like a hungry dog at a corpse.

The crowded maze of the rookery is even more crowded now. When the slum-clearers tore down a swath of tenements to build New Oxford Street, they didn't find this grubby lot aught else to live in. They just moved 'em on, jammed 'em tighter into what remained. Now they're five and six and ten to a room down here, where makeshift plank bridges lead from window to window, dank tunnels crawl beneath the streets, hidden doors lead into flash houses and slop houses and low lodging houses, where you pay a penny to scrounge a few hours' sleep on the floor or a shared bug-infested bed in a freezing airless shithole with no light. And in monstrous factories and power stations, workers inhale deadly cotton fibers, and dip matches in jaw-rotting poison, and shovel coal into hungry generators until they die.

And all in a world where they can hang you for stealing tuppence, and the price of bread's kept artificially high so the rich can get richer. *Things* matter more than people. It's enough to make you sympathize with them Frenchies chopping off their king's head and dancing around his bleeding corpse.

Heh. Nosy prickfaces like that idiot Temple should write about *this* in their fool pamphlets. Except, poor people dying slowly don't sell no papers. Never did. Never will.

I sidestep a wooden sewer trap, what looks like a sturdy cover only it's not. Step on that, and you'll fall to your death in a stinking pit. Traps like these—spring-loaded spikes, deadfalls, trip wires—are everywhere. If the crushers chase you in here, they might never come out. The Royal's fancy Enforcers, with their dumb clockwork justice? They don't dare even come here.

So everyone piles in, freaks and fortune-tellers, the fey and the fell, idiots and opium-eaters and them what's touched in the head by the *weird*. Some tell of a secret den called the Rats' Castle, a magical underground place where strange folk can go. Pish, says I. If it's real, I ain't never found it. Ain't no true fairy folk left, that's what I reckon, leastaways not in London. Years of witch-finders, greedy bounty-hunters, and plain bloody-fingered murder finished 'em off or drove 'em into hiding long ago.

But plenty of people can still claim fairy ancestors. If you've magic in your blood? The rookeries are where you hide. It's a laughing lunatic's idea of hell.

I cross Broad Street, where outside the bright-lit gin palace, an impromptu street fair is going on, a giggling riot of color. The crowd is a dirty rainbow, mismatched duds snatched from washing lines and pawnshops, the cast-off finery of dandies and high-born ladies. A mad fiddler in a crooked green top hat plays a raucous reel, competing with a bloke on a box who's hollering fine treasons about voting and workers' rights and how them bloodsuckers in the Commons don't stand for nobody nowhere.

"God save the Queen!" I yell, and a few people cheer. It ain't Her Majesty they've got a quarrel with.

Fire-eaters and sword-swallowers roam, and acrobats flip and tumble on long whippy limbs. A dwarf with a scaly face frightens passers-by for a penny with his cage of freaks. A pair of sinister carnies work an erotic shadow-play show, string puppets in silhouette behind a sheet doing all manner of dirt. On the corner, cheering folk circle around a cock-fight, and the stupid birds squawk and shed bloody feathers in clouds.

A change from the drab streets above, where everything's gray or black or cat-shit brown, and people toff about with noses held high. Here in hell, at least we know how to have a good time.

I shoulder through the smelly mass, heading for the Cock-atrice public house. Ahead, a pregnant Irish girl dances drunk in the gutter, singing about Molly Malone and her wheelbar-row. *"In Dublin's fair cityy . . . where the girls are so prettyy . . ."* I join in the chorus. *"Cockles . . . and mussels . . . alive, alive-OH!"* She grins at me, sharp-toothed. Her skirts are rucked up above her bare ankles, and a long tail like a rat's curls from under the hem.

A boy runs up to me, a dirty cap pulled down between his tiny sharp horns. He tosses blue fireballs from hand to hand, making them dance. "Penny for the flame, miss?"

I toss him tuppence. He scrambles in the shit for it, and I kick aside his accomplices trying to pick my pocket while he's distracted me and walk on.

In the shadow of the brewery's red-brick tower, a carved emblem of a winged dragon with a rooster's head crows down at me from a crooked stone lintel. I push the cracked door open and step into a blast of heat, stale breath, and liquor.

Sawdust crunches under my boots. The fug rolls at eye level, cigar smoke and hashish and blacker dreams.

I spy a bloke I recognize at the bar, so I elbow my way over, kicking some lushington who gropes my behind and pushing away a drunken dolly who thinks I'm some fine Sapphic gentlewoman looking for a bit o' rough.

No thanks, sweetheart. Only one bit o' rough interests Lizzie tonight, and his name is Billy fucking Beane.

The Cockatrice is what they call a flash house, a place where criminals of all kinds congregate. Cracksmen, magsmen, coiners and fakers, card sharps and forgers, snakesmen and canaries and fencers of stolen goods. They all come here to swap information, soak their sorry arses in gin, and show off, to whatever girl or boy or blue-spotted sheep takes their fancy.

Sly little baby-raping pimps, too, like Billy the Bastard Beane, not-guilty-your-honor-if-I-say-so-meself and the new fuck-the-coppers king of Seven Dials, at least for a few hours. Hang about here long enough, I'll bet my garters you'll see Billy here tonight, deep in his cups, drinking on his new-found fame while it lasts.

I squeeze up to the bar, and a wiry, sharp-eyed cove with a lurid purple coat and tangled black hair shoves a pewter cup into my hand and splashes it with gin. "Care for a tipple, madam?"

"Don't mind if I do, Johnny." I slap my cup against his, and gulp. Gritty fire spills down my throat and explodes, and holy Jesus, I just came alive. Eliza ain't one for the demon liquor, and she won't thank me in the morning, but sweet lord, Miss Lizzie likes a drink.

I clunk the cup down and burp, and my handsome gent pours me some more.

"Lizzie, my darlin', where have you been these dark and lonely weeks?" His words slur, and he flops a long arm around my shoulders and tosses me a glocky grin. Wild Johnny—so called because he raises hell—Johnny might act the fool, but his crooked eyes are quick, and like usual, he ain't near as plastered as he makes out. "When will you abandon your licentious ways and marry me?"

I wipe my mouth, artfully shrugging his arm off. Our Johnny's what country folk call *fey*, which is to say he's touched a bit odd. His eyes are a little too far apart, and his sharp-nailed fingers wrap further round that cup than they've any right to, and he smells uncanny sweet, of laudanum and rose petals over warm male skin. "You already got yourself a dolly, John."

He don't seem discouraged. "Yes, it is true," he pronounces dramatically, waving his cup in the air. "I am affy-onced, as they say on the Continent. Woe is me, my innocent heart caged like a dove by a vertible . . . a veritable shrew."

I wink along the bar at the shrew in question. Jemima Half-Cut, Johnny's squeeze, a gangly fifteen-year-old in a buttoned blue off-the-shoulder dress and shawl. So called because she usually is, though it beats me why a tart rolling in gin should be a matter for remark around here.

Jemima scowls and gets back to work, patrolling the crowd for trade. But her eyes are exhausted, her face wan. This is her night job, after ten hours scrubbing piss-stinking linen in some moldy underground wash-house.

Stupid compassion prickles my palms, and I wipe it off on my cherry skirts. Wild Johnny of Seven Dials is a catch, so he is, and a washer girl who sucks half a dozen cocks a night for sixpence apiece ain't got much that'll keep a man like him, if he gets another offer.

Johnny once told me he's a clergyman's son, on account of which he speaks so nice and spits on the ground whenever he walks by a churchyard. Maybe it's even true. When he was young, he went out with the swell mob, tall hat and cravat and his shock of midnight hair clipped short. But after a few seasons of fakement, the crushers get to know your face, and there ain't no point twigging yerself out as quality when the bastards in blue just cooper your lay every damn time. So now, a wise old man of twenty-one, he fences the swag, and word is there's nothing so dirty that Wild Johnny can't christen it clean.

Mayhap you're thinking I've a soft spot for him? Well, so I do. Johnny and I go way back, since I first started coming here as an angry sixteen-year-old hellcat and he were only eleven, and if I'd met him back then the way he is now? Sweet Jesus, I'd have been his dolly before he could flash those witchy eyes and say *how-d'you-like-it-darlin'*? His face is fresh and sharp, not yet rotted by phosphorous or pox-scarred to hell. He still has good teeth, what's left of 'em, and something about that mussed-on-milady's-pillow hair of his puts me in a mind to stroke it. I've a woman's heart, after all.

But I ain't playing that game, not tonight. I'm too old, too angry, too itchy inside with dark purpose to flirt with Johnny now.

I choke down another cupful. Wretched stuff, gritty like the barkeep pissed gravel in it, but it suits my mood. "I'm looking for Billy the Bastard. You seen aught of him?"

Johnny shrugs. His expression don't change. His cock-eyed smile don't slip. "What's it worth to you?"

I slide a pair of sovereigns his way along the bar. Johnny's in no need of my coin. It's just how business is done. The city's too full of snouts, and a flash gent like Johnny has a reputation to protect. Put it about that he can be bought for less than he's worth? His name'll be back in the mud before morning.

He makes the coins disappear, a swift shimmer of shadow, and scratches one oddly pointed ear. "I might have eyeballed the cove in question."

"And?"

"It's complicated, so it is."

"So?"

His dark eyes dance. "So kiss me and I'll tell you, sweet ruby Lizzie."

"Tell me and I'll kiss you, you fairy-arse tosser."

"Promise?"

"'Pon my honor."

He nods towards the pub's rear door and flashes me that winning grin. "He's out the back, playing loo. Now pay up."

"Complicated, is it?" I grin, too. "Johnny, you rakehell, will you deflower an innocent maiden with your tricks?"

"So I talked it up. You still owe me."

I grab his coat lapels and plant one on him. His mouth is warm and bold, a man's mouth, and his tongue tastes of gin and sorrow. Already his hands sneak around my waist, and his deft fingers are too long, strange, intriguing . . . but I draw back and pat his cheek affectionately. "Thanks, Johnny. You're a darling."

He blinks his wonky eyes, starry. "Sweet Jesus, I think I've gone blind."

I laugh and walk away, smacking my lips. Eliza would be scandalized, but do I care? A good, hard, breathless lesson in scandal from a rascal like Johnny is just what that strait-laced madam needs.

Me? What I need is none of your bloody concern. Just keep your mudlark mind on Billy the Bastard.

I shoulder through the crowd, picking up my skirts to avoid puddles of gin and vomit and whatever else. Jemima Half-Cut's sitting on some old bloke's knee, his dirty hand down her bodice, and her glare follows me, green with poisoned envy.

By the gin barrels, a toothless fortune-teller with a golden earring flips pornographic tarot cards for a penny, and a moth-eaten monkey in a tiny red waistcoat scuttles down his arm to collect the coins. A group of gin-swilling students raise a noisy toast, drinks splashing. "Hail to the King!"

The King of Rats, that is. His Majesty of the fabled Rats' Castle, lord of the fey underworld, duke of the downtrodden, prince of the perennially pissed-on.

Like I says before: pish. Revolution has an ill and blood-soaked history in this country, especially lately. Ain't no one gonna come riding in like King Arthur or Boadicea to avenge us. Not even some mythical rat bloke.

I edge through to the back room, down a couple of steps to where the illicit card game is in full swing by lamplight. Seven men around a rickety table, swearing and swilling gin over a heap of coins, collateral, and crumpled banknotes. It's a vicious game, loo, and fights break out more often than not. A whiskered dwarf in a green coat tosses his hand in, cursing in thick Irish, and beside him, an impossibly tall and thin cove with a hooked nose and a top hat hunches like a big insect on a stool and bets a fistful of silver half-crowns.

But I don't care a fig for them.

Because the ill-favored gent on the far end is Billy Beane.

Yes, it is. The Bastard, with his squashed hat, lice-ridden green coat, and skinny dog-whiskered face.

Filthy son of a sewer rat. My shiny steel darling thrums warmly against my thigh. Soon, sister. Soon.

I toss my cloak, revealing my bright skirts, and saunter in, hand on hip, twirling one curl on a saucy fingertip. I'm older than this scumbag's usual dollies, but watch and learn, because Lizzie has her ways.

I walk by Billy, trailing my hand over his shoulder. "I say, guvnor," I purr, "ain't you Billy Beane?"

"Fuck off, tart," growls the leprechaun.

Billy plays a queen of hearts—he's winning big tonight—and gives me the greasy eyeball. "What's it to you?"

"I heard you was a big man in these parts." I lean over, showing him my swelling cleavage—Jesus cried a river, he don't half stink—and slide my hand into his lap. A flick of my fingers and I'm in his trousers, and a dank and mossy place it is, too. Still, I've done worse. I fold my fingers around him, and it don't take but a moment to get his attention. "Mmm. A *very* big man."

Billy's gaze slides over the valley between my bosoms and back up to my face. He ain't so drunk—nor so dumb—that he ain't wondering what my game is. "You're a bold one. Never seen you before."

I rub him, and give a tart's sultry sigh of admiration. "But

I seen you. You's famous, so you is. I'll do it for free. Always wanted to fuck a king."

The tall thin fellow next to him grins, rotten teeth gleaming, and tosses in his last card. "Your lucky night, Bill."

The Bastard trumps the trick—cheating, I'll wager, cards up his sleeve or under the table—and the game is his. He laughs, uproarious, and drags the pile of loot in. "It's my fucking lucky year, lads!"

I smile and nibble his ear. Bite it, make him jerk and stiffen more. "What say we . . ." and I tells him a few choice tales about where he can put his business and what I'll do with it once it's there.

Thin Man sniggers. "It's got teats, Bill. Bit old for you, ain't it?"

"Nothin' wrong with full-grown cunny," says Billy loftily, "if it's dressed right. 'Specially when it's free."

Charming. Billy twists my hand loose, and soon we're stumbling out into the pub yard, where it's dark and stinking of old piss. I'm back against the yard wall, he's fumbling my skirts up. His breath is slimy on my collarbone. My heart growls, the old rage spilling out. Enjoy it while you're dreaming, arseface. I edge my hand up my thigh, to my garter where my pulse throbs eagerly against warm steel . . .

He gets his hand on me and grimaces. "You got hair there. Turn around, bitch."

And he tries to flip me face to the wall. Huh. *That'll* never do.

Time to improvise. I wriggle around him and drop to my knees. "Let me suck it."

"Be quick, then." He grabs my hair, drags my face in.

I take hold of him. He smells goaty, unwashed, and my blood boils all over again, those little girls crying, his grunts, his brutish hands . . .

I clamp my fist tight. Whip out my glinting silver sister, and jab the point into the sweaty crease beside his balls.

His skinny body jerks. "Whatthefuck . . . ?"

I squeeze tighter, yanking so it hurts, and grin my evillest grin. "Now, Billy Beane, let's play us a little game."

———◦◦◦———

Later, after I'm done with the Bastard, I'm flat on my back on a lumpy cushion in the Cockatrice, dizzy with gin and laudanum, gazing up at the eddying smoke. The crowd has thinned, men are passed out under the tables. Even the whores have drifted away, back to their cold penny lodging houses or the ratty beds of their fancy men.

Wild Johnny lolls his elfin head in my lap, and by now he *is* plastered, having matched me gin for gin and more. He's stripped off his coat—hot in here, or just the laudanum?— and inside his open shirt, his skin gleams, damp and luminous. He's a sight, let me tell you, sinew and sweat and smoldering fey eyes.

His hair spills over my cherry satin like India ink. I fondle it idly, watching with sparkly fascination as it curls around my fingers. My forehead feels tight, like there's a lump on it. For some reason, I taste cherries. There's blood under my nails, and a wet sticky patch soaking into my skirts, and my stiletto is snug back in my garter, humming contentedly, warm and sated for now.

But I don't have much longer. My stomach boils, and the

elixir's bitter taste repeats on me, stinging my mouth. My skin itches, like it don't fit proper. My muscles ache with fatigue, and already my thoughts stumble, fantasy and reality crushing together like jagged mirror shards. Dreams of blood and shadow, the smooth kiss of steel, a scream. I don't know if they're real no more.

I tip the near-empty bottle up into my palm, a brown trickle. Johnny licks laudanum from my fingers and groans, unrequited. "Be mine, Lizzie. Make an honest man of me. I can't live this way."

My head spins. "Go home, Johnny. Jemima's waiting for you."

He climbs me, fumbling, and rests his cheek on my chest. His starry gaze shines up at me. "Jemima's not you."

My vision blurs, mixing darkness and light and his dusty scent of flowers. The world swirls, an underwater rainbow. I'm dirty, drunk, stained by rage and resentment and Billy's horrid deeds, and my heart drums fiercely, mutinous, yearning for rebellion.

Soon, I'll have to go. I don't want to. Not back to my chains.

Slyly, Johnny eases his thigh across my skirt. I close my eyes, feel his rough cheek on mine, the catch in his breath when his long hand curls over the curve of my corset. He inhales, tasting my ear, my throat, and the laudanum should've dulled his desire but it hasn't. I can feel him—he's warm and insistent and wrong and I shouldn't but I want to and my blood burns with the terrible urge to corrupt, defile, destroy.

I don't have long. I should go home. Disappear into my dungeon, let those rusty shackles snap tight. Hide from the truth, which is that I'm a bad woman and I'll break this lonely boy's heart for the simple pleasure of watching beauty bleed.

But I don't care. About me, about Eliza, about anything. Let 'em come. Let 'em torture me, strip me raw, bare my black-rotted soul to the sun.

Johnny's sweet mouth hovers over mine. He murmurs, lips drifting apart in easy invitation, and I bury my hands in his hair—such lovely hair, Johnny, you fairy-arse tosser—and the world shimmers into light.

Darkness, the long empty echo of a wet Chelsea street. The artists' quarter, lonely and bleak. A doorway looms, wooden steps twisting upwards inside. Cold winter shadows prowl and hunch like beasts. No moon shines. The midnight sky's black with fog and dirt. Only my candle sheds light, a flickering halo of brightness in hell.

I edge forward, my heart thudding hard.

He's here.

I can taste it. Feel it in my fingertips like a long skein of wool unraveling, leading me to him. A bloodstain here, a fragment of cloth there. A smear of vermilion oil paint on a shirt; a telltale crimson hair, tangled in a dead woman's fingers; the unique shape and depth of the loving slices he's made in flesh. The homicidal artist whom the newspapers call Razor Jack has killed seventeen people that we know of. I should call for help. I should telegraph Inspector Griffin.

Anything but keep walking into the dark.

My shoes scrape on the threshold, unnervingly loud. My heart jumps like a frog into my mouth. I'm quivering, my candle's flame shakes. My courage is lost. I want Lizzie, her bold laugh, her fearless banter, that confident toss of her head.

But Lizzie's not here. There's only me, Eliza.

I climb the spiral steps, creak, crack. Wind whistles, bringing the oily smell of paint and solvent. I reach the landing. My candle gutters. An artist's attic boudoir, wide paned windows in the sloping roof. Palettes, brushes, pots of oil and pigments scattered on the floor amongst cushions and torn paper; silken drapes flung scarlet and blue over exposed rafters; a gilt-edged silvered mirror. Oil paintings stacked in the corners, propped against walls: Odysseus resisting the Sirens, triumphant Judith slitting Holofernes's throat, a waif in gossamer skirts dancing en pointe *in a pool of lustrous shadow that might be blood.*

His technique is startling, ferocious, the colors unbridled.

A half-finished canvas sits on an easel. It's drowning Ophelia, mad and beautiful, her pale hair drifting in cold black water.

The back of my neck prickles, and I whirl.

Glinting green eyes, wild-springing hair the color of blood.

I stammer, my pulse sprinting. He holds no weapon. He doesn't attack me. Doesn't move.

He just smiles eerily in the candlelight. "Hello, Eliza." His voice is lilting, gentle. An educated man. He's wearing black trousers, black waistcoat with four buttons in a square, white shirt with loose sleeves cuffed tight. That outrageous, indecently crimson hair springs over his collar, dances before his eyes. Too long, almost to his shoulders.

He has a sharp-pointed nose, a delicate red mouth that makes me stare.

He's only a few years older than I. Harmless. A beautiful monster.

I swallow, mouth dry. I was stupid to come here. But I—or was it Lizzie?—I had to see him for myself.

The moment stretches.

"I do apologize," he offers at last. "We've not been properly introduced. Malachi Todd, yours truly." He makes an elegant little bow.

I dip my head shakily. "Indeed we have not, Mr. Todd. I believe we can be forgiven for dispensing with formalities."

"I won't tell if you won't." He bends to light a glass-topped lamp, and the glow caresses him, velvety on his black waistcoat, warm in his eyes. "I feel I already know you, Eliza. May I call you Eliza?" He blows out the match and drifts closer to me. "You and your crafty shadow. You're both so . . . tenacious."

I back off in a hurry. He follows, matching my steps, a strange dance. My candle falls, dies. He kicks it away. Deftly he grabs my wrist, his fingers warm and strong. I stumble. He catches me, his hand on my waist. My back hits the wall.

And here we are, the talented Mr. Todd and I.

I can't help it. I'm breathing hard, my bodice is too tight, my pulse is on fire. I'm trembling.

But he's quite calm. "Ask me why."

"Please, I—"

"That's what you've come for, isn't it? To dance with my shadow?" A bright flash, the spring of steel. And a glitter-

ing warm edge kisses my cheekbone. "So. Let's begin. Ask me why."

It's the spine of his razor. Smooth, not sharp. Not cutting me. He's still holding my wrist, and slowly, he strokes my throbbing pulse with his thumb. A single, delicate search for reaction.

And he gets it, God help me. I lick dry lips. "Very well. The young lady in Mayfair. Why did you kill her?"

Softly, he slices off a wisp of my hair. Watches it drift to my shoulder. "She was rude. Ignorant. She corrupted her beauty. She had to die. You understand, naturally."

"The man in Whitehall?"

"Insufferable. Ugly manners. I can't abide ugliness. You're very pretty, Eliza."

"The art critic."

A sorrowful smile. "Ah. You have me there. Vanity, sadly, is my sin of torment. He called my Rape of Lucretia *too lifelike." He traces the razor's blunt end along my collarbone, a hot-cold tingle. "There's no such thing, you realize. Clearly, the man was deluded. I silenced him before he hurt someone."*

"And the little girl? She was only six years old."

"That was an accident." His fingers tighten on my wrist. His eyes flash darker, and my collarbone stings, a tiny shock. "These things happen. Shadow doesn't always behave. As you well know."

Trickle. A single, burning drop of blood.

His gaze follows it, lower, lower . . . until he catches it on the tip of his steel, just before it stains the edge of my bodice. "So where does your shadow go?" he whispers.

"Late at night, while you're sleeping? Of what does she dream? What forbidden pleasures does she taste?"

My stomach clenches cold. "I'm sure I don't know what you mean—"

"Oh, I think you do." A secret smile. "You know what she longs for. You've felt it. Always swallowing clever words, hiding your true thoughts. Restless in your bed, frightened and alone in a crowd. Bumping against a stranger, wondering what it'd be like simply to . . . act. To do whatever you please."

Suddenly, I'm aware of how warm he is. How close. How human. "Sir . . ."

"Tear off the veil. Strike the shackles. Live, instead of dying slowly, screaming into the silence. That's true beauty. Nothing is forbidden to people like us." He lifts the razor, my blood like a glittering ruby, and licks it.

Tastes me. Just because he can.

My heart hammers. I want to squeeze my eyes shut, but I can't look away.

And I take a deep breath and bolt.

But Mr. Todd is too quick. His foot snakes around my ankle, tripping me. He grabs my flailing hand and pulls, our bodies collide, only this time it's he against the wall with me in his arms and he's warm and strong and his body feels . . . well, it feels, don't you see. I ache and I shiver and his eyes glitter with dark purpose, and for some reason . . . I can't escape.

I can't breathe. I can't think. Has he bewitched me? Maybe it's because his wild hair gleams like fire and he smells of absinthe and sorrow and forbidden sin.

Maybe it's just the razor at my breast, threatening to slice my bodice apart and gut me like a rabbit.

But the beat of his heart against mine is more dangerous than any sharpened steel edge. God help me, I'm terrified, but I'm fascinated, and I want to blame Lizzie but I can't.

Because Lizzie isn't here.

"Do I disgust you, Eliza?" His whisper is small, forlorn. Tragic. And the truth slashes horror into my soul.

Mr. Todd is lonely.

Oh, sweet Jesus.

I open my mouth to answer, but for once in my life, I can't think of a single thing to say.

He glides the razor's edge along the line of the bone in my bodice. It whispers through a layer of golden silk, effortless. No resistance at all. "Do I frighten you, perhaps? You're thinking, 'What's the right answer? What can I say to convince this madman not to slice me up?'"

My voice withers, leaving only a dry whisper. "It . . . it had crossed my mind."

A tiny laugh. "No. You understand me better than that. You and your shadow. Admit it. We're the same."

A scream bubbles in my chest, and I choke it down. "You're wrong, Mr. Todd."

"And you're lying, Eliza. We'll work on that. You needn't be shy with me." His lips are so close to mine, and he eases closer, to brush a hot kiss on my ear. "I like you just the way you are . . ."

THE ILLUMINATION OF MATTER

•●•

ELIZA GASPED AWAKE, AND THE FAMILIAR DREAM-memory shimmered away like a ghost.

Uhh. Stale smoky stink sickened her. She pushed up on her elbows, raised a feeble hand to ward off the glaring sun . . .

From the left. Her bedroom window was on the right.

She groaned. She was still wearing Lizzie's cherry-red dress, too big around the chest now and greasy with sweat. Her hair tumbled in knots, most of the pins missing. Her skull ached fit to crack, and her stomach had peeled raw inside. Her mouth tasted like a small creature had died in it. *Oh, my. Did we get drunk again?*

She sat up, stretching cramped limbs. A whitewashed ceiling, broken wooden beams and soot. Her searching fingers met rough woolen cushions, the burred wooden edge of a chaise. Across the room, a bar, barrels of gin stacked three high, scattered tables and a few revelers passed out snoring on the floor. Some public house . . .

Lizzie must have had herself a fine night on the town. At least, thankfully, she'd woken alone.

Memory taunted her, dancing just out of sight. Warm whispers and laughter lingered at her mind's shadowy edges, a world of forbidden experience that Eliza secretly longed to taste.

She flushed. Such dark, unspeakable envy. Unthinkable . . .

Oh, many times she'd examined herself. Checked her body for signs of . . . well, of whatever Lizzie had been doing. But she never found anything. Always unbruised, unhurt, intact. As if the elixir *remade* her. Washed away Lizzie's sins, and kept Eliza innocent.

Except for this fearsome headache. What a pity Mr. Finch couldn't brew a potion to magic *that* away. And like a sniggering idiot in the basement lurked the uncomfortable notion that Lizzie knew a whole lot more about Eliza's doings than Eliza did about Lizzie's. Lizzie hovered every day in the back of her mind, waiting to spring alive . . . but when Lizzie was in control? Eliza slept, the fitful slumber of nightmares, and later, the events of those dark-lit nights seemed ghostly, confused, a fevered dream. Especially when Lizzie went drinking.

And Lizzie always went drinking.

Eliza scrambled up, tugging the red satin over her bust. It gaped annoyingly, the edge of her corset exposed, and a big stain had soaked into the skirt. She sniffed. It smelled like urine. Charming. But the pub was deserted. So far, so good.

She spied a dusty purple coat in a heap on the floor and slipped it on. It reached to her knees, and she wrapped it tight. It smelled strangely of flowers. For a moment, a glassy world of elusive memory swamped her, shapes and colors and textures tantalizingly out of reach . . .

She knotted her blond hair into a pinless chignon—was that her hat, trodden into the floor?—tugged her coat lapels up around her ears, and pushed the door open.

Cold air flared her headache afresh. Out on the street—where was this? Seven Dials? yes, there was the corner of Broad Street—pale dawn slanted through the narrow gaps between pubs and rotten tenements. Probably six o'clock, no later.

Vomit puddled on the threshold, and she sidestepped it carefully, lifting her skirts. Her ankles wobbled in Lizzie's too-high heels. Sleeping children made dark blobs in doorways, and blurry costermongers pushed woolly-edged carts on their way to buy fish or fruit at Covent Garden, or meat scraps at Smithfield Market.

She blinked, patting her belt for spectacles . . . Ah. No. She'd have to do without. But she knew her way home. She'd sneak back in before Molly came for her. A wash, a change of clothes, then a quick trip to Mr. Finch's on the way to work . . .

Hoarse shouts rang from the stinking side alley. A crowd babbled, adults and children jostling to see.

"Keep it back, there!" "Don't step on 'im!" "The man's murdit, I tell ya!"

Cold water flooded her guts. Compelled, she fought through.

A dead man sprawled in the dirt of the pub's backyard. Blood stained his trousers, crusted the ground, splashed the walls. She craned her neck, and her heart skipped a pace.

He wore a familiar torn green frock coat, with a motheaten patch on the shoulder.

She didn't need to see the dead man's skinny rat-whiskered face to know it was Billy Beane.

Billy the Bastard, murdered. In the very pub where Lizzie had spent the night.

Oh, my. Lizzie was furious when Billy was acquitted. Eliza had felt it, the poisoned tide of rage rising in her blood. Heavens, Eliza had been angry too. But surely not . . .

Determined, she pushed closer. She had to see the body, determine the cause of death . . . but above the heads of the crowd, a pair of dazzling blue eyes stopped her short.

Alarmed, she ducked, hiding her face. Out of uniform in an old dark coat, unshaven, his curling hair tucked under a cap. But even *sans* spectacles, she'd know those arc-light eyes and that arrogant chin anywhere.

Captain Lafayette.

Her spine prickled cold. The Royal, in Seven Dials? Surely not. They couldn't arrest everyone. No, Lafayette had some other purpose.

Something involving a dead child-rapist, and the person or persons unknown who'd killed him. And Eliza didn't fancy answering Lafayette's questions. Not wrapped in Lizzie's scandalous red satin, a borrowed coat, and the stink of gin.

Not when she didn't know the answers.

Her palms itched, frustration crawling like bedbugs under her skin, but she gritted her teeth and slunk away.

———◆———

The bell tinkled as Eliza, with Hippocrates in tow, pushed open the glass-paned door of Finch's Pharmacy on New Bond Street, just a few blocks from the stately homes in Grosvenor Square. The twin bay windows twinkled in the sun, polished to perfection.

The familiar, spicy scent of rare plants and chemicals greeted her. Rows upon rows of apothecary's drawers towered to the ceiling, each labeled in Latin. Bunches of fragrant herbs and drying leaves hung above the glossy counter. A wheeled stepladder on rails was shoved into the corner, where the obligatory portraits of Newton, Boyle, and Halley hung, the giants of times long gone. Behind her, glass-fronted shelves held phials of bright rainbow liquids—medicines and tinctures, philters and prophylactics, and poisons—and a coal fire shed a comfortable glow from a blackened iron grate.

"Mr. Finch?" Eliza shrugged off her mantle, wriggling her shoulders gratefully in the warmth. The morning sun had vanished behind a layer of yellowish London miasma, and on the cab ride from Russell Square, the cold dank air had crawled up her sleeves and beneath her petticoats. But the familiar, homely sights and smells of Finch's soothed her, as they always did. Even Lizzie relaxed, a contented sigh within. She was distant, sated, just a faint shifting presence in Eliza's heart.

This morning, she'd managed to creep up the back stairs unnoticed, hide Lizzie's stained dress and that oddly scented purple coat, unlock the bedroom door, and hop into bed before Molly came to wake her. The maid had dressed her and combed her tangled hair without comment.

But her head still hurt, her stomach scoured raw. She'd taken longer than usual to breakfast and make ready. Now she was late for work.

Hippocrates buzzed eagerly at her skirt hem, jigging up and down. She adjusted her spectacles, wincing. "Mr. Finch?"

"Eliza, my dear girl." Finch trotted from behind the leather curtain, dusting stained hands. He wore a white apron over his waistcoat and rolled-up shirtsleeves. Strange-smelling yellow smoke snaked after him, and he coughed and swiped the air. "Sorry. Don't breathe that in, my dear. My new cholera prophylactic. Works like a charm, I say!"

"Congratulations."

He beamed, his faded blue eyes vague through the pince-nez perched on his crooked nose. "Unfortunately, it's quite toxic. Kills rats, you know," he added gloomily, and then he brightened and ruffled his wispy white hair into a bird's nest. "Perhaps a new vermin bait. Aha! What a breakthrough! Smoke the vile critters from the sewers, say what?"

Eliza covered her nose and waved the smelly smoke away. "Genius, Marcellus. At least the dead rats won't have the cholera."

"Indeed," he said happily. Marcellus Finch wasn't yet fifty—he'd been very young when he brewed potions for her father—but he looked older, frailer. Like someone's doting grandfather. Quite mad, naturally. But her only confidant . . . at least, the only one she trusted.

"I received your telegraph," he announced. "Or rather, your little metal pet's telegraph. Where are you, tiny fellow? I've a sweet for you." He fished a barley sugar from his pocket.

Hippocrates bounced on his hinges, brass cogs spinning, and flashed his *happy* light.

"Hipp doesn't eat sweets," she reminded him. "He's made of metal, remember?"

A disconsolate *boing!* of springs.

"Oh. Well, never mind. I've something for you, too." Finch popped the sweet into his mouth and rummaged in drawer after drawer, tossing aside packets of herbs and pills and scraps of paper. He gulped the sweet and smacked his lips. "Aha! Here we are."

He twisted the lid from a cylindrical tin to show her the dark powder inside. "Fresh yesterday," he explained. "Same as before. Put twelve drams in half a pint of *aqua pura, mane et vespere.* It should alleviate your symptoms." He shot her an oddly shrewd glance. "How *are* your symptoms, by the way?"

She slipped the tin into her pocket. "Not good," she admitted. "The fever is worse. I'm having nightmares again."

"Hmm." He frowned. "I'd hoped the dependence would be easing. Have you, er . . . indulged?"

She sighed. "Last night."

"Oh, I say." Finch's eyes gleamed, confidential. "For how long this time?"

"At least eight hours. More, perhaps. And I think she might have . . ." Eliza shivered and glanced around, making sure no one was listening. She lowered her voice. "I think *I* might have done something unspeakable."

"Unspeakable," scolded Hipp, but his *happy* light gave a gleeful gleam. He wasn't helping.

"Really," Finch murmured coolly. "What kind of something?"

"A man was murdered. I don't know for certain, but . . ."

Finch poked his pince-nez. "Ah. Well, these things happen."

"These things *happen*? Is that all you have to say? I might have killed a man!" But even as she spoke, her own indignation rang false, and it made her shiver. Billy Beane had deserved his punishment. No one would miss him . . .

"But it wasn't *you,* was it?" Finch flicked a smear of ash from his sleeve. "I used to tell Henry the same. He'd get so dreadfully upset, you see. But Henry, I'd say, Henry, old chum, don't you understand? That's what the elixir is for. The shadow feels the rage so *you* won't have to. It sets you free."

Laughter, sighs, the heady scent of flowers, a hoarse male yell and a hot crimson splash . . . Her cheeks warmed. "But—"

"Take your remedy, Eliza." Finch patted her hand fondly. "Eat well. Build your strength, and we can keep these . . . accidents . . . to a minimum. Hmm?"

She swallowed. She'd been too young to understand or remember her father's experiments. Any truth in the scandalous gossip—that he'd done something appalling—had long since disintegrated into rumor. And Finch was a formidable secret-keeper. She'd long since given up fishing for information. But today . . .

"Have you ever tried the elixir, Marcellus?"

"Oh, bother me, yes." He waved a hand, dismissive. "A long time ago. Experimental, you see."

Hipp jigged at her feet. "*Nullius in verba*," he offered. "Scientific method."

"Precisely, tiny fellow, precisely. Henry and I had to be certain of the proportions."

"And?" asked Eliza.

"It was . . . fascinating. Such a night we had." Finch's expression darkened, troubled, but then he smiled and the shadows fled. "But you know I'm forbidden to tell you. When Henry died, the rest of us burned his notes, his equipment, everything. He was quite adamant. Now, your prescriptions."

He handed over a carton of glass phials, containing medicines for use in her daily practice at the madhouse. "As ordered. Tincture of poppy, infused with ginger and peppermint to settle the stomach *adstante febri*. A decoction of valerian root to cure hysteria. And, you know. *Ex tenebris*." He touched a fingertip to the cork of a narrow green flask.

It was an experimental medicine for the demented, based on the same active ingredient as her remedy. *Lux ex tenebris:* "light from darkness." In theory, if the shadow side could be kept at bay, even briefly, perhaps the lunatics would respond to further treatment.

She'd had mixed results. It didn't always work. And sometimes . . . Eliza suppressed a cold shudder. Sometimes, it even had the reverse effect and brought the darker side to the surface. Was her remedy similarly treacherous?

"Give them one small sip only," Finch reminded. "It's volatile. And . . ." He reached under the counter and produced a pair of black flasks. "Your elixir."

Her mouth dried. She wanted to flee. She wanted to rip the corks out with her teeth and gulp the lot right now.

"This is all I have left," he warned. "One ingredient in particular is scarce. From the Orient, you know. There'll be more. But not soon, so take care."

"Thank you, Marcellus." The flasks murmured in her hands, warm and clammy like flesh, and a hint of that glorious sharp-sweet scent teased her. Tonight. She could drink it tonight, sate her thirst, ease this burning need . . .

Sweating, she tucked the flasks into her bag and proffered a swab in a glass tube. "I've a sample I'd like you to analyze. I found this in a murder victim's mouth. Some kind of stupefying substance, fast-acting. Not fatal, at least not immediately or in small doses."

Finch held the tube to the light. His glittering pince-nez

polarized, prisming the light into rainbows. "Hmm. Not an opiate. Not an alcohol-based solvent, either. I smell . . . cherry blossoms, or . . ." He popped the cork, sniffed at the contents, and swooned, stumbling against the counter. He fumbled for his smelling salts and waved them under his nose. "Brr! Yes, I see your concern."

"I'm wondering if it's . . . well, you know."

"Hmm? Did you say something?"

Hipp's cogs whirred, an electric guffaw, and Eliza hid a smile. Marcellus was being even more vague than usual. "I said, do you think that substance could be unorthodox?"

"Aha! Alkahest, say what? *Ignis fatuus,* a splash of *aqua vitae*?" Finch beamed and wiped his dripping nose. "What did I say it smelled of, again?"

"Cherry blossom."

"Ah. Fascinating." He stuffed the cork back in the tube and scribbled a note. "I'll see what I can do."

"Thank you. Come along, Hippocrates." She turned to leave. "Oh," she added over her shoulder, casually, as if it were an afterthought, "I received a letter last night. From *him*."

Finch didn't look up from the berries and salts he'd started crushing in a little stone mortar. But his grip on the pestle whitened. "Oh? And what did *he* want?"

"He wants to see me. Tonight."

A tiny warm smile. "Be on your best behavior, then. Wouldn't do to upset him."

Ever since she'd grown old enough to wonder, it had baffled her that Henry Jekyll had left everything to this A.R. and not to her, his only child. Sometimes it hurt, distantly, like a long-healed wound. As if Father hadn't wanted her to be her own person. As if he hadn't trusted her. If she were a boy child, would he have done the same?

She'd often suspected Finch knew more than he was saying about her father's mysterious friend. But what if A.R. *was* Finch? Disguising his handwriting, hiding in shadow so she wouldn't feel in his debt? She depended on him enough already. Trained as a physician she might be, but she was no alchemist, to brew arcane potions.

And heaven knew, Marcellus had always been fond of her, watched over her, kept her secrets safe. It was he who'd taken her in when Henry died, wrapped her in a blanket before the crackling fire in his laboratory and placed a cup of strange-smelling tea into her chilled little hands. *I've a very sad thing to tell you, Eliza. Promise me you'll be brave.* He'd walked beside her in her father's funeral cortege, held her hand when she cried.

She lingered. "You and my father were close. Who do *you* think A.R. is?"

Finch continued his crushing, a little too enthusiastically. "Haven't the faintest idea. I correspond with him only by letter, and rarely at that. In my line of work, it's best not to ask too many questions."

"But—"

"No, there's simply no use in your fishing for information I don't have." He bashed harder at the mixture, seeds scattering. "You know the fellow wasn't named in Henry's will. It simply said 'my friend and benefactor,' and Henry had many strange friends."

"How vexing that no one thought to inquire."

Finch glanced up, arching his pointed white brows. "Well, the lawyer knew, obviously. Mr. Utterson, later called to the bar at Gray's Inn, like generations of scoundrels before him. Tiresome fellow. Always pestering Henry for this document, that codicil, the other signature in triplicate." He waved his pestle in the air. "Gabriel, I'd say, Gabriel, you obtuse old bean, leave the man alone. Can't you see he has higher concerns? Precious good he was when your mother passed, too," he added. "God rest her soul. We had the devil's own trouble convincing them all that Henry had nothing to do with it. Why does everyone assume it's the husband? It was a robbery gone wrong, nothing more. These accidents happen." Finch sniffed, indignant. "Pfft. God-rotted lawyers. Bottom of the Thames, say what—"

"Marcellus," she interrupted gently.

"Eh?" His expression cleared. "Oh, yes. Henry's will. As I was saying—you really shouldn't interrupt me, dear girl—as I was saying, Gabriel's dead these fifteen years. Buried in Highgate, you know, beneath the most spectacularly hideous black marble monstrosity. And no one else needed to know. Secrets were Henry's habit, especially towards the end. I know only that he trusted this 'friend' implicitly."

"As he did you."

Finch's gaze didn't drop. "Naturally."

She widened her eyes innocently. "What *is* that you're working on, Marcellus? I believe you've spilled it."

He looked down at the crushed berries and roots. A pungent leafy smell rose. "This? Another prophylactic. Not strictly conventional, my dear. Hush-hush."

"Against cholera?"

"Against a curse." He scraped the fragments into a pile using a folded paper, stuck one finger in, and popped it in his mouth. "Hmm. Needs more eel droppings. Oh, wait," he added slyly, "one more thing."

"Mmm?"

"Your Royal Society captain. Lafayette, was it? On the army list?"

She'd mentioned him in her wire. "Yes?"

"Arrogant gunslinger type, red uniform, smart mouth? Old money, East India Company, British army after the Mutiny, lately a bounty-hunter in darkest Bengal? Returned abruptly from the subcontinent under shady circumstances? Perhaps a tad too familiar with *la belle France* for comfort?"

"Yes?" She held her breath.

Finch winked. "Never heard of him. Good day, Eliza."

SUCH PRETTY LUNACIES

•••

BY THE TIME ELIZA REACHED BETHLEM ASYLUM FOR Pauper and Criminal Lunatics, it was nearly eleven o'clock, and clouds scudded along the horizon in a chilly breeze. The asylum's three-story edifice loomed, topped by a narrow green dome in the center between two long wings. The forbidding brick wall surrounding the complex was topped with spikes and broken glass and a coil of electrically charged wire spitting blue sparks and rust. More like Newgate Prison than a hospital.

She trotted up the steps, Hippocrates following reluctantly at her heels. Between the tall columns, beneath the twin statues of Mania and Dementia, their naked marble bodies contorted in chains, and into the stone entrance hall.

Poor Hipp scuttled straight into a corner, grinding his cogs forlornly and flashing his red *unhappy* light. He couldn't compute lunatics. They discombobulated his tiny brass brain.

"You can stay here, Hipp," she soothed. "Don't wander off this time." Sometimes, the more cooperative lunatics were allowed to sun themselves in the hospital garden. She'd found Hipp hiding beneath a hedge, fighting off a squealing girl who was convinced she'd found Snookums, her long-lost kitty.

"Stay here," Hipp muttered, and settled on folded legs with a sullen *click-click!* "*Felis catus.* Does not compute."

Eliza hurried along a narrow passage towards the office of the surgeon in charge. The stale air smelled of disinfectant. In the distance, an inmate wailed. Faded, forgotten photographs in frames stared down from the picture rail.

As always, she spared a glance for one in particular. In a dusty laboratory amongst his firebrand scientific associates stood Henry Jekyll, young and confident, wearing the black suit and elaborate cravat of the period. His expression showed that absent impatience she associated with thinking people and research scientists. *Not now, child, I've work to do. Run along and play.*

People said Eliza had his eyes. From the photograph, she couldn't tell.

The brass plaque on the open office door read SIR JEDEDIAH FAIRFAX FRCS. Eliza knocked, *rat-a-tat!* and entered.

Books and medical specimens in jars lined the walls on tidy shelves. A weak ray of sun dribbled in the narrow window. Above the desk hung a black-edged portrait of the late Lady Fairfax, a young and pretty woman wearing a white morning dress. On the desk itself—wooden, broad, not a speck of dust—sat papers and files, a single white rose in a tall vase, and a fat glass jar of preserving fluid, in which floated a pale, wrinkled human brain.

Mr. Fairfax—he preferred his surgeon's address, and never mind the knighthood, which he despised as the relic of a corrupted age he considered bygone—didn't look up from his journal.

"You're late, Dr. Jekyll." His neat steel-gray hair gleamed. Spotless black suit, an immaculate knot in his black cravat. Everything about him was tidy.

Eliza clutched her box of Finch's prescriptions under one arm. "My apologies—"

"When I agreed to take you on, madam"—Fairfax closed his book and meticulously set the pen aside on his blotter—"I did so for your late father's sake. Not for your amusing company. Certainly not for your superlative medical skills. Kindly be punctual in future."

A paper scrap dropped from her bag, and she scrambled to pick it up. "Certainly, sir. I'll do better."

"I'm sure you will." Carefully, as if he feared his face would shatter, Fairfax offered a smile. He had deceptively soft eyes, and the smile almost reached them. "I trust nothing alarming detained you?"

He was thin, she noticed. Pale. Faintly, she smiled back, and took the handwritten list he offered her. "Not at all. I'll get to work."

He rose. "After you, madam. I've rounds of my own to make."

"Oh?" She hurried beside him towards the stairs. He had a firm, energetic stride that belied his years, which had to be at least sixty. He was still physically vital, a skilled surgeon, and unlike his absentee predecessors in the asylum director's position, he preferred a radical, hands-on approach to mad-doctoring. Eliza remembered him from long ago as an arrogant but frustrated fellow—standing beside a childlike Marcellus

Finch in that photograph in the corridor—contemptuous of authority and driven by ambitious ideas. He hadn't changed, except perhaps by growing even more dismissive of idiots who got in his way.

"Indeed." Fairfax rubbed his bony hands, a hint of indecorous relish that made her shiver. "I'm testing a new treatment regime for the intractable lunatics. The potential is limitless."

"I see." She had to trot up the stairs to keep up, gripping her box under one arm, her bag in the other, with the list clutched in one fist. They passed a big woman in a dirty white nurse's uniform, carrying an armload of bloody sheets.

Fairfax made a careful frown. "Again, sister?"

"Yes, sir." The nurse kept her eyes down.

"Put her in the whirling chair, then, and do it properly this time. As I was saying, Dr. Jekyll, I'm not a believer in brain surgery. Believe me, I've tried it extensively and it's a lazy last resort at best. There's no such thing as incurable insanity. Only stubbornness and lack of will."

"If you say so, sir," said Eliza.

A pale glance. "Do you disagree?"

"Well," she ventured carefully, "I think that in certain cases, the lunatic longs for peace, but the cure is . . . more elusive than accepted medicine would have it."

"Ah, well!" Another eager rub of palms. "Then we must advance our medicine, madam, until it measures up to the task. Precisely what I'm attempting here. Would you care to observe?"

They reached the landing. The smell of filth and piss and the curious goaty odor of mad people washed over Eliza like greasy water.

A locked gate of iron bars sat immovable. Beyond, keepers in protective leather tabards strolled, steel cages like boxes on their heads and electric truncheons hanging from their belts. These were the common wards, where the non-violent lunatics could socialize, play games, dance, even be let out to spend an hour in the courtyard's chilly sunshine.

At Fairfax's nod, a warder unlocked the gate. This was the female section. Crowded, dim, noisome, the only light leaking in from barred slits too high to reach. A blunt-faced nurse with a bucket mopped at a dark wet smear on the floor.

A few of the women hooted and howled and plucked at their filthy smocks. Some just sat quietly, playing cards or reading, the kind who were neither violent nor truly mad. Just troublesome and inconvenient.

An old lady staggered in determined circuits around the room, shaking with palsy but holding her head high like a queen. Her frayed skirt was edged with ragged lace, and she twirled an imaginary parasol and nodded graciously to imaginary subjects. There were at least three queens in Bethlem, along with numerous duchesses and lords and even one genuine incarnation of God Himself.

Eliza dodged a ragged-haired woman who crawled on hands and knees, singing, her voice raw and ruined. *"She wheeled her wheelbarr-oow . . . through streets broad and narr-oow . . . cockles and mussels . . . alive, alive-OOOH!"*

In Eliza's head, Lizzie sang along raucously. *She was a fishmonger . . . and sure 'twas no wonder . . .*

Impatiently, Eliza nudged her to silence, resisting the strange urge to sweep up her skirts and dance. *For so were her father . . . and mother before . . .*

A girl with rough pink skin and trotters for feet drooled in the corner, plucking lice the size of small butterflies from her hair and stuffing them into her snout.

Eliza bent to touch her cheek. "Don't do that, Annie. They're not food. Sister, can we give this girl a bath, please?"

Annie the pig girl stared at her, baffled. The nurse grunted. "She's had one, Doctor. The lice just come on back for her. Like home for them, she is."

"And Lucy here? Is this necessary?" On the wall, a square metal frame was bolted, and from it hung a woman, shackled at wrist and ankle. Thin, but once her figure must have been shapely. Her smock was splashed with blood, and knotted dark hair fell over her face. Her fingernails were torn to the quicks. She didn't struggle or cry out. Just stared, blood dribbling down her chin.

"Necessary, as well as efficacious," reminded Fairfax. "This is not a prison, madam, but a hospital. We'll have none of Mrs. Fry's so-called reforms here. We do what works. A simple system of cause and effect. Action provokes reward, for good or ill. Wouldn't you agree, nurse?"

The nurse shrugged. "This one's been biting again. It's either this or solitary, and the cells is all occupied. Full moon in a few days. Drives 'em even more batty than they is already."

Eliza cleared her throat, self-conscious. Lucy was one of the patients on whom she'd tested Mr. Finch's remedy. *Lux ex tenebris*. She'd tried it only once. This bloodthirsty thing that burst out . . .

Fairfax lifted Lucy's chin with one finger. "Peace, my dear. You don't want the ice bath again, do you?"

"No." Lucy's voice was hoarse. Her gleaming eyes rolled, and she arched her body, lascivious. "Not the ice, sir. Please, I want to be warm and full inside. I don't care if it hurts. I'm starving in here. I need to *feed* . . ." She chewed her lip, drawing blood, which she swallowed with a lustful groan. At some stage, she'd filed her teeth to sharp points, and they glistened red.

Fairfax leaned in, an inch from Lucy's face. "No feeding, Miss Lucy. Not until you're pleasant to the other ladies. Then you can have a nice hot cup of blood. Would you like that?"

"Oh, yes, I'll be good, sir. I promise. So long as you let me drink from the nice one." Lucy writhed, passionate. "I want the nice one. He smells *goood*. Like an animal." She growled and snapped at Fairfax, missing his nose by a whisker.

Fairfax didn't flinch. "Nurse, put something between this woman's jaws before she hurts herself." And he walked away.

Eliza scuttled alongside. "Whom does she mean: 'the nice one'?"

Fairfax wiped reddish spittle from his face with a handkerchief. "Ah," he said lightly. "The bloodthirsty Miss Lucy has designs on young Mr. Sinclair. One of our keepers, a student of mine. It's quite harmless."

"I'm sure." Eliza stifled a smile. The nice one, indeed. She knew Mr. Sinclair. He was young, shy, good-looking. A kindly fellow who went out of his way to treat the inmates well. A lamb to Lucy's lion.

"But do you see? An incorrigible such as Lucy lets her compulsions rule her. Lack of will, Dr. Jekyll. Why would any of them *want* to be cured? If they remain mad, they don't have to face their sad little lives."

Eliza's arm tightened around her bundle. Her own treatment was based on Mr. Finch's theory of the shadow self, the darkness within—and her own desperate experience. Either you suppressed the shadow or you encouraged it. There was no middle ground. But who was to say which was "normal"?

Fairfax tugged her away. "I've no patience with shirkers. I intend to treat these unfortunate wretches, whether they like it or not. I shall defeat madness, whatever it takes." A shadow flitted across his face, the ghost of long-suffered grief, but it quickly disappeared. "Come along, you really must see this."

"And . . . er, what does your new regime involve?"

Through another barred gate, turning left towards the rear wing of the asylum, along a narrow brick corridor that stank sourly with vomit and fear. "It's comprehensive," explained Fairfax. "Electroshock, naturally. Hydrotherapy. Hypnosis. Extreme sensory control. Hot and cold, dark and light, noise and silence. All experimental."

Sinister electric lights flickered in wire cages. A barred gate loomed from the dark, guarded by a pair of heavyset warders, and beyond it, creeping silence. Broken only by lonely moans, and the wind, whistling mournfully through slitted windows.

The solitary wing. Killers. Cannibals. Bloodthirsty maniacs.

Eliza shivered, chilled yet burning, and the dank walls closed in. She was a trained physician. Madmen held no terror for her. So why was she filled with dread?

From the dark corridor came the sounds of a scuffle. Heavy footsteps, panting, the crash of furniture, a rough curse and a choking groan, as if a man had been punched in the stomach.

The tattooed warder with the shaven head nodded gruffly. Fairfax unlocked the gate with a key from his own iron ring. "After you, madam."

The scuffle grew closer. Eliza swallowed, and Fairfax waited, expectant. "The design is radical. Are you certain you wouldn't care to observe? I promise you'll find it educational."

She managed a weak smile. "You're very kind, but I'm already behind schedule. I really must—"

"Pity," said Fairfax blandly. "I imagined you'd be most interested in my first test patient's prognosis."

And a tall figure hurtled through the gate and slammed face-first into the wall, six inches from her nose.

She jumped back, heart thudding.

Wild crimson hair, the exact shade of the blood dripping from his nose. Black waistcoat, arms in dirty white sleeves shackled behind him with rusted iron at wrist and elbow. The warder jammed a crackling electric hoop stick around the man's neck, pinning him to the wall at a safe distance. The lunatic laughed and wriggled like a netted fish, earning himself a punch in the small of the back that knocked his breath away.

Every nerve screamed at Eliza to flee. But the narrow corridor left her nowhere to run. Nowhere to hide.

Malachi Todd grinned at her, green eyes sparkling with mischief. "Hello, Eliza," he panted. "Always we meet in such a crowd. Surely we no longer need a chaperone?"

A STUDY IN CRIMSON

• • •

GOOD MORNING, MR. TODD." SOMEHOW, SHE KEPT her voice strong. "Um . . . I trust you're well?"

"Oh, I'm capital. Most excellent." Todd licked blood from his mouth and smacked his lips. "I say, this is a first-rate establishment you've locked me up in. Very educational. I'm quite the new man."

"I'm pleased to hear it," she said faintly. He was even thinner than she remembered, his cheekbones hollow. His chin was colored with a few days of crimson beard—so improperly red, Mr. Todd's hair, ragged now in long knotted locks—and distantly she wondered who on earth dared to shave this man, and with what.

"You're keeping fine company, as ever," said Todd carelessly, his cheek still jammed against the wall. "Come to spark some life into me, Fairfax? Squirt me full of idiot juice? Or is it the ice bath today? I do so look forward to our little pain parties—"

"Shut it, dimwit," growled the warder, his thumb hovering over the button, and blue static arced in tiny forks in Todd's hair.

Todd's eyes glinted. "By all means, give me an excuse. Your face would make a charming lampshade."

"Now, Mr. Todd, keep it civil, please." William Sinclair bustled from the dark cellblock. Mr. Todd's keeper, he of Miss Lucy's sanguinary affections. Young face, dirty blond hair, a spot of blood staining his beard. He wore a smeared linen apron over shirtsleeves, and under one arm he carried a contraption of stiff canvas, trimmed with leather buckles and straps.

"Beefy Mr. Sykes here has a nervous disposition, you know that," added Sinclair. "Don't provoke him, or I'll have to take your books away again."

"Kind of you, William," remarked Todd. "Politely put. Manners appear to be in short supply this morning."

"Nervous, my arse," growled bristle-headed Sykes, and jabbed the electric stick in harder.

Fairfax waved Sykes back. "Enough. I don't want residual effects spoiling my treatment. Bring him to my new laboratory, Mr. Sinclair. Full restraints." And Fairfax marched away.

"Your funeral," Sykes grunted, and lumbered off, his glittering hoop stick fading into the dark.

Todd straightened, wriggling his filthy clothes back into place. He popped his neck, a crackle of stiff joints. Not easy, with his elbows pinned behind him. "Alone at last. How are you, Eliza? You and your shadow?"

His knowing gaze made her flinch. Mr. Todd wasn't fey, so far as she knew. Just very strange. "I'm sure I don't know what you mean—"

"Oh, never mind William," said Todd airily. "We can talk in front of him. He'll not speak a word of it. Too many wicked secrets of his own, you see. Closet hip-deep in skeletons. Shocking."

Will Sinclair smiled apologetically, his tea-brown eyes tired but bright. His cheekbone sported a yellow bruise, the relic of some scuffle. "He says that about everyone."

"He's secretly in love with me, you know," Todd confided. "It's embarrassing, the way he shuffles and stammers. I've told you before, William, I'm not your type."

"Woe! How ever shall I survive my broken heart?" A faint blush stained Will's cheeks. "If I take my eyes off you, will you run away again, Mr. Todd? Or must Dr. Jekyll and I tie you down to win a few moments of civilized conversation?"

"Now there's a diverting prospect." Todd tossed his wild red hair and grinned, feral. "By all means, you amorous beast. Civilize away."

"Thank you." Will made a little bow in her direction. "Hello, Doctor. Not often we see you in these parts."

"A habit I'd have preferred to keep," she said briskly. "I missed you at the most recent Sydenham symposium, Will. A demonstration of a pneumatic levitator. Only in prototype, of course, but it was amazing. Mr. Paxton proposes to build a railway across the Thames using this very idea. Imagine that."

Will's young face fell. "But it sounds wonderful. I'm sorry I missed it. I meant to go, but Sir Jedediah insisted. My surgery studies, you know."

Todd giggled. "Molding you into a little Fairfax, is he? What a revolting idea."

"No apology necessary, Will," said Eliza, ignoring Todd. "Next time, I'm sure."

"Definitely. One must endeavor to improve oneself in every possible way."

"I quite agree."

"I'm glad." Will fidgeted, rolling the canvas jacket in two hands. "Perhaps . . . you and I could attend together? If you're not too busy, that is."

She flushed. "Oh. Well. Ah . . . certainly. I'd be delighted."

Will beamed. He was only twenty-one, and his beard didn't make him look any older. "Excellent. Galvanism this time, isn't it?"

"I believe so. Animal electricity and its effects on the human form. It's highly anticipated."

"Oh, well done, Eliza," murmured Todd, an impish glint in his eyes that disturbed her. The symposium was merely a shared professional interest. And she liked Will. He was kindly and clever. But suddenly, she wished she could take it back.

Will hefted the buckled jacket. "Now, Mr. Todd, will you play nicely while we put this on?"

"Of course, old bean," said Todd. "So long as Eliza answers my question. Otherwise, I declare, I shall wail and kick and gnash my teeth, and our nervously disposed Mr. Sykes will come lumbering in with his whip and there'll be all that te-dious messing about with bridles and thumbscrews. And who'll have to wipe up the blood? Not I, William, I can prom-ise you that. I'm quite mad, don't you know. They don't trust me with mops and buckets—"

"Lest we be here all day," Eliza interrupted, the image of his elegant hands bleeding in metal clamps wriggling in her stomach like a snake, "I assure you, Mr. Todd, I'm perfectly well."

"And your shadow?" he murmured, intent. "I think she's troubling you. I read this morning's press. A most delicious revenge *tableau*."

Her throat corked, dry. How on earth did Todd know about Lizzie and Billy Beane?

"The ballerina, I mean," he added, watching her squirm. "I expect that's the theory your tragic Inspector Griffin is spouting. 'Revenge, sir! Vile enemies! Feuding families, ahoy!' Stupidly clever of him, I'm sure. Are you quite all right, Eliza? Your pretty cheeks are rather pale—"

"What do you mean," she cut in, "stupidly clever?"

Innocently, Todd lounged against the wall. "Oh, never mind me. I do claim a certain affinity with these matters. But I'm sure it's nothing . . ."

Mentally, she smacked herself. Classic lunatic behavior. Attention-seeking, self-aggrandizement. She should know better than to take his bait . . . "Explain, if you please."

An idle shrug. "It's all there in the reports. I'd hoped you of all people would read the signs. Your budding artist isn't angry or vengeful. Heavens, no. He's hopelessly in love."

"What?" Her senses eclipsed, and she fought to stand straight. *Whispers in her hair, the warm kiss of steel: let me show you . . .*

Will touched her elbow. "Come now, enough. No need to discuss such vulgarities."

"It's desperately romantic, Eliza," murmured Todd, "if not particularly elegant. His passion consumes his reason, and it's still hungry. If you don't soon find another . . . love letter scribbled in blood, shall we say . . . I, for one, should be all astonishment."

That's what you've come for, isn't it? A cold specter drifted from her memory. *To dance with my shadow?*

Will cleared his throat. "Thank you, Mr. Todd. As ever, your peculiar wisdom astounds. Now, I'm sorry to say Mr. Fairfax awaits—"

"Dr. Jekyll!" Bootsteps echoed smartly along the corridor. A determined, military stride.

With a sinking heart, Eliza turned.

"Dr. Jekyll, my dear fellow." Captain Lafayette of the Royal grinned at her. He'd freshened up since she'd glimpsed him that morning in Seven Dials. Clean-shaven, hat tucked under his arm, his coat a blaze of scarlet in the dank corridor. "Lady, that is. I'm so glad I found you. You must come at once . . . good God." He inhaled with a grimace. "This place stinks like a zoo."

Behind her—yes, there—Mr. Todd chuckled.

Eliza whirled, jittery. But Todd just stared at Lafayette, enthralled. "Oh, I say," he whispered. "Hello, shadow."

She swallowed. "I, er . . . I don't smell anything, Captain. What brings you here?"

Lafayette was still wrinkling his nose. "Whoever is this odd crimson fellow?"

Eliza smiled, dazed. Introductions in a lunatic asylum. This day just kept getting stranger. "Allow me, gentlemen. Captain Remy Lafayette of the Royal Society, may I present Mr. William Sinclair, student of surgery, and Mr. Malachi Todd, er . . . lunatic."

"Razor Jack." Lafayette studied him, hostile. "Fascinating. I thought you'd be taller."

Mildly, Todd met his stare. "A Royal Society lackey. Disappointing. I'd hoped you'd be smarter. Eliza, can we do without the lapdog?"

Lafayette bristled. "Nice shackles. Do they hurt?"

"Nice sword. Perhaps I'll try it out on your face. Do you think *that'd* hurt?"

Hastily, Will edged between them, lifting his hands in peace. "If you please, Captain, step away with your weapon."

"Why? He looks harmless enough to me." Lafayette didn't budge. Didn't shift his gaze.

Todd grinned like a hungry eel. "That's what they all thought."

"For heaven's sake, gentlemen," interrupted Eliza, "the miasma of male pride is choking me. Shall we draw pistols at dawn?" Firmly, she took Lafayette's elbow. "Come along, Captain. Thank you, Will, I'll see you on Tuesday morning at the Crystal Palace. Good day, Mr. Todd." And she hustled Lafayette up the corridor and away.

"Do visit me again, Eliza," Todd called after her, his voice fading into the distance. "When you find another. And give Harley Griffin my regards."

Eliza clutched her box of bottles tightly as she and Lafayette strode through the ladies' ward. Miss Lucy hissed at them, baring her chiseled teeth, greedy eyes tracking the impeccably dressed captain. "You smell *goood,* animal."

Lafayette cocked that single eyebrow. "Lovely office you keep. Such charming staff."

"Yes, well. Look to your virtue, Captain. They don't meet many dashing young officers in here."

"Lucky me," he commented dryly. "Do *you* meet many dashing young officers, Doctor?"

"Lately?" She smiled sweetly. "None."

"You wound me, madam."

"Really? How quaint. I imagine you as barely bruised."

A grin. "But you do imagine me."

"Don't push your luck."

"When I decide to push, Doctor, luck will not come into it." He glanced over his shoulder. "Whatever was that madman raving about, 'shadow'? And another what?"

"I haven't the faintest notion," said Eliza shortly, sidestepping the palsied old woman, who was still making determined circuits of the ward. "That's what 'madman' means. And mind your manners around him, if you please. Dignity is all he has."

"Weren't you the one who put him away? Didn't know you and he were friends."

She flushed. "We are *not* friends. I simply have no wish to make Will's job any harder than it already is. Rudeness upsets Mr. Todd, and when Mr. Todd gets upset, people get hurt."

"Fair enough. I apologize. The fellow back-combed my fur, I confess."

She waved at Annie the pig girl and smiled. "A descriptive turn of phrase. He has that effect on most people."

"But not on you." A sidelong blue glance.

"He's not my patient. I'm really not interested one way or the other." The warder unlocked the gate, and Eliza halted on the landing, gray skirts swirling. "Can you see yourself out from here? I have rounds to complete."

"Then complete them later." Lafayette was already tugging her down the stairs. "Come along, Dr. Jekyll. No time to lose. Consider your services retained by the Royal."

Evil visions of the Tower's dank electrified cells flitted through her mind, the rats, the rusted instruments of torture. Was he dragging her off to interrogate her? The box of Finch's alchemical tinctures under her arm suddenly loomed like a murder weapon, incriminating. Not to mention the two sniggering black flasks in her bag. God help her.

She tried to shake him off, bottles rattling, but his grip wouldn't shift. She stumbled over her skirts. "Whatever for? I assure you, I've done nothing—"

"Not for that. At least, not yet." Lafayette grinned, and it lit his eyes with disarming excitement. "It's another murder scene, Doctor. I think you'll find it familiar."

SCRIBBLED IN BLOOD

• • •

THE TALL FAUX-SANDSTONE COLUMNS OF THE EGYP-
tian Hall in Piccadilly swallowed the doorway in deep
shadow. Twin pedestaled colossi of ancient queens in
Egyptian headdress loomed above. Eliza stared up at them as
Lafayette handed her from the carriage, Hippocrates jumping
down at her side. The place looked like a tomb. "Another theater?"

"Just so. Come along." Lafayette ushered her down the
muddy side street, his hand at the small of her back. Behind
the Hall lay a bare stone courtyard, surrounded by a wooden
fence and overlooked by a pair of large black-painted windows.

Policemen milled about in their blue brass-buttoned coats,
protecting the familiar screen of bedsheets from a thickening
crowd. Scruffy boys, a pinch-faced governess or lady's maid in
a drab black dress, a haughty old lady wearing elbow-length
gloves and veils who looked down her nose when Eliza and
Lafayette shouldered through with murmured apologies.

Lizzie scowled. *Everyone loves a murder, eh? Villains in the
night, tragic heroines splattered in gore. Better than an opera.
Bloody vultures.*

On cue, Eliza spied Mr. Temple, the penny-pamphlet writer, lurking in a corner with his sketch pad out. She signaled to a policeman, secretly gleeful. "Constable, kindly escort this gentleman in the lime-green waistcoat from the scene. I believe he's contaminating the evidence."

"Oi!" Temple fought, but a grin played over his face, and he called over his shoulder as two uniformed men dragged him away. "This is an outrage, madam! I'm merely doing my job!"

"So am I, Mr. Temple. Good day."

She and Lafayette stepped around the barrier. Inspector Griffin motioned them over. A dead woman lay at his feet, a sprawl of blueberry skirts stained with blood. Young, pretty, tangled black hair stark against her death-white skin. Like Miss Pavlova, this woman had no feet.

And no hands.

Todd's words echoed uneasily in Eliza's mind. *I should be all astonishment . . .*

Her stomach rippled, sick. Every murder victim made her sad, angry, a little helpless. Much good her science did them now. All that remained to them was justice, and even that proved sadly elusive in a world where monsters walked free.

Aye, never mind, whispered Lizzie darkly. *Just another dead girl. And girls can be replaced, can't they? Can always get another wife. Another daughter to eat your food and spend your money, another housemaid to scrub and haul, another whore to make you feel good . . .*

"Still here, Griffin?" asked Lafayette breezily. "Outside your division, isn't it? Hadn't you better stick to Haymarket, where the crooks all tremble at the very twirl of your mustaches?"

"Lafayette, how nice to see you again." Griffin didn't bother to look up from his notebook. "This is still my case. The Commissioner insisted, I'm afraid. Sorry to disappoint you."

"Don't be, Inspector. You're so very good at it."

"Honestly, Captain, have you no male friends?" Firmly, Eliza pushed him aside. She, for one, was pleased to find Griffin at the scene, and not one of his rude colleagues.

She surveyed the body, pulling her optical from its bag and affixing it to her head in readiness. "Do we know her name, Inspector?"

"Miss Ophelia Maskelyne," said Griffin. "Known hereabouts as 'The Mysterious Disappearing Ophelia.'"

Memory flashed, an oil painting of a beautiful drowning girl, her flaxen hair swirling in dark water . . . She shook herself. This was no time to let Mr. Todd and his sly allusions muddle her mind.

Any more than he's done already, missy . . .

"She's a stage magician, playing at the Egyptian," added Griffin. "It's a family outfit. They're quite well known."

"A magic show?" Eliza glanced at Lafayette.

The captain shrugged. "I've seen their act. Garish but entertaining. They have the Royal's stamp of approval."

"And how does one earn such a precious jewel, pray?"

"By proving there's no magic in it, of course. You show the investigators the secret of every trick. Get it duplicated by our committee of experimenters. They document it, sign it off. It's quite simple."

"Wonderful," Griffin muttered. "You chaps take the fun out of everything."

"Fun is permitted. Just not dangerous superstition."

"Excellent. I'll remember that, next time the Royal burn some poor fellow in St. Paul's churchyard for speaking his mind."

"There's free thinking, Inspector, and then there's treason. Not the same thing."

"Really? My mistake."

"Truce, please," cut in Eliza. "Shall we help poor Miss Maskelyne tell her tale?" She bent closer to the body, careful not to disturb the pooling blood, and pulled on her white gloves. "Her face is bruised," she pointed out. "A black eye. Also her throat. When was her body discovered?"

"Time," demanded Hippocrates importantly. "Information please."

"Hush, Hipp, just record, please. Inspector?"

"Not until around midday. Possibly missing since late yesterday," added Griffin. He nodded towards a pale, dark-eyed fellow with dramatic elbow-length black hair and a bowler hat. "That's the brother, Lysander Maskelyne. Apparently she pleaded illness last evening and didn't go onstage."

"And no one thought to look for her since? Not a close family, are they?"

"Or simply late risers. These theater types do tend to over-indulge."

"A generalization, surely."

"Surely," agreed Griffin. "But the banal explanation is usually the truth. We need not seek criminal conspiracies under every rock." He shot a sharp glare at Lafayette. "Need we?"

Eliza stifled a smile. "The most likely explanation is the one requiring the simplest causes. The Occam's razor of crime. How illuminating."

Hippocrates ground his cogs. "Logical," he trumpeted happily. "Conclusion computes."

"Naught but weary experience, I'm afraid," said Griffin. "Besides, they say William of Occam was secretly an alchemist. How disreputable of him."

"Some say the Philosopher was an alchemist, too, in his day," reminded Eliza archly. "Just not a very successful one. Fools, obviously, I should say. What an outlandish notion."

Dramatically, Lafayette slapped his palms over his ears. "Tra-la-la. Sorry, what was that? I say, you vile rebels, carry on pretending I'm not here, long as you like." He wandered away across the yard, sniffing the air and humming to himself.

Griffin glanced after him, perplexed. "I'd swear that fellow's an idiot, but . . ."

"But," agreed Eliza. "I know exactly what you mean. Shall we carry on?"

She tilted her optical, ready to inspect the victim . . . but a chill threaded her bones.

A love letter scribbled in blood. What if Mr. Todd was right? What did it mean?

It means he's a friggin' lunatic, whispered Lizzie. *He just wants your attention. Forget him.*

A gulp of laughter threatened to escape Eliza's lips. Forget him? Todd was her recurring nightmare. The evil dream that never ended. The stain that never, ever washed out.

But avoiding the evidence didn't make a problem go away.

Briskly, she bent to inspect the woman's sliced legs through a magnifying lens. "Similar angle of slice relative to cut," she reported. "Same rolled edge of flesh and burr on the rim of the bone. And the forearms . . . yes. I would venture the same or similar instruments as our ballerina's murderer. And . . ." She swabbed the corpse's lips and added her golden solution from the dropper. The swab flooded bright green. "The same drug, whatever it is. We may indeed have a pattern. Or at the very least, an admiring imitator."

"The Chopper," indeed. Perhaps the bloodthirsty Mr. Temple would get his wish.

Your budding artist isn't angry or vengeful, whispered Mr. Todd in her ear. *He's hopelessly in love . . .*

But why would Todd help her? She'd stolen his freedom, locked him in a dark prison of madness and pain. Spoiled his art forever. He'd every reason to wish her ill.

Every reason, except . . .

Eliza chewed her lip, strange excitement tingling in her heart. What she had here was a multiple murderer. Killing women—surely, though two victims did not yet a *modus operandi* make—with meticulous, mathematical care. Evidence aplenty. Secret trails of tiny clues to unravel. A feast for a determined forensic investigator with unorthodox methods and no fear. These women would have justice. She'd make sure of it . . .

But she glimpsed Captain Lafayette of the Royal, resplendent in red, pottering about on the yard's edge, and shivered. A feast, but also a deadly trap.

A punctilious killer. A suspicious Royal investigator. A cunning lunatic. Each with the power to ruin her.

She didn't know whether to feel triumphant or terrified.

"Wonderful," remarked Griffin dryly. "Ten yards from the rear of a crowded venue, our hero manages once again to amputate limbs without arousing attention and to spirit himself away unnoticed. Hurrah! I do so enjoy a resourceful maniac—"

"Inspector, Doctor." Sergeant Porter strode up and tipped his hat to her. He was a gruff London man, all business, his graying mustaches bristling. "We've found the hands, sir."

Eagerly, Eliza followed Porter to a dark corner of the yard.

Two severed hands, dumped carelessly in the refuse pile. Smeared with dirt, the skin pale and bloodless. Carefully sliced off, halfway up the forearms, a pair of clean cuts.

Lafayette was already crouching, poking the appendages with a stick. His coattails trailed in the dust. "Odd," he commented, "that our man should trouble to cut them off, and then just toss them aside."

"Not particularly normal to carry them away, either."

"Illogical," buzzed Hipp, his red *unhappy* light gleaming mournfully. "Behavior does not compute. Culprit unreasonable."

Lafayette wrinkled his nose. "You say that as if it's worse than 'homicidal.'"

Eliza bent closer. "The fingers on the left hand are broken," she reported, pointing. "The flesh is badly lacerated. And there's bruising around both wrists. As if . . ." She flicked on a hand-held light, blue sparks showering. "Yes. Finger marks. I see the imprint of a ring on the left wrist. A broad one."

"She struggled when the killer subdued her," Lafayette suggested. "They fought, and her hands were injured."

"Perhaps." Eliza frowned. Cut them off, toss them aside. Maybe dropped by accident . . . "Put those in a bag, please, Sergeant Porter. And keep searching through this rubbish for the feet. Hipp, why don't you help him?" Hipp thrashed his spindly legs and leapt for the refuse pile with a gleeful *whirrr!*, leaves and sticks scattering as he burrowed in. "Crime scene," reminded Eliza after him. "Restrain your enthusiasm, there's a good boy." Hipp relapsed into kicking twigs aside one by one, muttering as he went.

"Perhaps?" prodded Lafayette, as Porter carefully scraped the appendages into a paper sack. "Speak your mind, madam."

Eliza chewed her lip. Her unscientific instincts itched, dissatisfied. "Let me present to you a different scenario. Miss Maskelyne missed the show last night, purportedly ill. But suppose—"

"Eliza?" Griffin waved at her from beside the body. "Come and look at this."

"First names, is it?" murmured Lafayette as she turned away. "Poor Mr. Todd. He will be heartbroken. You really are pitiless, aren't you?"

Her jaw clenched. "I'm sorry, *Captain,* did you say something?" She marched to Griffin's side. "Yes, Harley?"

Griffin hid a smile. "You are, you know."

"What?" Lately, he'd looked pale, she realized. Fatigued, his eyes bruised. As if he wasn't sleeping. But who did sleep, in this benighted city?

"Never mind. There's a letter in her bodice."

Sure enough, a folded paper poked from the neckline of Ophelia's dark blue dress. Eliza popped out her tweezers and eased the letter free. "Hmm. The page has been crunched up and smoothed out again. Retrieved from the waste paper, perhaps? And I smell something . . ." She sniffed the paper carefully.

"Violets," said Lafayette, without turning. "It reeks of them. Can't you smell it?"

She inhaled again. "Ah, yes. Violets. But . . ." She bent cautiously to sniff the woman's dress and hair. "Only on the letter. An expensive scent, is it not, Captain?"

"Very, in my experience."

"Purchase a lot of ladies' perfumes, do you?" murmured Griffin.

"I've had wild romantic impulses in my time."

"What a prehistoric prospect."

Lafayette grinned. "Violets are beyond the means of a stage actress, I'll wager."

"But perhaps not a gentleman admirer." Eliza shivered. *A love letter scribbled in blood . . .*

She unfolded the letter and squinted through her spectacles to read aloud.

> My dearest love,
>
> It breaks my heart to watch you cry. He does not deserve your loyalty. He will never cherish you as I do. He shall not keep us apart. Please, when can we meet again?
>
> > Your one and only
> > truthful servant,
> > G.

She held it to the light. "The ink is quite fresh, a day or two at most. And such lovely handwriting. Educated, I should say. Though rather too well-read among the bad novelists."

"So," mused Griffin, "suppose the mysterious Mr. G to be the guilty man. Ophelia receives this correspondence, she calls off sick from the show to meet him in this yard in secret . . ."

"Maybe that's his method." Lafayette walked over, dusting hands on coattails. "Same with the ballerina. He approaches famous ladies, pretending to be an admirer. Declares his love, and when they fall for it? Chop chop, thanks very much for your feet, see you later."

Griffin snorted. "Delicately put. Remind me again, Lafayette, what any of this has to do with you?"

"I'm the Royal Society, Inspector. Everything is something to do with me. Besides," added Lafayette airily, "I'm not convinced you can be trusted, old boy. Perhaps the 'G' stands for Griffin."

"You have me, sir. I am incorrigible. Clap me in irons at once."

"Don't tempt me."

"Truthful servant," murmured Eliza, abstracted. "How odd."

"How's that?" asked Griffin, still amused.

"Not 'true servant,' or 'faithful servant,' or 'yours truly.' It says, 'your one and only *truthful* servant.'"

"Hmm." Griffin stroked his mustaches. "Meaning . . . her other servants are false? Such as this 'he,' who shall not keep them apart?"

"Indeed. Show me your ring, Harley."

"I'm sorry?"

"Your wedding ring. Show me." The words came out before she thought, and inwardly she winced. It was a mark of the Griffins' modern view of marriage that Harley wore a ring at all. But Mrs. Griffin's health was frail, and had lately gone into decline. Eliza should ask after her. But it never seemed the right time.

Harley swallowed, pale, and held out his hand.

She turned it over, palm up. The silver band glinted around his middle finger. Broad, thick, the metal proud above the indentation of his knuckle. Definitely a man's ring.

"Now grab my wrists, as if I'm fighting you . . . Hmm. As I thought. Come, Inspector." She dragged him over to the gap in the linen barrier, where the striking Lysander Maskelyne still stood, arms folded over his long black coat, a stony expression on his handsome face.

"Mr. Maskelyne," she said briskly, "I'm so sorry for your loss. I'm Dr. Eliza Jekyll, Metropolitan Police. Do you mind terribly if the inspector and I ask you a few questions?"

Maskelyne looked down his hooked nose at her. He was about twenty-five. He wore his long black hair loose beneath his bowler hat, and like his sister's, it was dead straight, covering his ears. His dark eyes were arrogant, still lined with traces of stage makeup. Something looked odd about them. Improbably black, perhaps, too far apart, a little too large and liquid.

"I already told the constables everything I know," said Maskelyne coldly. "Ophelia is murdered. I can't help you beyond that." He had the grace to look grieved, his brow furrowing.

"I'm told your sister was ill last evening and didn't perform," prompted Griffin.

"She's frequently ill. She suffers . . . suffered terrible headaches. She doesn't often miss the show, but last night her discomfort was considerable."

"Oh, the poor child," said Eliza. "And how long do these, er, headaches typically last?"

"Days, sometimes." He eyed her insolently, her doctor's bag, her optical. "Women's troubles. I'm sure you understand. Or maybe you don't."

"Oh, I understand women's troubles," said Eliza with a cold smile. *Men like you, for a start.* "Tell me, Mr. Maskelyne, did your sister have enemies? Any person who might wish her harm?"

"We run a successful theater show. We've plenty of enemies." A note of unconscious pride.

"What about admirers? A particular male friend?"

His expression blackened. "What are you implying? Ophelia is a respectable girl."

Griffin touched Eliza's arm. "We don't doubt it, sir," he interjected. "But a young lady on the stage attracts attention, does she not? Sometimes from less than respectable men?"

"No doubt. But such *men*"—Maskelyne spat the word like rotten fruit—"must come through me, Inspector, and I do not shrink from unpleasantness, should it prove necessary. My sister's virtue is impeccable."

"So . . . there's no one you know of who might have written her a love letter?" persisted Eliza.

"Dozens, I imagine. She's a beautiful girl."

"How about a letter she'd choose to keep?"

Maskelyne tossed his head, stormy. "Certainly not. Now, if that's all, I have a show to run."

"Of course," said Eliza smoothly, and held out her hand. "Our apologies. I'm sure you and your wife work very hard."

"Indeed," muttered Maskelyne, and condescended to

touch her hand ungraciously, just for a second. No glove, and his oddly long hand was cold. On his middle finger shone a thick golden ring. "Do excuse me." And he stalked away.

Eliza watched him go. "A stubborn man, jealously guarding his sister's reputation. Interesting."

Griffin waited, expectant. "Well? Must I guess?"

"*He shall not keep us apart*'? Clearly, the endearingly patriarchal Mr. Maskelyne knows more than he's saying."

"Naturally. They always do. But—"

"Those bruises on Ophelia's face and neck are antemortem, Inspector. At least a few hours before death. Likewise the broken fingers. It's difficult to perform sleight-of-hand tricks in that condition, wouldn't you say?"

"Ah. The sordid truth emerges. Ophelia didn't miss the show with a headache."

"Indeed not. She missed the show because someone wearing a man's ring spoiled her face and broke her fingers."

"Perhaps an overly protective fellow who discovered her hiding a love letter he didn't want her to have?"

"Once again, you read my mind. Uncanny."

"Hmm." Griffin stroked his mustaches. "But no connection to the ballerina's case. And why kill his sister, if the argument was already over? A bad temper and worse manners don't make Lysander a murderer."

"No. But very possibly, he knows who is."

"Recall our vengeance idea, though," added Griffin. "I'd call a rival stage show a connection, wouldn't you?"

"What, you think Maskelyne could have had Miss Pavlova killed out of professional enmity?"

"I shouldn't think he'd hesitate. Did he seem the violently jealous type to you?"

"And what, risk giving himself away by hiring the same man to kill his sister? Don't even start me on hired killers going rogue and attacking their employers' loved ones."

"You suggested it, not I."

She fingered the letter thoughtfully. "Still. Creases smoothed out, carefully kept safe. Maybe Captain Lafayette's hypothesis still stands firm. Mr. G, the love-letter killer." *Scribbled in blood,* she almost added.

"Or, Lysander catches the couple at it and loses his temper. Kills Ophelia by accident. He's read about the ballerina's death in the papers, and mimics it to throw us off the scent."

"Now *that's* more realistic. It would make our amorous Mr. G at the least a witness to murder." She sighed. "So do our conjectures multiply, ever wilder. We must stick to the facts."

"Indeed." Griffin grinned. "Let's collect some more, then. I think we should track down this Mr. G, don't you, Dr. Jekyll?"

"I rather think we should, Inspector."

"Doctor?" Lafayette was messing about in the corner of the yard with Hipp and beckoned. "When you've concluded your mutual-appreciation symposium? You really ought to see this."

"What is it?"

"Come and see," he insisted. "Wouldn't want to miss my chance to impress you at last. Perhaps you'll call me by my first name, too."

"I doubt it. I find I've quite forgotten your name already." She strode over, but a hand on her arm stopped her.

"Doctor?" A pretty blond woman. Her green silken dress was fine but garish, the off-the-shoulder neckline trimmed in lace and covered with a light shawl that she clutched to her breast. Her lips were painted, her cheeks stained with peachy color. Her gaze darted, first to Lafayette, then Griffin. "I really shouldn't . . . I overheard you questioning my husband. I didn't want to talk to the detective, or to the other . . ."

But to another woman?

She caught Griffin's eye, drew the woman aside, and lowered her voice, confidential. "Mrs. Maskelyne? How can I help you?"

"My husband . . . perhaps he misled you a little." She touched her cheek, self-conscious. She looked at least thirty. Old to be Lysander's wife. But under the coating of face powder, her skin shone with an ethereal glow. "Ophelia has . . . had . . . an admirer," she whispered. "There were letters, flowers, gifts. It made Lysander very angry. He has quite a temper."

"I see."

"He's protective of his family," she said defensively. "Lysander is a very loving man. He only wanted the best for her."

"I can see that," said Eliza dryly. Perhaps those weren't just shadows under that makeup. "Did he and his sister, er, disagree last night?"

"I heard noises. Lysander was shouting, he wanted her to throw the letters away. I don't know what happened after that. I thought Ophelia went to bed."

Letters. More than one, then. "Did you not visit her? To make sure she was well?"

"Lysander wouldn't allow it. It was showtime. We had to cover for her. He said she was ill, hysterical."

"Mmm. And this . . . admirer? Did you ever meet him?"

"It was meant to be kept a secret. My husband didn't want it talked about. But we all knew."

Eliza waited.

Mrs. Maskelyne fidgeted. "I really shouldn't say. I can't imagine . . . He's a sweet, simple boy. Ophelia was lonely. It was harmless."

Eliza touched her shoulder reassuringly. "We need to talk to him, Mrs. Maskelyne. If he's innocent, he has nothing to fear. I'll ensure he's well treated." In fact, she had no such power. But unlike some of his Scotland Yard colleagues, Griffin didn't jump to conclusions. If the lad was blameless . . .

The woman breathed deep and nodded. "He started coming to the theater a month or so ago," she said in a low voice. "Hanging around after the show, sending Ophelia bouquets with little notes attached, things of that sort. At first she took no notice. Just another fan. But he persisted, and inevitably they became acquainted. Then a week ago a letter arrived that was . . . passionate. Indecent." Her face reddened. "My husband found it. He accused Ophelia of . . . well, you can imagine."

"I understand." A sudden dark vision of this woman's life spread before Eliza. Living with this Lysander, doing his bidding, observing his strict rules. Sharing his bed, being *touched* by him . . .

"She denied it, but Lysander refused to believe her. He's afraid she'll meet someone and leave the show, don't you see? She's the star of our act. It's not easy for people like us to get a Royal Society license. If she ever marries outside our circle . . ." She tugged her shawl straight, blinking her watery eyes.

People like us. Eliza recalled Lysander Maskelyne's strange eyes, his odd hands, the long dark hair carefully arranged to cover his ears. He put her in mind of the public house in Seven Dials, the scent of flowers, purple wool rough against her cheek . . .

"Mrs. Maskelyne, if you need help, I can get it for you. There are places where women can . . ."

"That won't be necessary." Mrs. Maskelyne patted her hair, self-conscious. "I just want this over with. The lad's name is Geordie Kelly. Medium height, dark hair, about twenty years old. I should say he has some decent living, from the cost of the gifts he sent her. That's really all I know, Doctor. I must go, my husband will be wondering . . ."

"Do you believe Ophelia was in love, Mrs. Maskelyne?" asked Eliza softly.

"I believe she was." The woman gave a faint, haunted smile. "Life's cruel like that, isn't it? Good day." And she gathered her bright skirts and hurried away.

Eliza turned to Griffin, who lurked by the yard's wall, eavesdropping. "Did you get all that?"

Griffin grimaced. "Not exactly. She was too far away—"

"Every word," cut in Lafayette, striding over from the corner. He finished scribbling in a notepad, which he'd evidently commandeered from a reluctant Sergeant Porter, and tore out the page to wave it in the inspector's face. "Honestly, Griffin, pay attention next time."

"Pay attention," echoed Hipp importantly from the refuse pile.

Griffin took the paper. "Thank you," he said through a clench-toothed smile. "I shall inform the Royal how pleasant and helpful you've been."

"Don't mention it." A smoldering Lafayette smile. He'd been standing much further away than Griffin.

Griffin swept his sharp gaze over Lafayette's penciled notes. "Your handwriting is a tragedy," he accused. "That 'T' looks like an 'F.' Don't they teach you properly at Eton, or wherever?"

"Harrow, actually. And truthfully? I've no idea. I was absent the day they taught anything other than cricket and thrashing smaller boys."

"Useful skills, to be sure."

"Foundations of the British Empire, old boy. Nothing more one needs to know."

"Careful, Captain. Your radical side is showing." Griffin frowned at the page. "So 'G' is for 'Geordie,' is it? Interesting. Was she convincing?"

"Very," admitted Eliza.

"Or a consummate actress," murmured Lafayette, abstracted.

"What do you mean?"

"Hmm?" He glanced up. "Oh. I don't know. Maybe I'm just accustomed to being lied to—"

"Say it isn't so," interjected Griffin swiftly.

"Appalling, I know." A flash of amused blue eyes. "But downtrodden wives, domineering brothers, secret assignations between innocent young lovers? All very convenient. We're in need of a suspect, so she gives us one. A tidy, uncomplicated one, who'll be easy to find."

Griffin shrugged. "This 'Geordie' could be an invention. Wives lie to protect their husbands all the time."

"Or to protect themselves *from* their husbands," suggested Eliza. "He could be forcing her to lie for him."

Lafayette grimaced. "Or maybe our timid Mrs. Maskelyne is the killer. Devoted wife, jealous of husband's beloved sister, defends the business at all costs, that kind of thing."

"Unlikely, surely."

That's what they all thought, whispered Mr. Todd in her mind.

"In my experience," said Lafayette, "it's the unlikely suspects who get away with murder. In any case, something doesn't smell right. And," he added slyly, "it isn't just that pile of electrical detritus by the fence."

Eliza's pulse quickened. "Burned aether? The same as Miss Pavlova?"

"Down to the melted stone." He grinned. "Admit it, you like me a little."

"How inappropriately fascinating."

"Thank you. Do I get the first name treatment now?"

"I meant the clue," she said coolly. *In my experience,* he'd said. What exactly *was* his experience of murder investigations? "But how telling, that you should think 'inappropriately fascinating' a worthy compliment."

A sidelong glance. "From you, my clever lady? I'll take what I can get."

Inwardly, she rolled her eyes. Charming, she'd grant him that. Pleasant to look at. His breezy over-confidence made her laugh. But she was no weak female, to be melted by a gentleman's smile. Especially not a man with the power to lock her up forever—or worse—with a single word.

Oh, don't trouble yerself, murmured Lizzie, with a dark giggle. *Sensible Eliza won't melt for a handsome smile. Hell, no. That takes love poetry and a straight razor . . .*

She forced a cool smile, but inside she was warm. "Wise of you, seeing as it's *all* you'll get."

"Famous last words, madam." Lafayette gave her the bright, unflinching version of his stare. A challenge?

Then, cheerfully, he clapped Griffin on the shoulder, knocking him off balance. "Unorthodox practices, Griffin old boy. Sounds like a matter for the Royal after all. You'll just have to put up with me a while longer."

Griffin sighed and straightened his hat. "Wonderful," he muttered.

THE EXCHANGE PRINCIPLE

•••

LATER THAT SAME AFTERNOON, ELIZA STEPPED OFF the Electric Underground at the new Covent Garden Station. The platform was crowded, the tunnel drenched with the stormy stink of hot metal. The tiny wood-paneled train carriage had been packed, its benches full and people standing in the aisles. The embarking and alighting crowds met and mingled, jostling her, and Hipp squawked in alarm and jumped into the crook of her elbow.

The doors slapped shut behind her, and with a deafening *bang!* and a shower of blue sparks, the train abruptly accelerated and speared away at top speed. Sky-blue lightning zapped along the tracks in its wake.

Her mind still tumbled with the details of the strange murders. Captain Lafayette was right about one thing, at least: no one's story rang quite true. But science never lied. Facts were facts. Both dead women had been drugged, both had their limbs severed by the same weapon. And both scenes featured this curious electrical detritus: a pile of burned aether and signs of extreme heat.

Like the electric train that just departed. Almost as if the sites had been struck by lightning. But there'd been no electrical storm in London for a month or more.

She'd collected samples of the aether, of course, now in little glass tubes in her bag. But she little knew what further tests to conduct. Perhaps her textbooks would enlighten her. She had a small library, tucked away in her study. All strictly orthodox, of course. The naughty books were hidden safely in Lizzie's closet, though Lizzie herself would have no use for them.

She recalled her father's laboratory, the bubbling flasks, the big coils glowing in their vacuum-sealed bottles. What would Mr. Faraday have had to say about this? Was the grit she'd collected really de-phlogisticated aether? Or would he have made some better, heretical explanation?

No point racking her brains about it now. She had more pressing matters to attend to.

Matters like Billy the Bastard, lying on a cold slab in the police morgue. Last known alive in the company of Miss Lizzie Hyde.

The irony was palpable. The ludicrous verdict at Billy's trial left Eliza in no doubt that he was a snout, a police informer. It was the only reason Billy lay in the morgue right now, his death being properly investigated, instead of left to rot in the dirt like every other corpse in Seven Dials.

Whoever killed Billy had, as Lizzie might say, really gotten someone's goat. But who?

Eliza's stomach quailed. She didn't want to know what had happened. But if Lizzie was guilty . . . what then? Could she cover up the evidence? Falsify clues? It was unthinkable.

Wasn't it?

She held Hippocrates tightly to her hip, lest he get trampled in the crowd, and he clucked nervously and clamped his spindly legs in. She let the crush wash her towards the stairs. Covent Garden Station had opened only recently, but already the tiled walls were grimy with soot. Electric lights buzzed and crackled in smoking sconces. Her tightly pinned hair tingled on end as she gripped the iron banister, the air bristling with static charge.

At last, she emerged onto Long Acre and gratefully sucked in the cold gritty air. Afternoon sunlight dribbled weak as water through the yellowish gloom, and fog wisped like lace around brass lampposts and the resting hooves of idle cab horses. It was nearly close of business, and commuters marched to and fro, satchels and leather cases under their arms.

Paper fluttered, a rain of printed leaflets like autumn leaves. She glanced up, but the fellow who'd dropped them from a rooftop had already vanished. The pages blew gently over the gutter, landing in puddles. The heading read THISTLEWOOD CLUB and A MEETING TO DEBATE PARLIAMENTARY CONCERNS.

Such seditious gatherings were banned. No one dared pick one of the leaflets up, but around her people muttered and whispered darkly to each other. *Thistlewood Club, there's no such thing . . . damned Jacobin rats, can't they just . . . the Lords rejected their petition again . . . must have a death wish . . . they'll shoot the poor bastards down like Peterloo . . .*

"Murder! Gruesome murder in Seven Dials! Killer on the loose!" A little boy in a peaked cap hollered on the corner, brandishing a pamphlet entitled THE BLOODY DEATH OF BILLY BEANE. Another of Mr. Temple's masterpieces. The cover was illustrated in garish detail, complete with knife-wielding hunchback, cringing victim, and gouts of blood. Another was entitled THE DYING DANCER, and featured a woman in ballet skirts swooning in a pool of gore.

"Murder," agreed Hipp gloomily from under her arm, and Eliza frowned, a sour taste in her mouth. She turned right along Bow Street, past the Royal Opera House, like a Grecian palace with its gabled façade and marble columns, and the domed glass pavilion of the Floral Hall. Men like Temple gloried in murder, the gorier and more detailed the description, the better.

But there was nothing glorious about death, about finding your loved ones discarded in the mud like garbage. No one had loved Billy Beane. That didn't make his death worthy of celebration. Did it?

The hell it don't, whispered Lizzie. *Why do you think your Mr. Temple's so popular? He's just speaking aloud what we're all thinking. Some folks deserve to die . . .*

It wasn't right. There was no excuse for murder. Eliza would bring Billy's killer to justice. And if Lizzie was involved . . .

The Bow Street police station loomed across the street, a dramatic four-story fixture in carved white stone. The Queen's symbol, with the ornate letters V.R. for "Victoria is Queen," stood in proud relief above the entrance, and white arc-lights glared in glass globes on either side of the door. Blue lights had been the norm for police stations until the Prince Consort died in agony in a blue room and Mad Queen Victoria had forbidden any reminder of her grief, especially *en route* to her beloved Opera House. So the lights at Bow Street were changed to white, and had been white ever since.

So were traditions born, at the whim of a grief-crazed widow. No one outside the inner circles of the palace and the Royal had laid eyes on the Queen for almost five years. She hid in her palaces, traveled in curtained carriages, concealed herself behind screens. People blamed her ersatz rulers—anyone and everything from Parliament suspending *habeas corpus* to the Royal Society's treason trials to the seemingly interminable Prime Minister, that senile Duke of Wellington, in his electric lung machine—for everything that had gone wrong. *God save the Queen!* had become an ironic catch-cry for radical reformers as well as royalists.

Perhaps the Queen was dead. Or kept as a lunatic, like so many unwanted women. Locked in a cold cellar on starvation rations, her screams unheeded.

Eliza strode up the steps, skirts whispering. The constable behind the entry desk was laboriously consuming THE BLOODY DEATH OF BILLY BEANE, running his finger beneath each line and mouthing the words under his breath. Like many of the Met's officers, he'd likely grown up in the slums, amongst the very people he now policed. A job was a job. Probably pure luck he hadn't ended up a criminal himself.

It didn't increase her faith in the justice system.

Hastily, he hid the pamphlet beneath his papers as she approached. His buttons were meticulously polished, his chin shaven clean. "Yes, madam?"

She flashed her police credentials at him. "I just spoke with Inspector Griffin. I need to examine a cadaver."

Not a lie, precisely. But the other inspectors weren't exactly her allies, and Griffin needn't discover her interest in the Beane case, not yet. Not until she'd established beyond doubt that Lizzie wasn't involved.

Or otherwise.

"Right you are, Doctor." The constable smiled uneasily. Like many people, he didn't understand the concept of a female physician, let alone a female police doctor and crime scene investigator. Possibly, he thought her a little crazy.

She gave her best maniacal grin and plonked Hippocrates down. "Come along, Hipp. Let's slice up some meat." And she flounced away before the constable had time to react.

The morgue lay downstairs, in a cold room lit only by electric coils. She shivered as she descended, Hipp's brass feet clanking on the stone steps. The door creaked open, and she was alone with the dead.

Two rows of slabs, six on each side. The bodies lay covered with pale sheets, all but a few of the slabs occupied. Harsh lights flickered, *bzzt! bzzt!* The sickly sweet scent of death wormed up her nose.

She lifted four sheets before she found Billy Beane.

There he lay, unclothed, his trademark green coat and hat removed. His thin body was pale, with dark patches of hair. His face was slack, untroubled in death. He looked smaller. Skinnier. Not so monstrous.

Arsehole, spat Lizzie coldly, and Eliza's lip curled, the shadows in her heart muttering black mutiny. Appearances meant less than nothing. Billy deserved to be dead. No one would miss him . . .

She shook herself, fighting the dark cloud that threatened to swamp her. *Lizzie, what did you do?*

But Lizzie just muttered dark curses and didn't answer.

Eliza pulled on her white gloves. The body had already been hastily washed, the trace evidence probably wiped away. The police had already seen whatever clues they could be bothered to look for. No time to lose. "Post-mortem examination, Hipp. Take a recording."

"Yes, Doctor." His little electric voice buzzed, fussy.

"Billy Beane, about thirty years old, dead since six this morning at the latest, probably longer." Hippocrates clicked and jittered, recording her words. "Visual examination. Our Billy appears to have been stabbed in the throat. Large bloody wound under the left side of the chin, angled towards the base of the skull, flesh sliced downwards on exit, not torn. The weapon stabbed upwards, then withdrew, probably releasing a large gout of blood. I'd say an edged blade."

Potentially not Lizzie's stiletto. So far, so good. And she'd noticed no voluminous bloodstains on Lizzie's dress. Still, it wasn't proof.

"In addition, three . . . no, four . . . more. Multiple stab wounds to the abdomen and chest. Some shallow, some deep, maybe three inches. Narrow weapon, sharp point. Bruises on the temples and ribs. Also the belly and private parts. He seems to have suffered some pain. What a shame."

She picked up Billy's hand. "Body stinks of gin, despite partial washing. Defense wounds, deep scratches on the palms and wrists of his left hand. He fought back, but with one hand only. The killer stabs; Billy clutches his bleeding throat with his right hand, fends the killer off with his left . . . Oh, hold on. Something's caught beneath his nails."

She peered closer, angling the dead fingers to the light. Billy's nails were disgusting, chewed ragged and stuffed with dirt. She popped on her optical, gazed through the magnifier, pulled out her tweezers, and carefully extracted . . . "It's hair. Coarse, yellow-brown in color, torn out by the root. Not the same color as Billy's."

She opened a brass flap on top of Hippocrates's head and slipped the hair onto the glass slide within. "Hair sample, Hipp. Identify."

Hippocrates flashed his lights, accessing his records of her sample collection. "Inconclusive," he reported. "Closest comparable specifications: *canis lupus familiaris*."

"This is dog hair? Are you sure? Could it be human?"

"Inconclusive. Require further data. Information please."

"Hmm. Perhaps his body was savaged by a starving animal. Even better than I thought." She popped the hair into a tube. "Moving on. Two long narrow wounds across the left shoulder and chest, probably the same blade . . . actually, no." She frowned. "These look like . . . ah." She brandished her tweezers again. "Another hair, similar in appearance, caught in one of the chest wounds. These have bled freely, their edges ragged. Not post-mortem."

She frowned. "Conclusion: Billy Beane was beaten, then stabbed to death. But before he died, he was clawed across the chest and hands by an animal. Through at least one layer of clothing, probably two."

How bizarre.

What did this mean? Did the murderer use an attack dog? Perhaps a fighting animal from the pits, or a ratter. Stranger things had happened in Seven Dials. And there'd be plenty of people who'd relish the idea of setting a dog on Billy the Bastard.

She bent to pick up the hessian sack that lay in shadow beneath the slab. "Billy's effects, put into a sack by the police. One black hat, squashed." She laid it aside, the greasy odor wrinkling her nose. "One shirt, one famously smelly green coat, both torn and bloodied, with other organic stains. Small puncture marks in the shirt, possibly matching the multiple stab wounds, measurements required. Small size of blood-stains suggests stabbings performed—"

The mortuary door banged open, and a short man with bristling mustaches and a bowler hat barreled in. "What the devil are you doing?"

She jumped back, and cursed inwardly. "Detective Inspector Reeve," she said calmly, though her heart was thumping. "How nice to see you again."

Reeve strode up, left thumb tucked in his braces, and chewed on his cigar. Just a little man, with a little man's inflated self-pride, and it irritated him to no end that Griffin had the Commissioner's ear. Griffin was younger, better educated, and well regarded by his superiors, which in Reeve's mind were three perfectly good reasons to hinder him at every turn.

"Oh, it's you," he grunted. "Griffin send you to poke your nose into my business, did he?"

"Merely doing my job, sir." Calmly she replaced the clothing in the sack. Someone's informer, indeed. Reeve was just the kind of man who'd give money to a beast like Billy Beane.

"No, *Doctor*"—Reeve salted the word with sarcasm and blew smoke into her face—"this is *not* your job. I'm about to close this case, and I'm damned if I'll allow some bookish missy who's been left on the shelf to meddle with my corpses."

The childish insult washed over her and away, rainwater on glass. "Indeed, sir," she said coolly. "You've done so well without medical evidence in the Moorfields Monster case, after all. How many victims now? Is it five?" A low blow, she knew. But his stubborn ignorance grated on her nerves. For a reasonably intelligent man, he certainly did a fine impression of a stupid one.

Reeve grunted. "Be damned to your swabs and squeezings, missy. Proper police work, that's what's needed, by proper police officers. We've found an eyewitness to the Beane murder."

Her heart skipped. "What?"

"Your fancy science didn't tell you that, did it?" He was practically crowing. "Yes, we have a little girly snout who saw the murderer. Or murderess, I should say, some uppity whore in a red dress. I'll soon find her, mark my words. It's open and shut!"

Her thoughts clattered like a rockfall. "But . . . how? Who is this witness? What did she see?"

"I can't reveal details of an official investigation to you." He chewed on his cigar. "Fancy yourself a police officer, don't you? Look, you just have to accept that girls don't have the wits for this kind of work. Stick to your embroidery. That's what you're good at. Leave the dirty jobs to the men, can't you? It isn't ladylike to have you grubbing around in the mud."

His patronizing tone stung. "Inspector, this man has been savaged by an animal. I believe there's more to this case than—"

"I didn't ask what you believe, missy, and I don't care. You can tell Griffin he'll not steal my thunder this time." Reeve stood aside and jerked his whiskered chin towards the door. "Now let me do my job, and get out."

Sweet rage whispered in her heart, and the urge to punch his arrogant face washed over her like a red tide.

Her fist clenched. She stepped up to him, her nose level with his. "If you're so eager, *Inspector,*" she spat, "you can tell him yourself. And I'll thank you to address me with respect, sir. It's 'madam,' if you please, or 'Dr. Jekyll.' I believe I've earned it. If you ever call me 'missy' again, I'll take that stinking cigar away from you and shove it up your nose."

And she slung her bag over her shoulder and stalked out, Hippocrates scuttling in her wake.

In the corridor, she stumbled against the wall, squeezing her eyes shut. Her pulse thudded, her blood coursing wild. She couldn't catch her breath. Crimson mist buzzed over her mind, an evil swarm of biting insects. God, she wanted to squeeze that horrid man's throat until his eyes bulged bloody . . .

She strangled a scream and slammed her fist into the wall. *Crunch!* Pain stabbed to her elbow, and the shock ripped her out into the real world.

The red mist dissolved like a breath, revealing the dim corridor, the single flickering arc-light.

She panted, trying to calm her sprinting pulse, control the angry shadow that threatened to smother her. She needed her remedy, Mr. Finch's powder, tucked away safely in her bag.

But so soon, after drinking the elixir only last night? Unprecedented. Something was wrong. Was the powder failing?

She shook her bruised hand. Ouch. Not very clever.

But Lizzie didn't think. She just reacted. And sometimes, when Eliza got angry, Lizzie bubbled to the surface like hot poisoned mud, ready to pop. Ready to protect herself at all costs from interfering guttersnipes like Reeve.

It felt good.

"Injury," reported Hippocrates, unruffled. "Seek medical attention."

"Thank you, Hipp." She had to calm down. Discover what Lizzie had done, exactly what Reeve's eyewitness had seen, what the clue of the strange hair under Beane's fingernails meant.

At the top of the stairs, she briskly straightened her skirts and arranged her professional face. "Constable?"

The avid reader glanced up. "All done, ma'am?"

"One more thing. I must follow up on the eyewitness statement for the Beane case. What was the girl's name and abode?"

"Name and abode," intoned Hippocrates. "Information please."

The constable frowned. "I don't think I'm allowed to tell that."

She glanced over her shoulder. Reeve was already emerging from the stairway. "Outstanding medical issues," she improvised swiftly. "Female problems, you understand. Did you know that a quarter of all women suffer paranoid delusions at the onset of their menses?"

His cheeks reddened. "No, I, er, never knew that."

"Well, then. It's a danger to society, you know. Hysterical bleeding madwomen roaming around everywhere. I must conduct a thorough internal examination of this girl's—"

"Right you are," he interrupted hastily, and searched through his papers, word by word.

Eliza fidgeted. *Come on . . .*

"Miss Jemima Clark," he read laboriously at last, "unfortunate." By which he meant "prostitute." "Age fifteen, Great Eel Street . . . No, Earl. Great Earl Street."

Frilled blue skirts, limp curls hanging over a low-cut bodice, a dull green stare of hatred . . .

I'll be damned, whispered Lizzie. *Jemima Half-Cut. That jealous cow.*

Eliza reeled. She knew the name. She didn't know it. She had no idea why this Jemima should be jealous. She had every idea.

But deep inside, her heart burned like poison, and she pasted a bland smile over her face and walked away.

Just before dusk, Eliza picked her way over the soil-stained puddles on Great Earl Street and stood before the Cockatrice public house.

Shadows stretched, the setting sun already hidden behind ramshackle buildings. The street was packed, strange-faced beggars and children with rat's tails and prowling whores with dirty skirts above their ankles. The slanting twilight threw an evil glint into every eye, turned every movement into an ambush, every whisper into a threat.

Lizzie had never minded the people, or the smell, which crawled like a living thing, damp and insidious. Eliza felt faintly sick, as if the air were poisoned.

The rooster-headed dragon above the crooked stone lintel stared down at her with insane, hungry black eyes, as if she were prey. Threatening. *Go away,* he seemed to growl. *I don't know you. You don't belong here.*

She shivered, suddenly sorry she'd taken her remedy, mixed with water just as Mr. Finch prescribed. The bitter powder had stung her throat as it went down. Now, Lizzie seemed but a distant haunting, her confidence a sadly faded dream. And this strange world—*her* world—was no longer homely or welcoming. Instead, it was filled with monsters.

Eliza clutched her bag strap tightly, mustering courage. Hippocrates crouched inside the bag, cogs clicking, his little head poking out from a gap in the flap. "Dragon," he grumbled. "Illogical. Re-examine evidence."

"Hush," she murmured, tucking him deeper inside. "We shan't be long. Just a few questions."

"Questions," he muttered reluctantly. "Home, one mile. Recompute."

She pushed the door open, and ripe warmth assailed her. Tobacco smoke swirled, mixed with the tart scents of gin and sweat. A scrawny fellow perched on a stool, playing an accordion, his bare feet dangling from trousers that ended a foot too short, and a few men already in their cups roared some filthy ditty.

They didn't appear to notice her. Didn't stop singing or sloshing their gin cups. But like a flower in the desert, her confidence wilted. She could feel their stares, sliding like fingers over her face, her well-nourished body, her clean dress.

She slid her hand deeper into the bag, grasped her electric

stinger tightly. This was foolhardy. But how else to discover what had happened? Anyone who attacked her would get a prompt dose of *zap!*, make no mistake.

A grinning white-haired fellow hunched over the pile of gin barrels in the corner, wearing only a smudged one-piece undergarment. On the floor, a mad boy with a bulbous forehead and no legs dragged himself up to her on a wheeled trolley. His arms were monstrous, over-sized. He leered, toothless, and poked his nose beneath her skirt. Startled, she shoved him away with her foot and edged up to the rough wooden bar.

"I'm seeking Miss Jemima Clark," she announced, to anyone who'd listen.

A one-eyed man behind the bar grunted at her, surly. His scar was angry pink, fresh. "Don't want no teetotaller mopsies here. Fuck off."

Her ears burned. Was that who she looked like? The Christian Temperance Union? "I assure you, good man, I've no wish to—"

"Who's asking?" Someone pulled her around by the elbow.

Instinctively, she back-pedaled a step.

Tall fellow, thin but healthy, a shock of black hair over sharp ears. He wore a dusty blue frock coat, and he surveyed her with dark, misaligned, oddly handsome eyes. He put her in mind of Lysander Maskelyne, only Lysander was chilly and unpleasant and this fellow was . . . not.

She took a steadying breath, a whiff of sweet flowers, and ghostly memory fingered the back of her neck. She knew him. She'd never seen him before. "I'm looking for Miss Jemima Clark—"

"Who? Reckon you've come to the wrong place." He glanced down at her skirts, her bag, up to her high lace-trimmed collar and neatly coiled hair. "I'd wager it, in fact."

"I don't mean to intrude. I merely wish to ask her a few questions . . ." Her words trailed away at the way he was staring at her. Frowning. Suspicious.

"Don't I know you, lady?"

Flashes of rough purple cloth, the vile taste of gin, a breathless laugh . . . "Me? Ha ha. I really don't think so . . ."

The one-eyed barkeep spat into the sawdust. "Just give her a slating and be done, Johnny. That rum rig will fetch a few bob on Petticoat Lane."

Still Johnny stared at her, scratching his untidy hair. "Indeed it would, Charlie."

She clutched her bag closer. Inside, Hippocrates wriggled, frantic. "Now look here—"

"Customers'll pay good coin for that fine mouth, too," observed Charlie the charmer. "Ain't every day you get sucked off by a *lady*."

"Speak for yourself," returned Johnny, eliciting a crude laugh.

Inwardly, Eliza cursed her foolishness, and whirled to run.

But Johnny's long fingers pinched her elbow cruelly. "Hell, Charlie, this is my drinking time. Just get out of my sight, woman. Go on, clear off." And he hustled her towards the door.

Hippocrates squawked against her hip. Somehow, she'd lost her grip on her stinger. How infuriating. "I say," she began, stumbling, "there's no need for—"

"Don't kick up a shine," Johnny hissed secretly in her ear.

"I don't know who you are, madam, or what you're about, but scuttle before you get fleeced, or worse. And don't come back." And he dumped her unceremoniously onto the street and slammed the door.

How rude. *Lizzie, who on earth was that?*

But Lizzie just murmured dreamily. Smothered by Finch's remedy, trapped in a dark miasma of slumber.

Damn it.

Eliza straightened her skirts, catching her breath. But her palms itched, and her skin crawled, and she raked her fingers through her hair and growled, frustrated. No one in this part of town would talk to her. Not without a policeman's authority, and probably not even then.

Lizzie, on the other hand, could navigate these treacherous waters with ease. Find this Jemima, discover what she'd seen. If she didn't get her red-skirted behind arrested by Reeve first. Not forgetting the irritatingly persistent Captain Lafayette, who had at least as much information as the police, probably more . . .

That rich, dangerous hunger burned inside her, scorching her resolve thin. Yes. Why wait for the relief she craved? She had the elixir ready. No time to lose. Prowl down here tonight, discover the truth once and for all. And it'd feel so good . . .

Her hands shook, sweating, and she clenched them. Not tonight. She couldn't, no matter how tempting the prospect. Set Lizzie free and she'd ooze off into Seven Dials and not come back until morning.

And Eliza needed to be home at midnight. To meet her mysterious A.R.

She hurried along darkening Broad Street towards the mist-twinkled lights of New Oxford Street, anticipation eclipsing the gnawing hunger, at least for the moment. How could she have forgotten? She had a bath to take, her hair to wash and curl, her best clothes to make ready.

It wouldn't do to disappoint A.R. Not at all.

A PROFOUND DUPLICITY

• • •

AT TWENTY TO MIDNIGHT, ELIZA EASED OPEN HER study door on the first floor.

Firelight gilded the bookshelves, the fringed carpets, her leather-topped desk. Plum-red velvet curtains hung floor-length over the window. On the mantel, above the glowing coals, a clock ticked, brass cogs clicking behind a cut-glass face.

She sat on the cream upholstered chaise, putting her candle on the table. Her light skirts puffed, and she smoothed them carefully. This was her best dress, pale golden silk with an embroidered bodice, tiny cap sleeves and matching gloves to the elbow. Something a young lady of not-quite-sufficient fortune might wear while she swanned around from *soiree* to house party to court reception for the season, trying to attract a lord's son or a rich officer.

Or on a dark midnight in a Chelsea loft, holding palaver with a murderer.

Her shoulders were almost bare, and a hint of cleavage swelled at her rounded neckline. She'd pinned up her hair under a pearl-studded net. All she needed was a feathery fan to bat her eyelashes behind.

She was just glad no one could see her. In any other setting, she'd have felt faintly ridiculous, not to mention fraudulent. But A.R. was old-fashioned. It pleased him to see her "ladylike."

Besides, he'd paid for most of this. Might as well wear it for him, if no one else . . .

But you did wear it for someone else, didn't you? You was due to meet A.R. that night, but instead you scuttled off on a killer's trail, and look what happened. Can you still smell oil paints, Eliza, even though the silk's long since cleaned?

. . . but with the receipt of A.R.'s letter, after so many months of being ignored, all the old questions bubbled once more to the surface. She fidgeted, the dress uncomfortable and strange. She'd eaten only the barest of morsels for supper, and the fire's heat made her sweat.

Who was he? What did he know of her father, the mother she'd barely known? Why did he spend so much effort and money on keeping an old friend's orphaned daughter, when a few simple financial transactions would have divested him of responsibility for her forever?

Keeping. The word bothered her. Like a museum exhibit. Or a pet.

Never ask about me, he'd whispered from behind the velvet curtain that first fateful night. *Never follow me. Stick your pretty nose into my affairs, princess, and I'll make you wish you'd never been born.*

Why had he forbidden questions? And why wouldn't he show her his face? Was he ugly? Deformed? Notorious? Did he fear she'd . . . what? Run, scream, make a scene? Go to the authorities?

And what if, one night, instead of obediently presenting herself to his summons . . . she sent Lizzie? *I want you to meet your new sister,* he'd said that night, as she trembled, the hot sweet scent of elixir watering her thirsty mouth. *Perhaps you've dreamt of her. Her name is Lizzie Hyde, and she wants you to be happy . . . but you mustn't ever make her angry, my sweet. You mustn't ever betray her. She won't understand.*

But the idea made Eliza blush. The things Lizzie would say . . . No, it'd never do. If A.R. wanted to see Lizzie, he'd say so. Wouldn't he?

So here she sat, in her ridiculous peacock outfit with pearls in her hair, while in Seven Dials, the hunt for Billy Beane's scarlet-skirted killer no doubt carried on. In her heart, shadows stirred like angry snakes. This was pointless. She should rush down there, winkle out this Jemima, find out exactly what the dirty chit knew . . .

"Don't go."

She froze, halfway to her feet. *Don't look. Don't turn . . .*

A warm draft puffed on the back of her neck, and her candle flickered, as the curtain behind her swayed. Leather, tobacco, a whiff of some bitter alchemical tincture.

She tried to breathe normally. "Uh . . . good evening, sir."

"Is it?" Gruff, roughened with liquor or sin. An edge of weird-city drawl. Kindly, after a coarse fashion. "Sit, why don't you? I don't bite."

She took her seat. The chaise pressed uncomfortably beneath her thighs.

A melancholy pause. "You look beautiful, my sweet."

She cleared her throat. "I, er . . . I was pleased to receive your letter."

"Were you?" A hair-tingling chuckle. "I think you'd like it better if I stayed away."

"Not at all, sir." It tumbled out in a hurry, and she gave an embarrassed little laugh. "I look forward to your visits. It's just that . . ."

"You'd prefer we met in public? Like normal people? Take tea and biscuits, make social calls?"

"It had crossed my mind."

"Ha! We'd make a fine spectacle in society, you and me." Cloth rustled, as if he sat or fidgeted. "Get ourselves invited to Lady Whoever-the-Hell's absurd summer ball. I'll parade you in on my arm and thrash the lights out of all the love-struck young fools who'd chase your hand. You'll wear silk and diamonds, and we'll dance the waltz by candlelight."

She gave a little laugh, trying to lighten the mood. "I'm afraid I'm a terrible dancer. Do you waltz, sir?"

He chuckled. "Bet your pretty ankles I do. Would you like that, Eliza? The clever little vixen and her fierce guardian angel of ruin. People would gossip that we're lovers."

She opened her mouth and shut it again. Impossible man.

But not for the first time, she wondered exactly what Henry Jekyll had intended their relationship should be.

"We can't ever do that, my sweet. Society, I mean." A bitter, wistful tone. "I'm sorry for you. If Henry were here, you'd be the toast of this god-rotted town."

Was that a flicker of shadow, in the corner of her eye? She laughed, shaky. "I really don't think so . . ."

"God's blood, girl, don't flay me with that smile of yours."

A jagged edge, bottled-up rage. How could he see her face? A reflection from some shiny surface, a window . . . ? "You look so much like your mother. May her ghost wander alone in the dark."

The sentiment shocked her. But the ever-present itch of questions was irresistible. "Did you know my mother well, sir? I'm afraid I barely remember her."

"*Know* her." His laugh was ugly. "Now there's a double-bladed question. The woman's dead and forgotten. Do you really want to dig up her murdered bones?"

She blushed. "I apologize. I didn't mean to pry." *Ask the question,* urged Lizzie impatiently. *What are you, a coward?*

"Never you mind. I hear you're having trouble with some strutting cock from the Royal."

As usual, she scrambled to catch up with his abrupt change of subject. Had Finch said something? "Oh. Yes, but . . . how did you know?"

"I know everything about you. For one, I know you met an old friend today. How did that make you feel?"

She shivered on the seat's edge, hardly daring to move. Finch knew nothing about *that.* "I'm not sure to what you're referring—"

"Entertaining, isn't he? An expert in his field. If you can stop him spouting rabid nonsense." A snort. "Always did have too many dreams in that tragic head of his. Did he ever show you his paintings? Now *there's* a zoo."

Unexpected connections dazzled her, and she struggled for clarity. Her father's associates, the photograph outside Mr. Fairfax's office. She didn't know them all by name. It was years ago; some were doubtless long dead. Was A.R. in the photograph? And as for Mr. Todd . . .

She suppressed the urge to rush to Bethlem to study the photograph. "I'm confused."

"No, you're just pretending to be stupid. It doesn't suit you."

"How do you know Mr. Todd, sir?" His challenge made her short.

She felt him smile, a warm current on the air. "I know everything interesting that happens in my town. And Todd's interesting, you have to give him that. Answer my question: How did he make you feel?"

She closed her eyes, counting heartbeats. Was it a trick question? A warning? "Uneasy," she whispered, as if in a trance. Was it only Todd of whom she spoke? "Lost. Frightened. He knows . . . too much."

"Mmm. Well, it's nice to have friends. Tell me about the Royal."

She blinked again at the bait-and-switch. "It's just routine. Merely a murder I'm investigating. They sent their man to pry."

"And you can handle this Royal's man, can you?" A derisive challenge, yet a strange note of pride.

"Of course. He knows nothing." But her heart stung that she might disappoint A.R. She wanted him to think well of her. How desperately she longed for that. Like any young woman, eager to please a father figure . . .

Flames danced in the grate, hypnotic like fairy lights. Her candle guttered, a spectral breath. "And Lizzie? How does *she* handle him?"

With both hands, whispered Lizzie slyly, and Eliza nearly splurted it out. "Uh. I'm not sure what you mean . . ."

But she knew. Lafayette was dangerous, and danger excited Lizzie. Made her reckless. But if a threat got too close? Lizzie acted swiftly to get rid of it. Or, so Eliza had thought, until that chilly night in Chelsea.

"Be careful, my sweet." A glitter of steel-edged threat. "No one wants a scene. But if I have to protect you, I will."

Her thoughts stumbled. What would A.R.'s "protection" involve? Would he petition important people on her behalf? Buy their silence? Hurt them?

"Now I've frightened you." A velvety rustle, the bitter scent of alchemy. "Let me give you something. Missed your birthday, didn't I?"

A cool caress feathered around her throat.

Her nerves crackled, electrified . . . but warm, rough hands pressed down on her bare shoulders, keeping her in her seat. His twisted shadow hulked along the bookshelves. The room suddenly seemed impossibly small and threatening, swallowing her in warm anticipation . . .

"This was your mother's. She'd have wanted you to have it, now you're old enough." His breath ghosted over the back of her neck. "I care for you, Eliza. Don't ever doubt it." His voice faded. "Even if sometimes I forget."

"Who are you?" she whispered, entranced.

A heartbeat of silence. "You know who I am."

She whirled. Gone. Just a sway of dark velvet curtains and the smell of leather.

She stumbled to the window. Open, a puff of cold midnight breeze. No one in the street. She stuck her head out, craned her neck. Nothing.

How did he do that? Did he . . . disappear? Just as the Chopper seemed to vanish without trace?

Ridiculous. No one *vanished*. Did they?

Eliza sucked in deep breaths, trying to calm herself, and speckled light danced across the wall. A reflection, starry fragments of golden flame. She fumbled at her throat. Smooth, ornate, the intricate edges of filigree.

A diamond necklace. The wedding gift in her mother's portrait. *May her ghost wander alone in the dark . . .*

What did he mean?

She fingered the jewels uneasily. They spilled over her collarbones, a flaming rosette in the warm firelight. Priceless . . . Abruptly, she tore the thing from her neck and dumped it on the table, as if it might bite.

It sparkled, accusing. *You'll wear silk and diamonds, and we'll dance the waltz by candlelight . . .*

Oh, no. No. It was all too perfect. Too convenient.

Suddenly resolute, she lifted her skirts and sprinted for the stairs. Down, two by two, careless of the noise. She grabbed her cloak and ran outside.

The door slammed behind her. Cold dark street, buzzing electric lamps, mist fingering the wrought-iron fences. She shivered and tossed the cloak around her shoulders. It covered her completely, hiding her delicate skirts under a velvety black swirl. No one around . . .

Her ears prickled. Tiny echoes, footsteps on stone.

At the junction with Bedford Place, a flapping coattail vanished around the cornerstone.

Yes.

She hurried after him, pulling the hood up over her hair. Moonlight spilled molten metal over the road and frosted the trees with silver. She was wearing her formal slippers, not boots, but her footsteps echoed, frighteningly loud on the stones. He didn't turn. Didn't notice her.

Chill seeped into her toes, crawling icy roots beneath her petticoats. Her breath didn't frost the clammy air. But her mother's absent diamond necklace still stung cold on her skin like a ghost. What did such a gift mean? Why had he chosen tonight to give it to her? And why had he avoided talking about her mother?

What d'you think it means? Lizzie humphed contentedly. *He's a dirty old pervert who thinks he can buy you with baubles, that's what. Told you so.*

She rounded the corner, the street still empty . . . but there he was. Almost a block ahead. He strode swiftly but unevenly, his shoulders hunched in a dark frock coat—black? dark blue? purple?—and a top hat yanked down on his head. She couldn't see his face, but he didn't look especially large or threatening. Just a man.

He was escaping. Disappearing into the mist. She broke into a trot. Around a corner, across a square, the wet grass soaking her feet. It was after midnight. The town houses were silent, no lights burning.

A hansom cab pistoned by on creaking brass legs. The cries and traffic noise of ever-busy city streets loomed closer. Arc-lights buzzed, the *clank!* and *boom!* of the Electric Underground beneath her feet, the stink of hot aether and horse dung.

She emerged onto New Oxford Street. For a moment she lost sight of him, and her heart bounced into her throat . . . but there he was, crossing the street, his strange shambling gait, his tightly jammed top hat. She hurried after him, dodging urchins and drunken revelers, costermongers already pulling their carts towards market.

Her quarry disappeared down Drury Lane and onto a side street. The shadows thickened, along with the stench. The street narrowed, walls closing in. Shouts and drunken song drifted. Ragged children slept in piles against walls and in gutters, their little faces pinched blue with cold. In a doorway, a man had his way with a prostitute, bunching her skirts around her waist. On the wall, someone had scrawled *Burn the Royal* in chalk.

Clawed feet scuttled behind her, and something growled, larger than any rat. Eerie laughter tracked her, echoing left and right, and sniggering breath ghosted across her cheek. A hooting thing leapt out at her, a bare-skinned man with long monkey arms and a sloppy grin.

She dodged and kept running. Breathing hard, the cold air aching her throat. She was losing him in the twists and turns. She ran faster. Her feet slipped in noisome effluent, and fruitlessly she tried to gather her skirts. Her best clothes were filthy. Molly would notice. Then again, she rarely wore this fancy gown. She'd have it cleaned by a laundress, replace it in her closet before Molly knew anything about it.

At last, A.R. limped up to a door across the street beneath a flickering blue torch and thumped it with his fist. *Bang-bang-bang!* The doorjamb rattled under his blows.

The door cracked open. Glinting eyes peered out, a red-lipped smile. A.R. disappeared inside, and the door slammed shut.

Eliza's spine tingled cold. Not a polite part of town. Fiery lights burned in the windows, and rough voices were muffled inside. The heady smell of liquor leaked out, as well as those of other, more dangerous substances, like seductive enchantments inviting her in. A woman screamed, and ill-made laughter followed, and abruptly the scream died. In the street, a fistfight had broken out between half a dozen men, and a tall thin fellow in a long coat was smashing another man's head into the ground, over and over. Another fellow already lay senseless in a puddle, face-down and bleeding. In the side alley, a prostitute did business on her knees, eliciting grunts and groans from her customer.

Clearly a house of ill repute. Stupidly, she flushed. What A.R. chose to do with his spare time was no business of hers. But what kind of "gentleman" was he? How had respectable Dr. Henry Jekyll even encountered such an ill-favored reprobate, let alone come to trust him as a "friend and benefactor"?

But she knew the answer.

She had Lizzie. Henry had his own shadow. A man who did dreadful things. Surrendered to dark and forbidden temptations. Made unsavory acquaintances . . .

You're just pretending to be stupid, A.R. had said. *You know who I am.* As if all the evidence she required lay right in front of her.

Go on, crooned Lizzie, seductive like a whore. *Stroll right up to that door and charm your way in. Dazzle 'em with a smile, flip 'em a coin or two, flash 'em some ankle. You'll find out what old mate's up to right enough . . .*

Frustration nipped at Eliza's cold fingers. She wasn't Lizzie. Look what happened at the Cockatrice. She'd never get past the front door of this place . . .

Maybe he wants you to follow him, argued Lizzie. *Ever think o' that? He's as tired of this secret game as we are. All that talk of waltzing and drinking tea. How many diamond necklaces he gotta give you before you figure it out? He wants you to see him, Eliza. Hell, he was right begging you to turn around . . .*

"That's ridiculous," she retorted.

Oh, aye. A husky chuckle. *He goes straight from your prissy parlor to a brothel. Who d'you reckon got him thinking along those lines?*

"Don't be disgusting!" Too loud in the gloom. Her fingers flew to her mouth, and she shuddered. God help her, she was talking to herself. Lunatics rotted in Bethlem for less. Were the voices her patients heard real, too?

But Lizzie's taunts stung like vinegar poured on a rash. Steeling herself, Eliza strode up to the door and knocked.

Rap-rap! The tiny sound didn't echo.

The door opened a crack. Firelight spilled out, the rich smell of wood smoke and old wine. Bloodshot eyes surveyed her with narrow disdain. "What's the word?"

"I'm sorry?"

"The watchword, idiot!" Crotchety, like a mad old man.

"Oh. Er . . ." Eliza tried to think, to imagine what such a word might be, but nothing came to mind. *How about, fuck off?* whispered Lizzie. *There's a fine watchword for you, you crazy old fool . . .*

"No word, no entry. Bugger off." A pernickety cackle, and the door slammed shut.

"I say, how rude." She rapped again, but the door didn't open.

She sighed and turned away. This place made her uneasy. What kind of place wanted a watchword?

Oi! Where d'you think you're going?

Determined, Eliza started walking.

Don't be a weakling, scoffed Lizzie. *Someone else might come along, and we can mooch in with them. Or at least wait 'til he comes out. He's gotta go home sometime. We could follow him, find out where he lives . . . or don't you want to know?*

Eliza huddled deeper in her cloak.

What are you afraid of, Eliza? Making Mr. Skulk-Behind-the-Curtain angry? Or finding out the truth about our precious Henry?

"Don't talk about Henry like that," she snapped. "He's my father, not yours."

Is he just? Where'd I come from, then? Not from that little black bottle, Eliza. I were always in here. The drink just lets me out . . .

"Shut up. Just shut up. You don't know anything!"

Coward, whispered Lizzie slyly.

"Am I, now?" snapped Eliza. "I'll remember that, next time I visit Mr. Todd. You remember Mr. Todd, don't you? Oh, that's right. You don't. Who's the coward now?"

Lizzie sniffed haughtily and didn't reply.

"Ha!" Eliza sniffed back. "That silenced you, missy. Not so clever now, are you?"

But the hot black aura of Lizzie's anger bubbled beneath the surface like a witch's brew, and Eliza rubbed her chilly arms and broke into a run.

IGNIS FATUUS

· • ·

THE NEXT MORNING, IN UNSEASONABLY WARM SUN-shine, Eliza hurried down the lane to the stage door of the Egyptian Hall, Hippocrates at her heels. A wisp of hair fell from her bun, and impatiently she tucked it back up.

Inspector Griffin was waiting for her, immaculate as usual in his dark morning coat and freshly brushed hat. His face looked pale, and sleeplessness drew dark rings under his eyes.

But he mustered a grin. "I say, Doctor, you look a little untidy. Late night?"

"You and me both." She covered a yawn, her eyes gritty. She'd slept barely at all, squirming in a mess of sweaty sheets and fevered dreams, in which the stinking maze of Seven Dials burned like the Great Fire, and she ran through flame-licked streets wearing a golden silk gown, chasing a shady personage she never seemed able to catch. Horrid demon laughter had echoed around her, evoking some elusive memory that she couldn't quite recall. A cold corridor in her father's big old house on Cavendish Square, creaking floorboards, whispers from a darkened bedroom, the slow *drip-drop-drip* of blood . . .

She'd swallowed another dose of her remedy an hour ago. It hadn't helped. Shadows squirmed inside her like trapped snakes, hunting for a way out . . .

"By the way," said Griffin casually, "I've received a complaint about you."

Lizzie snorted. *Little Mr. Left-on-the-Shelf, I'm thinking.*

She sighed. "Don't tell me: Inspector Reeve."

"Uncanny! The very same. He has this peculiar idea that you serve at my beck and call at all times. Interfering with strange bodies, indeed."

"'Missy,'" trumpeted Hipp, imitating Reeve's condescending tone. "'Fancy yourself a police officer. Stick to your embroidery.'"

Eliza stifled a giggle. "It wasn't a 'strange body,' Harley. I was simply doing my job."

Griffin's gaze darkened, serious. "Then do it carefully, Eliza. Reeve is a vicious little man who still has friends at the Home Office. If you step over the line, I won't be able to help you."

I'll bloody well help meself, then, snarled Lizzie, and Eliza's blood warmed with the seductive prospect of revenge. *If that little cigar-chewing bastard crosses me, he'll be sorry . . .*

"Very well." Eliza yawned, properly this time, but the rage bottled up inside her, prickly and dangerous like a cactus in a bag. "So, what am I doing here? Did we finally get a court order to search Disappearing Ophelia's quarters?"

Griffin fielded imaginary applause. "Thank you, it was nothing. Creaky old Magistrate Turpin dickered and muttered and scratched himself as usual. Until I tossed out the words 'Royal Society.' That cleared away the cobwebs."

"You used Captain Lafayette as a threat?" She glanced around the alley, half expecting Lafayette to leap out. "Now he'll be truly insufferable."

"Not in so many words. I merely pointed out that now the matter has engaged the Royal's interest, I'd be sure to mention His Honor's name as the man who stalled my investigations."

"What was the problem, in any case? I expected the search to be done by now."

"The charming Mr. Maskelyne and his entourage of strange and beefy friends wouldn't let us in. He said his sister was killed in the yard, not in the theater, so it wasn't a crime scene, and seeing as his lady wife had conveniently told us everything anyway, a search wasn't required, and would we kindly clear off. Or phrases to that effect."

Eliza winced. She didn't envy Mrs. Maskelyne her husband's temper. "So where is our ever-helpful captain, anyway? Not hovering over your shoulder today?"

"Before noon? Shouldn't think he'd strain himself."

"You realize he has authority to enter where he wishes? We could have made this search yesterday."

"Yes, well, consider it my good deed for the day. You noticed Lysander's odd ways, didn't you?"

"Certainly. Horrid man."

"Undeniably. But as yet he's done nothing wrong by law. Did you see his eyes? I've no idea how he fooled the Royal the first time, let alone a second." Griffin shrugged, ingenuous. "Perhaps there are places our tenacious captain needn't go. Don't you agree?"

Chastened, she nodded. Just because Lysander annoyed her—*back-combed your fur, did he?* whispered Lizzie smugly—didn't mean he deserved to have his livelihood destroyed. "Didn't think you believed in magic, Inspector."

"The Royal believes in it. That's what matters." Griffin held open the door. "After you . . . I should say, after him," he added, as Hipp darted inside and vanished into the dark.

Inside, a narrow, musty corridor led into the bowels of the Hall, which doubled as exhibition space, gallery, and museum as well as a small theater. Curtains, sudden corners, ladders lurching upwards, wooden steps twisting down into the dark.

Sergeant Porter led the way to the stairs, which took her up to a narrow landing with a series of doors. "First one along," he said gruffly. "We've left it just as it were, sir."

"For what it's worth," muttered Griffin. "Maskelyne has long since stripped everything he doesn't want us to find."

"We shall see," said Eliza firmly, pulling on her white gloves. "Every contact leaves a trace. Let's see what Ophelia and her brother have left for us."

A tiny window let in a shaft of dim light. Wardrobe, rug, wrought-iron washstand with a half-empty jug. A full-length mirror hung on a hinged frame, covered in a white satin shawl. A few books leaned on a shelf. *Oliver Twist. The Age of Reason. Jane Eyre. The Faerie Queene. A Vindication of the Rights of Woman.*

Shimmering costumes in garish colors lay flung over the couch and hung on hooks along the wall. The dressing table was cluttered with little glass pots of rouge and stage makeup, like lurid oil paints, green and blue and orange.

A tall screen covered in golden Chinese silk hid Ophelia's bed, which was a narrow one with a ghostly lace canopy. Neatly made sheets, but the white quilt was creased and flattened, as if someone had lain atop it without getting in.

Hippocrates snuffled at the pillow and buzzed. "Attention. Trace substance detected."

"Well done, Hipp." Eliza poked her tweezers at a tiny rust-colored stain on the satin pillowcase. She flicked a filter on her optical and snapped on her ultra-violet light. The stain glowed eerily. "Blood," she confirmed, and pushed her optical away. "Still, it could be from a nosebleed or a scratch. And certainly not enough for the kind of surgery our killer performs."

She sniffed the sheets. The smell of rose petals and oriental incense hung, a faded memory. "A single bed," she commented. "No other girls in the family?"

"Correct. Just Lysander and Ophelia."

"Poor girl." She pinced a single black hair from a crease in the quilt and held it to the light. "Coarse, with a slight curl. Ophelia's was fine and straight. Still, it could be hers. I'll do a comparison." She popped the hair into a sample tube.

"Too short to be Lysander's," added Griffin.

"In the bed? Let's hope so." Eliza poked at the ashes in the incense burner, checked the wicks in the old-fashioned oil lamps. "At least a day old. If someone's been in here, they brought a candle."

Griffin sorted through the contents of the dressing table drawer with his pencil and fished out a slip of writing paper. "Same handwriting, would you say?"

Eliza peered over his elbow and read aloud.

I watched you disappear tonight. It was better than I could have hoped. You were fabulous, and I wished we could vanish together. Perhaps one day we shall.

I live in hope.

Your loving
G.

She smelled the paper. "Violets again."

"A threatened elopement?" Griffin mused. "Strange, that Lysander should leave this letter and take the others, if he's so protective of his sister's reputation. Left here for us to find?"

"Or perhaps we're giving Lysander too much credit for cunning." A bunch of dying white roses sat in a vase on the dressing table. She lifted one out, and crispy petals fluttered to the floor. "White for purity," she commented, "not red for carnal love. Neatly cut, stems undamaged. A florist, or someone with garden implements. Expensive."

"Roses, white," piped up Hipp. "Threepence per bunch."

"Expensive, indeed. Or stolen."

Her brows lifted. "Mrs. Maskelyne said she thought this 'Geordie' to be of no uncommon means. But perhaps he's merely a thief. A con man of some sort. Lafayette's love-letter killer?"

"It would explain the alleged expensive gifts. Which, by the way, I don't see here." Griffin poked through the glass jewelry box on the table. "It's all costume, for the stage. Not a genuine piece among them."

"Raided by the loving Lysander?"

"The gifts? I expect so. If they ever existed at all."

"Don't tell me you're suspicious."

"Do you see anything that contradicts the Maskelynes' story?"

"Not in particular," she admitted.

"That's what I mean. It's all too convenient." Griffin grimaced. "Awful as the prospect is, I'm rather beginning to agree with Captain Insufferable—"

The door banged open, and a young servant girl in a black dress and white apron halted in her tracks. "Oh. Sorry, ma'am, sir. I'll come back after . . ."

"Not at all," interjected Griffin, swiftly moving so she couldn't back out. "Come in, please. What's your name, child? Are you the housemaid here?"

"Mary, sir." The girl dipped a curtsey, hastily tucking a loose curl under her cap. "I clean up after 'em, sir. Make the beds, take out the rubbish, bring water."

"And who dresses—dressed—Miss Ophelia? Is there a lady's maid?"

"Well, there's Missus Maskelyne's maid . . ."

"I mean for the theater. To help with the costumes."

"No, sir. They all put on their own. Sometimes I help," Mary added with pride. "I curl Miss Ophelia's hair just how she likes. She says to me, 'Mary, whatever shall I do without you?'" Her smile faded. "I'm not in trouble, am I, sir? Because I never done nothing . . ."

"It's all right, Mary," soothed Eliza. "You've done nothing wrong. I say, those are lovely flowers, aren't they?"

"Very pretty, ma'am."

"A gift from a friend?" suggested Griffin.

Mary shuffled, twisting her hands in her apron. "I didn't see who brought them, sir. Miss Ophelia is much admired."

Something in the girl's tone rang false. "Are you sure?" asked Eliza. "Do you know a boy named Geordie? A friend to Miss Ophelia?"

Mary fidgeted. "Everybody knows Geordie. He hangs around the theater all the time."

"Why?"

"Well, he wanted a job, only Mr. Maskelyne told him no. But Miss Ophelia were nice to him."

"In what way?"

Mary blushed. "She talked to him, is all. Such a nice hand-some boy, and most people just kick 'im out o' the way, but not her. He's . . . well, he's kinda sweet on her," she admitted, with a sigh straight from a melodrama. "I told 'im it were no use, but . . ."

"But what?" pressed Griffin gently.

"But he won't listen. He watches her on the stage, and he thinks she's so pretty and magical-like, and I . . ."

Lizzie smirked. *Aww. Sweet little thing's in love.*

Inwardly, Eliza rolled her eyes. "And you what?"

"Ma'am?"

"It's all right, Mary. You won't be punished."

Mary twisted her hands. "Promise you won't say nothing to Mr. Maskelyne. He'll have my hide."

Eliza and Griffin exchanged glances. "We promise."

"I just wanted Geordie to like me." The girl was nearly in tears.

"Mary, we can arrest you if we have to. Do you think Mr. Maskelyne will keep you on if that happens? Just tell us what we want to know, and nothing need be said. You have my word."

Mary wiped her face, resigned. "Sometimes I snuck him into the theater for free, so as he could watch her. And I bringed him things. Of hers, you know. Old flowers, ribbons. Things she throwed away. I don't mean no harm."

Awkwardly, Eliza patted her shoulder. "Thank you, Mary. You can go now . . . Oh, one more question. Did Geordie ever write letters to Miss Ophelia?"

"Letters, ma'am?"

"Like that one." She pointed to the letter from "G," which still lay open on the table.

Mary shrugged. "Sometimes he give me papers for her."

"Was that one of them?"

"Dunno, ma'am. I can't read."

"Do you know where he lives?"

"He never said. But he must have a place somewhere. He's always clean."

"Thank you, Mary. You can go."

The girl curtsied and scuttled out.

Griffin watched her go. "Boy falls for stage actress, bribes housemaid for access, actress brushes him off . . . I suppose it's plausible."

"Surely more plausible than 'jealous housemaid kills actress over unrequited love affair'?"

He winced. "Truly horrible. And I thought hatchet-wielding ballerinas and rogue hired killers were the worst we could come up with."

"And what was all that about the roses? 'I didn't see who

brought them,' she said. Not 'I never seen who brung 'em,' or some such."

"Indeed. Such elaborate secrecy from Mrs. Maskelyne about an admirer that apparently everyone knew about. And then a clumsy lie about a bunch of flowers."

"'Miss Ophelia is much admired,'" mused Eliza. "As if the maid had been taught what to say, if anyone should ask."

"Mmm."

"So why not just have her claim the roses were a gift from this Geordie?"

Griffin tugged his mustaches. "Because Geordie's involvement is a recent invention, that's why. No, this Flower Man is not Geordie. He's some person they don't want us to know about."

"Someone they're covering for?"

"Or someone they're ashamed of. But that doesn't mean Geordie can't be the killer."

Eliza tucked her heavy optical away in its case. "Hmm. Flower Man, Geordie, the mysterious 'G.' So do our suspects multiply."

Griffin scribbled a few more lines in his notebook and flipped it shut. "Are you busy this afternoon? I think it's time to pay a visit to the Imperial Russian Ballet. Perhaps our vengeful Muscovites can shed light on the matter."

"Diary," reported Hipp in his tinny electric voice. "Three o'clock, Bethlem Asylum. No further appointments."

Swiftly, Eliza sorted through her day. Tonight, she'd send Lizzie to the Holy Land, find out what this Jemima Clark knew about Billy Beane. She had patients to attend at Bethlem, but they could wait, and she'd no wish to face Mr. Todd again.

Her thoughts fluttered, dancing, lured by a distant will-o'-the-wisp. *A love letter scribbled in blood.* What had Todd meant? *Your budding artist isn't angry. He's desperately in love . . .*

But with whom? Miss Pavlova? Then why keep killing? Or Ophelia? Todd had spoken before her body was discovered. Perhaps he really was prescient.

Aye, muttered Lizzie. *Or mayhap he's just foolin' with your mind. Wouldn't be the first time . . .*

Eliza shook herself, determined to concentrate on the case. "I'd be delighted."

At her skirt hem, Hipp rocked on little brass feet. "Delighted," he echoed smugly. "One o'clock, Imperial Russian Ballet. Make greater speed."

Griffin raised his brows. "Keen, isn't he?"

"Naturally," said the theater manager at Her Majesty's, an hour later. "Everyone here knows Geordie Kelly."

His name was Underwood, and his craggy, deep-wrinkled face seemed a hundred years old. He was fabulously tall and thin, hunching over on a slender black cane that quivered under his weight, ready to snap. His creaking black hat sported a net of cobwebs on its brim, and a tiny brown spider scuttled underneath into his scraggly white hair.

Eliza tried not to stare. Behind her skirts, Hippocrates gave an electric titter.

Griffin coughed to cover a smile. "Everyone? Why? Does Geordie visit the theater often?"

Underwood's snow-white brows bristled. "Take me for a fool, do you? I still have my wits, you know. I already told that other young fellow all about it. Smart chap, fine red coat. A detective from India, you know. Tigers and nabobs, say what?"

Inwardly, Eliza groaned.

Lafayette sauntered in the office door, resplendent, hat under his arm. "Dr. Jekyll, my dear lady." Hippocrates clattered up to him, his *happy* light flashing, and Lafayette gave him an indulgent pat on the head. "I say, Griffin, we really must stop meeting like this. People will think we're working together."

Underwood blinked. "Yes, that's the chap. Told him all about it. No stone unturned, all that."

Eliza smiled faintly. "Excellent. Hipp, come here, please. Mr. Underwood, sir, would you mind telling us what you've told the captain?"

"About what? Oh. Yes, this Geordie. Theater nut. Harmless fellow, really. Well, except for . . . Ah-CHOO!" Underwood wiped his nose on a vast scarlet handkerchief that he dragged from his coat pocket. The spider dangled from its web into his eyes, and he batted it away. "Confounded crawlers! Sorry, what was I saying?"

"Geordie," prompted Griffin.

"Who?" Underwood peered vaguely at Eliza. "I say, young lady, have we been introduced?"

"Indeed we have, sir. Eliza Jekyll, Metropolitan Police."

"Not you," he said crossly. "The other one. Saucy girl, dark hair."

Faintness washed her mind thin. Was Lafayette glancing at her oddly? "I'm sorry, who?"

"Who what?" Another sneeze, louder and wetter than the last. "Never mind. What were you saying?"

Griffin smiled patiently. "The boy is harmless, except for . . . ?"

"The showgirls don't like him, for certain. He spies on them, they say. Steals things from their dressing rooms. Never saw it myself. The filching, that is, not the spying. Of course he spies. Dancing girls with no clothes on, eh? Who wouldn't spy?"

"And the late Miss Pavlova?"

"Who?" Another bristling white frown. "Oh, yes. Russians, dead girl. Terrible thing. Their *Giselle* was so popular. Now I'll have to find another show for my theater, I suppose. Acrobats, I'm thinking. Whistling about on the flying trapeze, ahoy!"

"You were just telling me," interrupted Lafayette, with a steel-edged smile, "that Geordie had admired the late Miss Pavlova. Sent her flowers, that kind of thing."

"Poor girl didn't speak a word of English, but that didn't stop him. The more exotic, the better, that's our Geordie."

The spider on Underwood's hat climbed down its thread towards the old man's coat lapels, and Eliza resisted the urge to grab it and pull. Perhaps he'd unravel. "So he's . . . an obsessed theater lover?"

"You could say that. Once, we had an opera diva from darkest Africa. Lovely young thing, six-octave voice. Sang like an angel. He mooned after her for weeks. Poor lad was heartbroken when her company moved on."

"He's a regular patron?" suggested Griffin.

"Good God, no." Underwood's eyes crinkled, incredulous. "Are you all idiots? He works here."

PIECES OF GIRLS

•••

"**W**HAT?" ALL THREE OF THEM SPOKE TOGETHER, and Eliza saw Griffin hide another smile. At last, something Lafayette hadn't been able to find out first.

Underwood scratched his flea-bitten hair. "In charge of the electric lights. Swings about in the rafters, flicking switches on and off all night and making puppy eyes at the leading ladies. Moons about in the corridor outside the dressing rooms, picking up feathers and sequins from the girls' costumes. As I said: harmless."

"How frightfully convenient of the lad," murmured Lafayette in Eliza's ear. His hand on her waist made her jump. "Tell me you're not buying into any of this."

Hippocrates whirred, indignant. "Impertinence," he trumpeted. "Inappropriate manners. Recompute."

Coolly, Eliza ignored Lafayette and plucked the letter they'd found in Ophelia's dressing table from her pocket. "Could this be his handwriting, Mr. Underwood?"

"Shouldn't think so," said Underwood briskly, without glancing at it. "Boy's an idiot. Dull-witted. A fuse loose. Whacked with the glocky stick. I doubt he can read or write."

"Care to discuss your thoughts?" whispered Lafayette. "I'm free this afternoon. Your little brass idiot seems an efficient chaperone, if you're bothered with that sort of thing. Or we can just call it an interrogation."

She fought strange laughter. *The very devil in scarlet . . .*

Her cheeks flamed, and she elbowed him in the ribs. "Stop it," she whispered fiercely. "This is serious."

"So am I. You smell fabulous, by the way. For a revolutionary."

Griffin cleared his throat. Eliza smiled weakly at Underwood. "I see," she said loudly. "Thank you. Can you, er, tell us where Geordie lives?"

Underwood's spider crawled over his lapel and disappeared inside his shirt. "Right here, of course," said the old man. "A loft in the rafters. Our very own Quasimodo!"

They bustled in single file through corridors crowded with machinery, old scenery, piles of lumber, and tools. Looms of electrical wiring hung along the walls, clumped with dust. The air was musty with the smell of old makeup and sweat. Eliza and Hipp dodged harried servants, small boys with buckets and brooms, dancers in rehearsal costume. Many of the dancers were fey, with graceful spindly limbs and huge eyes, their long-suffering feet crammed into pretty satin ballet shoes.

Craggy old Underwood halted in the stage wings, at the foot of a huge red velvet curtain. He pointed with his stick at a rickety iron ladder that climbed the wall on metal pins, stretching upwards into the dark. "Rafters. Lads swinging about like gibbons, eh?" His top hat slipped down over his eyes. He fumbled it back, and wandered off, muttering,

"Watch out for rodents. Hungry critters, size of small dogs. They spread madness, you know."

"Apparently," murmured Eliza. She peered up the ladder and glanced down at her skirts.

Lafayette was already grinning.

She eyed him sternly. "Don't even say it."

"I wasn't going to say anything."

"Why don't you wait down here, Doctor?" Griffin suggested. "I'll call if I need you."

"That won't be necessary." Briskly, she tugged her satchel tighter over her shoulder. "Wait here, Hipp. After you, gentlemen, please."

"Wait here," agreed Hippocrates eagerly, and folded his legs with a happy *whir!* of cogs.

"Good dog." Lafayette vaulted up the ladder, climbing swiftly. Griffin followed. Eliza gripped the highest rung she could reach, and started to climb.

The air grew warmer, the light dim. The curtain beside her grew dustier. Ropes creaked, wind whistled in the roof above. From the stage below, piano music rippled, the bright notes of a *pas de deux*. The ladder creaked under the combined weight of three. Her heartbeat quickened. She fought not to grip the rungs too tightly. *Don't look down. Don't look down . . .*

Lizzie giggled, and clapped invisible hands. *Whee hee! Now here's some fun . . .*

"Landing," called Lafayette from above.

Sure enough, after a few more rungs, a narrow wooden platform stretched along the wall, where a dozen ropes were wrapped onto a rack of belaying pins, like those on a ship's deck. The web of ropes stretched out over the stage, echoing the spider's weavings on Underwood's hat. Curtain ropes, plus others holding scenery and lighting arrays that swung over the stage on wooden beams.

Eliza dusted off her hands and peered downwards. Her vision swam. Why was she always compelled to look down? Twenty feet at least to the stage, where dancers twirled and stretched to the music. Nothing to stop you from falling. She craned her neck upwards, pushing back her spectacles. In the dim light, she could just make out criss-crossing rafters, disappearing into the gloom.

"There's another level." Griffin squinted up, resting his hand on the next ladder. "This Geordie must be a veritable monkey . . . I say, who's there? Stop, man—oof!"

Griffin stumbled. Lafayette swore. A shadow slipped by, just a blur, too fast to see, and something hard banged into Eliza's shoulder.

She overbalanced, arms waving, and the earth beneath her dropped away.

Her stomach shriveled. She flailed desperately but caught nothing but air . . . and then *wumph!* A hanging beam slammed into her chest. A bone in her corset snapped, and she clung there like a barnacle in billowing skirts.

The beam swung wildly to and fro, creaking under her weight, and at one end, the knot holding the rope began to unravel. *Oh, bother.*

She heard Griffin cursing. Lafayette scrambled to the landing's edge. "Hold on, Eliza. Don't let go!"

"Wasn't planning on it . . . uh!"

The beam swung again. The sharp edge of a light fixture dug painfully into her upper arms. Something fell from her satchel, hit the stage and smashed. Somewhere below, Hippocrates squealed and screeched, "Danger! Danger!"

Her arms ached with fatigue, weakening. Her heart lurched, sick. *Don't look down. Don't . . .*

Dizzy depths, swirling into blackness.

Her grip slipped, and Lizzie yowled like an angry cat. *Pull yourself together, girl. You'll not get rid of me like this. Climb!*

Gritting her teeth, Eliza heaved herself up. But her muscles must have turned to water while she wasn't watching, because her arms just strained uselessly. The beam swung wildly, banging against the landing, and her spectacles dislodged and fell into nothing.

Wonderful, snarled Lizzie. *Climb, you useless mopsy, or I'll climb for you.*

And the familiar, raw sickness clutched at Eliza's guts. Her pulse cartwheeled. *Not now . . . not now!*

But her muscles spasmed, a shuddering cramp of pain and pleasure, and bright electric rage raced along Eliza's nerves. It was her, Lizzie, *it's me,* me, *you stupid girl, are you so afraid that you can't even save your own life?*

My face is quivering beneath hers, like the real face under a mask. My skin's juddering, my hair's springing alive, desperate to escape, to *change.* That Captain Lafayette is leaning over the edge and his knowing gaze meets mine, a stinging blur of color, *her* eyes and *mine* and *hers* again and I can't breathe and I can't think and God fucking help us if this happens *now.*

"Eliza! Give me your hand!" He's barely holding on while he reaches out to me. One hand gripping a rope, the other teetering above nothing, Captain Smart-Pants Lafayette of the god-rotted Royal in his scarlet coat and oh-so-pretty chestnut curls, only there ain't nothing pretty or weak about him now. There's fire in those heaven-blue eyes, fire and hatred and screw-it-all defiance that lights a familiar flame in my heart.

He knows pain, this golden soldier-boy. He knows death, and today, death's picked the wrong man to screw with.

The ancient knot at the beam's end slips some more—who tied this bleeding thing anyway, Noah?—and I grab the wood and haul my body up, up, hand over hand. My muscles screech at me, whining like pampered babies, but they can just shut the hell up or *die,* and Lafayette strains for my hand and his knuckles bang mine and finally, his big fingers clamp my wrist like a Newgate shackle and don't let go.

My elbow wrenches. The beam tries to swing back, away, yanking my shoulder joint apart, a white-hot spike of *ouch.* Lafayette heaves, and I let the beam go and come flying onto the landing, ker-*bang!* into a knot of tangled skirts and pounding pulse and holy Jesus, I'm still alive.

I lie panting on my back, sweating. The beam crashes to the stage, *bang!* Glass shatters. A girl down there screams. *Eliza* screams, clawing at my face, struggling inside me, over me, *through* me, our skin crawls and our guts twist into knots and I writhe and fight and open my mouth to yell . . .

Air rushed into Eliza's lungs, and she jerked upright.

Her heart galloped, her breath in deep gasps. Her bodice was soaked with sweat. Her stomach ached, her insides felt weak and stretched, as if someone had wrung her out to dry. But Lizzie was gone.

For now.

"Are you hurt, Doctor?" Lafayette scrambled up beside her.

She let him haul her to her feet. Her legs shook. She gripped the wall for balance and pushed him away, catching her breath. "Just a little shaken."

"Pleased to hear it."

She blinked, short-sighted. She'd have to fetch her spare spectacles from home. She dusted off her dress. A bone in her corset had snapped. She'd have to get it mended. "What hit me? One minute I was standing there, the next . . ."

"Our glocky-sticked Geordie, presumably." He regarded her strangely. As if he'd never seen her before.

Her throat crisped. Had Lizzie . . . come out? Had her face changed, her hair? "What? Kindly stop staring, sir."

That flashlamp smile. "So that's what your eyes look like."

She arched stern brows. "Hardly the need to fling me from a landing to discover that . . . Goodness, Harley, you're bleeding!"

Griffin lay on the landing, clutching his side. His hat had rolled into a dusty corner. Blood oozed between his fingers. "Are you all right, Doctor?"

"Never mind me. What happened?" She knelt and peeled his fingers away. More blood gushed.

Griffin clenched his teeth. "The little rat stabbed me. I'm all right. Don't fuss."

"Hush. I'm a doctor, it's my job to fuss."

Lafayette peered over the landing's edge, sniffing the dark air. "Well, the little rat's gone now."

"Wonderful." Griffin tried to get up.

"Not a chance. Let me look." Eliza eased his bloody shirt aside and poked her nose close so she could see. A glance along the flesh below his ribs: not deep, but it looked painful.

"You're growing thin, Harley," she said brusquely as she folded a swab from her satchel over the wound and pressed his hand over it. "Hold here. You work too hard, you know," she added without thinking, and immediately wished she hadn't. She wasn't the only one who threw herself into her work to avoid thinking about other, darker things.

"Physician, heal thyself," muttered Griffin. "I'll live."

"Foiled again." Lafayette hopped onto the second ladder and started to climb. "Shall we see what our knife-happy idiot is hiding?"

Eliza glanced after him, then back. "I need to stitch this, Harley."

"I shan't bleed to death." Griffin waved her ahead. "Don't let him mess it up. And try not to fall off this time."

Casually, Eliza rearranged her satchel, and when Griffin wasn't looking, she swiftly pulled out a phial of remedy and took a gulp. Warmth flushed from her belly to the top of her head. Sweat dampened her skin. She wanted to squirm, to press her legs together. How undignified.

Her stomach boiled, indignant, as if the substance wasn't welcome there. Strange. This last batch of mixture tasted different. Spicier, stronger. Had Marcellus changed the formula without telling her?

Defiant, she gulped a second mouthful, tucked the phial away, and followed Lafayette into the dark.

Cobwebs crawled over her face, dry skeletal fingers. She brushed them away, shivering. *Don't look down. Don't . . .* Another landing loomed, the ladder leading through a hole cut in wooden boards. She grabbed Lafayette's hand and let him help her to her feet.

She popped the switch on her little aether-powered electric light, and the coil buzzed and bloomed, throwing a bright ring against the dusty wall.

The landing was about ten feet square, small enough to make her swallow and shuffle away from the edge. A blanket lay heaped in the corner on a tatty straw cushion. Atop the bedding sat a dirt-smeared brown felt rabbit, one solitary ear flopping over its face, a leg and one eye missing.

Along the wall, above a splintery trestle table, stretched a row of rusted electrical levers. The hinges were coated in corrosion and dust bunnies. Electrical potential buzzed amid the faint stink of burned aether.

Someone below threw a switch somewhere, and goose pimples sprang on her arms, her hair standing on end. Her coil flickered and burned brighter, absorbing the power.

Lafayette cocked his eyebrow. "Is that thing certified?"

He knew it was. They both knew it was. Her nerves were still wound tight like a fishing reel, from the fall and from Lizzie's sudden strength. Lizzie had never forced through on her own like that before . . .

. . . and if he looks at me like that again, I'll kick his pretty arse, Lizzie whispered slyly.

"So arrest me," snapped Eliza. The remedy hadn't worked. Lizzie was still right there, just beneath the surface . . .

"Perhaps I shall." Lafayette didn't drop his sky-blue scrutiny. "There's more to you than is evident, Dr. Jekyll."

She shivered, angry snakes still wriggling in the pit of her stomach. Her yearning was unsettling, unconscionable. To laugh like a madwoman, twirl until her skirts flew out like pinwheels, scream to "hell with it," and just *change* . . .

"Oh, I don't think so, Captain," she said lightly. "You give me too much credit. I'm insufferably dull when you get to know me."

"Mmm. You're rather good at this, aren't you?"

"What's that?"

"Lying." His gaze didn't drop. It burned, certain. Indefatigable. Whatever he'd meant, it wasn't an insult.

"I'm sure I don't know what you mean."

"I'm glad you're on the side of the law. You'd make a formidable murderer."

"Don't be ridiculous. And I'll thank you to cease your unseemly behavior, sir. You are far too forward." She spun away, cheeks aflame. Her remedy was failing. What would she do without it? The urges would strengthen inside her, a poison vine taking root, she'd hunger and thirst and *want* until her skin burned and her blood screamed and she couldn't hold Lizzie inside any longer . . . and then . . .

And then . . . what? She couldn't go out in public, not with Lizzie about to pop out at any moment. She'd have to stay indoors. Become a recluse, like her father, his wits rotting inexorably away, going slowly mad in his laboratory while the world forgot him . . .

She sucked in a deep breath. Ridiculous. A moment of panic, that was all. She'd nearly fallen to her death. Completely understandable. She'd talk to Marcellus. He'd alter the formula, make her remedy stronger, more reliable. No need for dramatics.

In the meantime? Joking about it with Lafayette was a very bad idea.

So that's what your eyes look like, he'd said. But whose did he mean?

"Eh? What?" She shook herself back to reality.

"I said, come look at this." Lafayette was fingering through a pile of clutter on the trestle table. "Our Geordie's a collector."

She peered, blinking, wishing for her spectacles, and held her light closer. Ribbons, fabric scraps, sequins, feathers . . . "Pieces from the girls' costumes?"

"And pieces of girls." Lafayette showed her the broken-off bottom of a glass bottle. Fingernail clippings, still sporting flecks of pink paint. Locks of hair, carefully tied with string. Different colors, blondes, brunettes, a redhead. "I don't see any feet in this collection. Rather less ambitious."

Eliza wrinkled her nose. "I can test those samples, see if any belong to Miss Pavlova. Or to Miss Ophelia, for that matter."

She angled her light further. A shard of looking-glass sat upright on the table. Beside it, a comb, scissors, an old razor. Her shoulder brushed Lafayette's coat, and inside her, warm shadows stirred and sighed . . .

She jerked back. He'd see her. Smell her, with that sensitive nose of his . . .

"Vanity?" she suggested calmly, though her pulse skipped.

"Lysander's wife said he was a good-looking boy. It could be part of his method. Ladies do such wild things for a handsome face."

Warm steel in her palm, deft artist's fingers on her cheek, a single drop of blood. "Let me show you . . ."

"Do they?" she asked tightly. "I'm sure I wouldn't be so foolish."

His smile twinkled. "Don't shoot. I surrender."

She flicked dust from pressed flowers, ribbons, old makeup pots scraped clean. "So what do you make of this jumble?"

He ruffled his chestnut hair. "Treasure."

"Hmm?"

"Everyone has keepsakes. Trivial things that mean the world. Pitiful, isn't it? A man reduced to locks of hair and nail clippings."

"That sounds like the observation of experience, Captain." She flipped casually through the items with her tweezers. "Were you truly a detective in India? Or did you invent that to impress Underwood?"

He laughed. "Nothing so fascinating. I was a hunter. Disappointingly commonplace."

"What, no romantic tales of dashing piratical exploits? One immediately suspects you of hiding something."

"Maybe I'm just being mysterious and seductive."

"Mmm. Half a victory to you, then. You've piqued my curiosity, at least. I imagine you stalking through the jungle wearing a safari suit and pith helmet, brandishing muskets and blunderbusses and taking pot-shots at anything that twitches. A hunter of what, pray? Tigers and nabobs?"

He measured her, a piercing probe of blue. "Of treasure, at first," he conceded. "The conventional kind. Gold and silver, lost cities, the overflowing jewel chests of despots and thieves." He made a mock bow. "Captain Lafayette of the East India Company, seeker of fame and fortune in darkest Bengal, scourge of villains and honest men both."

"Now *that* I can believe."

"Everyone's young and stupid once." He poked at a dried

rose pinned to the wall, agitated, as if he were compelled to speak. "As I said: commonplace. Then the Rebellion happened, and overnight our happy little slave colony exploded into a lawless zoo. Enter Captain Lafayette, bounty-hunter."

Rebellion, he'd said. Not *mutiny.* "And then what? Why return to England?"

He rubbed his wrist, that odd silver-sealed bracelet she'd noticed the first time they met glinting in her lamp's light. Was it a memento? A lucky talisman? How unscientific.

"Wanted men hide in evil places," he explained. "Bloodthirsty holes where the demons that devour us are made real. I encountered things I'd never believed existed. It . . . changed me."

Well, *that* was obvious. She'd already met two Lafayettes, the flirt and the fighter. If she dug deeper—slid under his skin, slow and careful like a warm needle—would she discover another?

"For the better, I trust."

He shrugged. "If you wallow in filth long enough, it stops washing off. I'd seen enough. I had to leave."

His tone clanged, a tell-tale discord of untruth, and the compulsion to pry itched like a growth in her belly. *The very devil in scarlet.* Lizzie's whisper drifted back to her, colored afresh with rosy intrigue . . . and on its heels, Mr. Todd in Bethlem, watching Lafayette with that mischievous twinkle in his eyes. *Hello, shadow.*

She shivered, a ghostly chill shifting on the air. She should let it alone. Before she exposed things best left buried . . .

"And now you hunt heretics for the Royal? An odd career choice, for a man who believes in demons."

"I believe in what I can see, madam. Believe me, some creatures deserve to be hunted." Lafayette poked at a jar of dried black greasepaint and wrinkled his nose. "Well, if this is our love-letter killer, I don't see any ink or paper. Or books, for that matter."

Subject closed, then. "According to Underwood, Geordie's illiterate," she offered. "So whence the letters?"

"Perhaps he pays a scribe to write his awful poetry for him."

She glanced around the dirt-smudged loft, weary. Her head was beginning to ache, what with no spectacles, no food, the strange-tasting remedy . . . "With what, dust bunnies? How much do you think Underwood pays a live-in rafter-monkey?"

"Likely nothing at all. How shrewd of you."

"And I see no weapons or tools. No knives or bayonets. Nothing that could have made those curious electrical burns at the scenes, either."

"Another fascinating observation. Congratulations."

Her head swam, and her throat felt coated in hot spice. "You don't believe Geordie has anything to do with this, do you?"

"No, madam, I do not. Assumptions make idiots of us all."

"Despite the robe of devil's advocate that you seem to have slipped on in the last two minutes."

He curled a severed lock of yellow hair around one finger-tip. "I don't have a scientific explanation for you, Doctor. It just doesn't smell right. I don't scent murder here."

Another wave of faintness. Her stomach burned distantly, a sure sign her need was gathering pace, and like a shedding snake's, her skin rippled. She wanted to writhe, scratch at it, peel it off, make the horrid sensation stop. Sprint for home, break open her secret cabinet and gush that warm bitter elixir down her throat . . .

She fought to steady her breath, quell her rising panic. She needed to see Marcellus. Now.

But she couldn't leave. Not until the evidence was examined. Until she ensured Lafayette couldn't follow her. "You can scent murder?" she said lightly. "How quaint. If only investigations were always so simple."

"They are, after a fashion. I've known compulsive killers in my time. Men with monsters inside them."

"Creatures that deserve to be hunted?" Things like Mr. Todd, or Billy the Bastard.

Things like me . . .

A dark smile. "Precisely. They come in two types. Either they cover their tracks immaculately, like our Chopper friend, and you get not a whiff of them until they strike again . . ."

That's what you've come for, isn't it? whispered Todd in her memory. *To dance with my shadow?*

"Or," added Lafayette, "you find them at the end of a short but lurid trail of gore. Sometimes, they're even standing over the corpse, drenched in terror and blood and wondering what in the world just happened. Which group do you think Master Glocky-Stick here would fall into?"

Eliza picked up the brown plush rabbit and tweaked its nose. Its single ear flopped. "A simple lad who sleeps with toys," she mused. Her palms left damp marks on the worn velveteen. "It does seem unlikely. Still, I'll match the samples. One never knows." She popped the rabbit back on the cushion and tugged a paper bag from her satchel to collect the hair.

"Aren't you supposed to wear gloves when you do that?"

She dropped the locks into the bag. "It's the size and shape of the hairs that concern me here, not any other substances that might be present. One day, perhaps, it will be possible to lift finger marks from surfaces and identify the person who left them. They're unique to the individual, you know. But not yet."

"Compelling idea. But wouldn't you need a copy of everybody's finger marks first, with which to make comparison? Seems authoritarian to me."

"Only if you have something to hide." Like Lizzie, the lady in red, who'd lured Billy Beane into the dark and . . .

(*hot flesh, sour sweat, dirty hair smearing her fingers, a yell and a bright flash of steel . . .*)

. . . and stabbed him in the throat? Fended off his feeble struggles with a laugh and watched him bleed to death? Did Eliza really want the truth? What then of her precious justice?

Lafayette eyed her, incredulous. "Do you actually believe that? What happened to 'innocent until proven guilty'?"

"You work for the Royal. You tell me."

"I enforce the rules, madam. I don't make them."

"And do *you* actually believe *that*?" She thrust a glass tube in his direction. "Make yourself useful for once, won't you? Put those fingernail clippings in here."

"Lovely. I get all the fun jobs." He popped the tube's cork and carefully tipped the clippings inside. "I was serious about this afternoon, by the way. We have things to talk about."

"Do we?" she said, with false composure. "I can't imagine what."

"Oh, I think you can. The matter of your orthodoxy has taken an unexpected turn, wouldn't you say?"

"I've no idea what you're talking about."

"I can arrest you, you know. I'd prefer not to, in my current mood. But my moods change. It would serve you well to . . . satisfy me."

His tone was careless, unthreatening. Flirtatious, even. But she didn't believe it for a moment.

He'd seen her *change,* back there on that dangling beam. He'd seen Lizzie flashing in her eyes. And like a dog with a ragged-meat bone, he wouldn't let it go.

Eliza squared her shoulders. Two could play at that game. She was stubborn, too. God's blood, *we're* as stubborn as they come, she and I, and we'll not sleep until we've wrested that god-rotted bone back and swallowed it whole. And if Captain Smart-Pants won't let go, why, we'll just have to *deal* with him, won't we, a wink and a flash of sweet steel . . .

Eliza's stomach knotted, and she shuddered. Good God, she had to get out of here. "What a shame," she said smoothly. "I have another appointment. Perhaps next week." And she snatched the tube from Lafayette's hand and scrambled down the ladder.

By the time she reached Finch's Pharmacy, Marcellus wasn't there.

New Bond Street rattled and clanked with traffic, the late afternoon sunshine glinting on polished shop fronts and lanterns. The paper blinds in the twin bay windows of Finch's

Pharmacy were pulled down, the blue-painted door barred. He'd closed early for the day.

Marcellus never closed early. Not even on a Sunday.

Eliza shivered, chilled. And Lizzie giggled in sly anticipation. *Not long now . . .*

Hippocrates whistled and popped, his lights flashing, and he hopped like a jumping bean on his two back feet. "Finch," he muttered. "Eight until six. Does not compute."

"No, it doesn't, Hipp." Eliza peered through the window, shading her eyes with one cupped hand. Perhaps Marcellus was working on one of his more exotic concoctions and closed the shop to avoid interruptions. Maybe he'd gone out for supplies. Maybe he'd simply forgotten to get out of bed this morning. But all she could see was her own reflection, her eyes dark and eerie and too large, and for an instant, Lizzie winked back at her.

She whirled and started for home. But her stomach lurched as she threaded the crowded streets. Her remedy was failing. Lizzie couldn't be trusted. And Mr. Finch might not return until . . .

Cries rang out. "Make way! 'Ere, watch it!" Iron brakes screeched, and metal carriage feet scraped the flagstones. Horses skittered, nervous. The crowd jostled, knocking her sideways. And an evil-looking black carriage thundered by. Drawn by four black horses in sable plumes, its driver hunched in a black coat and tall hat. The wheels were edged in brass, the windows draped in black, and the brass-etched emblem of the Royal Society gleamed on the lacquered doors.

Eliza tugged her skirts back into place, but the latent fever in her bones melted into sick heat. The President of the Royal Society's carriage, hurtling on its way to the Tower.

The man never appeared in public. Some said he was terribly old and frail. Others whispered stranger, more dangerous suggestions, that he emerged only at night, that he couldn't stand the sun, that his own bizarre scientific experiments had made him into a monster. Eliza didn't believe the wild tales for a moment. But whatever the case, the Royal's shadowy agents had the Mad Queen's ear—and just like that carriage, the power to sweep from their path anyone who disagreed with their precious Philosopher or otherwise displeased them.

Rage boiled Eliza's blood, and she spat on the pavement in the hideous black carriage's wake. People stared. She didn't care. Always hiding, always skulking in secret, nothing proven but always suspected. Forever living in fear. Why couldn't the stinking Royal just leave people alone? None of their god-rotted business what folk got up to in private.

Viciously, Eliza tugged her sleeves, hard enough to pop stitches in the seams. For once, she and Lizzie were in agreement.

At the theater, she'd spent an hour tending to Griffin's wounds—Harley was stubborn, but no match for her when there was treatment to be done—and another messing about impatiently, waiting for Captain Lafayette to be gone. She didn't want him following her to Finch's. But Lafayette had hung around like a disease, questioning the theater staff and dancers with that annoyingly insouciant air, throwing her the occasional grin, as if he knew precisely what she was waiting for.

Why didn't he just arrest her and be done? Drag her away to the Tower, hurl her in with the rats and begin with the pain, the thirst, the erosion of will, the excruciating mind games that would make her beg to tell him everything, invent things if she didn't know, and weep when she could tell him no more?

But somehow, the image of Lafayette the torturer grated on her sensibilities, the way a bad oil painting offended the eyes. The captain was . . . straightforward. Spoke his mind and damn the consequences. She couldn't picture him duplicitous and cruel, playing sick torment games in the chilly dark . . .

Cowshit. Lizzie slipped effortlessly forwards, itching on the tip of her tongue with no more trouble than a cramp of her stomach and a hot flush. *He ain't got nothing on us, that's all. Either that, or it ain't arresting us that he wants.*

"Nonsense," muttered Eliza aloud. "What else could he possibly want?"

If you don't know, I ain't explainin'. Lizzie mooched along beside her, a phantom in the corner of her eye, in translucent red skirts and jaunty hat.

Swiftly, Eliza glanced aside . . . and the apparition vanished. Or did it? Was it even there?

Seeing things, now. Excellent. How sane.

"Don't be ridiculous," she said shakily. "I'm not an idiot, Lizzie. The captain flirts for a purpose. He's barely half the things he pretends, and 'aimless' and 'stupid' he certainly isn't."

To be sure, Lizzie agreed. *The man has a plan. Ain't you itching to know what it is?*

"Not particularly," Eliza lied. A passing servant girl eyed her oddly, and she gave a weak smile.

Oh, right. Sure. You keep telling ourselves that.

"Aimless," echoed Hippocrates, scuttling to block her path. "Wrong turning. Home, three-quarter mile. Retrace steps."

"What?" Eliza halted, confused. She'd wandered two blocks past her turning, lost in conversation with a figment of her imagination. Brilliant.

"Sorry, Hipp," she offered belatedly and turned about, hurrying around the correct corner towards home.

But was she really lost in thought? Or had she walked by on purpose, reluctant to face what had to be done? She'd business in the Holy Land tonight. Dark, thrilling business that only Lizzie could attempt.

And if she let Lizzie out again—twice in three days—what price her remedy then? How shaky her recovery?

How desperately weak her control?

A dark chuckle. *Come now, sister, it weren't so bad. We had some fun, didn't we? Me and handsome Johnny and Billy the Bastard . . .*

"Stop it!" She clutched her satchel tighter to her chest. Her vision blurred, worse than no spectacles, an evil red miasma of doubt and fear where monsters lurked. Flesh's iron-sweat scent, a whiff of sweet flowers, the clench of fingers, the hot-shock flavor of a kiss . . .

Pain bloomed a fresh sunflower in her forehead. She tripped, skinned her palms on the flagstones, staggered on.

"Don't remember," she mumbled, unsteady, wiping her nose with the back of one hand. Something foul on her fingers, sticky. Her mouth burned with guilty memory, but it lurked just out of her reach. "Did we do bad things, Lizzie? Did we . . . ?"

A sultry laugh, warm like candle flame. *Very bad, Eliza. Deliciously bad. But don't fret. You could use a little badness now and then . . .*

And Eliza stumbled home, lost in darkling dreams. The steps of her town house loomed abruptly from the mind-fog, a familiar thing made threatening by the shadows gibbering in her head.

She fumbled with the door, let herself in. Lurched up the stairs, tripped over her skirts, banged her kneecaps on the landing. Mrs. Poole didn't emerge.

She should pour the elixir down the drain, take her remedy, go to bed . . . But she needed desperately to know what Lizzie had done. Even if it meant losing control.

Mr. Finch—wherever he was—couldn't help her. And she wasn't a murderess. Not she, Eliza Jekyll.

You and your shadow, whispered Mr. Todd, a curl of alchemical smoke in her memory. *Admit it. We're the same. Let me show you how . . .*

Her bedroom was dark, the fire not yet set. She tossed her bag on the bed, heedless. Shadows oozed through the window, crawled over the carpet. Clawed at the coverlet, skeletal black fingers reaching for her soul.

Trembling, sweating, she pulled the candlestick. *Clunk!* The door swung open, maddeningly slowly, and as usual her heart shrieked, the terror-stricken doubt of addiction. What if she'd miscalculated? What if there was none left? What if . . . ?

Two bottles hulking on the shelf, right where she'd left them. Winking at her, gloating black glass eyes. She grabbed one, thumbed off the cork. The evilly warm liquid bubbled, as if it laughed at her, and dark thirst shivered her skin like contagion.

She gripped the bottle's neck tightly, the glass smooth and inviting. Tonight, she'd see. Tonight, she'd know.

And when Lizzie was done? It was high time Eliza got rid of the meddling Captain Lafayette. Flirting might be amusing, but no point in courting danger. Find this Chopper, and Lafayette would have no reason to hang around.

All the more reason to close the case quickly.

Oh, we'll get rid of him, Eliza. One way or the other. And I've a feeling tonight will be a long, dark night. My little steel sister is stirring. Who knows? Maybe we'll meet, the blue-eyed captain and me . . .

Horror salted Eliza's tongue. "No," she tried to say, "Lizzie, leave it alone . . ." But the thirst savaged her throat, shredding her will, ripping her voice to husky nothing. And as the weak winter sun slipped below the rooflines, relinquishing her bedroom to the darkness, she tilted her head and gulped the bitter elixir down.

LEAPING IMPULSES AND
SECRET PLEASURES

···

AT LAST.

Quickly, I strip off Eliza's stupid clothes. Her dress falls in a damp heap, and I kick it aside. My pulse thunders, pounding black helldrums I can't ignore, and freedom is sweet but it don't satisfy me tonight. My fingers tremble, my palms are clammy, a flea-bitten itch creeps under my skin that I can't scratch away. Sweet lord, Miss Lizzie needs a drink.

I grab a dress, any dress, a swish of wide skirts. Crimson velveteen gleams darkly in the mirror as I fumble the buttons tight over my corset. My eyes glint back at me, a greedy reflection of hunger, and I *glitter,* my skin glistens, it's as if my hair's aflame, a bright-stung fey halo that prickles with anticipation or warning.

I twist the curls up under a little top hat, stuff some pins in, and jam my muttering stiletto into my garter. Peace, sweet sister. All in good time.

A few seconds more, and I'm gone.

By the time I reach Seven Dials—it really is a seven-way crossroads, an evil omen if ever I seen one—the city's a corpse, shrouded in chilly darkness. Clouds blot out the bloated moon, and eldritch light glimmers from broken windows, under doors, dragged out like bright river water by that invisible moon's tide. Stray wisps of false fairy fire dance, blue and green on the mud at my feet. Tomorrow, that greedy moon will be full, and latent energy tingles through my flesh, an invisible electrical charge. I can feel it, taste it, crackling on the tip of my tongue: there's magic on the air tonight.

I hum a ditty off-key—*cockles and mussels, alive, alive-ooh!*—as I splash through puddles of shit and diseased water, and it's like I'm surrounded by a bristling bubble of don't-fuck-with-me, because dirty children dodge me in the alleys without trying to pick my pocket, and a mugger in a greasy black overcoat eyes me off and then slinks away, clawing his beaver hat down over one gleaming eye. Even the starving curs cringe in the corners with their ears pinned back as I stride by.

I smile, hungry. If the crushers want 'emselves a murderess in a red dress? Here I am, lads, come get me if you dare. Miss Lizzie's on a mission. The world knows this. And when Miss Lizzie's on a mission, you don't interfere. Not if you want to stay pretty.

The Cockatrice is open, golden warmth leaking from the shuttered window. The carving above the lintel leers at me, cock's head on a dragon, and I salute it, with a wink and a fingertip to my hat brim. "Cock-a-*trice,*" I say, and laugh. "The beast with three cocks. Congratulations, sir."

Mr. Cockatrice has nothing to say.

Inside, firelight licks the broken walls, gloats along the bar like a lover's lies. It's packed tonight, a herd of rum-swilling idiots singing a rude sea shanty, something about *the good ship Venus, by Christ you shoulda seen us,* and any glocky fool can finish *that* fuck-me-clever rhyme. A skinny cove wearing naught but a stained white undergarment crouches muttering by the bar, grabbing at his ankles and scratching his shock of white hair. A bunch of swells sprawl limp on the cushions in a stupefying hashish cloud, and that ugly little bloke with no legs trundles around them on his trolley, filching trinkets from their pockets as they sigh and drool.

Like a lazy laudanum dream, the beautiful stink of gin crawls up the walls of my mind.

I shoulder the crowd apart, cursing and kicking and prying rough hands off my backside, and push through to the bar. Scarfaced Charlie the barkeep gives a hateful grin and splashes me a tot from a dirty bottle. Eliza had Charlie's measure right enough. He ain't got no redeeming features, except maybe greed, which makes him easy game when you want something. I toss him two pennies—drunk for a penny, dead drunk for tuppence—and sink the drink in one gulp.

Fire explodes in my belly. I shudder, delight spreading along my limbs as if I just . . . well, never you mind. I just want more, again, forever, molten gold and flame, bitter chemical oblivion. God's innards, this stuff'll be the death of me, like it's murdered so many others, cold-blooded and relentless as any razor-glitter lunatic, only you won't make no front-page story drinking yourself to ruin.

We're all hurtling towards death. Some of us just run faster.

"Lizzie, my darlin'." Wild Johnny waves a sloshing gin bottle in my direction. Already bright-eyed with booze—or is he?—he stumbles against the bar beside me, and rights himself with a rakish bow that'd charm a lesser woman's corset off. "You flay me. Your radiance is more than I can bear. Let's get drunk and misbehave."

"If you're buying, I'm in."

"Naturally, madam. What do you take me for, some ha'penny sneak thief with no class?" He plonks the bottle on the bar and lets out a happy burp. "I'll have you know I'm the classiest gent in this bar."

"Too right. A ten-quid sneak thief is what you is. Nothing but the best."

"I'll drink to that."

But my stomach knots, spoiling my high, and for the first time, his suggestive rosy scent squirms tiny roots of threat into my veins. I might have teased Eliza with what we done, but truth is? I were deep in my cups t'other night. I don't right remember what went on, only that Johnny and me was sharing gin and laudanum, and he kissed me and it tasted of sadness, and something about his pretty hair and then Eliza woke up on the cushions, alone.

Damn it. Eliza would scold me for a fool. And for once, she'd be right.

We clink cups and swallow, and he feints at me with his flirtiest grin. He's wearing a different coat, a long dusty blue one, and too late I remember Eliza took the other. Shoulda brought it back. Shoulda left a lot of things the way they was.

But Johnny ain't never so plastered—nor so vague—as he makes out. He studies me with crooked black eyes and scratches behind one pointed ear like a puppy, his tangled hair flopping. "What?"

My skin itches. I ain't got time for about-last-night. I need to quiz him about Jemima, find out what the hell happened to Billy Beane.

Because I ain't right sure about that, neither, despite what Eliza might think. I like gin, for sure. But I never claimed it for my friend, and like a treacherous lover it keeps secrets from me.

I sigh. "Look. Um . . . what happened, t'other night? You and me, I mean."

He licks his teeth, considering. "What do you want to have happened?"

Jesus, Johnny. Why you gotta be so damned *nice*? "How about . . . we wiped ourselves clean on laudanum, and passed out?"

A loose-limbed fey shrug. "Then that's what happened."

Is he lying? Did his gaze slip? I'm too damn tired and antsy to know. I gulp another gin and snort. "Yeah, well, while we was busy not happening, your bloody squeeze turned snout, didn't she?"

His warm gaze crackles over with frost. "What?"

"Jemima told the crushers I did for Billy Beane."

"Did you? What a shame. Sounds like a win all round to me."

"That's as may be, but I ain't swinging for something I never done." I lean over both elbows on the bar, and glance sideways and back again before I lower my voice. "Billy was a crusher's moll. They can't let it go unpunished. They'll find someone to blame. You have to help me, Johnny."

And I know he will.

I play with him. I use him. I break his lonesome heart. But

I know in my crusty black soul that this sweet-natured lad won't never let me down.

Johnny, God love him, is my friend. And more fool he.

My eyes burn, and I blink them clear.

Johnny shrugs again and drops his voice, too, that practiced criminal's murmur that carries over flash house noise, but only to the person it's meant for. "You asked me where Billy was, then I never seen you for maybe a quarter hour. That's it. Don't know anything more."

"And you heard nothing?" I demand softly. "No hue and cry? Weren't no blood, nothing like that?"

"Nope. You had dirt on your dress and a bruise on your forehead. I figured you walked into something. You know how bloodthirsty doorways can be around here."

I frown, poking my foggy memory for what I *do* recall. The yard, damp night air on my bare thighs, stinky Billy a-fumble under my skirts. Greedy steel murmuring in my hand . . . and *wumph!*

Distant pain swells my forehead, an echo of injury past, and a ghostly green shadow blots out my breath.

My mind reels like a drunken fiddler. "Someone came into the yard and hit me," I blurt out. "Not Billy. Someone else. They must've seen something."

"Well, it weren't Jemima," says Johnny. "Not while you was out back. She and I held a short but fiery palaver. I'm ashamed to say that bad words were spoken." He tugged his hair, sheepish. "Such is love."

"But the crushers still think I done it." I slam twin fists on the bar, dazzled like winter sunshine with fresh anger. "Jemima better keep her eyes peeled for me."

Johnny slops more gin into my cup and swills his own. "Be easy on her," he says, but a shadow over his voice tells me Jemima better look out for him, too. "She might be glocky, but she's not blind."

"Thought you said nothing happened." But my face feels hot, and it ain't no virgin blush. I could snaffle Jemima's fancy man in an eye-blink, and don't she know it. I'd have done the same as her, if some uppity skirt were sniffing her snotty nose around my bloke. In Seven Dials, a girl fights for what's hers, or in a twinkle it ain't hers no more.

"*You* said nothing happened. Can't speak for what 'Mima thinks." Johnny edges closer, a sly thief's glide. "But I've a thing that might interest you, so I do."

"Oh, aye? What'd that be?"

He unfolds one long-fingered hand. In his palm lies a pocket watch. Mother-of-pearl face and black hands, dirt crusted around its dented silver rim.

I squint, puzzled. "A cheap ticker? You shouldn't have."

"A ticker, cheap," agrees Johnny airily. "Recently belonging to Billy the loudly lamented Bastard. Passed on to me this morning—in good faith, naturally, the fellow must've dropped it, these things happen all the time—by my fine friend . . ." He sighs artfully. "Well, perhaps you ain't interested after all. Let me buy you another gin, sweet ruby Lizzie, and we'll wallow the night away in decadence and gay abandon."

His suggestion is too alluring. Too tempting, when you're drowning, to scream *damn it all* and sink to your death.

But I need to swim. To stay sober, or thereabouts. Because Eliza needs me.

Fancy that.

Secret starlight warms my heart. I'm used to being the dark half, the beast in the closet, the mad wife in the attic with fleas in her hair. But Eliza needs me now. And screw me raw if I'll let her down.

I'm teetering on a precipice, breathless on the brink of a chasm of dark unknown. And it feels . . .

I clear my throat. Hell, we've only got one body between us, right? If the crushers bone Miss Lizzie, it'll be Doctor Eliza in the Bow Street lock-up come morning, and from there it'll be questions and fists and a swift bumpy ride to the Tower, courtesy of the god-rotting Royal. Even Eliza's hoity-toity detective friend can't help us, once they tumble to what we is.

If they burn her, I'm just as dead. Right?

I sigh and pull out a golden sovereign, let it catch the light.

Johnny's smile gleams. He makes the coin vanish—no, really—and now the watch is gone, too, into his pocket or up his sleeve or who knows where. I catch a flowery whiff of spelldust.

"Sally Fingers," says he.

"The moll buzz?" I know her, by reputation at least. Half the trick in picking pockets—especially ladies' pockets—is looking as if you belong, and it ain't only the lads who go out square-rigged with the swell mob.

"The very same. Seems you wasn't the only one after a slice of Billy's hide that night."

"What d'you mean?"

He shrugs, as if that particular piece of gossip is beneath him, and drinks. "Ask her yourself. She's working the Strand tonight with Jimmy the Chink."

"I'll do that." I drain my cup, bang it down, stretch my neck with a *crunch!* Time for a nice evening stroll. Little Sally Fingers better 'fess up quick, for Miss Lizzie and her shiny steel sister ain't feeling patient tonight.

"Lizzie? Can I ask you something?"

And here it comes.

"I already told you," I grumble for cover, "I ain't marrying your sorry fairy arse."

"And right sorry my fairy arse is for it, too. But not that." Johnny's lopsided gaze is shrewd again, sharper than the gin he's swilling should allow. Not for the first time, I'm envious. Sweet lord, the lad can put it away, only Johnny drinks because he can, not because he must. "A lady came looking for Jemima yesterday. Pretty yellow hair, in a gray dress. Don't suppose you know aught of that?"

Foggy memory haunts me, shadows behind glass. *Don't I know you, lady?* And then he'd turfed brave Eliza into the street, out of harm's way.

Protected her, when he could've fleeced her for every bright thing she carried and dumped her in a gutter for the rats.

Does sweet Johnny wonder where I go? Where I vanish to, for days or weeks on end, never to be seen? Then all of a moment I'm back, swilling gin and flirting like no time has passed at all.

And then Eliza shows up, a creature of sunshine with shadows in her heart—with *me* in her heart, chewing around like a specter hungry for souls—and Johnny's delicate fey senses light up like fireworks.

He *knew* her.

Shit.

I shrug, faking like I don't care, but cold spiders scuttle down my spine. "Nope. Why?"

"Thought I made her face, is all." He shrugs again. "Maybe some lady I tooled over once."

"Aye. Some copper's fakement, most like."

"Most like." He watches me a breath longer, then jerks his head towards the door. "Get on with you, you'll miss Sally."

I bite my lip. He don't have to believe my lies. "Johnny?"

"Mmm?"

So many things I ought to say. Tell him some lie about Eliza, shake him off this dangerous scent. Tell him to go home, buy Jemima a trinket or a new dress, take her to bed and forget about me, because I can't never be his, not when I'm only half a person and the lesser half at that.

Tell him the truth. If one man in this ugly world would stand by Miss Lizzie through anything . . .

Or even just say *I'm sorry.*

But I ain't. Miss Lizzie ain't sorry, any more than she's sober. And somehow, that stings sharpest of all.

I muster a grin, and my cheeks ache with the lie. "Thanks for the gin." And I walk out before he can reply.

The streets are black and grimy, thick with smoke and the expectant scent of a storm. Shadows leap and snigger down dark alleyways and beneath the eaves of crooked tenements, and the unseen moon drags a swell of excitement from my blood. The outdoor air feeds the fire in my soul, and I sink comfortably into my skin. That aching stab of conscience seems a distant dream.

I skip a few steps and twirl, my skirts fanning out. My stiletto murmurs and winks against my thigh. I realize I'm laughing, wild and high-pitched laughter like a madwoman's, and I cover my mouth to make it stop.

When you *change,* like us, the moon calls to you, and like that old Greek bastard in Razor Jack's painting—what's-'is-name, the cove who sailed his ship past the Sirens—if you don't rope yourself to the mast and stuff beeswax in your ears, you'll jump to your death.

Bittersweet fever licks me a-shiver inside, but it ain't me who shivers at the thought of *him.* It's Eliza, and her secret, wistful dreams.

God help her. Miss Lizzie likes a challenge, so she does, and I admit I ain't averse to a tasty slice of forbidden fruit. But when it comes to that bloodthirsty red-haired loon, it's Eliza who's blind. I've told her often enough—screamed at her, Jesus, that razor blade against her cheek I won't soon forget— but she don't listen. It's as if she don't even *hear.*

I know what Todd is, see. The Greek bloke in the painting was the clue, tied to the mast with that heartbroken look in his eyes.

Mr. Todd is what happens when you jump.

Or if you fall.

I stride through the barrows and rickety stalls of Covent Garden Market, dodging jugglers and fish-sellers and fey-faced fire-eaters, children selling piles of bread crusts, old fruit, pans of dripping, eel skins they've scrounged from middens. The rotten stink invigorates me. This place I know. This place I understand. Prostitutes wink and swagger in dirty skirts, buttons undone and poxy flesh on show. In a corner, two greasy blokes are kicking a third bloke senseless, blood and teeth in the mud. Somewhere, an accordion plays a raucous Irish tune, and a pair of dwarves in little frock coats and top hats dance a tipsy jig.

Cold fingers whisper over my shoulder.

I whirl, fierce. No one. No pickpocket, no lumbering fey idiot with a sloppy grin and a magic trick, no greasy customer who thinks I'm for sale.

Only shadows, and the smell of thunder.

But my breath is tight. My senses scintillate like angry fireflies. I can't help feeling that someone's following me.

"Follow away, whoever you are," I mutter, and stride on, skirts flouncing. I've got business tonight.

The Strand is a dark throng of carriages and omnibuses, electric lights glittering bright amongst gas lamps and torches. Horses snort and kick in their harnesses, disturbed by the relentless tick of clockwork. It's only early, and shop windows shine like wreckers' beacons through the dark, their fashionable wares luring folk to ruin. Well-dressed gents and their ladies promenade up and down, snotty noses in the air.

A line of god-rotted clockwork Enforcers strut along the middle of the street, and everyone makes way for them as if they've got the Black Death. Boxy brass soldiers, their gemstone eyes a-glint. More of 'em every week, the way things is. One pulls a big brass cage on wheels, and inside it, a skinny fey girl lies sobbing and howling. But Enforcers don't never listen or show mercy. Whatever spellwork she's done, it ain't helping her now.

Compelled, I scrape up a handful of horse dung and hurl it at them. "Nice work, chaps," I yell. "The streets sure is safer now. I feel so much better."

They don't stop. One turns its blank white face to look at me. I give it a rude gesture. Its red eyes flash, and it turns away once more.

"Heh," I mutter, hot-faced at my own stupidity but still feeling good. "Shows what *you* know."

I make my way through the clatter, keeping a sharp eye. The crowd is massive, surely I'll never find Sally Fingers amongst this lot, but in truth it don't take me long to single her out. I've an eye for the swell mob, so I do. I know their formations, one in front, one behind, a lookout off to the side, and here's Tom o' Nine Lives and Jimmy the Chink, sailing along in fine coats and cravats, nice as you please. Jimmy's even got a cane, and he flourishes it like a dandy, tipping his ridiculously tall hat to some simpering lady, who eyes his dusky half-Oriental skin and practically pops a rivet in her corset.

A yard or two away in the crush ambles a thin woman in a pale green dress and matching hat. She's familiar. Sharp nose, pinched face, long hands in lace gloves. Greasepaint is plastered over a blight of pox scars on her cheek.

Sally Fingers, moll buzz and Beane-thief extraordinaire.

Tom o' Nine Lives—so called because with that handsome face, he can talk his way out of anything—Tom halts abruptly, peering into a window, and the lady behind bumps into him.

She stumbles, her creamy crinoline bouncing. Handsome

Tom apologizes, so sorry, madam, forgive me, la-di-da. And light as a brothel girl's feather, Sally Fingers lifts the purse from madam's belt and passes it to Jimmy the Chink, whereupon they each drift off into the crowd in different directions, while Tom's still steadying blushing madam's elbow.

Simple, but it pays. I ease into the crush and fall into step beside Sally. "Nice pull."

Sally spears me on a leaf-green glance, but she's too experienced a hand to reply. She ain't pretty or clever. Ain't even fey. Just a girl, faded brown hair twisted up under her fancy hat, and I can see the ragged ends where she's once hacked it off, to sell or to rid herself of lice. She smells of stolen perfume, a rich lady's scent.

"I ain't no snout, Sally Fingers. Wild Johnny sent me."

"Who?" Casually, she gazes around, like we're not talking. Informants are everywhere. You never know who's watching, or what they'll tell they seen.

"Billy Beane's watch. You fenced it on Johnny this morning."

"Was that Billy's? Well, I never. I picked it up out of the dirt. Sold it fair and square." She smiles, nods at some imaginary acquaintance, glances in a window. Changes her story without a blink.

"And now Billy's dead."

"Is he? Hadn't heard. Cholera, was it?"

"Oh, I think you heard." I link arms with her, easy, two friends on an evening stroll. "He's murdered, Sally. Stabbed in the neck like the bag of offal he was. But you knew that."

"Don't know what you're on about."

She pulls away, stiff. But I squeeze her forearm hard enough to grate the bones. "Word is that Billy was on your shit list. What, did he shove his hand up your skirt?"

"None of your damn business—" .

"I think you killed him, Sally Fingers. Stabbed him and left him dead in the dirt. What do you say to that?"

"Don't know nothing." She struggles, wild. "I seen you that night. You're the skirt from the Cockatrice. Lemme 'lone, okay?"

"How did it feel, Sally, jabbing your knife into his skinny neck? Did he squeal? Did the light in his eyes die while you watched?" My breath shortens, I'm sweating. God help me, I'm enjoying thinking about this. "Was his blood warm on your face? Did he shit himself, when you twisted that blade—"

"He was already dead, all right?" A flush rises in her cheeks. "I went for him but the arsehole was lights-out on the ground when I got there. So I snaffled his coin and his watch, and scarpered."

"Don't believe you."

"Don't care. It weren't me." She's crying now. Real swollen-eyed tears, not the crocodile kind you shed to play the helpless girl for the crushers. "I wish it was, but it weren't, so just fuck off and lemme 'lone!"

Startled, I ease my grip. It's the look on her face, hate and frustration and empty anger that'll never be satisfied. I know that look . . . and with a jolt, I recall why she's so familiar.

Billy's trial. In the gallery, throwing fruit and weeping while he laughed. Sally were stalking him, all right. Someone else just got there first.

"What'd he do, Sally? Did he . . . ?"

"Not me." The electric streetlamp washes her face green. "My little sis. She's five."

"Bleeding Christ." Red mist sparkles before my eyes, and I close my fists on empty air. My palms sting. Now, I wish even harder that I'd killed him. "Did you see who done for him?"

"No, I told you. He were lyin' on the ground when I got there." She swipes smudged eyes. "I got mad. Might've stabbed him a few times, just to make sure the scum-fucker was dead." Her chin trembles. "All right for him, innit? He don't have to suffer no more. I shoulda raped his stinking corpse with a stick. There. Happy?" And she grabs up her stolen skirts and hustles away.

Uh-huh.

I weave my way back through the crush, thoughts spinning over and under like a broken clockwork toy. Sally didn't do it. Sally didn't see it. And Sally didn't see me.

So what happened?

Do I even care?

I duck around a snorting horse and his carriage full of quality—Mr. Horse's tail quivers, and the fine fellow lets loose with a glistening pile of turds, thank you very much—and I wonder if I shouldn't just let this be.

Billy ain't touching no more little girls, and good riddance. If hell's real, he's in it. As Johnny said: a win's a win.

But the coppers are hunting me, the lady in the red dress. I've no alibi, no defense. Just a pub-full of folk who seen me slink out to the loo game, and jealous Jemima Half-Cut turning Queen's evidence. What they used to call "telling the Royal," before that came to mean something worse.

I am, as they say at St. James's Palace, screwed. And I'll need to do better than *Gosh, Constable, it weren't me, I swear!*

I don't give a damn that Billy's dead. I do care that I'll hang for it. And so will Eliza, who never hurt no one in her life, not even scumbags like Billy who deserve it.

Not even crimson-haired crazy men who've killed seventeen people already and won't never stop, not so long as they're alive and free.

I slip from the crowd, into the darkling side alleys where folk are wild and the dogs hungry, down shadowy Southampton Street back towards Seven Dials. So now what? How will Miss Lizzie wriggle out of this one?

Eliza would know what to do. Eliza would stick to the facts. Someone stabbed Billy Beane in the neck that night. Was it me?

Seems to me I'd remember ripping out a man's throat, no matter how much gin I'd sucked back. Seems to me my clothes would remember, too, and I know that no blood ruined my dress that night. And I've got Johnny to back that up.

Look at me, eh? I can read them clues, just as good as Eliza. And the clues say Miss Lizzie didn't do it.

So who else wanted Billy dead?

I skip over a piss-stinking puddle and chortle. Big help *that* is. Everyone, that's who. Man like that keeps a lot of enemies. Folk from St. Giles to Covent Garden have riper reasons than mine to off the Bastard.

A creditor, waiting for him to get out of Newgate so they could hush him. A rampsman, craving Billy's coin. Someone who found out he's a snout. Someone like Sally Fingers, who don't like child-rapers.

Someone who wanted to kill Billy so bad, they swiped me out of the way . . .

I halt, my breath sucked dry.

What if I'm chasing down the wrong rabbit hole? I wanted Billy dead: he's dead. What if this mysterious cove didn't kill Billy instead of me?

What if he killed Billy *for* me?

Someone who didn't want me to dirty my hands. Someone protecting me. Watching me. *Following* me.

Like Mr. Shadowy No-One-There from earlier this evening. Like the shiver under my skin t'other night, when I snuck out of Eliza's fancy town house. Like . . .

The dirty old man's voice slithers back to me, glittering with Eliza's romantic notions but steeped in dark-bitter threat. *No one wants a scene. If I have to protect you, I will.*

Jesus in a jam jar.

Well, screw it. I ain't gonna find out who killed Billy by *thinking*. Stick to the facts, says Doctor Eliza, and Lizzie can dig them little bastards up just as fine as she can. Sort of. I ain't got her fancy opticals and swabs and bottles of goo. But I've got eyes, and attitude. Those'll have to do.

Beneath scudding clouds, I cross the Dials, where the usual trade of drug-sellers, footpads, and gin-soaked dollies parade like circus beasts. Flitches of moonlight slant though gaps in the smoke to caress my face, and my pulse quickens, that warm tide tugging deep.

I slink in behind the Cockatrice, towards the yard where Billy the Bastard met his deserved end. Flames flicker against one wall of the pub from a burning pile of rubbish, and two spindly-fingered urchins shiver and warm themselves. Twigs grow in their tangled hair. One has webbed feet, his green toes spreading like a frog's in the mud. Right Rats' Castle material, they is, if that place were real, which it ain't.

The yard's fence is low, with broken planks, and it ain't much to vault over the top. My skirts billow as I land, and black puddle-muck splashes my velveteen. The yard stinks of piss and kitchen refuse. It's dark, but I can make out the spot where Billy and me had our romantic rondy-voo. I poke the scuffed dirt with my foot. It crumbles, crusted with blood. Here lies Billy, child-raper and all-round arsehole, sorely missed by precisely no one.

I squat and poke at the ground. The yard's empty. If there were a murder weapon, a knife or sommat, it's long gone now, stolen and sold. Sally Fingers took Billy's watch and his coin, and his moldy boots wasn't in that bag at the mortuary, but not even corpse-robbers wanted his louse-stinking green coat . . .

Aha. The tortoise to Eliza's hare. I'm slow, but I get there.

The killer left Billy's goods behind. So whoever offed Billy weren't in it for profit.

I sniff, a sharp scent freshening my nose. What's that? Smells like the Electric Underground. Hot metal, sparks, a whiff of singed skin . . .

Cold iron kisses the back of my neck.

I jerk, chilled to the spot.

Zap-click! An electric pistol primes, and now the barrel's warm against my skin. Eerie purple light wells. My new friend's shadow leaps on the wall, lean and hungry, and I curse inside that I never seen him coming. Beneath my skirts, my stiletto buzzes angrily, but what can I do? He's got me dead to rights. Copper or killer, it don't matter. What a dumb-arsed way to go.

I hold my breath and wait for the light.

But what I get is an easy male laugh.

"The famous lady in red," says he, and my blood sparkles alive. "We meet at last."

THE DEVIL IN SCARLET

•●•

ILIFT MY HANDS, TO SHOW THEY'RE EMPTY, AND RISE.
The pistol follows me, singeing the back of my neck.
Carefully, I turn, edging away.

Rough-spun coat, dirty shirt revealing an ungentlemanly expanse of tanned throat. Strong chin, hair curling over his collar, a smudged hat tipped to shade his face. But I can still see his bright hunter's eyes. Stained with midnight madness now, by the pistol's purple glow, but I happen to know they're cry-to-heaven blue.

"That's close enough." Captain Lafayette aims his sparker at my chest. "What's your business here?"

My thoughts skip, a stone across water, unable to penetrate the depths. He don't recognize us. Not yet. This is good.

But what in hell is he up to? Eliza's nemesis, handsome as the devil, keeper of torture dungeons, burner of weird-folk and on the trail of a killer he thinks is me. Out of twig—it's a damned fine look, mind you, Lizzie enjoys a man in uniform but he's dead lovely all roughed up like this—and roaming around Seven Dials after dark. No Royal Society trappings, outside this damned pistol that's spiking hot fight into my veins.

Against my thigh, my sweet steel sister whispers black murder. My fingers itch. If he wants a fight, I'll give him one. He knows far too much. And while Eliza might mind her manners around him, he don't scare Miss Lizzie one whit.

Badge and commission be damned. In these stinking alleys? Lafayette of the Royal is just one more corpse.

Quick as clockwork, my plan ticks over. Lose the sparker. Disarm him, get him talking instead of threatening, and then . . . well, it ain't no accident that Miss Lizzie hides her weapon beneath her skirts. And the world knows she ain't got no shame.

Besides, I like the fire in his eyes. Hell, I've stuffed my hand down worse pairs of trousers.

"Could ask the same of you, sir." I cock my chin, feint at him with my saucy black eyes. "Lurking in alleys like a garroter instead of courting me as a proper gentleman should. Oh, wait. It's just my fortune you're after? You heartbreaker. Say it ain't so."

His aim don't slip. "Don't dissemble. This is a murder scene. But you knew that, didn't you? The police are looking for you, Miss Redskirts."

"Are they? Jesus, I just shat meself." I lower my hands, plant them on my hips, lean forward to show off my chest. "Look, I ain't got all night. If you're a copper, nick me and be done. If you ain't, then get your god-rotted sparker out of my face, and let's talk."

My heartbeat thrums. It's a gamble. He might just shoot me. But I don't think he wants to, not his mystery lady in red. He's too much the adventurer for that.

His smile flashes, brighter than Wild Johnny's and twice as dangerous, and hell if I ain't charmed to the teeth. "Fair enough," says he, and lowers the pistol—but he don't power it down. "Consider me unmasked, madam. What's your name, pray?"

I give a crooked smile. "You first, handsome."

An ironic little bow. "Remy, to you."

Silently, I taste it, rolling the "R" on my tongue. Exotic, foreign-like. And not a lie. Intriguing. "What's that, froggie? *Vive la révolution,* and all that?"

"Hardly. Third-generation English, I'm afraid. And you are?"

"Lizzie Hyde." I lift my chin, insolent. Nothing fancy or foreign-like here, and if that ain't good enough for his exotic arse, he can just piss off.

As if I care what he thinks of me anywise.

But he just dips his devilish head, like we're introduced in some snotty salon. "Well, *Miss Hyde*—" He sharpens my name, as if he's mocking me. "Care to tell why you're sneaking around a murder scene after dark?"

"What's it to you?"

"Oh, you know. Truth, justice, crime doesn't pay, that kind of thing."

Moonlight slants through a gap in the clouds, and my tongue gallops off before I can rein it in. "Cowshit."

Bugger. But he ain't on Royal's business tonight, and damn it, but I'm itching to find out what he's up to.

He arches an appreciative eyebrow. "To the point, aren't you?"

"Saves time." Inside me, Eliza wriggles in protest. I should run away, lose him in the maze of Seven Dials. I should just kill him and be done, get him off our backs for good. Why is nothing ever simple?

"Save more, then, and tell me, Miss Hyde: if you had nothing to do with this murder—as I feel sure you're about to insist—then why are you the Met's chief suspect?"

I open my mouth to answer before I realize that my words don't matter a damn to him.

He's watching my face. Cataloging my every tic and twitch, like one of Eliza's clockwork measuring devices, searching for a glimpse of guilt.

My cheeks burn. Damn it. Handsome plus charming don't equal harmless. He's playing my own game on me, and he's winning. And just because he's no crusher don't mean he can't arrest my scarlet-skirted behind, only the Royal don't need murder or thieving or ringing the changes. Looking at him the wrong way will do.

"It weren't me, if you must know," I say at last, giving him another eyeful of my bosom. "Some stupid snout dropped me in it because her fancy man made eyes at me. Not my fault her bloke's got good taste."

Inside, Eliza whispers fiercely at me to back off, for heaven's sake, before he recognizes us or arrests me anyway for the suspicion of it. She's near the surface tonight. Too near for my liking.

But dark mutiny mutters in my blood. I ain't backing off. I've had enough of his insinny-ations. If he's got words for me, he can bloody well say 'em and be done.

"So," says I. "You believe me, or do we have a problem?"

A knowing smile. "I find your half-truths quite convincing. Even without the view."

I have to laugh. "Was wondering if you'd noticed."

"I'd have to be dead not to."

"And how do you like it?" I inch closer, daring. I like him. I think he likes me. No dancing around the issue tonight.

He allows himself a good look, and then it's back up to my eyes, a fresh smolder of interest. "I like it well enough to know you're using your charms to distract me."

Heh. He's good. A man who knows how to get what he wants. But still, screw him and his attitude. He'd never dare speak that way to *her*. Am I so far below her?

"Is that so? From what?"

"Oh, I don't know," says he, offhanded. "Evidence. The murder scene. Breathing."

The nerve, sniffs Eliza in my ear. *Lizzie, he flirts with anything in skirts. Don't lower yourself.*

Oh, aye. As if you ain't thought about it, missy.

I cough. Lower meself, indeed. Rich gents like him want women like me, no matter what they all pretend in their fancy salons and soirees. That's what they come here for: to shed their virtuous mask and be real. Wife for duty, dolly for desire. At least whores get paid, for all the wife gets is grief.

But envy glitters in my blood, green like fairy fire. Damn her. Is it so hard to believe he'd mean it?

Now, I'm itching inside. I want to flirt back. I want to punch his arrogant face. "So what's your game, sunshine? If you're no crusher, why d'you even care about the Bastard?"

Lafayette toys with his pistol's charger, a restless *hiss-flick, hiss-flick*. He squints up at the cloud-wreathed moon and pops his neck bones. "Truthfully? I couldn't care less."

"Then—"

"But I do care for the manner of his death." Steel glints in his violet-blue eyes, same as I seen on that dangling beam at

Her Majesty's, and it's a side of him I like. "I care for that very much. So I'd appreciate it if you'd tell me what you know."

The manner of Billy's death? Stab, slash, die. Ain't no mystery . . . But an ugly thought strikes ice into my bones. What if Lafayette killed Billy? And now he's back to clean up some clue or other? Cover his tracks, eliminate all the witnesses?

Well, now. That'd be interesting.

But why the hell would he kill Billy Beane? No. It ain't true. Not he. Because everyone knows that handsome plus charming never equals killer. Right?

I finger a loose curl. "And what if the coppers are right, and I killed him?"

"If you killed him, *Miss Hyde*"—he holsters the pistol at last, as if he's decided I'm no threat—"then you'd be just the woman I need to speak to, wouldn't you?"

I drift closer, and I can't help but admire the strong line of his throat, the tempting shape of his lips. My, he's pretty, for a torturing son of a dog. He smells dark and warm, the inviting scent of *stranger*. "What, you don't believe me?"

"That you're a murderess? And you'd admit it to me? Not for a moment."

"But clearly there's reward in it. If you're so interested in how Billy was done . . ." I trace a fingertip over his shoulder. Time to show your quality, Captain Blue Eyes. ". . . Maybe we can come to an arrangement?"

"Mmm. What did you have in mind?"

I slip my finger inside his shirt, where his bare skin is warm. He swallows, but he don't back off, and my mouth sours. He might talk fancy and polite to Eliza, but down here in the slums, he's the same as all the rest. Just a man with an itch, be it gin or gambling or girls who don't say no.

Either that, or the lady in red's just next on his murder list.

"I could show you evidence." I ease my skirts higher, rub my stockinged ankle against his calf, a kitten purring to be stroked. "And you could help me get away with it. Y'know, if I was real nice to you."

He grips my waist, and now I can feel his heartbeat, invasive against my breast. An enemy that wants to take me, force me, mold my rhythm to match its own.

Shit. I recoil, but he yanks me in, possessive, a crude gesture of *mine*. A shaft of moonlight spills over his face, illuminating it with eerie living fire, and like a genie sucking back into a bottle, his refined façade melts away.

"And I should be nice to you in return, is that it?" His whisper is rough, almost a growl. His fingers clamp tighter on my waist. He ain't polite. There's a wild, primitive glint in those heaven-blue eyes that says he ain't playing by the rules no more.

Well, now. Suddenly I'm hot, itchy, thirsty for vengeance and destruction.

"Oh, most definitely," I whisper. "I warn you, I'm armed."

"You'd best hope so."

My laughter bubbles, seductive. I knew it. He's the very devil, make no mistake. A violent man, just like all the rest. Is this the side of him they see when they're chained in the Tower to a rusty dungeon wall, weeping and begging for their lives? Because this bloke here—this shadow-Lafayette with the beast behind his eyes—he could torture them to death and skip home afterwards for tea and kisses.

Eliza thinks the captain's a civilized man. That when the time comes, she'll be able to reason and cajole and parley. That he'll listen to sense and let her go.

Eliza don't know shit about the real world. And this is what I'm here for.

I pull his hand beneath my skirts, between my thighs, an inch above my garter where the stiletto sings. "See?" My breath is sultry against his neck. "Told you I had a weapon."

"Consider me ambushed." His palm on my skin is big, hard, a little rough. His fingers are long and warm and he *strokes* me, sweet Jesus, just a light touch but it pleasures me deep, I'm hot and eager and my breath comes faster and can't we just . . .

No. No, we can't. I curl my fingers around the warm hilt and whip out my blade.

But he grabs my wrist and twists. Pain spikes up my arm. I cry out. Damn, he's quick.

Easily, he wrenches the stiletto from my grip. I struggle and kick, but his other arm's like an iron bar in the curve of my back and for an instant here we are, chest to breast and a *knife* between my legs, and I must say, that weren't what a moment ago I'd expected to find there.

"Predictable," he hisses, just a lick away from my mouth. "Don't bait me, Miss Hyde. You might not like what you catch."

His eyes glitter, demented. He knows what I'm thinking. No one around here will help a woman yelling. He could bleed me out in the dirt, stand there and watch me die. Rape me with the blade and swallow my screams. Eat me alive.

I can do what he wants, or die.

I want to scream at the stupid injustice. Evil drums thunder in my head, drowning out my reason. This is what it's like to be insane. I work up some spit, ready to launch it into his face.

But he just shoves me away and tosses my stiletto into the dirt. "Get out of here."

Careless. Contemptuous. Like I don't matter.

Dizzy, I scrabble for the weapon. I'm sweating, trembling. Moonlight glares, dragging that hungry heat through my flesh, it's the shadow, the ugly black beast is strong tonight and Jesus, what's that bleeding racket now?

Wildly, I swat at my ears. Beneath the drumming, Eliza is screaming. She's been screaming a while now. I just didn't hear. Shut up, you bitch. Enough.

I snarl and brandish my blade. I'm struggling to be still, to calm my shrieking soul before I kill him, take him, tear his pretty face off and goddamn him for treating me like scum . . .

But Lafayette won't look at me. He's breathing hard. He swipes a forearm across his cheek, and I realize he's sweating, too. Fidgeting. Glancing up at that greedy moon as if he's got somewhere to be, someplace to go, and never time enough to get there.

I know that look.

He swallows, throat glistening. Damp curls stick to his face, and sweat trickles over one cheekbone, moonlit silver. Our gazes lock, and in his eyes, something wild and impossible catches alight.

Oh, hell. Eliza fights, yelling at me to stop it, run, get out of here. For once, I agree with her. We've got nothing, no one. It's always been that way. We can't share our secrets.

But like a murderess plagued with guilty dreams, I burn to tell. To scream my truth to the heavens, drag all my squalid secrets into the light and finally be *free*.

Damn him. I want to stab him in the throat for threatening us. I want to shake him, demand to know why the devil he's bleeding harmless folk to ruin for the god-rotted Royal when clearly he's got problems of his own. I want to crush his hair in my hands, drink the threat from his skin, kiss the danger from his lips, strip off that rough-spun coat and feel his battle-scarred body under mine . . .

Eliza wails in denial, and her voice dazzles me. My hair wriggles and springs tight. My bones shudder, something *ripples* under my skin, and for a moment, my vision blurs like water.

My pulse screams useless warning. Short-sighted eyes. *Her* eyes. Oh, Jesus.

Lafayette stares, pale. "Good God—"

"Get away." I stumble backwards. I don't want her here. I don't want her bloody conscience dragging me back from the precipice.

I don't want him to hurt her.

My temper flames like touch paper. Damn him for existing. For tempting me to sin, for scaring my Eliza so bad, she jumps out to protect *me*.

Me, Lizzie Hyde. Some lousy big sister I turned out to be.

He lifts his hands, palms out. "Listen, you don't understand—"

"Stay away from me, hear? Or I swear to God, I'll hunt you down and knife you in your black-rotting heart."

I grab my skirts in sweaty fists and run.

And I don't stop running until I reach Russell Square, where I stumble up the back stairs and into Eliza's study. I'm muttering, tearing at my hair. It's cold, no fire, no light. I fumble for a lamp. My breath is burning, and my muscles scream, spent. But I have to tell her. I have to keep her safe, or we'll both go down howling and it'll all be my fault.

I grab a pen and scribble furiously. The nib rips the paper, and ink blotches my fingers like blood. The pen snaps in my grip. I hurl the useless thing away and run to Eliza's bedroom, where I huddle under the cold white quilt in the dark and wait for the sun.

QUITE THE FASHION

∙•∙

THE NEXT MORNING, ELIZA HURRIED ALONG NEW
Bond Street, wincing in the weak light. Shopkeepers
swept spotless thresholds, pedestrians chattered,
church bells rang, every sound a hammer across her temples.
Hippocrates bounced along beside her, whistling brightly at
the morning, his *happy* light flashing, and she suppressed a
raw urge to throttle him.

She had to see Mr. Finch. Now.

Windows glared, town houses and lawyers' chambers and
upmarket shops. Her spare pair of spectacles wasn't quite
right, and the strain only made her head ache harder. Her
doctor's bag hung heavy, a millstone on her shoulder, weigh-
ing her down. Her muscles hurt ferociously, as if she'd run for
miles.

She remembered more than she wanted to. Gin's brash
burn on her tongue, a pair of crooked black eyes, the Strand's
bright lights, and a skinny woman in green skirts. Dirt beneath her fingernails, rooting around in a stinking muddy yard
for . . . what? A fright, the *hiss-flick* of an electric pistol, a
man's hand invading her skin, dizziness, clammy heat . . .

And then, in the dark of the morning, she'd jerked awake in her own bed.

Lizzie had come home.

Eliza had dozed, then, a fitful slumber, jagged nightmares intermixed with gasping, sweating wakefulness. Time seemed to reverse, morning creeping ever further away like a thief. Strange smells tortured her as she tossed and writhed, blood and flowers and gin and other, more compelling things she couldn't quite identify. Memory taunted her, dancing at the tips of her fingers and away again.

Now, Eliza hopped over the gutter and across the street, to where the windows of Finch's Pharmacy flashed in the sun. This time, the blinds were raised, and behind the counter Marcellus scuttled about, his wispy white hair trailing as he collected prescriptions for a customer.

Hippocrates jigged, kicking his brass feet. "Finch," he announced. "Normality restored."

Relief like laudanum flowered in her veins. She'd scarcely dared hope. She'd telegraphed Finch yesterday, twice, and no reply. Where he'd been, she didn't know. It surprised her to imagine he had a life beyond drugs and potions.

Her fingers smeared the glass door. The bell clanged, scraping at her fragile nerves.

In one damp fist, she clutched Lizzie's note.

She'd discovered it this morning, amid a mess of paper and ink smears on the study floor. The broken pen lay hurled into the corner, the ink spilled in a sticky black blot. She'd read the scribbled words with a skein of hot dread winding tight in her stomach.

BILLY wasnt me Some one SAW LaffaYETT KNOWS kill danger poiSoN KILL mister TODD jumped ship TODD shadow SHADOW

The note was covered in smudges and finger marks. The paper was torn through where Lizzie had pressed too hard, with a fat ink splash at the bottom where she'd thrown the pen away and fled.

Lizzie had been furious. Or terrified.

But what did it mean? The lines about Mr. Todd . . . well, she knew what Lizzie thought of Mr. Todd. As for Billy . . . ?

Snakes knotted in her mind, refusing to wriggle free. How bewildering.

All except the line about Lafayette. Couldn't get much clearer than that. Eliza shivered, remembering the theater yesterday, his knowing blue gaze on her as she *changed* . . .

Lafayette knew.

How terribly vexing.

But it was also a strange relief. The matter was settled: she couldn't tolerate his interference for a moment longer. Action was imperative. One way or another, she'd have to get rid of him . . .

Finch's door tinkled shut. Warmth washed over her, the fire burning merrily, light gleaming over the glossy counter and pharmacist's drawers. She sucked in a grateful breath of herb-sweet air. She was safe. Everything would be all right. She'd explain to Marcellus about the remedy, have him prepare a new and stronger batch. And then she'd go home. Pour the last of her elixir down the drain. Get on with analyzing the evidence from Geordie Kelly's loft. They'd solve the Chopper case, and Lafayette would leave her alone, and then she'd stay out of trouble forever . . .

Her gaze focused, and the bottom of her stomach dropped out.

Oh, bother.

———◆◇◆———

Marcellus Finch beamed at her behind the counter. "Eliza, my dear girl. We were just talking about you. I believe you know Captain Lafayette?"

Inwardly she cursed, worthy of Lizzie herself. Was the insufferable fellow to pop up everywhere she went? "Captain, how nice to see you again," she said coolly.

But her mouth stung with bitter betrayal. Finch and Lafayette. Had Marcellus deceived her? But why?

"Likewise, madam." Lafayette smiled sharply. Clean and immaculate in uniform once again, everything tucked neatly into place. "How pleasant that we keep meeting like this. I shall have to write 'stumble over Dr. Jekyll' into my daily schedule." He bent to pet Hippocrates, but his gaze never left hers.

Hipp jittered, his cogs spinning in alarm. Eliza felt like doing the same. "Oh, there's no need. I've already included 'secretly stalk Captain Lafayette' in mine."

"I should be so fortunate."

"Should you? Perhaps an additional entry reads 'test new untraceable murder technique.'"

He laughed. "A point in your favor, I'd say. The proper scientific method."

The comforting smells and sights of the pharmacy suddenly jarred. Good God, you could smell the alchemy in this place. It reeked like a medieval sorcerer's dungeon. Surely, she was revealed, and Marcellus, too . . .

Still, she had a professional excuse for meeting with Finch. The Chopper case, the strange drug on the victims' lips. So long as she didn't panic . . .

But at the sight of Lafayette in her safest place—spotless red uniform, polished Royal Society badge—the swirling shadows of last night's events took dark, threatening shape in her memory.

God's blood. Lizzie had tried to kill him. With chilly calm that Eliza had thought belonged only to people like Mr. Todd. Get rid of Lafayette, yes. Stop him from troubling her. But murder?

No. She must show him there was nothing to see here. No whiff of unorthodoxy. Get him to conclude his investigation, and he'd leave her alone. It was the only way.

She unearthed a feeble smile. "I didn't realize you gentlemen knew each other."

"Merely a passing acquaintance," said Finch, an ironic glint in his eyes. "The captain was good enough to ask my advice on pharmaceutical matters."

"Indeed." Lafayette made a polite bow. "You're quite the fashion, Mr. Finch, among circles I frequent. I couldn't resist coming to see for myself."

"Capital. A fresh customer, say what? Always glad to help our *dear* friends at the Royal." Finch finished wrapping a measure of yellow powder in paper and pushed it across the counter. "As ordered, sir. Ha-ha! What an achievement! A first of its kind, I'm certain. An ounce dissolved in hot water, if you please, when the need strikes. Can't say I can promise anything. But we'll know soon enough, eh?"

"I daresay we shall, Mr. Finch."

Eliza blinked, uneasy. What was that powder? And what did "pharmaceutical matters" mean? "I trust you're not ill, Captain? Is there anything I can do?"

"As enticing as I find the prospect of your ministrations, I assure you, I'm in the best of health." Lafayette pocketed the parcel and slid a handful of golden sovereigns across the counter.

Finch dismissed the payment with an indignant wave. "Don't be foolish, dear boy. I ought to be paying you. Rodents as test subjects do have certain communication problems. I adore a good experiment, don't you? *Nullius in verba*, all that."

"All that," agreed Lafayette. "One does one's part for progress . . . I say, Doctor, you've gone quite cheesy in the face. Are you well?"

"Oh, yes," said Eliza faintly. "Just a little tired." But that familiar itch grew beneath her skin, and she wanted to scratch her arms raw. To scream at Lizzie to go away, to cease these lascivious, murderous thoughts and let Eliza be.

What game was Finch playing? He'd never betray her . . . would he? She lingered, pretending to search for something in her bag, impatient to talk to Finch alone. Would Lafayette never leave?

But the captain just nodded pleasantly, as if they'd met by chance in the street and stopped to chat. "You do work rather hard, if I may say so. You should take the air, brighten up those cheeks of yours."

"How clever of you. A useful prescription in almost all

cases. You should become a society doctor, you'd have ladies queuing from here to Cavendish Square." The old resentment bubbled up in her chest. She'd struggled to maintain her medical practice in the face of doctors who preferred to offer their patients popular, rather than efficacious, treatments.

"Alas, quackery still sells better than good science. On that, at least, we can agree. But do I detect a note of envy?"

"Quackery," muttered Hippocrates at her feet. "Incorrect conclusion. Re-examine evidence."

She nudged the little fellow with one toe. "Hush, Hipp. I believe it's a note of contempt, Captain, but call it what you will."

Lafayette grinned, easy. "So what brings you here? Mad-doctor medicine? Poison to slip into my tea?"

Inscrutable man. If he'd connected her with Lizzie—with the woman who'd tried to *stab* him, for heaven's sake, who'd offered him flesh and seduction and black treachery—he was giving no sign.

Hot fingers brushed at the skin of her memory, elusive. There'd been something strange about him . . . something not quite right . . . *Lizzie, what happened? Why did you run?*

But Lizzie didn't answer.

"Er . . . no," she offered lamely. "Not this morning. Mr. Finch, I've come to see about those tests . . ."

"What's that?" Finch peered vaguely over his pince-nez. "Ah! Your murder case. Corpses aplenty! A delightful mystery, say what?" He scratched his wispy white hair, leaving a yellow smear. "I'm afraid I'm still isolating the ingredients. The drug's composition has proven most difficult to crack. Get a good lungful of it and you're out in seconds. My investigations haven't been helped by the fact that incidentally to its stupe-fying effects, the substance is an anterograde amnesiac."

"A memory suppressant?"

"Of not insignificant power," added Finch happily.

She frowned. "Anterograde? What does that mean? The patient won't remember what just happened?"

"Not at all. It means they won't remember what happens *next*. A tiny sniff to test the reaction state, and I come to my senses twenty seconds later with no idea. Ha-ha! Most incon-venient, say what?" Finch waved towards the leather curtain that hid his laboratory. "I'm performing another electrolysis now, if you'd both care to observe?"

For heaven's sake, Marcellus. "You're too kind," she said through a tight smile. "But I'm in a terrible hurry. Perhaps another time."

"What a shame," murmured Lafayette.

Finch sniffed, doubtful. "I suppose it is rather a mess back there . . . well, never mind. I say, you two look quite the pic-ture together—"

"Lovely to see you, Mr. Finch. I'll stop by another time for those results." Invisible ants nipped at her toes, stinging. No remedy for her today. Curse it, why wouldn't Lafayette leave her alone?

But he just held the door, and she stalked into the crowded street, Hippocrates at her heels. Horses and clockwork car-riages veered too fast, instilled in her mind with fresh reck-lessness. Cogs over-speeding, the animals' eyes rolling in fear. The air was sour, gritty, a boiling cloud of frustration.

Lafayette fell into step beside her, gazing carelessly into the bright sky. "Such a lovely morning for a walk. May I?"

"If you must, sir," she replied with ill grace, "you may walk with me as far as the station."

"Excellent." Either oblivious to her reluctance or pretending to be so. The sun flashed on his iron badge, licked over his polished weapons, gilded his hair. She waited sickly for him to offer her his arm. She didn't like the idea of touching him. Of triggering dark memory, a scent or a familiar sensation . . .

He didn't. Just ambled beside her, hands tucked behind his back. "I wanted to ask your advice on another murder case. An intriguing scenario."

"Mmm?" As they strolled—an infuriatingly slow pace, with Hipp muttering "make greater speed" at her skirt hem—passers-by sidled away, giving them a wide berth. Most avoided eye contact with Lafayette, and she hid an ironic smile. Served him right. That was what the Royal's badge got you.

Lafayette just smiled gaily at them, nodding to the ladies. "Perhaps you've heard of the victim. William Beane?"

Her pulse quickened. "Oh. Yes. Horrid fellow. I gave evidence at his trial."

"Yes, I know."

"Well informed, as usual," she remarked coldly. "Did he die? What a shame. No doubt they're weeping from here to Newgate."

"I also know you already examined his body." He shrugged, an arrogant apology. "As you say, Doctor: well informed. What I don't know is why you'd lie about it."

She flushed, wishing for Lizzie's facility with bending the truth. "I did not lie, thank you very much. I merely withheld certain facts. You of all people should understand that distinction."

"I also understand when someone's avoiding my question."

She sighed and countered with a half-truth. "If you must know, Beane's murder is not Inspector Griffin's case. I examined the cadaver without authorization, and there are men at the Bow Street Met and elsewhere who'd happily see the last of a 'lady' police doctor on any scrap of pretext they can unearth. Surely you understand if I don't care to make a fuss."

"And you imagine me to be one of those men."

"On the contrary. I remained silent because I imagined you not caring about me or my career, one way or the other."

"Oh, please." He grinned, dazzling. "Aren't we past that? I've nothing but admiration for your skill."

"And nothing but disregard for my schedule, apparently. Really, Captain, I'm in something of a rush—"

"Then I'll keep it brief. I found burned aether at Beane's murder scene. Scorch marks in the wall, same as the other two crimes."

Her breath sucked dry. Lizzie scraping in the dirt, fingers sliding over rough charcoal burns, the smell of thunder.

Lizzie had cornered Billy Beane that fateful night, stiletto in hand, ready to do him all manner of harm . . . and the next thing she knew, she was back in the flash house, drinking gin, and Billy was dead. Time lost, memories vanished, events never recorded.

They won't remember what happens next. Marcellus's words stained bright with fresh meaning. Anterograde amnesia.

Billy's murderer had drugged Lizzie. Just like the Chopper.

But why would the Chopper choose Billy Beane?

"How unexpected," Eliza covered brightly. "Do you think it can mean . . ."

"I'm not sure what else it could mean. Unless, of course, we're missing the point, and the aether has nothing to do with anything."

"Zero correlation improbable," mumbled Hipp, subdued. "Recompute."

"Indeed," agreed Eliza smoothly. "Don't tell me you believe in coincidence, Captain."

"I believe in material causes. Which rather tend to cancel out coincidence."

"Well, I hope to find out more about those causes. Tomorrow morning I'm attending a galvanic demonstration by Dr. Percival." She named the eminent scientist whose class she and William Sinclair were planning to attend, and her cheeks warmed faintly. She'd forgotten about Will and his shy affections, if that was what they were. "Percival's an expert on the latest electrical technologies. I'm hoping he might know what kind of machine could produce such a singular discharge."

"Excellent notion. Do let me know how you get on." Lafayette's smile tweaked. "Perhaps your Mr. Todd could enlighten us. He seems to know a lot about it."

"He is not *my* Mr. Todd," Eliza retorted. But she squirmed. How much of that conversation had Lafayette overheard?

"He certainly thinks he is, madam. You should pay more attention to the hearts you break."

"Sir, I really must protest—"

"In any case," continued Lafayette, as if he hadn't changed the subject, "there are other similarities between Beane's assailant and the Chopper."

She frowned. "But the B—but Beane wasn't mutilated in

the fashion of the other victims. The wounds I found on his body were entirely different."

"Odd, isn't it?"

"Nor was he drugged."

"Doubly odd. What could be going on?"

She smiled wryly. "Come into my parlor, said the spider to the fly."

"No traps, Doctor. Merely an observation to which I'd like your response."

"Whatever do you mean, sir?"

"Oh, nothing." He tugged at his coat front, almost sheepish. "Just that I can find only one other connection between Irina Pavlova, Ophelia Maskelyne, and Billy Beane."

Hipp perked up. "New data. Information please."

Casually, she fiddled with her gloves to gain a few seconds, and thought desperately. The theater, Geordie the simpleton, severed limbs, stupefying drug . . . nothing that pointed to Billy. The other two victims were female, famous, talented, beautiful. Billy was none of those. And Billy alone had yielded the coarse golden hair, the scratch wounds.

"I can't see what that could be," she said at last. "Other than the aether, nothing seems to—"

"Actually, it's you, Dr. Jekyll." A dark glint of threat in his gaze. "Intriguing, wouldn't you say?"

A WHIFF OF CHERRIES

··•··

A SICK YELLOW CLOUD BLOTTED OUT THE SUN.
Shadows bubbled hot under her skin. She wanted
to scream. Grab him, smack his annoyingly handsome face, tell him to stop being so damned obtuse and just
tell me what you know, you god-rotted lying son of a dog . . .

Eliza fidgeted, sweating. "Well, naturally. I work for the
police. Murder victims do tend to crop up."

"Oh, I think it's more than that."

"Kindly explain, sir."

"You went directly from the ballerina's crime scene to the
Old Bailey for Beane's trial. Where he was found 'not guilty,'
incidentally, despite your eminently learned and scientific evidence, when everyone within a mile of St. Giles's steeple
knows he was anything but."

And then, Lizzie had prowled to the Holy Land in search
of Billy. Where someone had stepped in at the critical moment and killed Billy in her place.

Eliza reeled, seasick. Murderers had been known to lurk
at their own crime scenes, enjoying the fun. Maybe someone
had followed her from the ballerina to Billy's trial and thence

home. Someone who'd seen Lizzie slip out of Eliza's house, and followed her, too . . . and then . . .

Confusion misted, treacherous as any yellow London fog. And then what? Stabbed Billy Beane in the throat? What on earth for? Who was this person who seemingly knew her secret, yet did nothing to blackmail or endanger her? What then was his purpose?

No one wants a scene, whispered A.R. in her memory. *If I have to protect you, I will . . .*

Oh, my. She fought rising panic. Deny. Obfuscate. Insist she knew nothing. If Lafayette dug too deep . . .

"I fail to understand what Beane's acquittal has to do with the Chopper murders," she countered.

"So do I. Abjectly. Infuriating, isn't it?"

Her mouth had already opened to deny whatever accusation he'd been about to make. Foolishly, she clamped it shut.

"But these are the facts with which we must deal," he added. "Our killer took time out of his busy and suddenly urgent limb-chopping schedule—two in two days, in case you hadn't noticed—in order to smite an undrugged, unmutilated, unfemale, unfamous, and otherwise equally unrelated victim."

"I'm glad you admit it seems random and ridiculous," she said tartly.

"But for your involvement in all three cases."

"Astonishing. Truly, my nefarious exploits range far and wide. When you discover how I am an accessory to these murders, please be sure to let me know."

"Oh, I shall." A bright smile. "Depend on it."

"And what of our charming Inspector Reeve's chief suspect?" she added daringly. "Beane was Reeve's informant, did you know that? He's determined to catch Billy's killer at any cost. Where does his famous 'woman in red' fit into my evil plans?"

"I believe her to be innocent."

"Oh?" She feigned only polite interest. "How so?"

"I questioned the lady. She convinced me she's no murderess. At least, not Billy Beane's."

Eliza's palms prickled, relief and disquiet in equal measure. "Clever of her. How hard did she have to try? I didn't pick you as a man to be baffled by a pretty smile."

"Didn't you? How inattentive you've become. I find I'm routinely baffled by yours."

She laughed. "A word of advice, Captain: cross 'pretending to be a fool' off your list of interrogation techniques. It becomes you not at all."

Lafayette cocked one eyebrow. "Madam, I've just given you far more information than you gave me. If this is my interrogation technique, I ought to look for another job."

"Yes, perhaps you should," she retorted. "Seeing as your current one is such a dangerous waste of time. Really, Captain, I must be going—"

"What exactly did you discover on Beane's cadaver?" he cut in coolly, abruptly all business. "I'm finding your reluctance to share disappointing. If you have information that tends in another direction, I strongly suggest you tell me now."

She halted, heedless of the milling crowd. At her feet, Hipp quivered, belligerent like an angry cat. Defiantly, she folded her arms. "Or what?"

A steady blue stare. Not threatening. Just . . . calm. Un-ruffled. Certain. "You really don't want that answer."

Icy wire spiked her veins. Had she truly imagined she could trust him? He'd hurl her in the dungeon in an instant if it suited his purposes.

Her stomach boiled. Lafayette might seem intelligent and easy-going, but he was just a man in the end, using bullying and brute force to get what he wanted from those weaker than he.

She'd known that all along. So why was she disappointed?

"Claw marks." Her voice was small, dry. What point in dissembling? He'd find out, one way or the other. "Billy was stabbed in the throat, you see. That was the cause of death. But I found claw marks, and hair fragments from an animal."

He stared. "I see," he murmured at last. "What species of animal?"

"Canine. I've no sample that precisely matches. But the animal was large. Perhaps a bear-baiting dog."

"Thank you, Doctor. I appreciate your cooperation."

"I *feel* appreciated," she said coldly. "Truly."

He ruffled his hair beneath his hat and sighed. "Look, you don't understand. It's a matter of some urgency for me—"

"Oh, I understand, Captain Lafayette." She yanked at her gloves, hard enough to make the leather snap. "I *understand* that you've done little but threaten me since we met. And I *understand* that you're accusing me of involvement in some outrageous cover-up of murder, if not the murders them-selves. The next time you need a crime scene investigator? Call someone else. Good day." And she stalked away, fuming.

He didn't follow. She barely noticed. God's blood, she'd been so *stupid*. She should never have trusted him for a moment . . . well, she hadn't trusted him, had she? Her fists tightened. That was the most infuriating part. She hadn't trusted him, yet she'd tolerated his presence anyway.

What kind of fool was she?

Should have let me kill him, whispered Lizzie.

"Then why didn't you," snapped Eliza waspishly, "if you're so clever?"

Don't give me that. You know why.

Her cheeks flamed. "Don't you *dare* put this onto me—"

A crowd swarmed out of the Underground, knocking her almost flat. Hippocrates squawked and scuttled to keep up. She shoved with belligerent elbows towards the entrance. "Come along, Hipp."

A shoulder bumped her off balance. Heavy hands caught her, gripping too tight.

"I say, let go—oof!" A hard object jabbed into her stomach, punching her breath away. Hippocrates screeched. Something black dropped over her head—a bag?—and she sucked in air to scream, but too late she recognized the smell. *Cherry blossoms . . .*

And her senses blotted like wet wool, sinking her into warm, fevered darkness.

THE CLEVEREST MAN IN ENGLAND

·•·

T HE WORLD TILTED AND SWAYED, LURCHING ELIZA from drugged insensibility. Thundering hooves, squeaking carriage brakes. It was still black as night. Her head ached, as if she'd indulged the night before. She fumbled for her face to tear the bag away. But two pairs of rough hands grabbed her arms, dragged her from the carriage, set her swaying on her feet.

Blind, she stumbled in her captors' grip. Where was she? Who had her? How long had she been traveling? She couldn't remember. She clutched for her bag, but it was lost. Hippocrates was lost. Everything.

Dread watered her muscles cold. She opened her mouth to yell, but only a garbled groan came out.

Distant street noise filtered through. They dragged her struggling up stone steps and inside. A heavy door slammed. She was trapped.

Her stomach knotted. Was this the Tower? Lafayette had turned her in at last. Damn him.

Her teeth clenched, fury all the hotter for its impotence. Typical, that he'd walk away and leave the dirty work to someone else. Despite his brash façade, the man was a coward. She should have known he wouldn't have the guts to face her.

But her chest ached with bitterness. She'd thought he valued her skills. Respected her as an equal.

How deplorably, stupidly *female*.

Up another stair, her boots slapping on wooden boards. Hinges creaked. She was unceremoniously dumped in a soft upholstered chair. The bag was ripped away, and a door clicked shut.

Candlelight stung her eyes, a fire's warmth on her face. Clean coal-scented air, a hint of floor wax, the tang of fresh-brewed tea.

She blinked, and the world reappeared. A man's library, sparsely furnished, drapes covering tall twin windows. Desk in the corner, her sofa on a Turkish rug before the fire. All four walls covered in glass-fronted shelves stuffed with books. A tray of tea steamed on a small table. On the marble mantel, below a framed seventeenth-century portrait, a pearl-faced clock steadily ticked. A quarter past five. She'd been out for hours.

Eliza stared, befuddled. An odd torture chamber, to be sure . . .

"Oh, I'm not in the business of torture, Dr. Jekyll."

Her head jerked up. She hadn't noticed him. Hadn't heard him move. Yet there he lingered, in the mantel's shadow.

"Though I've servants who are," he added, stepping into the light. "Perhaps you've met a few."

Slim, not especially tall, wearing the smart coat and gloves of a gentleman. Neither old nor youthful. Rather, ageless. Long hair, curling to his shoulders in the antiquated fashion, not gray but colorless, as if the pigment had drained away. His skin looked brittle and held a similar translucent cast.

He studied her with timeless eyes the color of rain. Bottomless, like staring back into a ghostly past.

Eliza smoothed her skirts, wary like prey. "Where am I, sir?"

"The Tower."

Her pulse skipped. "Then this is—"

"Of course."

"And you are . . . ?" Her gaze flicked back to the old picture above the fire. The man seemed familiar. He put her in mind of Finch's Pharmacy, the dusty likenesses of the Royal's long-dead heroes on the wall, Boyle and Halley and . . .

Oh, my.

That imperious gaze, cast aside from the viewer, as if he'd already noted everything interesting about you and moved on. The arrogant tilt of his mouth, his proud nose, the dark blue coat and pale, unfashionably long hair . . .

"Come, madam, think it through," said the Philosopher impatiently. "I don't have all day. We've business to discuss."

Eliza's heart fluttered, awestruck. To meet the great Sir Isaac himself, face-to-face . . . But impossibility thudded in her mind, obliterating all else. "You . . . you died more than a century ago," she stammered. "Everybody knows that. They held an enormous funeral, there's a monument in Westminster Abbey . . ."

"Yet here I stand. What a marvel."

"But . . . how?"

"What are you, a schoolmistress? Don't weary me with questions to which you know the answers."

At her baffled expression, he gave a sepulchral laugh. "Come, did you expect any less? I've injected poisons and jabbed needles into my eyes in my quest for truth. Upon whom should I have tested my *aqua vitae,* if not myself?"

"You succeeded," she said numbly. "You found the elixir of life. Where everyone else had failed for centuries. Did you transmute matter, too?"

"Spare me your thick-headed nonsense." He stalked before the fire, and the coals flared brighter, as if absorbing unseen energy. "I proved there is no *God,* madam. Life is no miracle, for it can be trapped in a bottle and absorbed at will. A *little* more perilous a question than turning lead into gold, wouldn't you say? Now, shall we get on with business?"

"But . . ." She stumbled over her words, struggling for coherence. "If you know that alchemy works, why persecute it? Why destroy the very thing that keeps you alive?"

A nasty grin. "Oh, I'm not destroying it. I'm keeping it out of the hands of the mob. Science and magic are weapons. Look what happened in France when the rabble decided they knew best: a perfectly good revolution spoiled by buffoonery and superstitious bunkum. I can't have just any fool on the street meddling with my dangerous toys. Who knows where it might lead?"

"But the new science belongs to us all," she protested. She wanted to be sick. She felt betrayed. Deceived. Lied to. "You can't stop people from experimenting because you're afraid of what they might find."

"But I already know what they'll find. A clockwork heaven with no one winding the mechanism—to which I alone hold the key." He caught her glance, and smiled. Properly, this time, and it made him look young again. "Oh, I'm not in the business of burning down churches, Doctor. At least, not without help. You should see some of the submissions we get at the Royal. Now *that's* the stuff of revolution. There's one called 'On the Origin of Species' that particularly suits my purposes. We'll see some fun when the world hears of *that*."

The Philosopher linked hands behind his back, with a theatrical sigh. "But egad! My wide-eyed wonder lures me astray once again. Shall we proceed? I have a job for you."

"Job?" she repeated stupidly. Potions, mad science, unorthodox gadgets. He cared nothing for them. Just using it all for his own bizarre power games.

"The man who controls you. Where is he?"

She struggled to think quickly, all too aware that in that department he outclassed her. "What? Who? No one 'controls' me—"

"We can begin the unpleasantness whenever you like." That same impatience, a man weary to the core of explaining himself to lesser men. "The fellow who claims to be your guardian. Where can I find him?"

Her blood spiked cold. "You mean . . . A.R.?"

"Is that what he calls himself? Amusing. But yes, I mean the King of Rats."

Her mind tumbled, a rock in a bottomless crevasse of denial.

The strange elixir. A.R.'s curious disappearances. The smell of alchemy that always surrounded him. His mysterious jaunts into the Holy Land . . .

"But this King of Rats is a myth." She mustered her wits at last. Dissemble. Lie. Put him off the scent. "Why on earth would you imagine my humble guardian to be he? What evidence have you?"

"I have my spies. This King and his foul inbred brood cringe in their stinking hole and plot against reason and liberty. I require . . . how does one say it? An 'inside man.' Or woman, rather."

Spies. He meant Lafayette. Surely, the captain had been following her after all . . .

Sudden and fierce loyalty burned in Eliza's heart. A.R. had done her no evil. He'd supported her all her life. She wouldn't give him up to this power-twisted genius. Not without good reason.

Such as . . . the fact that A.R. might be a murderer? *No one wants a scene . . .*

"My guardian always comes to me," she burst out, improvising. "I don't know where he lives."

A sharp smile. "Find out."

"Why?" she countered swiftly. "You've plenty of minions. Get them to do your dirty work." Minions like Lafayette, who'd betrayed her mercilessly at this horrid man's bidding. What a gullible fool she'd been.

"In that vile part of town, amid trip wires and poisoned deadfalls? Where the mortality rate of my agents has been uncomfortably high? I think not." Sir Isaac sat opposite her, crossing his legs and carelessly arranging his coat skirts. Absently, he twined one finger in his hair, a shy young man's gesture that belied the cunning gleam in his eyes. "Besides, you're a scientist. Show me *your* evidence. If your guardian is not the King of Rats? Prove it."

She faked a laugh. "I've better uses for my time, sir. Fairy tales don't interest me." But her treacherous blood itched to know the truth, and she suppressed a curse.

"The point yet again escapes you. Allow me to explain." He poured tea into a pair of china cups, holding the lid on the pot with a scarred fingertip. Unwilled, she recalled Henry Jekyll's hands, marked with cuts and chemical burns. An experimenter's hands. "I make the rules here. Not Her Majesty. Not the Prime Minister, nor those witless clowns in the Commons. And I will silence this King of Rats, madam, as I have silenced princes and upstart so-called scientists before him."

"I'm sure," she muttered. "Poisoned by sorcerers, indeed. Do that yourself, did you?"

A knowing grin. "A necessary evil. The Prince Consort had the Queen's ear. Dangerous, but in the end a fool. This King of Rats, I fear, is the first but not the second, so I'm sorry to say he cannot be suffered."

His damnable arrogance made Eliza bold. She was already in his power. Nothing more to lose. "And who are you to decide who may or may not be suffered, sir? I don't recall anyone putting you in charge."

"And at last, we reach the point." He replaced the teapot and fastidiously wiped his fingers on a napkin. "This is not France, and this King of Rats is certainly no people's champion. We will have no revolutionary nonsense here—until it's *my* revolution. When blood runs in English gutters, madam, it shall belong to bishops and sorcerers and anyone else who dares to defy the truth. *My* truth. Do you understand?"

She nodded mutely. There seemed little to say.

"Excellent." The Philosopher dropped in a cube of sugar and stirred. "Now, either you'll do as I command, and give me this King of Rats, along with his plans, by . . . shall we say, Sunday next?" He tapped his spoon against the cup's rim and placed it on the tray. "Or you'll spend your few remaining hours stripped naked in a freezing dungeon before I burn you alive alongside every misbegotten wretch who's ever had the ill fortune to be your friend." He offered her a steaming cup and smiled politely. "Tea?"

NEITHER DIABOLICAL NOR DIVINE

•●•

THREE HOURS LATER, AND I'M STILL BLOODY ANGRY.
I'm lurking in a doorway's shadows, peering out at the arc-lamps and gleaming windows of Tottenham Court Road. Waiting for my quarry, and he's taking his sweet time.

I'm antsy. I can feel that fat greedy moon's pull, lacing fire through my blood an hour before he even rises. My fingers itch to punch someone, to wrap around my sweet steel sister and jam her deep into some fat aristocratic throat.

Damn that creaking old bastard. I wanted to hurl that scorching cup of tea into his eyes and watch him scream. But Eliza just sipped and sat there, tight and anxious, waiting for it to be over so she could rush home and decide what to do. Turning over options, making plans. *Thinking.*

Well, screw thinking. Lizzie don't care about no lecherous old guardian or King of rot-bleeding Rats. She wants to act. And it's just a pity that even I can't sneak into the god-rotted Tower. Because if I could, I'd murder that crumbling relic of a scientist in his sleep and piss on his corpse. Put an end to the whole fucking thing with one slice of my blade . . .

Still, part of me wonders if there's a reason why that mean old bonehead don't die. A sneaky, bitter reason in a shiny black bottle, some dark *aqua vitae* that ate away all the nice parts of him and left *that*.

If in years to come, Eliza will . . . fade. Dissolve, like a weary ghost, to haunt no more. And there'll be only me.

The back of my neck prickles, a premonition. I poke my head around the doorjamb. There he is. My prey. Lafayette, out of twig once again in the same dirty coat and hat. Curse him for turning us over to his masters, even though Eliza's done her damnedest to be his friend.

He'll pay for that. This time, I won't be weak and girly. This time, he's mine.

Lafayette glances about in purple twilight. Lamplight shadows his face, pale and damp as if he's falling with a fever. He tugs his hat brim over his eyes, and then he's off at a quick clip towards the Euston Road.

I stroll into the street, tossing my cloak over my red skirts, and follow.

Marcellus Finch, see. The crafty old bean's playing both sides, and when Eliza got home, a telegraph was waiting for her, with the address of Lafayette's lodgings.

This time, she'd the wit not to fight me. I'm our courage, see, and I'm better at this part—the sneaking-around-in-the-dark part—than she is. A tiny gulp of elixir later, and here I am.

Finch enjoys his funny little games. So I'll play, this time. I'll find out what Lafayette's up to, mark my words. And then, maybe I'll march back to Seven Dials, winkle Mr. A. Rat-King Esquire from whatever stinking coal-hole he's skulking in—Rats' Castle, indeed—and ask him what the golden fuck's going on.

The street's thronging with rich folk, strolling in the cool evening, in wide skirts and frilly bonnets and neatly tied cravats. I saunter by, winking at the gentlemen, and the ladies poke their noses in the air and pretend not to see me. They're all too canny with the fancy whores who screw their husbands up and sideways, naughty French tricks and spankings and wild abandon, when all they get is the pox and a few rigid fumblings in the dark.

My fists quiver. I want to poke their eyes out, watch them fall and wail and bleed. "You ain't so special," I mutter.

This one lady must have heard me, because she shoots me a poisoned glare. Too high and mighty to acknowledge I exist, other than as some dirty object in her way.

"Aye, you." I bare my teeth, a maniac's grin. "You ain't better than me, lady. If you got your legs sliced off and died bleeding in the mud? Your so-called gentleman would just get another, and she'd poke her nose in the air and pretend the whores ain't there, too."

She gapes at me, dumb. And I tip my hat to her blustering fancy man and hustle on.

I stroll faster, chasing Lafayette through the crowd. He's in a hurry, thirty yards or so ahead, and I almost miss him as he ducks down a street and across a gardened square. Past the gloomy broken towers of Trinity Church, where fake beggars mimic frothing fits to earn a penny and revolutionary rabble-rousers yell about freedom and the vote and evolution, and he's heading into the dark expanse of Regent's Park.

Damn, he's in a rush. I hurry after, picking up my skirts. In the park, no one's around. The tree-lined avenue of Broad Walk is deserted, the sunlight nearly gone. The old, weak gaslights are few and far spread. Glimmering mist licks my boots, creeps under my skirts to lead me astray. In the dark, strange fairy fire dances and my bones zing with warning.

Jesus, the man's got a death wish. If this place ain't brimming with footpads and rampsmen and mad-arsed fey killers, I ain't Lizzie Hyde.

But Lafayette ain't slowing. He's practically running now, and every few seconds he glances up at the sky, searching, as if he's expecting it to crack open and swallow him. Ahead, the tall iron fence of the Zoological Gardens shimmers from the dark, a mist-wreathed mirage.

I pull out my stiletto and hold it in my hand—no need to look like easy game—and take off after him. If I lose him in the dark, it's all been for naught.

A black shape lurches from the fog, and *whoosh!* the cosh swings down.

I twirl aside on one heel. The weapon falls harmlessly, and I laugh wildly and stab with all my might. *Squelch!* My blade finds flesh. Compelled, I stab again. *Squick! squock!* and I twist and shove and the robber thumps into the ground, gurgling.

The stink rises, dirt and rotgut rum. Is he dead? Bad luck, idiot. You had it coming. No one threatens us. His bald ugly head glistens, his bowler hat fallen off. I jump on it, and kick him for good measure, and run on, blood spraying from my blade. There's something warm and wet on my face. I wipe it off with my forearm.

Strange, liberating power gleams in my heart, and I laugh.

Ahead, Lafayette's climbing the fence.

No joke.

He's scaling the fence into the zoo, leaping upwards like a monkey and swinging himself over the spikes. He drops on the other side into a row of green ferns and disappears into the gloom.

Shit. I run up to the fence and peer in, a vertical bar in each fist. The gap's too small for me to squeeze through, what with my bosoms the size they are. Eliza might fit. Me? Not a chance. I sheathe my blade and haul myself up. It's a good ten feet to the top, and my arms ache, the rough metal rips at my palms. My skirts hook on the spikes as I clamber over. *Zzzp!* Silk rips as I yank it free, and I drop into the damp garden.

Wet ferns brush my face. I giggle. This is fun. Ain't never been to the zoo.

Clouds scud, bruised bloody with the light of the soon-to-rise moon. I snap on Eliza's little blue-shaded lamp—her stuff comes in handy sometimes—and peer about in the mist. The foul stink of old straw and shit crawls up my nose. Good. It'll mask my smell from that uncanny nose of his, though I fancy he's too distracted tonight to notice me anyway.

Creature scuffles echo from the dark, whines and word-less chattering and the *craw-craw-craw* of a lonely bird. Something screeches, and running hooves rumble on the dirt. A lion roars. The animals are awakening.

A white antelope goggles at me from behind a fence. *Honk!* says he, and skips skittishly away.

"Honk to you, too, handsome," I say gaily. He don't answer.

I take off up the main path after Lafayette, past a big

smelly pond thick with lily pads. A pair of darling little striped horses are charging about in their cage, black eyes rolling in fright. Their hooves kick up mud, splattering it over the walls. They don't have enough room to be what they are. Tension stings the air, a taste like thunder, and the beasts can sense it. Hair stands up on my arms. Something's about to break.

Iron clangs, a gate slamming. I run, the purple light swinging crazy from my belt, making the world sway. Gravel crunches under my boots. I can't lose him now.

The painted sign on this enclosure reads CARNIVORA. I duck inside, panting, along a narrow brick corridor that smells of blood. It's lined on one side with barred cages, and pairs of gold-lit eyes shine at me from the dark.

The cages are small, only a couple of yards across, floors covered in straw. The beasts prowl to and fro, growling and stretching their shaggy jaws, and something's groaning, an animal in pain. Memories of Bethlem madhouse break like glass, and I shudder and try to forget. Don't know how she puts up with that hell. I'll take lions over lunatics any day.

A shadow lurches at the corridor's end. I scrabble for my blade, but it ain't no escaped lion.

It's Lafayette. Ignoring me, if he's seen me at all. He's wrestling like a madman with a cage, rattling at the lock, *bang-bong-twang!* and at last he yanks the iron-barred door open and jumps inside.

What in bleeding hell is he up to?

I run, torn skirts swishing, past the watchful eyes of prowling monsters, but it's too late. The cage door clangs shut, and locks, and I skid to a halt with a death grip on the bars and brace myself for ragged screams.

But only Lafayette's inside.

He huddles in the dirty straw, knees to his chest, shivering like the creeping death. His hands shake, fingers curled white. His face shines bright with fever. Sweat drips from his hair. He's already hurled his coat aside, and his shirt's slicked to his body like a wet second skin.

Ain't that hot in here. Eliza's the doctor, not me, but Jesus. Whatever powder Finch gave him? It ain't working.

I tear at the gate, but it's locked. He's tossed the key into the corridor, where it glimmers alone on the bricks. What's his plan for getting that back? I don't know. But he ain't inventing this as he goes. He knew he was coming here.

He's been before.

"What the hell are you at?" I blurt out. I don't go for the key. Something's weird's going on.

Now he sees me. "You shouldn't be here," he hisses. "Go away." Fresh moonlight pours down, dragging sweet sensation from my blood and setting his gaze afire.

"Not until you tell me what's . . . holy Jesus." I stare, and the silver-edged night sucks my breath asunder.

Because Captain Lafayette is *changing*.

———◆———

His pupils slam wide. A groan forces between his teeth, pure agony. He's shuddering fit to explode, and muscles bulge and ripple under his wet shirt, more than they've any right to. Like rats in a sack, fighting to escape.

"For God's sake, get away." No rage in his voice. No hatred.

He's pleading with me. Begging. He don't want me to see.

In the next cage, the lions are going nuts, slavering and growling and poising to spring. Likely they got the right of it.

But I can't leave. I have to see. I *need* to.

Sinews strain in his neck. His spine arches backwards, an impossible curve. Bones pop and crackle, and he flings his bulging arms outwards and howls for blood and something's happening to his *face*. His beard sprouts thick and golden in a matter of seconds. His nose flattens and widens. Wicked teeth split his gums, spearing long and sharp, and blood spills over his chin.

His hands contort, stretching, long fingers with knobbly knuckles. His nails curl three inches long. His knee joints pop backwards with a horrible *crack!* He tears at his shirt, shredding it, and his body was always lean but now it's stretching, changing, muscles roping tight over a rib cage that narrows and elongates as I watch. His furred ears twitch, and his hair springs long like a lion's mane, tarnished with silver and gold.

He howls again, and there's a flurry of straw and torn fabric and then he's hurling himself against the cage bars, rattling them fit to snap. Silken fur ripples along his back, over his chest, down his legs and arms . . . or, should I say, *front legs*.

Naked. Inhuman. Magnificent.

I stare open-mouthed like an idiot. Captain Lafayette of the magic-hating Royal is a monster. He's cursed. At the mercy of this greedy moon, just like us.

Just like me.

It all fits. His sense of smell. The powder from Finch, a prophylactic against a curse. The odd way Lafayette acted last night, when clouds scudded away from the moon . . .

"Well," says I, after a moment. "This is awkward."

Laughter tickles me. This is fucking fantastic. I want to flee, scream for help like a girl. I want to stroke that rich golden pelt, howl beside him to the moon.

I want to strike that lock away and set him free.

He hurls himself against the bars again, fur bristling. His hand—paw?—swipes at me through the bars. I jerk back, and those magnificent claws miss my nose by a whisker.

He tumbles into the straw and howls with frustration and blind need.

My fingers itch. What if I did? What if I opened the door?

Would he hurt me? Kill me? Claw me aside without a thought? Or is some shred of human thing still lurking inside, the man who had all the chance he wanted t'other night to kill me—yes, or have me—and walked away?

He—still a "he," somehow, never "it"—he's at bay now, crouching, lean muscles a-quiver. Breath rasping, tongue lolling between cruel saber teeth that glisten wet in the moonlight. Golden-lashed eyes, fixed on me . . . and still improbably sky blue.

There's a look in 'em, rage and hunger for sure, but something else, and with a jolt of ice in my blood, I realize the person inside him is ashamed.

My nails slice into my palms. What does he think, that I'll turn him in? Call men with guns to shoot him dead?

Or is he afraid I'll let him out?

Fuck it. Why should such a magnificent creature be caged?

We're all killers, when it comes down to *them* or *us*. Let him be what he is.

But he don't want that. He's shackled his shadow in iron, the way Eliza shackles me. And my heart burns with his pain.

What damage has he done, this shadow beast? How many people has he hurt, alone and hungry, the way only a beast can be hungry, that mindless, insatiable need?

I grip a bar in each hand. "Don't be scared. Can you underst—"

Crash! He slams into the bars, spraying spit and blood.

I back off, palms outwards. "Remy, calm down. I won't hurt you." I've never said his name aloud before. It tingles my tongue like gin. Remy. Secret, somehow, just for us. Just another thing Eliza won't dare.

He just whiplashes from the floor and charges me again. *Clang!* The iron rattles, and I sigh, frustrated. What did I think, that he'd curl up like a lapdog at my feet? That I'd bring out the man inside the beast? That he'd find new strength and overcome his curse, because he *likes* me?

I snort. Ridiculous. What is this, a children's tale? But something cold aches in my chest. What if *she* was standing here?

Around us in the moonlit dark, the zoo's going wild. Animals screech and squawk, fighting in their cages. I fold my arms and watch as Captain Wolf Thing bounces his furry frame off the walls, tries to climb the bars—no thumbs, good luck with that—claws at the floor howling, and snarls at the lions, who snarl back. Crimson flows down his snout, between his claws, through his beautiful golden pelt. He's hungry. His blood's up. He's desperate to get out.

But I can't set him free. I owe him—the human him—
that much. And when the moon slinks away, and Lafayette
the man emerges?

I sit, crossing my legs beneath my skirts. "I ain't leaving," I
announce. "Roar at me all you want. You won't get rid of me
that easy."

And I wriggle myself comfortable and wait.

For hours, his shadow rages. My heart beats. My eyes
grow sandy. Inside me, Eliza stirs, wakeful, and I rub my aching stomach and grit my teeth and hold on. Just a while longer, Eliza. Let me be.

Eventually, the wolf-man sleeps, his drooling chin on his
paws. His bristly tail twitches. His breath is rough, tense, just
a wink from springing awake. I wish I could stroke him, feel
those delicate furred ears, catch his breath on my fingertips.
I want to lie down beside him, curl my body around his, and
share his fitful slumber.

But I can't.

And eventually, when sick yellow pre-dawn grazes the sky
and the swollen moon has ebbed away, he stretches, baring
his belly, and gives an enormous wolfish yawn. The golden fur
ripples and dissolves. His limbs shrink and straighten. His
face reshapes.

And Lafayette huddles shivering in the straw, naked and
streaked in his own blood.

I don't speak. I just rise and unlock the door.

Hinges squeak. He don't move. I kneel beside him, straw
crackling against my silken skirts. His hair is warm and wet
under my fingertips. He swallows, a tortured sound. I can smell
him, blood and exhaustion and dark male sweat.

I trail my fingers to his shoulder. His bare skin is smooth fever. He jerks away, and I grab his chin and make him look at me.

Blue eyes, brimming with shame and self-loathing. My stomach flushes, sick. It ain't right. It ain't fair. I want to yell, shake him, smack his head into the wall that's already splashed with his blood and make him understand, make him feel all the years I've spent fighting for my *life,* for my *existence* in a world that don't want me.

Even Eliza don't want me. Night after night, I've struggled on alone. And here he is, swallowing their lies. Believing he don't deserve to live.

Crack! My palm stings. I've hit him. He don't recoil.

Enraged, I hit him again. My nails rake angry marks across his cheek. "Don't look at me like that. You got no right. I'm here, don't you get it? Don't you *dare* shrink away from me." And I grab his curly hair in both hands, and my muscles burn to slam his head into the floor, but somehow his scent fills my nose and the lure of his strangeness drums fever into my blood, and I yank him to me and our mouths collide.

His teeth slice my lip. The shock tastes like blood and tears. He's rigid, disbelieving. I open my mouth, murmuring with no words, and something in him *melts* and he kisses me back. Rough, raw, hungry, that dark shadow-born thirst. Only I can understand. Only I can know. I'm a bad woman, right enough, only he's a bad man, too, a monster just like me, and it ain't the badness that's quivering him wild.

He's afeared he *likes* being bad.

He yanks my hat from its pins. My hair tumbles. I push him down and climb onto him in a pile of ripped red skirts.

His body is hard under my palms, perfectly remade, and my mouth waters. I want to taste him, *eat* him, see how it feels to be *known*. I lick his throat, he's salty on my tongue, taut in my teeth, and the sound he makes—half-purr, half-growl—makes me shudder and gasp and thank Christ he's already naked because I don't think I can wait for this. I fumble under my skirts. His thighs are slick between mine, his flesh hard and insistent. He feels nice in my hand, all smooth and burning, and I ease into the right place and push.

Oh, my. I push more, and the hot gladness eases deeper, tingles of starlight that I know are only the beginning. I move, and he moves with me, and for once I ain't drunk or stupid on laudanum and my every sense is singing.

His beauty stabs me breathless. Such perfect skin, such rich golden-brown hair. So blue, his eyes. So clear and stripped bare of pretense, my heart quails. I feel small and scared, as if I'm in the wrong place. As if this should be *her*, not me. As if it's her he really wants.

He pulls me down, kissing me, locking his fingers in my flowing hair. He makes love to me urgently, with purpose, seeking my pleasure, and I groan and let it take me. I can feel *her* stirring, awakening, and rebellion sparks fresh fever in my blood. Get lost, you hear me? Go away. This is mine. *He's* mine.

And it must be true, because what we're doing don't take long but it's sweet, so sweet. I shudder and gasp, fireworks falling, and it must be true, because nothing she can imagine could feel this good. It must be true, because as he finishes, his lips bruise my face and his fingers tighten in my hair and the name he whispers into my mouth is mine.

TRIMMING THE MIDNIGHT LAMP

• • •

THE CRYSTAL PALACE GLINTED IN MORNING SUN, A vast oblong structure of glass and steel, its arched gables soaring to the sky. Eliza hurried from the railway station tunnel and along the paved path across the park. She'd missed the early train and was running late again—this time for Dr. Percival's electrical demonstration, where she'd promised to meet William Sinclair.

Here on the city's outskirts, the air stank less of coal smoke and human waste, and more of green grass and sunshine. A few ladies and gentlemen strolled between elms and oaks in the grassy park, frilled parasols flittering in the breeze. One young lady in a blue crinoline led a pair of spaniels, while her servant wheeled a baby's pram.

Eliza quickened her step, inspecting the graying horizon for rain. She hadn't yet had time to visit Marcellus and retrieve Hippocrates, who according to Finch's telegraph had turned up at the pharmacy a few minutes after her abduction, yammering about heads in bags and strange men and *does not compute*. And she'd dropped her doctor's bag in the street, and it was lost. Her medicines for lunatics. Her precious optical, irreplaceable. All surely stolen or scavenged by now. She'd never get them back.

Without them, and without poor hysterical Hipp, she felt nervous. Exposed. Unclothed.

Her cheeks flushed guiltily. She hadn't slept last night— Lizzie had held on until dawn, whereupon she'd wandered dreamily along Oxford Street until Eliza had fought to the surface and hurried home, trying to hide ruined red skirts under her cloak. Not an ideal morning.

On the train to Crystal Palace Station, the carriage had been warm and stifling, the rocking motion soporific, and Eliza had dropped into an exhausted stupor. Her dreams were . . . troubling, to say the least. And now she tingled all over, hypersensitive, as if she were coming down with a chill.

She knew what Lizzie had seen. What she'd done.

She'd felt everything, distantly, as if she peered through fogged glass at her own ghost. And like an accidental murderess, staring in horror at the blood dripping from her hands, it was too late to take it back.

The thing was done.

Her stomach churned. How could she ever face Lafayette again? How could she face her friends? She'd acted abominably. It was enough to ruin a woman for life.

But no one will ever know.

The dark whisper tickled inside her, tempting her to further sin. How could anyone know? No one had seen her. No one had watched her climb onto a naked, bleeding man in the filthy straw of an animal's cage and indulge her darkest needs . . .

Inside the Palace, conservatory gardens rambled, a mass of

overhanging leaves and exotic, brightly colored blooms. Statuary was dotted throughout, white marble cherubs and fountains and mock Egyptian ruins. The sun-warmed atmosphere made her sweat, the scents of tropical flowers cloying. Surely, her face was the shade of tomatoes. Someone would see, make some remark, humiliate her in front of everyone . . .

But the door attendant said nothing, only glanced at her, uninterested.

She paid her shilling and briskly straightened her dove-gray skirts. Ridiculous. No one could see. People did worse than this all the time, and it wasn't written across their faces. If she'd learned anything while assisting the police, it was that criminals looked just like everyone else, only happier.

But was she happy? Or disgusted? Mortified?

She hurried through the maze of garden paths, where butterflies flapped their rainbow wings and fat frogs croaked on shiny green lily pads. At the end lay a small amphitheater with steeply raked bench seats, similar to the operating theaters she'd attended during her medical studies. A crowd had gathered for the demonstration, mostly shabby students, plus a few fashionable ladies eager for titillation. Dr. Percival was popular, and few empty seats remained.

Amongst the crowd, no doubt, government agents lurked in disguise, ready to descend if the meeting grew too large or unruly. Any meeting larger than fifty souls was illegal. Royal Society agents, too, poised to arrest Percival if he showed the slightest deviation from orthodox science. She shivered, recalling the Philosopher's empty smile, his unveiled threats. *Alongside every misbegotten wretch who's ever had the ill fortune to be your friend . . .* And then he'd let her finish her tea and go. Just like that.

But the mean old man expected her cooperation. That was clear. Give him A.R., and soon, or . . . well, she didn't doubt the Philosopher's power to ruin her with a wave of his bony finger.

Her stomach squeezed tight, a horrid sensation like crunching glass. What to do? How could she betray the guardian who'd been so kind to her? How would she even find him, let alone learn his plans? *Stick your pretty nose into my affairs, princess, and I'll make you wish you'd never been born . . .*

To complicate matters, she still had investigations to make. Inspector Griffin's men were hunting Geordie Kelly for the Chopper murders. Harley was fair minded, not one to hang accusations on an innocent man. But once a suspect was in police custody, the evidence tended to stack up. And she knew that the Commissioner—that stuffy old cigar-chuffing gentleman who'd adopted Harley as his latest *protégé,* but only as far as Harley's success lasted and not for one moment longer—the Commissioner and his conservative Home Office paymasters would demand a quick result.

But there was more to this case than a lovesick simpleton. She was certain of it. And it wasn't just the piles of electrical detritus.

Shamefully unscientific, she knew. But somehow—and was it Lizzie's dark whispers, the intuition of a woman sly in street ways and half a criminal herself when it suited her?— Geordie Kelly just didn't *feel* right.

The demonstration was about to begin. Percival and his assistant were on the stage, fiddling with wires and arrays of electrical equipment. Eliza spied William Sinclair by the entrance, his hat in his hands, and hurried over. "Will, I'm so sorry to be late."

Will's face brightened. He wore a clean brown suit, and he'd scrubbed his Bethlem-scarred hands until the fingernails gleamed. "Eliza. I'm so pleased. You look radiant."

Like a harlot, her mind added, and she flushed again. "Oh. Thank you. Listen, Will, I've been meaning to talk to you about—"

"Ah-*choo!*" Will sneezed wetly, covering his nose. He had a bruise under one eye, another relic of Bethlem. "Ah," he said indistinctly. "Sorry. The flowers, you know."

"Bless you. I trust you don't have a chill."

"It's nothing. Just the garden . . . What?" He'd seen her expression. "Oh. I ran into an old friend a moment ago. I hope you don't mind if he accompanies us. May I introduce—"

"The Doyen of Dreadful himself." Eliza smiled coolly, but her heart sank. "Mr. Matthew Temple. What an enchanting surprise."

Temple grinned his pointy-chinned grin, cracking dimples like a goblin's. "Dr. Jekyll, how serendipitous. Did you read my latest pamphlet? You're in it. *Slaughter at the Egyptian! A Tale of Magical Murder!*"

"No, Mr. Temple, I did not. I daresay I shan't, either."

"Oh, come," said the writer easily. Despite his glaring orange waistcoat and necktie, his dark morning coat made him look almost respectable. Even if his hair did still stick up like a porcupine's needles. "It's a fantastic tale. The Chopper strikes again! Suspense! Mystery! Just the right amount of gore!"

"Bloodthirsty as ever. Did you ever consider publishing some responsible news?"

"One writes to an audience. If I make it boring, no one will read it. And even a sensational report is better than these poor women's deaths going unnoticed. Don't you agree?"

His sentiment surprised her. "Quite. I never imagined you cared."

"I'd say there's plenty about me you've never imagined, Doctor." Temple winked. "I'll even send you a free copy, since you're such a devoted fan."

"Would you? Truly, sir, I'm all aflutter." She fanned herself mockingly. But her tight muscles eased a little. She was anxious about spending time alone with Will. Surely, if he had romantic intentions, he'd never have asked Temple to stay . . .

Temple just laughed, good-natured. He had lively eyes. "The day I set *your* heart aflutter, I'll give up publishing for good."

"Heaven forbid." Will sneezed again and wiped his nose on a huge white handkerchief. "Are you two already acquainted? Small world, isn't it? Matthew and I attended classes together years ago."

Eliza cocked her brows sardonically. "A medical student, Mr. Temple? Who knew you could be so useful?"

"A failed one, sadly." Temple scratched his autumn-leaf hair, making it stick up even further, a gesture that would have been endearing if she'd liked him. "Never could figure a spleen from a gallbladder. Examinations *viva voce* were never my forte, either. I hold you educated folk in awe." He winked. "Still, medicine's loss is literature's gain, eh?"

"And what a loss it's been," she replied sweetly. At least he was making an effort to put work to one side for the day. "I believe the demonstration's about to start. Shall we take our seats?"

The three of them edged around the amphitheater to a vacant spot. The spectators fell into an expectant hush, and just as Eliza took her seat, Dr. Percival began.

"Animal electricity," he announced. He was a tall old man with curling gray mustaches, dressed in a dark tailcoat and top hat. Beside him sat his electrical apparatus, a boxlike battery festooned with dials, levers, and glass-fronted needle gauges. His assistant, a young woman in a black dress, fiddled with a sheet-covered table.

"I'm sure many of you are familiar with Signor Galvani's work, animating frog's legs with electrical fluid," Percival continued. "And the famous demonstration conducted by Signor Aldini on the hanged murderer, Forster."

Percival went on to describe that particular experiment, in which electricity had been applied to a cadaver, with famously grotesque results. The dead man's face had contorted dreadfully, and horrid sounds had issued from his mouth. People had fainted in the theater. One audience member even died of shock, believing the corpse had come alive.

Eliza glanced at Temple, expecting him to look bored. But the writer watched Percival intently, absorbed. He wasn't scribbling notes. He didn't even have his recorder with him.

A science fan? To be fair, she didn't really know the man or his interests, outside lurid crime reporting and asking annoying questions. But she couldn't help the squirming suspicion that he'd known she'd be here.

Had Will mentioned her to his old friend? Had Temple attended with the intention of . . . what? Ambushing her with gruesome questions, as usual? Ingratiating himself into her good opinion?

Or had he a more sinister objective?

She glanced the other way, at Will, and he gave his boyish smile. He smelled of lye soap and disinfectant, and she could see a tiny spot of blood on his shirt front. Bethlem was a dirty place, and like most students, Will was poor and didn't own many clothes. Temple, on the other hand, was dressed well, if eccentrically. Something such as Mr. Todd might wear.

Her throat tightened with the urge to ask after Todd. Fairfax's new treatment regime hadn't sounded pleasant. Shock treatments, ice baths, all manner of sensory assaults. The thought of Todd's fragile body wracked with shock . . .

A flourish on the stage dragged her attention back. Percival had whipped the sheet from the table, exposing a pale cadaver. The audience gasped as one. Ladies fanned themselves. One fainted.

Eliza leaned closer, fascinated. The dead body—a young man's—was dressed modestly in a shirt and trousers. Dozens of fine wires sprouted from all over his clothing, connected to the battery machine with copper clips. The assistant fussed around, arranging the wires and checking the distance between with a pair of calipers.

"In this new experiment," announced Percival, as he shrugged his coat off and rolled up his shirtsleeves one by one, "we go further. By applying the electrical fluid in carefully controlled quantities to discrete parts of the form—to individual muscles, no less, requiring a precise anatomical map—we find we can animate the mechanical structure of the human body ever more accurately." He hung his coat over a chair, and placed his hat on a table. "As you can imagine, this is a very dangerous procedure. We must ensure the machine is calibrated correctly. Miss Morton, are we prepared?"

Miss Morton—the assistant—stepped away from the cadaver, skirts swishing. She was about Eliza's age, her dark hair pulled tightly at the nape of her neck. "You may proceed, sir."

"Observe, ladies and gentlemen." Percival pulled a large lever on the machine, and *bang!* it slotted into place.

Sparks flashed. Eliza's hair stood on end, the air zinging with electrical potential. The wires attached to the cadaver quivered and crackled with tiny blue lightning. The body jerked, every muscle rigid, its face pulled into an ugly rictus.

And then, it came alive.

Jerkily, like a grotesque marionette, the cadaver sat up. It raised its arms, pointing straight ahead. Its hands folded and unfolded. One knee rose, then the other. And, woodenly, it turned and stood.

"Oh, my," murmured Eliza, entranced. Temple whistled under his breath. Will's fingers gripped hers, and she squeezed his hand back.

A murmur raced around the crowd. One woman screamed and abruptly exited the amphitheater.

"Keep back, ladies and gentlemen." Miss Morton ushered the more enthusiastic spectators back to their seats.

Percival manipulated his machine, and awkwardly, the corpse plodded forward. One step, another. Its bare feet slapped the floor. Its arms levered back and forth, a parody of a living thing, and a horrid wheeze—*erk, erk, erk*—emanated from its grinning mouth. When it reached the chair, it shuffled around and sat, carefully, the crackling wires sprouting from its front. The chair creaked under its weight.

Eliza stared, her chest tight. Truly amazing. The thing hadn't fallen or slumped into the chair. It had seated itself precisely, all movements controlled.

Beside the dead man, Percival's brushed top hat sat on the table. The cadaver reached for it, grinning, its dead eyes pearlescent. Its fingers folded around the brim without a single fumble, and it set the hat on its head.

The crowd applauded raucously.

Percival raised his hand for quiet. "As you see, the muscle contractions are precisely measured. The animated flesh, as we call it, can execute complex movements, even perform simple tasks such as you see, while under my control. However"—he glanced swiftly around the amphitheater, as if to forestall accusations of sorcery—"it is not living. Observe what happens when I cease the flow of electrical fluid."

He grabbed the big lever again and slammed it in the opposite direction.

Snap! The quivering wires fell limp, and the body tumbled to the floor. Flaccid. Dead. Just a lump of flesh and wires.

"Astounding," murmured Eliza. Amid more applause, Dr. Percival and Miss Morton hoisted the cadaver back onto the table. Limbs flopped, and the head lolled to one side, the face once more at peace.

She realized she was still holding Will's hand, and it seemed he did, too, because he let go and cleared his throat. But his face shone. "That was brilliant," he announced. "Truly, there are no limits to what we can achieve."

"Brilliant," agreed Temple, that mischievous grin playing.

"But no limits? Tosh. The fellow's dead, isn't he? Can't bring him back to life with a spark up his arse."

Eliza smothered a grin. "Delicately put, Mr. Temple."

"Oh." He had the grace to blush. "Forgive me, Dr. Jekyll. I am but a crude creature of the street."

"I doubt that more every time we meet. But I've heard the word before."

"Is that what it's labeled in your anatomy texts?" Temple's eyes twinkled. "But my point remains. Death is death, and it's final. You've seen enough corpses to know that."

"Oh, use your imagination, Matt," said Will gaily. "Just because we can't do something *now* doesn't mean we never shall. Progress is inevitable, if we but seek to better ourselves. Have we not conquered pain? The scientists of our future might yet conquer death."

An image flitted through her mind of the ageless Philosopher, a hundred years dead yet calmly drinking tea in his drawing room and selecting just the right blood to flow in his gutters, and a sense of dumb *wrongness* tingled her spine. Conquer death, indeed—but at what cost?

"Hush, Will," she whispered. "Someone will hear you."

"You mean your red-coated shadow?" suggested Temple slyly.

Her thoughts scattered like marbles. Coincidental choice of words? She recalled her inkling that Temple was following her. "Who?"

"You know." Temple glanced at Will. "Your latest admirer. Captain Fancy Royal Society. Where is he this morning? Or did you brush him off already, now that you've got what you want?"

And what was *that* supposed to mean?

But she knew. Horrid worms crawled under her skin, and the shining glass walls glared, accusing. God, she wanted to disappear. Surely, everyone was staring . . .

Will flushed. "Come, Matt, don't be impertinent."

Carefully, she smiled, certain her face was as red as Will's. But inside, she boiled. "I've no idea where the captain is. I'm not his keeper. Perhaps he's at home, reading about himself in *Slaughter at the Egyptian.*"

"Oh, I hope so," murmured Temple. "I wrote nice things about him. Such a multi-faceted character."

Her skin prickled. Was he threatening her? What did he want in return for his silence? Or did he just enjoy watching her squirm? Wouldn't be the first time he'd fished for information by pretending to know more than he did.

Abruptly, she tired of the game. "Pleasant as this is, gentlemen, I have business with Dr. Percival. Thank you, Will, for a most interesting morning. Do excuse me."

She hopped down the steps, skirts whisking about her ankles. The crowd was dispersing, and the scientist and his assistant were coiling up the nest of wires and putting the machine to bed.

"Dr. Percival," she called. "I'm Dr. Eliza Jekyll, it's so interesting to meet you." She grabbed the old man's hand and shook it, pretending not to notice he was taken aback. "That was a most absorbing demonstration. I've never seen its like."

"Thank you, Doctor." Percival studied her with pale, intelligent eyes. "Any relation to the late Dr. Henry Jekyll, perchance?"

She hadn't expected the question. "He was my father. Did you know him?"

"A little. A team of his colleagues were doing work on electrical phenomena." Percival shrugged into his coat. "I attended some lectures Henry gave at Barts one summer. Most interesting. Your father was an excellent scientist. Quite the visionary. I was sorry to hear of his passing."

"Thank you," she murmured, because it seemed appropriate, and because suddenly her heart stung afresh with the loss. "Dr. Percival, may I avail myself of your expertise?"

"Certainly . . ." *Bang!* A starburst of sparks caught his attention. "Clara, make sure you isolate those two main lines properly."

Miss Morton toggled some switches and arched dark brows.

"Better," agreed Percival. "Now, Doctor, what can I do for you?"

Eliza produced the sample tube from her pocket. "What kind of machine could produce an aetheric discharge like this? I believe the reaction makes a sound similar to an arc-pistol."

He shook the tube, dislodging the clumped black powder. "How much does this weigh?"

"This sample? Half an ounce."

"And the purity?"

"Eighty-seven percent." She'd tested it. It was high. Whatever the machine was, it consumed its fuel very efficiently.

"Something with a voltage gap like so." He held his thumb and forefinger about half an inch apart, and handed the sample back to her. "As you say, an arc-pistol, or perhaps a large immobilizer. Even a malfunctioning electric valet. It could be many things. Why do you want to know?"

"And what if there were twelve ounces?"

Percival's expression blanked. A muscle in his cheek twitched. "I'm sure I can't help you," he said coldly. He retrieved his hat from the floor, where it had fallen from the cadaver, and bowed crisply. "Good day, madam."

"Dr. Percival . . ." Her voice trailed off as he marched away, and she sighed. "What did I say?"

"Are you with the Royal?"

Eliza turned. "I'm sorry?"

Clara Morton busily coiled wire and didn't look up. "If you're accusing him of unorthodox practices, then why don't you just say so?" she said brusquely. "We've answered your questions many times already. We don't take kindly to interference around here."

Eliza laughed. "I assure you, Miss Morton, nothing could be further from my purpose. Did you help build this wonderful machine?"

"What if I did?" Clara was a serious-looking woman, whom some might call *plain*. Her skin was unfashionably healthy instead of pale, her nose proud instead of buttonish, her cheeks narrow instead of daintily curved. Her dress looked coarse and well-worn, something a girl in service might wear.

But Clara's dark eyes were sharp, missing nothing. "Women can be scientists too, you know," she added coldly. "We aren't all hysterical damsels in distress."

Memory scratched with tiny claws. Had they met before? "I realize that," explained Eliza. "I'm a physician myself. Your demonstration was simply amazing. I wanted to ask—"

"Well, you can't," snapped Clara, whipping the wires tightly. "Think you can win him over with your feminine charms? Use your pretty face to get whatever you want? How many times must you people be told? He doesn't wish to respond to your ridiculous accusations. If you don't like it, come back with one of your fancy Royal warrants."

Under the Royal's suspicion already, then. But for what? "You misunderstand," said Eliza patiently. "I'm not a Royal agent. I'm a police physician. My name's Eliza. Eliza Jekyll." She held out her hand.

Clara just regarded her rudely. "Police, are you? Why don't you go catch some killers, then?"

Eliza blinked, taken aback. "That's why I'm here. I found this aetheric residue at a crime scene. Please, I won't take up much of your time. I just wish to—"

"We can't help you. Kindly leave." Clara stared her down.

Eliza stared back, hurt. But Clara didn't relent, and finally, Eliza shook her head and walked away.

Will Sinclair waited at the amphitheater's entrance. He winced at her expression. "Wouldn't answer your questions, eh?"

"No," she admitted as they walked away side by side, along the gravel path back into the garden. She looked for Temple, but he was nowhere in sight. "But who says I was asking questions?"

"You're always asking questions. It's one of the reasons I like you."

"Only one?" she teased, and immediately wished she hadn't.

"Shall I make a list?" He grinned. "Don't worry, I shan't. Your humble quest for self-improvement is quite safe with me."

"What a relief." She watched a pair of butterflies, tumbling and fluttering in the sun, their wings brushing together in an intricate dance. "I was seeking information for a murder case," she admitted, frustrated. "Electrical apparatus might have been involved. How rude some scientists are when invited to share. I don't understand it at all."

"You know," Will ventured after a moment, "if you're interested in electrical machines, you might . . ."

"Yes?"

He fidgeted. "Perhaps I shouldn't say. It's really none of my business."

"William," she warned.

"Well, it's only that Mr. Fairfax is experimenting with electroshock, as you know." He gazed airily around the garden, as if the matter were of no consequence.

"And?"

"And if some of his research was . . . not quite orthodox? Not that I'd know anything about that, of course. I'm merely a humble student. Quite beyond my feeble understanding."

"Of course," she murmured. "These things can be so confusing."

Will plucked a leaf from an overhanging branch and inhaled its perfume. "The asylum has quite a library," he remarked idly. "Why, a madhouse could be a good place to hide documents you don't want found, don't you think? Or so I've heard."

"Have you, indeed?"

They reached the entrance, and Will held the door for her. Outside, the park was busier now, couples strolling to and fro, children frolicking on the lawns under their nursemaids' watchful eyes. A swirling breeze rustled between the tall trees, and clouds on the horizon threatened rain.

"Well, I must to work." Will eyed the rain clouds with a long-suffering sigh. "Lunatics in bad weather sleep for no man. I imagine I'll be there until quite late this evening. Perhaps I'll see you, next time you happen to visit Bethlem. You never know what you might find." And he made her a little bow and was off.

She watched him go, unsettled. This aetheric discharge was a vital clue to the murderer's identity. If Fairfax's library contained books that could unravel the mystery, she had to see them. Even if it meant leaving her uncomfortably in Will's debt. And besides, what if . . .

She hesitated, but the thought was too compelling, too bittersweet.

Too many of Mr. Todd's idle remarks had proved accurate. What if his bizarre insights really could help her trap this murderer?

She shivered, flame and frost. Well, what if he could? Asking why was pointless. The real question was: would he help?

And what would he take in return?

She trailed back towards the railway station, feeling strangely alone without Hippocrates scuttling at her ankles. The pale sunshine barely warmed her, and she huddled in her cape against the breeze. Ducks quacked on the pond's edge, and beside the brick-edged path, a little golden-haired boy in a blue-and-white sailor suit rolled in the grass, giggling. A young governess in an unadorned gray gown called to him, demanding he put on his coat at once . . .

Bells chimed in Eliza's mind, resolving into a perfect chord.

A drab gray dress, as a servant girl might wear. A governess, she'd thought, or a lady's maid.

Clara Morton had been among the crowd at the scene of Ophelia Maskelyne's murder. The scene from which, in full public view, Eliza had collected the very aether sample she'd just tried to show Clara.

But Clara pretended she'd never seen Eliza before. *Why don't you catch some killers?* she'd snapped. Hostile. As if she were dismissive of the failure. Or . . . gloating?

Eliza shook her head, trying to sort her thoughts clear, but they scattered like blown leaves. Percival's denials, Temple's sly remarks, Will and his forbidden books. And now Clara Morton.

This morning, it seemed, everyone had something to hide.

CURA TE IPSUM

•••

ELIZA HURRIED UP THE STEPS INTO BETHLEM ASYLUM in the dark, with a cold blustery breeze tugging wisps of her hair loose. Heavy clouds purpled the sky, blotting out the moon. It had rained, and her skirts were splashed with mud from a puddle she'd stepped in when she'd jumped off the omnibus.

Her wet boots did nothing to warm her numb feet, and she stumbled on the stone steps as she climbed to the first level. Fairfax's corridor was dark and silent. No nurses walked the halls. Only the groans of lunatics kept her company.

But at the top, a male keeper in a wire mask grunted at her. A large man, brutal arms stretching his shirtsleeves. "A raw night, Doctor. They're up and about. What's your business?"

"I must see William Sinclair, up in the solitary cells. He telegraphed earlier, you see. I'm afraid it's an emergency." She clutched her bag to her hip—a spare bag, which she didn't like nearly as much as the original—as if it contained something important. In fact, it held only a notebook and pencil, plus a few basic medical supplies. She'd gone to Mr. Finch's to collect Hippocrates, and the little fellow was so excited, he nearly popped a spring, but she'd left him at home for this visit. Even the placid lunatics made him squeal.

She grinned weakly at the keeper, wishing for Lizzie's courage. But Lizzie slept still, the smug slumber of a well-fed cat.

Down the corridor, frightful wails echoed. The keeper turned to lumber away. "Sinclair? I'll fetch him."

"I think not," said Eliza quickly. "He's the only one down there tonight, and this man I must see is very ill. Will can't leave him unattended."

The keeper scrubbed at his cropped hair. A bug scuttled out. "Aye. But you're not going unescorted. This place is a frigging zoo tonight."

She wished he hadn't mentioned the word *zoo*. He led the way to the female ward, unlocked the iron-barred door, and ushered her through, gripping his electric whip in one enormous hand.

The madwomen danced and howled, a shabby circus act. One banged her head against the wall, leaving a splash of blood. The rain-soaked air zinged, heavy with anticipation, and the lunatics drank it in, feeding on its energy. An old woman lay on the ground and screamed, over and over, pausing only for breath. One girl tried to climb the walls, tearing her nails on the rough bricks. Every time she fell, she moaned and sobbed, reaching bloody fingers for the high window.

Eliza and her escort strode through, unhurried. It was best not to aggravate the patients with any sudden movements. Annie the pig girl rooted in a pile of dirty straw and swatted at another woman who snatched a handful of stalks and stuffed them into her mouth. A girl with bedraggled hair grabbed Eliza's arm and hissed something unintelligible in her ear.

The keeper flung the woman away. It was Miss Lucy, she of the sharpened teeth. She raked back her hair and grinned, blood oozing down her chin. *A nice cup of blood.* Was it her own?

Eliza was glad when she'd left the ward behind her. Ahead, shadows whispered and beckoned. The keeper locked the gate, grunted, and lumbered back to his post.

Alone, she hurried down the corridor. Invisible fingers floated over her skin, danced in her hair. Ahead, an electric lamp gleamed sick yellow in its wire cage. Screeches pierced the dark, grunts, the retching sobs of a man weeping his heart out. The air stank of blood and urine, but it wasn't the smell that made her fight for breath. The air stretched tight with questions unasked, chances untaken, anticipation she daren't feel.

She peered through the barred gate. "William?"

Abruptly, the sobbing ceased.

"Will?" she called again, louder. Wind moaned in the window slits. Somewhere, an owl hooted.

The darkness stirred, and William emerged, holding his lantern aloft in a pool of golden light. "How unexpected," he said with a grin.

"I happened to be passing. What a happy coincidence." Her clammy sleeves clung to her arms, and she shivered. "A foul night."

"Not for madmen." Will fished a chained key ring from his pocket. He wore the same dirty apron over stained shirt-sleeves, and his unruly blond hair was crusted with workaday grime. "Bad weather brings out the funny in these fellows. Some of them are true comedians. They ought to be on the stage."

The heavy lock clunked, and the gate creaked open. "Fascinating, isn't it?" said Eliza, as he relocked the gate behind her. "I've often wondered what excites them so about a storm."

"You want my unlearned opinion? A frustrated physician, condemned to the lowly hell of surgery?" A joke, but touched with bitter truth.

She knew what it was like to be looked down upon. "You're as learned as anyone when it comes to lunatic behavior, Will."

"It's the aether in the air. They absorb the energy somehow. But it's also the idea of indiscriminate destruction. A power greater than us all that doesn't care if we live or die." Will shrugged. "That's the difference between a sane man and a lunatic. We strive for order, they yearn for chaos."

She thought of Lizzie, laughing in her gay red skirts, dancing, flirting. Doing exactly what *she* wanted . . . "Is order so desirable?" she found herself asking. "Couldn't we all do with a little chaos in our lives?"

"Well, that's the question, isn't it?" The electric lantern-light glinted in Will's eyes. His cheeks looked hollow. "How much chaos can we bear before we scream for order?"

How close he was standing. Close enough that she could feel his warmth . . .

Instinctively, she tugged off one glove and pressed the back of her hand to his forehead. Slick, clammy. "You're running a small fever, Will. Perhaps you should go home."

Perhaps they should *both* go home.

But Will backed off in a hurry. "Gosh, I'm sorry. It's been

a long day." A pale smile. "The madness rubs off on me a little when I'm tired. Forgive me."

And he led the way into a long wide hall lined with cells. No bars here, only brick walls punctuated with stout iron doors, each bolted and padlocked, pierced with a tiny viewing slot covered in a lockable metal slide. A single electric light buzzed. No windows, save for ventilation slits a few inches wide, out of reach just below the ceiling. The wind moaned and whistled, *aaah! oooh! aaah!*

Deep in the cells, a man sang along with the wind, his voice ragged. He was making up words, strange syllables that held no sense. Another man yelled in a Cockney accent and cursed at him to shut the fuck up.

In the anteroom's corner sat Will's desk, piled with papers and study notes. An illustrated medical text lay open, a drawing of a sliced brain. No pens or pencils, nothing sharp. A chained metal rack bolted to the wall held electric whips and hoop sticks. Somewhere—that wooden door at the end?—a storeroom held leather restraints, buckles, manacles, hoods, the tools of the madhouse.

Will laid his lantern on the desk, shoving aside a pile of papers. She caught a glimpse of one of Mr. Temple's pamphlets—SLAUGHTER AT THE EGYPTIAN!—and Will hastily tucked it under some lecture notes. "I'm so pleased you could come. I don't get much reliable conversation around here. Do you hear old Mr. Matthews wailing?" he added irrelevantly. "He's been in here a very long time. That'll teach him to embarrass the Foreign Office with all that peace-with-France nonsense. Mad now, of course. Forty years in here would drive anyone out of their mind."

She pulled her glove back on and hugged herself, shivering. "Why do you work here, Will? No windows, no fresh air, all this noise in the dark. Don't you find it . . . disturbing?"

He smiled shyly. "I like taking care of them. The smallest kindnesses can make them so happy. I guess it's a nice antidote for being a surgeon, where all you do is hurt people all day."

"What's that you're studying, brain anatomy?"

He wrinkled his nose. "Yes. A matter of conjecture, if you ask me. No one knows the truth of it, not even Mr. Fairfax."

"Don't tell him that."

Will laughed. "I wouldn't presume. Did you know that's supposed to be his wife's brain in that jar on his desk?"

"You don't say."

"That's what the staff told me. Poor Lady Fairfax went mad before she died, and he's been trying to discover what caused her madness ever since."

With a pang of sympathy, Eliza recalled the black-edged portrait in Fairfax's office. "Do you believe it?"

"Well, he's certainly dedicated to curing brain sickness. You wouldn't believe some of the things he's tried."

"Perhaps I wouldn't. Does he really keep his library here, in your cells?"

Will nodded towards a door near the end. "Ingenious, isn't it? Only the books he doesn't want anyone to see, of course. He's spent years making sure everyone knows he's as orthodox as the Russian pope."

"Isn't it a little damp for keeping books?"

"Certainly. All the more reason no one will come looking." Will seemed about to say more, but cleared his throat instead.

"Anyway. Your Chopper case, eh? Must be quite exciting. Being a police doctor, I mean. What did you say this was about?"

"Electrical machines."

"Ah, yes. I've one particular book that might interest you. A scientist's experiment journal, with diagrams, technical specifications, and the like. It's old, unfortunately, and the damp isn't good for the books, as you say. But . . ."

She frowned. He was fidgeting, evasive. "Is something wrong?"

"No. I mean . . . Are you sure you want to . . . ?"

"William." She fired him her warning glare.

"It's just that . . ." Reluctantly, he met her eye. "You know I allow Mr. Todd to read."

Her nerves wriggled, but found no escape. "It's very kind of you. I'm sure he appreciates it."

A lunatic let out a fearful cackle. The other fellow was still singing, louder now, and the groaning wind raised its voice.

"Oh, he does." Will gave a fleeting smile. "Mostly, I give him newspapers and the like. He especially enjoys Matthew's pamphlets. But sometimes . . . well, he's so dreadfully clever, you see. And he gets so bored . . ."

The ghost of warm breath tingled in her hair. "Will, tell me what's going on, or I shall shake it out of you."

"This morning, he was in a good mood, so I put him in with the books." Will's cheeks reddened. "I might have let it slip that you were coming. And now he won't come out."

Eliza wiped sticky palms on her skirts. "Open the door. I'll talk to him."

The singing lunatic wailed, the pitch rising. Will took out his keys, selected one, and unlocked a door. *Clunk! Clonk!*

He yanked the bolt, *screech!* The door squeaked open an inch, and light welled from the crack.

"Mr. Todd?" called Will. "You've a visitor. Are you decent?"

No answer.

Will shrugged and backed off towards his desk. "All yours. I'll be right here if you want me," he added. "Just yell."

Eliza swallowed and pushed the door open.

The room smelled of mildew and old paper. An electric hurricane lamp threw shadows up the walls. The ceiling was lost in darkness, and the outlines of piles of books edged from the gloom. Somewhere, a rat scuttled.

"Mr. Todd?" Her knees shook, and she steadied herself on the rough wall. Shadows snaked across the bricks. Instinctively, she stepped towards the light.

At her back, the door squeaked shut.

She whirled, stumbling backwards, away. And behind her, gentle hands caught her waist and set her on her feet.

Her heart jittered. His breath was delicate on her hair like a spider. His body's strange warm aura, that tiny sound as he licked his lips . . .

Sweating, she jerked away and turned.

From the corner, Mr. Todd gave her his secret green-eyed smile. As always, the light seemed to seek him out, curling over his thin frame, his stained white shirt, licking his crimson hair with fire. He held a book, one finger along the spine to mark his place.

No shackles. No chains. Nothing.

"How the raindrops glitter in your hair," he remarked. "Jeweled like a medieval queen. Shall I compose a sonnet to your loveliness?"

She realized she was crushing her bag and forced her fingers to relax. "A poet as well as an artist? I'm impressed."

"And I'm flattered, but it's a matter of cruel necessity." He rubbed his red head against the wall, *scritch-scratch,* and tapped an agitated fingertip on the bricks beside his thigh. "I have no paints. No *tools.* My inspiration overflows and runs to ruin. Alas, one must make do. And now here you are," he added with a cunning grin. "My muse, delicate as a rose and clever as thorns. And all I have are words. What a shocking waste."

"Will doesn't allow you to paint?"

"William? He'd positively adore a painting, especially one of you. No, no, it's Fairfax. Afraid I'll stab him in the throat with a paintbrush." Todd looked faintly disgusted. "Honestly. Of all the revolting ideas. I say 'one makes do,' but . . ."

She swallowed, avoiding his direct gaze. "What are you reading?"

"Ah. The lunatic educates himself. What could it be? Machiavelli, you're thinking? Rousseau? De Quincey, perhaps, on the art of murder?" He showed her the book's frontispiece. "Merely Alhazen, *De Aspectibus.* A frightful translation, but it gets the gist. He pointed a telescope at the stars five hundred years before Galileo."

"And what did he see?"

"Stars, of course. What did you expect he'd see?"

How long since Mr. Todd had gazed up at the stars? Since he'd seen the sky?

He put the book aside. "Did you know that Mr. Newton would have tossed his new color-corrected reflecting telescope in the closet and forgotten about it, if his friends hadn't presented it to the Royal Society on his behalf? If only the fellow had stuck to optics," he added slyly, "instead of all that futile messing about with *aqua vitae*. What a world we'd be living in."

He caught her gaze at last. Bloodshot green eyes, ringed dark with fatigue. A burn shone angry and wet on his forehead. He wiped his nose, smearing blood.

Her breath caught. "You're injured. What happened?"

Todd smiled at his bloodied hand. "Ah. Fairfax's idea of hospitality. He has this peculiar notion that electric shocks will make me like him better. Perhaps he should try boiled sweets."

Eliza's skin wriggled, a living coat of worms. "Does it . . . is it painful?"

"Pain is life, Eliza. It sharpens the appreciation. He tries to hypnotize me, you know," he added carelessly. "What a charlatan. Forces frightful purple concoctions down my throat and peppers me with erotically charged questions about blood and razors and such. Fairfax, I told him, you execrable excuse for a human being, you've no need to ply me with narcotics to get your way. If you require instruction, all you have to do is ask."

She recalled Fairfax's description of his horrid new regime. How she longed to grab Todd, examine him, quantify the damage. He could have a concussion. Blood clots. Nerve damage. Worse.

She twisted her hands. "What exactly has he done to you?"

"This morning, you mean? Didn't he tell you? I call it 'Fairfax's Fun with Wire.' Anything you can jab an electrode into is fair game." Todd sneezed, and more blood splashed his hand. He wiped it on his already filthy sleeve, clicking his tongue in annoyance. "I say. Anyone would think me a common convict."

She laughed shakily. "Mr. Todd, I assure you, you're far from common."

"You're too kind." He tugged a singed red lock over his forehead, frowning at it cross-eyed. "William insisted on cutting my burned hair. Dear boy, he finds any excuse to touch me. Do you like it? Tell me. I won't be affronted."

His hair had always fascinated her. Rude, almost. Too outrageous to be real. Today it was shorter, the ends snipped raggedly, but still it sprang wild, refusing to be domesticated, a rakish lock falling over one bruised cheekbone. Vividly, she recalled the fresh, clean scent of it, the softness as it brushed her cheek . . .

"Uh . . . certainly," she stammered. "Most fetching. I say, Will mentioned a certain book—"

"I do apologize for my appearance, you know. Ordinarily I'd never court a lady in such a shabby state."

She tried to keep it light. "How scandalous. Is that what we're doing, then? Courting?"

"A tryst in a secret library, no less? Alone by electric light, amid the perfume of blood and excrement, the howls of lunatics our serenade? What else would you call it?"

Sweat trickled into her collar, and she wished for Lizzie's courage, to obey her instincts, do as she pleased. She wanted to run. Yell for Will. Sink her fingers into that scorched crimson hair, soothe that bruised skin . . .

She shivered. *Lizzie, help me.*

But Lizzie didn't answer.

"After all," added Todd softly, "you chose the venue. 'Not guilty by reason of insanity.' What an odd thing for you to say about me. Anyone would think us enemies."

His accusation stabbed her, a guilt-poisoned blade. But guilt for what? Condemning Todd to this sordid den of despair? Or because her testimony had saved the life of a multiple murderer? "We all do what we must, Mr. Todd."

"Don't we." He walked towards the light. "William tells me you're searching for certain books."

A knot in her stomach loosened, just a little. "Yes. I'm investigating a case, and . . ."

"So I've heard." He grinned, glittery like false gold. "I did enjoy Mr. Temple's garish little tract. *Slaughter at the Egyptian! A Tale of Magical Murder!* Flamboyant fellow, isn't he? Temple, I mean, not our friend 'the Chopper.' I should say *his* talents run more to the aesthetic."

She thought of Todd's painting of drowning Ophelia, that beautiful corpse drifting in black water. "How did you know about that?"

"William brought me a copy. He and Mr. Temple are great friends, you know. Or perhaps you didn't." Todd sniffed. "I don't like the fellow, frankly. He wrote about me, you'll recall, in most uncomplimentary terms. 'Lurid' was the word he used. One could speak of stones and glass houses."

She made a mental note to ask Will: Had Temple recently visited Bethlem? And why? "I didn't mean the pamphlet. I meant the second victim. You knew this miscreant would repeat his crime in similar fashion. How?"

"I say, it's getting rather late. You look tired." Todd leaned idly beside a stack of books. "After such a sleepless night, too. Your shadow's been busy."

She laughed, shaky. "Such things you say, Mr. Todd. One wonders if you invent them on the spot."

"Come, you know me better." He flicked a speck of grime from his sleeve, but his handsome mouth twisted at the corner. "I confess I'm envious. It must be so exciting for you, watching from a distance. Tell me: Do you think she's tempting you? Or trying to frighten you away? I found that a difficult dilemma. For a while."

She had to look away, trembling. The impossibility of his insight terrified her. Surely, he was only teasing . . . "I'm sure I don't know what you mean."

"You're lying." Suddenly his tone sliced exquisitely. "Don't insult me."

Silence stretched, just the lamp's fairy-fire gleam and the beating of her heart.

"Your trace evidence will lead nowhere," added Todd blandly, as if he hadn't digressed, and the tense silence snapped like spun glass. He picked at the brick wall and examined his fingernail with a frown. "If you're going to catch your man, you must first understand him."

"But how?" Her courage shrank. Understanding a killer. She'd edged far too close to that already.

"Come, it's elementary. Just watch what he's doing. He's a shy fellow, can't you see, but he thinks things through."

"I don't follow you."

Todd sighed. "How would you characterize the murder scenes?"

"Well, the victims are—"

"No, no," said Todd impatiently, "I said 'characterize,' not 'describe.' Who is this fellow's god? What guides him? To what does he aspire?"

A dull ache flared behind her eyes. Was this a test? "No blood splashes, no mess," she said at last. "It's all very tidy. He aims not to shock, but . . ."

"But what?"

She squirmed under his scrutiny. "His method is elaborate. He's spent time selecting these victims, developing his method, looking for escape routes. It's . . . precise. Mathematical."

"Just so!" A taint of sarcasm. "The effort he puts into planning his scenarios is special. He likes order. He likes things to be just as they should be. What does that say to you?"

She stammered. "Well . . ."

"It says that he *cares,* Eliza. He wants this very badly. His killings are acts of seduction. This is how your artist makes love."

"But . . ." Frustration gripped her, a dull student who couldn't follow her master's lessons. "If he's in love with his victims, why kill them? Anger, perhaps, he finds he can't perform as he wishes . . ."

"Oh, I shouldn't say so." A bright red smile. "The *tableaux* positively exude joyous abandon. He's happy with his results. Your Moorfields Monster, *au contraire?* Now *there's* an angry lad. Such primitive duality dwells in the human spirit. It's enchanting."

"Jealousy, then. The victims loved other men . . ."

"The hands were damaged," interrupted Todd, "did you see that?"

"I'm sorry?"

"Disappearing Ophelia's hands. They were disfigured somehow, yes?"

"How did you know that?" she demanded breathlessly, for what seemed like the dozenth time that evening. "We kept that little fact out of the papers. And Mr. Temple's pamphlet."

"Have you ever studied a ballerina's feet, Eliza?" Todd's sharp nose twitched. "How those ladies suffer for their art."

"I don't follow."

"Try harder." Todd reached out one palm. A scar glistened on his wrist beneath his sleeve, the mark of a manacle. "Show me your hands."

He hadn't moved. Hadn't edged closer. But suddenly the walls shuddered inwards. The cell threatened, frighteningly dark and cramped.

"Come, I shan't kill you with a paintbrush." A delicate grin. "Supposing I had one handy."

She held her breath and offered her right hand.

He took it, and light as a butterfly's wing, eased away her glove. Traced one fingertip over her palm, that all-too-familiar search for reaction.

She gasped. So sensitive. His fingertip so smooth and warm. What if he touched her face, as he'd done that night long ago, his strange scent alive, his breath tingling on her cheek, until . . .

Or maybe he'd kill her. He'd no weapons. It didn't matter. Doubtless he could end her life as easily with his bare hands. Artist's fingers, well-trained, so precise as they sought that fragile place in her throat and *squeezed* . . .

Mr. Todd trailed his finger over her knuckles, where her skin was roughened from work. Over the edge of her forefinger, tough from holding scalpel or curette. Between her thumb and fingers, where an old cut still stung faintly, unhealed. She wanted him to press harder. Press his lips to the aching spot and taste her, the way he'd tasted her blood long ago . . .

"Look," he whispered, "at what your work makes of you. *Now* do you see?"

A doctor's scars. A ballerina's tortured feet. And poor Ophelia's broken hands . . .

"He's removing the damaged parts," she blurted out. "He's making them perfect."

Todd smiled faintly and tucked his hands behind his back, and Eliza realized she'd snatched her hand away.

Fresh bitterness stung her heart. He lived alone here, in the dark, his only company Will and Fairfax and broken men who screamed. Her visit, this conversation . . . probably the most interesting thing that had happened to him for weeks.

Of course he'd try to fascinate her. He wanted her to come back.

"But the next victim could be anyone," she covered in a rush. "We could search for injured women, deformed women, those in the public eye somehow . . . but it's a long shot. I must know how he's doing it." She tugged back an escaped wisp of hair. "This electrical machine he's using, I must know what it is. Will mentioned a scientist's journal . . ."

"Oh, you mean this?" From behind him, Todd produced a blackened book.

The tooled leather cover was scarred, burned. Sinister. "What is it?"

"I had an inkling you'd be interested. Do you read German?"

"Only a little."

"Well, never mind. There are illustrations enough, and what Latin he uses is tolerable. The man was a visionary, for certain." A twinkle of knowing eyes. "I should have liked very much to see his inventions brought to life."

Her fingers tingled, eager. "Who's the author?"

"You'll see." He made no move to give it to her. "When you discover your Chopper, what will you do?"

She blinked. "Well, I imagine we'll arrest him. Collect the evidence, send him to trial."

"Testify that he's insane?"

She swallowed. "Perhaps. May I have that, please?"

"He knows what he's doing. He has his reasons. He's orderly, in control. Why would you testify to such nonsense?" Todd hid the book behind his back. "Who knows? Perhaps one day I'll meet him, on the other side of my cell wall. We could swap 'how Eliza lied about me' stories. Wouldn't that be amusing?"

"Well," she said faintly, "I'd have to examine his particular case, and . . ."

"I let you into my *house*. We *talked*. I thought you understood." He hadn't moved. Hadn't raised his voice. But the lamplight lent a monstrous gleam to his hair, a dark and sinister shadow under his cheekbones, a baleful fire to his eyes.

She wanted to back away, escape that glittering green stare. She'd condemned him to this prison, the shock treatments, the squalor and ugliness. Was Bethlem mercy compared to facing the hangman?

Her hands trembled. "Mr. Todd—"

"Would you like to dance with my shadow? It's the perfect evening for it." He licked his lips, that tiny sound. "So. Let's begin. My turn, I think, with the questions. You had your chance to end me, Eliza. I'm still here. Why?"

How many people must you kill and dismember before you're a madman? Mr. Temple's jest clanged, hideous now. She gritted her teeth. The very definition of insanity was failing to comprehend that cutting people up with a straight razor was unacceptable. Todd didn't live by ordinary rules. He existed in a secret, perfect world of his own. That was what "insane" meant.

Admit it, Todd had whispered that night in his loft, *we're the same.* And Eliza had insisted he was wrong.

But the day she'd stood in the witness box in that chilly courtroom, under the scrutiny of an outraged London that clamored for his hanging, she couldn't help glancing at the prisoner in the dock. He'd given her a tragic little smile, and with a flash of dark certainty, she knew she'd never forgive herself if she let him die. Her testimony, for good or ill, had saved his life.

Now, in the dimly lit cell, her eyes burned. Was his special world real? Or had he fooled her, with his odd charm and twinkling eyes and swift heartbeat against her breast?

What if it was all just a game? A seductive illusion that she'd wanted desperately to believe, simply because it meant she didn't have to face the truth?

What if he was just an ice-hearted brute who delighted in blood?

"It was a legal matter," she said shakily. "Nothing personal."

"The law's the law, is that it? *Fiat justitia ruat caelum.*"

Though the heavens fall, indeed. "Exactly."

"Admirable," murmured Todd, "but I wasn't referring to the courtroom."

Her heartbeat skittered. "I'm sure I don't know what you mean—"

"And you're lying again. I told you we'd work on that." His gaze stalked her, lurking in shadow. "We were alone, that night in my studio. I confess, you'd surprised me. I was defenseless. The quarry you'd chased for months, at your mercy. Yet I'm still alive. Why?"

Warm lamplight, the silvery flash of his blade, the tiny throb of his pulse beneath her fingertips. His fingers closing around hers, inviting her to strike. *Do it,* he'd whispered. *Let me show you what freedom means. Let me show you how . . .*

"It wasn't my decision to make," she said shakily. "I believe in justice, not retribution."

"We both know that's not entirely true."

She swallowed, desperate. "I was afraid . . ."

"No excuse. You came to me, alone, in the dark. You're the bravest person I know." A step closer, the predator preparing to spring.

"You're stronger than I, I couldn't . . ."

"I put the razor in your hand, Eliza." Todd's whisper sliced the shadows, deadly as that blade. "I gave you my life. And you gave it back. Don't pretend it was because you didn't *want* it."

Eliza's body burned. She'd had her chance to end him. To slice him open, drain his hot crimson life away. To put an end to his nightmare world of murder. She'd have saved countless lives, brought a criminal to justice, solved the impossible case.

Let me show you, he'd whispered, the lamplight caressing his face. His fingers had wrapped around hers, guiding her hand, pressing the glittering blade against his throat.

Let me show you how I love you.

Mr. Todd smiled. Indecently red, just like his hair. And silently, he held the journal out to her.

Shivering, she grabbed it and fled.

STARTLING BLASPHEMIES

••

A
N HOUR LATER, RAIN PELTED FROM A BLACKENED sky, fat drops that left oily streaks on her clothes. Eliza stomped up her town house steps in wet boots, her skirt hems slopping with mud. Her cape was sodden and grimy, and the evening chill had soaked deep into her bones.

Inside, delicious smells of supper curled from the kitchen in delightful warmth. Rain streaked the windows and hammered on the roof. Hipp greeted her, hopping on the spot, trying to climb her dirty skirts. "Welcome," he yammered, flashing his lights. "Welcome. Possibility of rain. Make greater speed."

"Down, idiot." She petted him, but her weary bones ached as she put down her things. RIOTS IN HYDE PARK, read the rain-smudged headline on her evening edition. RABBLE MARCHES ON PARLIAMENT. SHOTS FIRED. MILITIA FORCES DEFEATED BY CAVALRY. The Thistlewood Club, it seemed, had received a hard lesson in public order—what would Sir Isaac make of that, she wondered, with his talk of revolution?— and she'd ridden home from the station along puddle-splashed streets that were lined with armed soldiers and possessed by the strange, unearthly hush of fear. Despite having taken a cab, she was saturated.

The unnamed scientist's diary, too, huddled in Eliza's bag, mysterious and compelling, but all she wanted was supper, a warm bed, and sleep, free of dark dreams.

She shuddered. She had an inkling what her dreams would be about tonight. Glittering green eyes, a fevered embrace, sparkling steel . . .

She hung her sodden cape in the closet. "Mrs. Poole?"

The housekeeper emerged from the kitchen, wiping her hands on a dishcloth. "What time do you call this? Your little brass critter has been nagging me all afternoon. How do you quieten a dog who won't chew a gumdrop?"

"Critter," announced Hipp happily, "critter-critter-critter . . ."

"And a good evening to you, too." Fruitlessly, Eliza shook her wet skirts.

"Look at you, you're drenched. That cape is quite ruined. And your hair's coming down." Mrs. Poole tutted and fussed, taking Eliza's sodden gloves. "The bedroom fire's lit, not the study. Unless you're planning to stay up past dawn again."

"How thoughtful," said Eliza faintly, and turned to close the door on the foul night.

Footsteps splashed on the stairs. "Dr. Jekyll?"

Hipp scuttled into the corner, muttering.

Not now. Please, not tonight. She longed to slam the door, pretend she hadn't heard. Run upstairs and hide. But her soaked skirts suddenly seemed to weigh a hundred pounds.

Captain Lafayette stood dripping on her threshold. His hair was plastered wet to his cheeks in sharp tendrils, and his eyes shone too brightly in the night. He looked young, harmless. A boy lost in the rain.

"You're home," he said unnecessarily. "I, er . . . that's good."

Words wouldn't come. Burning heat, roughened breath, damp skin sliding on skin, fingertips and palms and thirsty mouths colliding. Golden fur, claws, moonlight glinting in wild blue eyes, the horrid *crunch!* as his bones stretched . . .

Eliza swallowed, her mouth dry. What could she possibly say? Lafayette was . . . well, she didn't quite know *what* he was. As a child, she'd read with delight the garish tales of lycanthropes, wild beast-men of the forest. She'd never heard of one who locked himself in a cage when the change came.

Distantly, she recalled the claw wounds in Billy Beane's corpse. The hair sample she'd taken still sat in its glass tube on her desk. Coarse yellow-brown hair, torn out by the root. A dog's, Hipp had said.

A wolf's?

Lafayette was a monster, certainly. But a dangerous one? A killer? Had he connected her with Lizzie? Did he remember . . . ?

Pointedly, Mrs. Poole cleared her throat.

Eliza knitted her cold fingers. "Captain. I . . ."

"Rude of me, I know, to visit at this hour." For once, Lafayette didn't smile. He held out a large object wrapped in a damp hessian bag. "I just wanted to bring you this."

She unwrapped the bag's corner and gasped in delight. Her optical. Undamaged and polished, the brass spotless, lenses gleaming red and blue. "Oh. I say . . ."

"And to offer you my apology." Lafayette's blue gaze glowed, clear of deceit, and her stomach filled with hot dread. She squirmed. How she wanted to disappear. Vanish in a puff of *this never happened* . . .

"I'd ask if you're all right," he added, "but clearly you are. I heard you were taken, and I'm sorry. I know you won't believe it wasn't my doing. But I'd never have left you had I known what they planned. Forgive me."

Relief staggered her, and she grabbed the doorframe lest she fall.

He was talking about her abduction. The Philosopher.

Did she believe him, that he'd had nothing to do with it? It didn't matter. After all that had happened—the Tower, Mr. Todd, the mess Lizzie had made—she'd almost forgotten she and Lafayette had argued, that she'd as much as ended their acquaintance. That the Chopper and Billy Beane's killer were the same person. Or *creature*.

Oh, my.

She held her optical tightly, abruptly aware of the incriminating arcane diary in her bag. "Where did you find this?"

A raindrop trickled down his cheek. "I called in a few favors. Recovering stolen goods is simple if you know the right people. A device so unusual doesn't go unnoticed."

"Oh." Not so simple as he pretended. Recyclers and fences were a greedy lot. Doubtless it had cost him dear even to find the right one. He'd gone to a lot of trouble for her . . . but was it just part of his ruse?

She fidgeted. *Captain, we really should talk. Convince me I should believe you that you aren't the Philosopher's agent trying to trick me. Explain why you're chasing me up and hither for the Royal, when clearly they'd burn you alive if they discov-*

*ered what you really are. Prove to me that the hair I found on
Billy's corpse is nothing to do with you.*

*Promise me you don't realize that the woman who gave her-
self to you in a pile of dirty straw last night was me.*

"Thank you," she added lamely.

"The least I can do." He tucked his hands behind his back,
squishing water from his soaked coat. "Um. Well, I'm glad I
found you at home. Sorry to intrude so late."

The silence stretched. Compulsion gripped her to say
something, anything. Apologize, call it a misunderstanding,
let him know they could still be friends.

"Er . . . Might I offer you an umbrella?"

Well, *that* certainly wasn't it.

At last, a flash of his old smile. "A little late for that. Good
night, Doctor." And he vanished into the gloom.

Eliza closed the door and leaned against it with a thudding
heart. Relief. Confusion. Guilt. She didn't know what she felt.

What to do? Either Lafayette was determined to pretend
nothing had happened . . . or he didn't realize she and Lizzie
were the same woman. Should she go along with it? Had he
truly been innocent of her abduction? If he'd wanted to arrest
her—or get rid of her—he'd had ample opportunity. That didn't
mean he wasn't delaying for some dark purpose of his own.

A prophylactic against a curse. Mr. Finch's words echoed
back to her, glimmering with fresh meaning. *Can't say I can
promise anything.*

What if Lafayette was trying to cure his affliction? What
if there really *was* a cure? If she could get rid of Lizzie for
good . . . would she?

A flick on her shoulder startled her. "What?"

Mrs. Poole swatted her again, dishcloth flying. "Don't 'what' me, young lady. Who on earth is *he*?"

Him? Oh, he's a moon-crazed wolf-man. My lover. Might I have some tea? "No one. It doesn't matter." Eliza clunked her optical onto the hall table and wiped water from her sleeves. Her fingertips were wrinkled and clammy.

"Obviously not," said Mrs. Poole blandly, producing a fresh hand towel as if by magic and pressing it into Eliza's hands. "What a ridiculous notion. Fine-looking gentlemen call here soaked to the skin in the middle of the night all the time. Utterly of no consequence."

Eliza snorted and swabbed her dripping hair. "Captain La-fayette of the esteemed Royal Society"—she waved her towel grandly, splashing water drops—"was merely returning my property, soaked to his bullishly thick skin or otherwise. And it isn't the middle of the night, even if it feels like it. It's barely eight."

"You allow he's fine-looking, then."

Eliza tossed the damp towel at her. "Do you think so? I hadn't noticed."

"Single, is he?"

"Given his insufferable arrogance, I should imagine so." She realized with a pang that she didn't know. He wore no ring and flirted incessantly. That meant nothing. For all she knew, somewhere there lived a Mrs. Lafayette, who stead-fastly tolerated her husband's absences and his easy ways with other women, counting herself lucky to be able to spend his fortune—and happily oblivious that he burst out into fur and fangs whenever the fancy took him. Or even when it didn't.

"Rich?" pressed Mrs. Poole.

"Odiferously, I suspect."

"Charming, too."

"I'll take supper in my room, if you please. I'm finding the conversation down here quite vapid this evening."

"Whatever you say," agreed Mrs. Poole happily. "If the good captain comes by again, I'll give him your best."

"You do that." Wearily, she climbed to her bedroom and stoked the dying fire.

She peeled off her damp clothes, heaving a sigh as she unhooked her corset. Wet hair snaked on her shoulders. She pulled on her nightdress and turned to hang her gown before the fire to dry.

The closet door—Eliza's closet—hung open an inch or two, and a hint of scarlet cloth peeked out.

She'd dressed in a hurry this morning to make the Crystal Palace train and had tossed Lizzie's clothes in the bottom of the closet, with no time to open the cabinet and hang them properly. Fine. She'd put them away in the morning.

She bent over to tuck the cloth out of sight. Lizzie's corset was thrown in on top, the steel hooks gleaming—and as she closed the closet door, she caught a glimpse of fine gold.

Caught in the curl of the topmost hook was a single golden-brown hair.

Breathless, she plucked the hair out between finger and thumb. Firelight licked it with a warm yet sinister gleam. It was about four inches long, not a hint of wave.

Captain Lafayette's hair was curly. Longish, true, but not *that* long. This was the hair of a large animal.

A wolf's hair.

She snatched up her candle and hurried downstairs to her study.

The sample sat innocently in its glass tube on her desk. She popped the cork, tweezed out the contents. Laid the two strands side by side on the blotter.

The hair from Billy's corpse, short and coarse, uniformly yellowish along its length. And the one from Lizzie's corset, long and fine, brown at the root, golden at the tip.

She didn't need a microscope to see they weren't the same.

Her knees buckled, and she gripped the desk's edge.

Dear God, she'd been convinced he was the murderer. She hadn't realized. So deeply convinced, she'd lapsed into disbelief, a refusal even to consider the truth. That the *thing* she'd

(*made love to*)

trusted with her life was a mindless beast.

But the hair wasn't his. Lafayette the wolf had, as Lizzie might say, wriggled off the hook.

Which left her once again with no clear clues. No answers. Nothing.

Deflated, she gripped her candlestick with chilled fingers and slunk back to bed.

The room was blessedly warm, the glowing coals hypnotic. She climbed into bed, intending to sit up and wait for Mrs. Poole and her supper. But restless slumber ambushed her, and she tossed and muttered, trapped in dark dreams of Bethlem Asylum, its stone walls running with fresh blood.

Warm steel hummed and whispered in her hand. In the shadows, a pair of glinting green eyes danced, beckoning. She knew she must reach him, stop him, let her thirsty blade drink, but even though she sprinted until her chest burned, the monster lurked just beyond her reach, mocking. *Let me show you,* it growled. *Let me show you how I'll devour you. Make you ache. Make you bleed . . .*

She snapped awake, a cry on her lips.

The fire had burned out. She dragged back sweat-crusted hair. Her palms stung, and she unfolded cramped fingers to find red crescent moons where her nails had dug in.

She fumbled with the bedside lamp. *Pop!* Yellow light glared, the faint smell of hot metal. Her bag made a dark blob on the carpet by the bed. Shivering, she reached for the diary. Her fingertips tingled as they touched the cover. The bumpy black leather felt smooth, alive with possibility, the invisible tracks of Mr. Todd's fingers zinging like fairydust. It looked as if part of the book was missing, torn out, leaving a ragged gap in the spine.

Todd had wanted her to have this. To what end?

Did she care?

Huddling in the twisted quilt, she opened the cover with a creak of old binding and hunched into sweat-fragrant pillows to read.

ABSENCE OF EVIDENCE

•·•

AT NINE O'CLOCK SHARP THE NEXT MORNING, SHE strode into Inspector Griffin's office at Bow Street and dropped the open diary onto his desk. "Harley, you must look at this."

Griffin's tiny office was tucked at the top of the stairs, with no windows and the desk jammed in one corner, almost blocking the door. Maps, drawings, and scribbled notes covered the walls, lined up and neatly pinned at each corner. Like the whole building, the room smelled of stale coal and cigar smoke, though Griffin didn't smoke and likely never would.

She'd spent the dark of the morning poring over the diary's contents. Handwriting, old-fashioned copperplate; neatly ruled diagrams, labeled in black ink on moldering paper. *A visionary,* Mr. Todd said. Whoever the diarist was—the title pages were torn out, frustratingly, any indication of the author's identity obliterated—whoever this man or woman was, he or she fell not far short of genius . . . or lunacy.

Griffin shifted in his old wooden chair, grimacing. She'd known he'd be at work. Even a knife wound wasn't sufficient to keep him away. His top hat still sat on the desk, beside neat stacks of letters and telegrams. His pen was wiped clean, his blotter unstained. "Eliza—"

"Look," she insisted, stabbing her finger at the diagrams. "This is the source of the electrical detritus at the crime scenes. This is what he's built. It's brilliant!"

"Brilliant," chirped Hipp, muffled in the depths of her new bag.

Griffin glanced at the inked page. "Eliza—"

"Dr. Percival said a voltage gap of half an inch. But this machine generates twenty-four times that. Twenty-four times!" Her excitement made her sweat, and she tugged at her tight collar. "No wonder it sounded like an arc-pistol. More like a brace of cannon—"

Griffin leaned forward and gripped her hand, stopping her in mid-flow. "Eliza!"

"What?"

On his blotter lay a letter decorated with the Home Office's fat wax seal.

Her stomach curdled. She didn't need to pick the letter up. "It's Reeve, isn't it?"

"He filed a report. First you examined his precious cadaver without permission, and now you've been arrested by the Royal. I didn't say anything," he added, forestalling her with a raised hand. "He found out all by himself. You've given him one excuse too many."

That little weasel, snarled Lizzie, freshly awake now. *I'll rip his nose off.*

How did Reeve find out? Had he set someone to follow her? "But they let me go before you even called on them. No charges were laid."

"Do you think they care, down at Whitehall? You've made the Home Secretary look foolish. A cardinal sin." Griffin shrugged, resigned. "I'll contest it, of course. There'll be a hearing. They can't keep you out forever. But for now . . ."

"I'm off the job." Her mouth soured, the rich flavor of Lizzie's anger mixing with her own. She wanted to spit it out, scream their unladylike rage to the sky. Stalk Reeve down a dark street, dance our fingertips across his shoulder, show him what it means to be lost and alone . . .

Griffin squeezed her hand gently. "I'm sorry."

"It's not your fault." But her guts felt hollow, as if a burning brand had scoured them out. She pressed her fist hard onto the table, lest she punch it. Damn Reeve and his smug woman-hating nonsense to hell. "Fine," she said stonily, and swept around to depart.

"Leaving already? What about the case?"

She halted. "I thought I was excluded from 'the case.'"

Griffin quirked his brows. "This is my office, isn't it? No rule says I can't entertain a civilian guest. Do take a seat, madam, how kind of you to visit. Perhaps you'd like a tour of the station?"

She hesitated. "Harley, you'll only make trouble for yourself."

He leaned back in his chair, as far as the tiny room would allow. "Oh, I'm merely delivering bad news in person. It's only polite. If anyone should ask, you were just leaving."

"Thank you. You're a good friend."

"Don't mention it." His eyes were reddened and ringed with shadow, his cheeks pale. He looked as if he hadn't slept. She should ask after Mrs. Griffin's health. Somehow the subject never seemed appropriate. Like poking at an open sore.

She sat, not bothering to smooth her skirts or cover her

ankles, and dumped her bag on the floor, eliciting an indignant *clunk!* and *whir!* of cogs. Her blood still boiled, and she forced herself to slow down, take a breath. She wanted to thrust the book into Harley's face, make him see. "You really need to look at this book. It changes everything. I assume you're still chasing your lovesick idiot?"

"Have to follow every lead, and right now he's all we have. He can't have wandered far. I have constables hunting for him for streets in every direction. He'll turn up."

She hesitated. "Should you be at home? Is Mrs. Griffin . . . ? Is there anything I can do?"

He shrugged, but the ghost of incurable sickness haunted his smile.

"Harley . . ."

"I can't bear it, Eliza." He swallowed, hard, and for once, a fraction of his grief spilled into his eyes. "Do you think me cold? I suppose I am. But she's fading and I can't bear to just stand by and watch. She can't speak, or see. She barely knows if I'm there. Better to fight battles I can win."

"Indeed." Eliza cleared her throat. "Very well. What shall we do when we catch this Geordie?"

"Question him. It is possible he's guilty, you know. Occam's razor, and all that." Griffin scraped back his already impeccable hair. "But you're not convinced. Lafayette's theories getting under your skin?"

"It's not that. Please, you have to look at this." She shoved the diary closer.

"Is that German? I'm afraid I don't—"

"Never mind the words. Look at the diagrams. Remember the burned aether at the scenes?"

"Left by some electrical equipment, you said."

"The very same. A machine requiring extremely high voltage, with some function important to our killer."

She waited, expectant.

Bemused, Griffin peered at the page. "It looks like the contraption on the top of a train carriage. Forgive me, this isn't my expertise. I'm not sure I follow."

"Consider our Chopper's purpose," she said earnestly. "He kills his victims with a drug and a blade. So the machine isn't for that. By the time he activates it, the women are dead, and he's gotten what he came for. What subsequent aim must a murderer have?"

Griffin thought for a moment. "To get away undetected. No one saw him go. Just the sound of a pistol shot."

"Just so." She pointed at the diagram, triumphant. "This is how he escapes. It's—"

"Inspector!" Sergeant Porter hurtled in, short of breath. He stumbled into Eliza, all but knocking her from her chair. He steadied her, and straightened his hat. "Sorry, Doctor. We've found him, sir. The Kelly boy. Skulking in the market, begging for scraps."

Griffin was out of his seat before Porter had finished. "Where is he now?"

"In the cells, sir. He legged it, but we nabbed him easy."

"Good. Don't let anyone else in. If the boy is as dull-witted as they say, it'll be too easy to put words into his mouth." Griffin jammed his hat on, and plucked up his notebook. "Do you have confirmed identification from a witness?"

"Four of 'em, sir." Porter couldn't resist a gruff little grin. "Everyone knows this Kelly lad."

"Excellent. Good work, Sergeant." Griffin glanced at Eliza. "Perhaps you'd care for that tour of the station now, madam? Our cells date back to the previous building, you know. Eighteenth century. I'm sure you'll find them fascinating."

Deep beneath the station, the dank stench stifled her, and she covered her nose. Ahead, Griffin ordered Porter to light more lamps. Their footsteps boomed on the stone stairs, then trailed away into darkness.

Electric light flared. Dripping stone walls, a row of iron-barred cells on each side. Dirt floor puddled with muck, the sour stink of human captivity. The first few cells contained several men each. Their clothes were muddy, their faces unshaven. Most had been beaten bloody. Not all policemen shared Griffin's civilized attitude towards investigation.

Curses and rough words greeted her. One or two of the men leered and made coarse gestures. Others ignored her. One spat in the dirt at Griffin's feet and called him a frightful name.

"Leave my good lady mother out of it, Mr. Frost," said Griffin easily, "or I'll scratch out that drunken affray charge and write 'treasonable assembly.' Fancy a trip to Newgate? I hear it's full of your radical friends."

The prisoner glared, sharp as prussic acid, but lapsed into silence.

"What a pleasant fellow," murmured Eliza.

"To be fair, one can understand his ill temper."

Eliza pursed her lips, torn between sympathy and disgust. The conditions were horrible, but even the lunatics at Bethlem had an excuse for their behavior. Most of these fellows were merely crude. Common criminals, who acted thoughtlessly and without reason better than greed . . .

Oh, aye? Lizzie piped up, prickly as a pear. *And who the hell are you, missy? Easy to be law-abiding when you've got everything you want.*

Everything I want, have I? Inwardly, Eliza snorted. *I work for what I've got. You don't see me stealing and cheating.*

Don't see me doing it, neither, said Lizzie craftily, *'cause I'm way too good.*

Griffin followed Porter along the narrow corridor, past outstretched hands and hostile stares.

Picking her way through the filth, Eliza followed. One cell lay empty, separating the lone man in the next from the others. Geordie Kelly sat cross-legged in the mud, fiddling with a stick. Black hair fell across his forehead. His frock coat's skirt flopped in the muck, once a fine blue fabric but now old and torn. His trouser hems hung ragged. Somewhere he'd lost his boots—stolen?—and his bare feet curled, long toes twitching.

He didn't look up as they halted in front of his cell.

"Thank you, Sergeant," Griffin murmured, and Porter dipped his hat and strode away.

Eliza's throat tightened. Questioning was important. If Griffin made a mess of it, they'd get the wrong answers. Kelly was innocent. She was sure of it. A scapegoat.

But whose? The Chopper's? Or someone else's?

"Geordie." Griffin spoke softly, so as not to alarm.

Geordie looked up. A boy, really, barely in need of a shave. He blinked, bewildered. A bruise reddened one slanted cheekbone, and his nose was crooked, an old break. Handsome lad, even with a few pox scars.

"Is that your name? Geordie Kelly?"

The boy nodded—three times quickly, *down-up-down-up-down-up*—and fiddled with the stick in his lap.

"You're in the Bow Street cells. My name is Detective Inspector Griffin. I'm a policeman, and I'm going to ask you some questions. Do you understand?"

Down-up-down-up-down-up.

"Where do you work, son?"

"For Mr. Underwood, sir." Not the rough weird-city drawl. More of a West End accent, as if he came from a good family. "At the theater. I work the lights."

"Are you acquainted with Miss Ophelia Maskelyne?"

Geordie rocked back and forth, clutching his knees.

"When did you last see her?"

He rocked harder, his head down.

Eliza crouched, heedless of the muck, and gripped the bars. "Geordie, look at me. You're not in any trouble. We just need to know when you saw Ophelia last."

His soft mouth trembled. "She was so pretty. I liked her. She was nice to me, and now she's dead."

"What happened to her, Geordie?"

"I saw her lying in the yard. There was blood. The police were there. I ran away." Tears leaked, unheeded. He didn't seem to realize he was crying. Perhaps he cried a lot. "Someone did something bad, ma'am. Will the police find them?"

"I'm sure they'll do their best," she murmured. "Why did you run away, Geordie? Were you afraid?"

"The other lady was there. She'd chased me away. She always chases me away. She doesn't like me."

She glanced up at Griffin, who nodded slightly: *go ahead*. "Do you mean Mrs. Maskelyne?"

"The other lady," Geordie repeated, and gulped a big wet swallow. "Miss Ophelia's friend."

Eliza's memory bounced back to the crime scene. Clara Morton, in her plain gray servant's dress. "Do you know her name?"

A vague shrug. "Miss."

"What does she look like?"

He wrinkled his nose. "Pointy face. She frowns all the time. Not pretty like Miss Ophelia."

"And what was she wearing, this other lady?"

Geordie nodded at Eliza's dress. "Like you, only not as nice."

Eliza's skin tingled. Clara, then. An electrical expert. "And what about the night before Ophelia died? Did you see Ophelia then?"

Down-up-down-up-down-up. "In the yard. I waited, by the fence where I always wait. She was crying. The other lady arrived, and they . . ." He muttered something under his breath, his face darkening.

"They what?"

"Don't know." He rocked again, gripping his knees. "Don't know."

"Did they argue, Geordie?" offered Eliza gently. "Is that what you saw? Were they fighting?"

"Miss Ophelia cried. Her face was all bruised and bloody. The other lady tried to get her to leave. Then Mr. Lysander called, and Miss Ophelia went back inside. The other lady left."

"What happened then?"

"I went back to Her Majesty's and I swept the wings and the dressing rooms, like always. Then I went to sleep."

"In your loft?"

His gaze slid aside. "Don't know."

Griffin scribbled in his notebook. "What time was this, when you saw Miss Ophelia in the yard?"

Geordie squinted, confused. "It was dark. The ballet was finished. I'm not allowed out until the ballet's finished. I work the lights, see. Without me, there's no lights."

"Sometime after eleven, then. Which makes it after the magic show had ended." Griffin made a note. "And what time did you go to bed?"

A sullen shrug. "Don't know."

"Well, you must know, lad. It's what, a fifteen-minute walk back to Her Majesty's?"

"Don't know."

"How long does your cleaning usually take?"

"Don't know."

Eliza sighed. His hair was dark, coarse, long like a choir-boy's. Just like the strand she'd found on Ophelia's pillow. "Tell the truth, now. You didn't sleep in your loft that night, did you?"

"Don't know," he muttered again, tucking his chin to his chest.

Instinctively, she reached through the bars and touched his hand. He was sweating, his skin warm under her palm. "It's all right. You can tell me. You won't be punished. Did you go back to the Egyptian?"

"She wasn't there!" More tears washed his cheeks. "I went in to look for her, but she was already gone. I only wanted to make her smile again."

"She wasn't in her bedroom?"

"No."

"But you lay down on her bed, didn't you?"

He sniffled. "It smelled nice," he said indistinctly. "I didn't mean anything by it. Please don't tell Mr. Underwood."

"We won't," she soothed. "What did you do then?"

"I stayed until morning. I hid, but she didn't come back. When I came out, the police were in the yard."

"And did you hear any strange noises in the night? Say, a gunshot?"

He shook his head.

Wordlessly, Griffin handed Eliza his notebook and pencil.

Eliza offered them through the bars. "Will you write your name for me, please?"

"Uh?" Geordie stared blankly at the paper.

"Your name," she prompted. "Can you write 'Geordie Kelly'?"

He took the pencil and wiped his nose on his sleeve. Balanced the book on his knee. His brow furrowed with concentration, and he chewed his bottom lip. "There," he said at last, and held it out to her proudly.

His sweaty hands had stained the paper, and the pencil lead was smudged. His handwriting looked like an eight-year-old's, irregular, with some letters larger than the others. He'd drawn the "K" backwards at first and crossed it out.

A flash of memory, Lafayette scrawling on Sergeant Porter's

notepad: *Your handwriting is a tragedy.* If anyone's writing was tragic, it was Geordie's. His name was likely the only letters he had. Not the same hand as Ophelia's correspondence, by any stretch.

If Geordie was faking, he was extremely good.

Griffin retrieved his notebook. "Did you ever give Miss Ophelia gifts, Geordie?"

"What's gifts, sir?"

"Flowers, jewels, presents. Such as a gentleman gives a lady."

Geordie's brows crunched together. "Once I found some pansies in the street. But I gave those to Miss Irina."

"I see," murmured Griffin. "Nothing else?"

"No, sir. I don't have anything like that. Mr. Underwood only gives me sixpence a week."

Eliza frowned. A straight answer, in fact.

She recalled the flowers in Ophelia's room, the house-maid's rehearsed response: *Miss Ophelia is much admired.* It seemed Mrs. Maskelyne had told only half the truth. But if the flowers weren't Geordie's—then whose?

"One more thing," she added. "You operate the electric lights at Her Majesty's. Can you tell me how they work?"

He nodded vigorously. "I pull switches, and they come on and off. Sometimes they go bang, and there's a fire, and I have to use the sand bucket."

"Indeed. How many amperes does the array draw?"

A puzzled pause. "I pull switches," he repeated.

"What kind of power source is it? An aetheric generator, or a rack of galvanic batteries?"

Geordie just frowned, bewildered.

Griffin touched Eliza's shoulder. "I think that's enough for now."

She stood, dusting her skirts. "Thank you, Geordie. We'll be back."

Back in Griffin's office, she waited until he closed the door before she rounded on him. "Tell me you still think he did it."

Griffin perched on the desk's edge, leaning back on his palms. "Well, in the absence of more evidence, he's still our chief suspect. I can't let him go. But I admit, it doesn't seem likely."

She laughed. "Harley, the boy can barely write, and he has no money for a scribe. He doesn't even have the wit to invent a convincing lie." She ticked the points off on her fingers. "One: those letters to Ophelia aren't his. Two: he didn't give Ophelia the flowers. But Mrs. Maskelyne wanted us to think he did. Three: he has no clue how an electric light works, let alone a more sophisticated machine. And four: the 'other lady,' who tried to convince Ophelia to leave the night Lysander beat her? Whom Geordie saw at the crime scene? That's Clara Morton, assistant to the scientist Percival, whose electrical demonstration I attended."

Griffin frowned. "What's that to do with anything?"

"Clara lied to me. Pretended she didn't know me, or Ophelia. And she's an expert on high-voltage electrical apparatus. Not many machines will produce the type and weight of discharge we found at the scene." Eliza pointed to the open journal. "I did some research. This is how the killer is getting away." She took a breath. "It's a teleporter."

"A what?"

"An instantaneous long-distance travel machine." She showed him the diagram. "You build two machines, one positive, one negative. The power source attaches to this one, the main system. The other is portable. You activate that one *here*"—she pointed—"and the machine transports you back home to *there*." She looked up, triumphant. "With a very loud bang, and a pile of black aetheric discharge. This thing has a spark gap like this." She held her hands a foot apart. "No wonder the stone in the wall was melted."

Griffin studied the page. "Where did you get this?"

"It's unorthodox. I'd rather not say."

He stroked his mustaches. "Very well, I shan't press. But there must be several scientists with sufficient expertise to build this. Imagine this Clara Morton to be the killer. She's supposed to be Ophelia's friend. What's her motive?"

"Lysander beats Ophelia, Clara tries to convince her to run away," mused Eliza. "Ophelia refuses, out of family loyalty, so . . . better dead than unhappy?"

Griffin winced.

Eliza sighed. "I agree, it's flimsy."

"Also, what's the connection to Irina Pavlova?"

"Well . . . what if Clara isn't the killer? What if she's just helping the killer? He needed a method of escape, so he hired her to build this machine for him. She's short of money. She might very well take such a job."

"Or the killer blackmailed her somehow and forced her to help him."

"Clara's under investigation by the Royal, or at least Percival is. That's an easy threat for a blackmailer."

"Hmm." Griffin considered. "She poses as Ophelia's friend, lures her into the killer's clutches . . . ?"

"Maybe she did the same to Miss Pavlova."

"Far-fetched but possible. But then who's 'G,' and how is he involved?"

"I don't know. Maybe he isn't. Just an unfortunate admirer, in the wrong place at the wrong time." Eliza smoothed her hair absently. "Hmm."

"Oh, dear," said Griffin dryly. "I know that 'hmm.' It means trouble."

She bit her lip. "It's probably nothing . . ."

"But?"

"Do you recollect what Geordie said, when I asked what Ophelia and Clara were talking about in the yard?"

Griffin didn't need to refer to his notebook. "He said, 'Don't know.'"

"The same thing he said every time he wanted to lie. As if . . ."

"As if he knew, but didn't want to tell us?"

"Exactly." Eliza tucked the diary under her arm. "He might not be our murderer, but he's definitely hiding something."

"Could it be the same thing that Mrs. Maskelyne was trying to cover up? The identity of the real secret lover? The mysterious 'G,' in fact?"

"I think it's time I paid Miss Morton another visit, don't you?"

Griffin grinned. "I couldn't possibly say, madam. This is a police investigation, I'll have you know. But suddenly, I find myself strangely powerless to stop a civilian asking questions."

Eliza grinned back. "For shame, Inspector. At this rate,

the Met will be hip-deep in private investigators before sun-down."

"Scandalous, isn't it? Do take care, Eliza. If Reeve catches you, the Home Secretary won't care how many razor murder-ers I've caught. There'll be nothing I can do for you."

A MOST SINGULAR PERSUASION

• • •

D R. PERCIVAL'S EXPERIMENTAL LABORATORY WAS at the Royal Institution, a grand edifice fronted by fourteen marble columns, quite near Mr. Finch's shop in Mayfair. Eliza hopped up the steps, clutching her bag close, and Hippocrates scuttled inside after her, towards the rear of the building.

She hadn't telegraphed ahead or made an appointment. She wanted to ambush Clara, give her no chance to absent herself. And sure enough, when Eliza ducked under the low doorway to approach the array of buzzing electrical machinery by a row of soaped windows, there stood Clara, sleeves pushed up to her elbows, cleaning a pair of bright silvery anodes with a chemical-soaked rag.

Hipp beeped, his lights flashing double-time. "Off you go," she murmured, and he dashed away under the tables, hunting rats.

An electric light hung low from a hinged metal arm, casting a pool of light around Clara Morton as she worked. She wore the same drab gray dress, her hair arranged in a tight coil. Her freckled face looked sallow, drawn with fatigue. Perhaps she, also, worked too hard. It wasn't easy for a woman who wanted a career in science. You had to be better than your male colleagues, brighter, more determined.

"You again." Clara didn't cease her polishing. "Clear off."

"I'm sorry we seem to have gotten off to a bad start," Eliza began, with a harmless little smile. "I don't mean to intrude. As I said, I'm a police physician, and—"

"What do you want?" snapped Clara, not looking up. "I'm very busy."

The woman's attitude stung. "Then I'll keep it short," said Eliza rudely. "I need to ask you some questions about the murder of Ophelia Maskelyne."

Clara just scrubbed harder at the anode, liquid splashing in her pail. "Poor woman. An actress, wasn't she? I don't know anything about it. Just what I read in the papers."

"Well, that's strange, because I saw you at the crime scene, on the very morning Miss Maskelyne was found dead." Eliza plonked her bag on the table, atop a pile of handwritten notes, and folded her arms. "And we have a witness who saw you arguing with the victim at the theater, just hours before she was killed. Obstructing a police investigation is a crime, Miss Morton. Care to revise your story?"

Clara halted, and then she sighed and let the anode slip from her hands into the liquid. "We talked, that night," she said, in a small voice. Did her chin tremble? "I left the Egyptian sometime after one, and that's the last I saw of her. I don't know what happened. Please, Ophelia was my friend. I really don't want to talk about it."

"I understand," said Eliza gently. "But two women are dead, possibly more. We have a murderer to catch. Can you think of anyone who wished Ophelia ill?"

"No. Everyone loved her." A catch in her throat. "But it's not always those who hate us who cause the most pain, is it?"

"What do you mean? What did you talk about, that night in the yard?"

Clara wiped her hands on a towel. "Her brother was in the habit of mistreating her. I urged her to stand up to him."

"By doing what? Finding a husband to protect her? I understand she had a sweetheart."

Clara laughed, bitter. "Another man, to beat her as Lysander did? To lock her in her room and order her about? Trust me, Ophelia wasn't the marrying kind."

"Then what would you have had her do? What was the fight about?"

Still, Clara avoided her gaze. "She didn't want to leave. She could have, you know. There are places such women can be safe."

Deft fingers tugged at the back of Eliza's mind, a thief's hand at her skirts. But she couldn't grab it. "Could she have lodged with you, for instance? Where do you live?"

"I have a room at a ladies' hostel near Sloane Square."

"But she refused?"

Clara shrugged.

Eliza recalled Ophelia's letter. *I wished we could vanish together. Perhaps one day we shall . . .* "And what happened then?"

"Lysander called for her, and Ophelia went back inside. I walked home. I'm afraid I don't know anything else . . ."

"Are you acquainted with a young man named Geordie Kelly?"

"Geordie?" A little laugh. "A feeble-minded lad. He followed Ophelia around like a lost lamb, making eyes at her. A pest. Harmless, I suppose."

"He told me you don't like him. That you would chase him away."

"Yes. He became tiresome. Always eavesdropping on our private conversations."

"Could he have been eavesdropping that night, in the yard?"

Clara's expression froze. "I didn't see him if he was."

Eliza held out a sheet of paper. She'd copied the teleporter diagram from the old diary, minus the technical notes. "Do you know what this is?"

The scientist leaned closer, frowning, but color flooded her cheeks. Relief at the change of subject? "Looks like an oversized capacitor, or . . . I say, this is a very strange design. Where did you get this?"

"What might such a machine be used for?"

Clara shrugged, opaque. "It looks like something an electrical chemist might use. For plating anodes such as these here, or synthesizing new chemicals."

Images of a certain apothecary's laboratory fizzed in Eliza's mind. Galvanic cells, wires coiling from beakers of fluid, voltmeters, vacuum flasks, unorthodox spectrometers . . .

Marcellus Finch had been her father's colleague, privy to his secrets. And he knew enough about electrical fluid phenomena to synthesize alchemical solutions, at least. Was Marcellus involved somehow? She'd perused his hidden cache

of books at New Bond Street before and never found anything like this.

What if Finch was still in league with Fairfax? Henry
Jekyll's old cabal, still hiding their secrets? Storing their most
provocative codices at Bethlem, where no one would ever
think to look?

Eliza's mind boggled. Finch's strange medicines. Fairfax's
radical treatments. What was going on?

"But this machine is far too large to be practical," Clara
added. "The resistance alone would fry the circuit in minutes."

"It could function only for a limited time?"

"Yes. A few minutes only, even if you had an extremely
efficient voltage discharge method."

"Such as what?"

"A heat sink the size of this room. Or a directed explosion.
A lightning strike, if you like. Where did you say you got this?"

"That's confidential." From her bag, she pulled the diagram's other half. Beneath the bag, Clara's notepapers piled,
their edges curling. Ornate handwriting, the letters swiftly
but finely penned, with careful flourishes and swirls on the
capitals . . .

Eliza's heart skipped.

Harley's words from Ophelia Maskelyne's crime scene
echoed in her mind. He'd been twitting Lafayette about his
handwriting: *That "T" looks like an "F."* No one drew their
letters in exactly the same fashion.

The initial at the foot of Ophelia's correspondence, for instance. A simple 'G.' Or, with a swirling flourish at the bottom . . .

Oh, my.

She held the diagram out to show Clara, damp fingers sticking to the paper. "What if you paired such a machine with this one? What purpose might it have then?"

Clara stared. "I insist that you tell me where you got this."

"Why? Does it look familiar?"

Clara's cheeks pinked. "No, I just . . ."

"Worried someone might have stolen your ideas?"

"Don't be ridiculous."

Eliza watched her closely. "It's easy to do, especially from a woman. No one would believe you had priority, would they? They'd assume you were taking the credit for some male scientist's work. Look, I'm not from the Royal, Clara. You can tell me. Have you built something like this before?"

Clara sighed. "Not exactly . . ."

"Not exactly. A smaller, more rudimentary one, then, for the stage. For Ophelia's vanishing act."

"I don't know what you mean."

"Oh, come." Eliza unfolded Ophelia's letter from her pocket. "'I watched you disappear tonight,'" she read. "'It was better than I could have hoped. You were fabulous, and I wished we could vanish together. Perhaps one day we shall.'" She showed the letter to Clara. "This is your handwriting, isn't it? And your initial 'C' at the bottom? The perfume of violets that you bought for her?"

"What if it is? We were friends. There's no crime in that." But Clara's square chin quivered, and her fierce eyes glistened, wet.

"'My dearest love?'" Eliza quoted from memory. "'Your one and only truthful servant?'"

"I think you should leave now."

"What really went on between you in the yard that night? What did Geordie Kelly see that he was too scandalized to tell me?"

Grief washed green like cholera over Clara's face. "You horrid thing. Get out of my laboratory."

Eliza's heart brimmed with sympathy, but she resisted it, with a spike of Lizzie's coarse practicality. Now was the time to be brutal, to move in for the kill. "An illicit liaison. My, my. The Maskelynes were very keen for us to believe that these letters came from someone else. And now I discover you're building the very type of machine the killer is using to escape the scene of his—or her—crimes. It smells of cover-up, wouldn't you say? I should think my inspector will be pleased to hear of this."

Briskly, she tucked the papers into her bag. "Thank you so much for your time, Miss Morton. That will be all for now . . ."

"Do you know what it's like?" The rage in Clara's tone roasted Eliza in her place. "For women like me? They call us mad, or hysterical. They lock us up. When I was sixteen, my mother was so ashamed of me that she took me to see a doctor. He suggested I have relations with a man immediately, to 'set me right,' or I'd have to be put away."

Eliza blanched. She knew all too well the fate of women who loved other women. The Bethlem cells were frequented by those who harbored "unnatural desires." "Miss Morton . . ."

"Yes, I loved Ophelia." Viciously, Clara wiped her nose, but the tears kept streaming. "And she loved me. Is that so hard to stomach? Are you disgusted, *Doctor*?"

"Not at all," said Eliza steadily. "I'm sorry for your loss."

Clara stared, white. "You know," she said at last, her voice small and trembling, "you're the first person who's said that to me."

The injustice burned at Eliza's heart like poison. Had Clara been a man, she'd be inundated with messages of condolence. To live forever in secret, never sharing, never admitting the truth . . .

She swallowed. "I don't mean to pry, Miss Morton. All I want is to find out what happened, and catch the murderer."

Clara wiped her swollen face and nodded.

"The family didn't accept you." Not a question.

Clara snorted. "Her brother is a beast, his wife just as bad. They loathe me. Can't abide the scandal. Their darling girl's *unnatural*. You'd think she'd sprinted through the streets naked."

Eliza's palms itched at the callousness of it, and she wanted to scrub them clean. Mrs. Maskelyne's story was a spiteful half-truth. Lafayette was right: so much for the downtrodden wife. *Miss Ophelia is much admired,* they'd taught the housemaid to say. Pointed the finger at an innocent half-witted boy. All to cover up the scandalous truth: Ophelia's secret lover was a woman.

"Lysander and his wife as much as told me your letters were from Geordie Kelly," Eliza admitted angrily. "They'd let him go on trial for murder to keep their secret."

A flat, humorless laugh. "Forgive me if I'm unsurprised. Lysander had already threatened to marry her off against her will. They'd shackle her to anything in trousers if she'd have it, but she point-blank refused. And word was getting around.

None of Lysander's cronies would have her. That night, he found her with my letters and lost his temper. Told her he'd marry her to the old man who cleans the latrines if she didn't 'come to her senses.'"

"And later, you came to see her?"

"I wanted her to leave with me. She wouldn't. Afraid of what might become of her without her livelihood, I suppose." Clara wiped her reddened face again. "As you can imagine, I didn't see it quite like that at the time. We argued. I left. That's the last I saw of her. I returned the next morning to make it up to her, and there she was in a pool of blood, surrounded by a police barricade. I swear to you, I don't know what happened."

"I believe you." The grief and distress crumpling Clara's face looked real. Briefly, she wished for Captain Lafayette's canine facility for sniffing out lies. "And the disappearing machine . . . ?"

Clara shrugged, rueful. "A party trick. It didn't really work. All it did was momentarily disrupt the aether and make it look as if she'd vanished. You needed a mirror and some tricks with the lights to get the effect."

"I see." Eliza considered. "Do you think it could work, though? In principle?"

"A vanishing machine?" Clara made her best effort at a smile. "It does sound far-fetched. But the new science makes anything possible. I suppose if the apparatus were large enough . . . well, who knows?"

"Who indeed?" Eliza tucked her bag under her arm. "One more thing. Are you acquainted with Sir Jedediah Fairfax?"

"Not personally. Surgeon, isn't he? A knighthood for tending some princess's brain fever? I recall Dr. Percival mentioned something about it."

"What about Marcellus Finch?"

A blank look. "The name isn't familiar."

"He's a galvanic chemist. Among other things."

For a moment, true fear shadowed Clara's gaze. And then
she visibly composed herself, her cold mask dropping into
place. Apparently, some types of scandal scared her more
than others. "I don't know anything about those other things,
Dr. Jekyll," she said smoothly, arranging her skirts. "Now forgive me, I'm very busy. Good day."

Two hours on a traffic-blocked Strand later, Eliza burst back
into Inspector Griffin's office, with Hippocrates and her precious diagrams tucked safely in her bag. "Harley, I . . ."

Inspector Reeve waved at her from behind Griffin's desk,
chewing on a cigar.

She halted, thoughts whirling. "Where's Inspector Griffin?"

"I'm afraid Griffin was called away. His wife has only
hours to live, they say. Tragic." Reeve didn't sound as if he
cared one whit.

Eliza's stomach knotted, sick. "I'm sorry to hear that."

"I'll take on his cases in the meantime, naturally. The
least I can do for a dear friend." Reeve puffed stinking smoke
at her. "I believe you're trespassing, madam. Good day."

"But I have evidence in the Chopper case. I—"

"That case is closed. We have the murderer in custody."

"Geordie Kelly?"

"The very same."

"Inspector, with all due respect, I've questioned him and I believe—"

"I don't care what you believe. The boy confessed an hour ago."

Her mouth soured. She could imagine how Reeve had likely elicited that "confession." "But it can't have been Geordie. There's an electrical machine—"

"The case is closed," interrupted Reeve, propping his feet on Harley's desk. "You no longer work here. Good day."

But his gaze flickered, a tiny slip in confidence, and suddenly she spied a different Reeve. An old-fashioned police officer, who'd always relied on the ways of the street, tip-offs and pay-offs and confessions by brute force. Whose job was skidding out from under him, usurped by brighter and younger men, altered beyond recognition in a new world of strange technology and politics he couldn't comprehend.

Bizarrely, she felt a twist of sympathy, then stamped on it. He was still a bitter little woman-hater. "But—"

"Shall I have you escorted from the building?" Reeve didn't look up from the file he was reading. "Believe me, madam, it'll hurt you more than it hurts me."

"That won't be necessary." Eliza squared her shoulders and resisted the temptation to punch him in the face. "Good day, Inspector. We'll talk again when the next woman is murdered." And she pushed past Sergeant Porter, who hovered at the door, and strode out.

She stamped down the stairs, conflicting thoughts scrapping like angry rodents. Harley Griffin, praying at his wife's bedside. Clara Morton, red-eyed and grief-stricken. Geordie Kelly, quivering in the lock-up, thrashed into a confession he didn't understand.

Bright sparks of rage blinded her. *Curse that Reeve for a stupid ape,* hissed Lizzie. *Let me at him, I swear . . .*

She took a deep breath, trying to be calm. She needed a plan, not a berserker's fury. The killer would soon strike again. And all she had to go on were a diagram of an impossible teleporting machine and the perverted insight of a razor-wielding lunatic . . .

Fuming, she stalked out into the busy street. Late afternoon sun glared along the roofline. Her eyes swam and watered, and suddenly Lizzie's eyes focused, sharper than a blade . . .

Thwack! She collided with a hard body and stumbled, skirts dragging in mud. Her vision wobbled, a bright wash of fever, and Lizzie crouched like a tiger, ready to spring . . .

Matthew Temple steadied her, one hand on her waist, and straightened his cap. His bottle-green waistcoat dazzled in the sun. "I say, Doctor, are you all right? How fortuitous. Just the lady I need to see—"

"Not now, Mr. Temple," she snarled, and pushed him aside.

But he grabbed her elbow, jostling her bag against her hip. "I really must speak with you." An odd note of pleading spiked her attention. "It's urgent. It's about your murder case—"

"Are you following me, idiot?" She rounded on him, thrusting her face in close, and he jumped back in alarm. "You've been at every crime scene in remarkably quick time this week. Perhaps you do have information about the case. Perhaps the murderer is you."

His face greened to match his waistcoat. "That's ridiculous—"

She lifted one finger in warning, and he fell silent. Her rage bubbled over, and her muscles juddered eagerly. Grab him, close her fist around his skinny throat, and squeeze . . .

"Just stay away from me," she growled, and whirled away.

People scattered from her path as she strode up towards Long Acre, barely watching where she was going. Shouts and strange laughter echoed, a tornado of confusion. She reeled, stumbled, fought on her way. Was that others laughing? Was it Lizzie? Was it herself? Her bag slipped and fell, papers and bottles scattering. Blindly, she scooped them up, and Hippocrates gurgled and shrank from her touch. She stuffed him back in the bag and hurried on.

Conflicting urges collided, dragging her in multiple directions. Her wits stretched thin like rubber. Her head swelled, threatening to burst. The bitter taste of her remedy repeated on her, flooding her mouth with burning bile.

Something was awry with her prescription. No doubt about that now. And only one man could tell her what was happening.

She waved down a cab, and it shuffled to a halt on brass legs, purple electrical coils snapping sparks. She jumped in. "New Bond Street," she spat, "and make it fast."

About time, whispered Lizzie. *He's been playing you all along. Will you ask the tough questions, or shall I?*

The cab rattled along, legs pistoning, and the rocking motion made her seasick. Did she have the courage? Did she really want the answers?

In the depths of the darkened cab, she sucked in a deep breath for nerve and let Lizzie out.

AN ENGLISHMAN'S HOME

∙•∙

WHEN WE GET THERE, THE STREET'S DARK, AND SO is the shop, the blinds drawn. The front door's locked, and the door to upstairs too. He's hiding.

I want to kick those smug polished windows until they shatter. Inside me, Eliza squirms, unwilling yet compelled. I know how she feels.

But I'm angry. I can't breathe in this damn dress. And I won't be stopped by some prissy locked door.

So I suck in the biggest breath I can, stretching my laces a little. I wander casually into the entranceway, where no one can see me in the shadows. I yank a pin from Eliza's swept-up hair-do—Christ, I must look a sight—and shove it in the lock.

They ain't much, these cheap door locks, and I've learned from the best. In half a minute, *pop!* The door clicks open in my hand.

I take the narrow stairs three at a time, *hip! hop!* The landing has only one door, and I shove it open and stride in.

He's reading in his little chair by the fire, wearing a purple smoking jacket, pince-nez perched on his nose. Yellow stuff is plastered in his milky hair, as if he's wiped his hands in it. The room's stuffed with books, teetering shelves packed to bursting on every wall, and there's paper and ink bottles and all manner of mess.

I grab him by his fluffy jacket. *Slam!* Into the bookshelf. A few books tumble, and his glasses fall to the floor. I hold him there—he's right skinny—and grin my maddest grin.

"Marcellus Finch," says I, "you sneaky little bastard."

Marcellus grins, just as mad. His heart is racing. I probably outweigh him, and he knows it. "Lizzie, my dear—"

"Don't you 'dear' me." I bang him a little harder into the books. He smells of alchemy, of burning wood and melting gold. "What've you done to our remedy, you white-haired loon?"

His baby-blue gaze glints, mischievous. "Couldn't possibly say—"

The old man's got courage, I'll give him that. I grab his scrawny neck, twist his chin higher. "You *will* bloody say, or I'll keep right on squeezing. Hell, I don't know my own strength these days."

His throat jumps in my palm. But there's fire in his eyes. "You're magnificent," he chokes. "Just as I told Henry you would be. Remedy, be damned. Why do you even care?"

He makes a good point. A week ago, I might have agreed. But things are different now.

"I don't, you old buffoon. But you're upsetting Eliza, and that I can't have." I squeeze tighter, threatening. "Now tell me what's going on, or you'll see just how magnificent I am."

Finch's eyes bulge. "Ugh-mmph. Aant halk."

Another good point. I loosen, just a little.

A wet splutter. "He made me, all right? He wanted to see what would happen—"

"He who?" I demand. But rich inevitability scorches in my soul.

"*Him.* Your guardian. He's the kind of man you don't say 'no' to."

"You've worked for him all along," I accuse. "Why did you lie to her? Jesus, Marcellus, she *trusts* you."

And so did I.

Never had much doing, Marcellus Finch and I. Once, when I was young and stupid, I tried to turn him, get him on my side. He refused me. Now I stay away from him. He's Eliza's friend, not mine, and I see now he's a loyal man. Just not to us.

"That was the arrangement," he protested. "I was never to tell. I was to let you . . . her, that is . . . I was to let *her* have *you,* but on *his* terms. One needs to ease into these things. Accidents can happen."

A strange chill ripples through my belly, echoes of long-forgotten childhood memory. Shivering in my nightdress in a midnight corridor, fierce whispers coming from the bedroom of a dead woman. *An accident, Henry . . . Poor pretty lady . . . happens all the time . . .*

"Oh, aye?" I venture, just to see what he'll say, but I'm uneasy, twitchy, reluctant. "Accidents like our mother's death?"

Marcellus blinks. "You'd best ask him about that."

Oh, lord. What the hell's gone on here?

I cover my trouble with a sneer. "Right. And what about Captain Lafayette and his medicine? Did you just want to 'see what would happen' to him, too?"

Finch's gaze flickers, sullen. "That wasn't my fault. Curses like his are myriad. I tried. I just got it wrong."

I laugh, though it ain't funny, and let him go. "Whatever you say. Just tell me where I can find my precious *guardian*." I salt that last word with sarcasm. Fine job he's made of it.

Finch shakes himself, straightening his clothes. "The Rats' Castle, of course. I thought you knew."

My mouth gapes. The King of Rats. That creaky old skeleton from the Royal had it right . . . and like a midnight-black rose, a shadowy new world opens before my eyes.

"Don't tell me," I say at last. "The place with the blue light and the stinky-arse door-keeper." Not a brothel after all. Now that I've finally figured it out, I can't wait. I'm dying to see this place. Maybe, I'll finally find where I belong.

"Just so." Finch peers blindly at the floor, searching.

But I find his pince-nez first. He grabs for it, but I hold it away out of his reach. "What's tonight's watchword?"

He gives a cunning serpent grin that puts me in mind of Mr. Todd. "You're a clever lady, my dear. You figure it out."

I snort in disgust and hurl the glasses at him.

He catches them, surprisingly nimble. "Just one thing," he calls, as I whirl to leave. "For your own sake."

"What?"

"Let Eliza talk to him."

I halt and glance back.

He's earnest. "I swear, I never meant her harm. Things are more complicated than you know. Just let her ask the questions."

"Why?" I grumble. "Does he think he's too good for me, too, same as everyone else?"

"Because Madeleine was her mother, too."

And that, even I can't argue with.

———◄•►———

Eliza's feet hit cold flagstones, and behind her, a cab rattled away.

"Wha—where are we?" She peered down a dark, narrow street littered with garbage. The smell assaulted her, rotten meat and excrement. Rickety buildings teetered inwards, broken shutters dangling over the street, where beggars and sleeping dogs slumped in the muck and drunken fellows sang and staggered. And at the end, a doorway with a flickering blue light . . .

Rats' Castle.

No time like the present, whispered Lizzie. And of their own accord, Eliza's legs began to walk.

"Oh, no. Lizzie, don't. He made us promise not to pry, remember?" *And the Philosopher promised to burn us if we don't . . .* Her muscles cramped. Try as she might, she couldn't control them.

Be buggered. We're going in.

"Lizzie, what are you doing?" But before Eliza could think or do anything, her legs had marched her along the muddy street to the doorway.

Rap-rap-rap! Her fist thumped the door. "Open up, you crusty old bastard!"

Her blood burned. Her skin stung, alive. She hadn't *changed.* Not all the way. But it felt . . . exciting. Exhilarating, to let Lizzie have her way.

The door lurched open, and the same crotchety fellow

glared out, red-eyed. "You again. Didn't I tell you to bugger off—ugh!"

Eliza (*Lizzie*) grabbed his skinny throat and slammed him against the wall. Her nails dug into greasy skin, and his pulse throbbed against her palm. "The watchword is 'screw you, rat-squeezer,'" she snarled. "How'd you like that?"

The fellow spluttered and nodded rapidly, eyes bulging. Beyond him, a dark stairway descended, lit with blue arc-lights that zapped and hissed at the darkness. The faint smells of smoke and hot metal beckoned.

This wasn't a house. It was a tunnel. But to where?

"I'll take that as a yes." She hurled the door-keeper aside, banging his head against the wall for good measure, and hopped inside. The door slapped shut behind her. And like that, she was in.

Eliza stumbled on the steps, stomach churning. Her dress felt too tight, as if she'd grown a size. She couldn't breathe. No air. Frantically, she tugged at the top of her bodice, popping a clip to loosen it, and gasped gratefully. "What did we just do?"

Lizzie's chuckle writhed under her skin, ready to burst free. *Just a little practical persuasion. Always here to help.*

Eliza tossed her cloak back. Her hair crackled, alive with static. "That's enough of your help, thank you."

Oh, for sure. You take it from here. Just lending a hand.

Eliza swallowed, defiant. She'd walked alone into a lunatic's lair and emerged alive. Twice. She could surely face this. But A.R.'s threats resounded in the murkiest part of her brain. *Poke your nose into my affairs, princess, and I'll make you wish you'd never been born . . .*

Steeling herself, she walked into the dark.

The wooden steps mocked her as she descended, *creak, creeeak!* The blue glow dimmed, the electric lights set further and further apart. In the distance, an Underground train rattled and banged. The pressure in her ears grew, the warm blackness thickening. How far down was down? She'd lost count. Above her head, water gurgled, the sewer or a subterranean river. The smell of hot iron grew stronger.

Abruptly, the tunnel switched to the right, and the light died.

Blindly, she edged forward. One step, another, fingers outstretched . . . and then, rough leather gave under her touch.

A curtain. Her fingers prickled in warning, and her tongue stung with a sharp, familiar flavor . . .

Spelldust, warned Lizzie, and for once Eliza was grateful for her insight. *There be hidden fey traps here. Beware.*

Slowly, Eliza pushed the curtain aside.

Light dazzled, a wash of sweet-scented warmth. Her ears popped. A shiver rippled over her skin.

The world telescoped, sights and sounds hurtling away to an invisible pinpoint. Eliza staggered, deafened, her head spinning.

Everything beyond six feet away was a whirling blur. At her feet, a fat white pig hove into view, snuffling for scraps along the sawdust-covered floor. A leash dangled from his collar, attached to the slender arm of a lady who wore long lacy gloves and a ruffled silken gown the color of verdigris.

The woman peered at her through silver opera glasses on a stalk. Her eyes were impossibly large and liquid, the verdant green of summer leaves, and her skin and the frothing hair that fell to her waist *glowed,* illuminated from within by some strange fairy-green light.

Eliza smoothed her own dress, self-conscious. The green lady was astonishingly beautiful. Never could she pass for ordinary. Likely, she was a prisoner here, chased underground along with anyone else who was fey-struck or talented or just plain strange.

"In or out, sprite," the lady said crossly. Her perfume was like spun sugar, delicate and mouth-watering. "Are you a cat, to be stuck halfway? Don't let in the draft."

"Oh. I'm sorry." Bewildered, Eliza shuffled inside. The curtain dropped behind her, and as if a spell had broken, the world crashed back into focus and noise erupted like a volcano.

The room was vast, lit by fires and torches both, ceiling and floor lost in cavernous darkness. Galleries ringed the enormous space, stacked four or five high like boxes at the opera, teeming with people and beasts and creatures of a like she'd never seen. Costumes of all kinds, from ratty frock coats covering half-naked bodies to the glossiest peacock finery. She saw clothes from bygone eras, periwigs, ruffs and farthingales, polished suits of armor, and garments of unfamiliar shiny cloth. Softest silk, roughest leather, lace and satin, in a glittering prism of colors, sky blue and sunshine yellow and brightest forest green.

Ladders and flimsy wooden bridges criss-crossed in all directions, joining galleries, stretching between levels at giddy, impossible heights. Urchins and fey-fingered creatures swung from ledges, crawled across beams, sat cross-legged atop poles and yardarms.

The noise was incredible. People ate and fought and laughed like lunatics. They danced and whirled and kissed like lovers. They jumped and cavorted and held deep conversations in smoke-filled corners, drank from carafes of rainbow liquids that sparkled and misted like magical potions.

Music battered her from all directions, here a fiddler, there an accordion, over there a wailing singer, a hurdy-gurdy, a brass band. Smoke drifted, sparkling with purplish spells and scents that dizzied and entranced. She peered left and right, trying to sort through the enormous crowd, but her mind just boggled. How would she ever find the man she sought?

"He's down there." The green lady pointed with her opera glasses, down a puzzle of twisting ladders to the heaving crowd below.

"Who?"

But the green lady had already followed her snuffling pig away.

Eliza blinked, bewildered. It didn't seem beyond possibility that the lady could read her mind.

Lizzie shrugged gaily. *Well, we're here now.*

"Yes, we are." Eliza picked up her skirts and started down the ladder, boots slipping on the rickety rungs.

Unseen hands gripped her waist and whisked her down to the landing. Breathless, she turned to see who had aided her, but they were gone into the carousing crowd. Fey children darted between a forest of legs and skirts. Next to her, a frog-fingered boy slipped his hand into an impossibly fat woman's purse, and a pointy-nosed fellow with a beetroot face hissed at the boy and flung him away empty-handed. "No thieving in the Castle," he growled.

"The Castle? What's that?" Eliza struggled to keep her feet as a gaggle of dancers whirled by, screaming their excitement.

"This is." The beetroot man yanked his top hat on tighter, and tilted his head to peer along his nose at her. "The Rats' Castle. Ruled by the King. Where we odd rats run, heh heh." He paused. "You don't look odd."

"I'm sorry?"

"Odd. You don't look it." His beady eyes narrowed. "Odd's good."

Eliza's guts burned like fever. She loomed over him— easily, as he was half her height—and her vision juddered and zoomed. "Oh, aye? How's this for *odd*?"

The little red man's face blanched to pink. "Very good. The King will see you. He's that way. Follow the carousel tune." And he scuttled away, sniffing at the floor like a bloodhound.

Heh. Lizzie grinned, satisfied. *Told you I'd come in handy.*

Down another ladder, across a crowded landing where a raucous gambling game was going on, a pair of pennies tossed in the air amid cheers and curses and the clink of wagers being paid. Unseen hands grabbed hers, whirled her through the crowd, passing her on to the next pair, and the next, helping her on her way.

Down again, a carnival in full flight. Acrobats cartwheeled amid fire-eaters and fortune-tellers. Clowns mimed and cavorted.

A big brown bear danced at the end of a rhinestone-studded leash and a tiny elephant honked, his trunk curling.

Here, a fighting ring with wooden rails, crushed in by spectators. Grunts, snarls, flesh smacking on flesh, punctuated by the splatter of blood on the wooden floor. A cheer erupted as the fight ended, and money changed hands in enormous quantities. Other wagers, too, involving drinks, kisses, body parts being shaved. The crowd parted, a limp and bleeding man was dragged away, and the next fight started.

In the distance, an ornate carousel spun slowly, dream-like. The painted plaster figures—stately unicorns, poodles, dolphins, over-sized rats with grinning teeth—were festooned with tiny electric lights in rainbow colors. The organ ground out a melancholy waltz in a minor key. Atop the carousel, twinkling arc-lights were arranged in the outline of a crooked crown.

Or a court jester's belled hat.

The crowd ebbed and swelled, as if the music, heady smells, and laughter pushed them from side to side. Everyone seemed taller than she, looming over her. Eyes flashed, sinister now, the electric light casting an evil glint.

Lizzie's invisible hand tightened on hers, comforting. Blindly, Eliza fought her way through, clawing at gossamer skirts, leather coats, bare skin. Intoxicating scent engulfed her, sweet and tart like absinthe, and she swayed and fell to her knees.

All of a sudden, the crowd parted.

She was isolated, alone. The carousel's lights glittered, spinning, and a tall shadow fell across her bunched skirts.

The shadow of a structure made of wire, broken electrical circuits, hinges and forks, and fragments of metal machines. All twisted together in tight knots to form a chair.

A throne, to be precise.

Dizzy, Eliza looked up.

SATAN'S SIGNATURE
UPON A FACE

• • •

THE MAN—THE CREATURE—UPON THE THRONE LOOKED neither old nor especially young. Ageless. His old-fashioned frock coat was the color of plums, over gray doeskin trousers and scuffed black boots. Grayish hair was cropped short beneath his battered top hat. His shoulders hunched, lopsided, and he toyed absently with his gold-topped cane in one big callused hand.

But something was wrong with his face. Handsome, with a compelling strength, yet . . . warped. Corrupted. Mouth just a little too cruel, eyes too sunken and bruised. As if something beautiful had spoiled.

Eliza swallowed, dry. His gaze hadn't unlocked from hers. The color of storm clouds, alive with rage and afire with deep-seated hatred. Her father's eyes.

Her eyes, alight with living hell.

"Eliza, my sweet." That rough, not-quite-respectable drawl prickled her skin.

As if her name were a signal, a hush descended—or was it

some magic spell? Around her, the crazy party danced on, but it was as if a glass wall had solidified between them. Though the figures howled and cavorted just the same, the sounds were muted, as if from a great distance.

She was still on her knees. Should she rise? At his feet, his lackeys fawned. A sharp-eyed lad with rabbit's ears; a stunted fellow with sharp teeth and a bulbous belly; an ogrelike woman in a chain-mail suit. Another skinny creature was shackled to the throne by a chain around his ankle, his bare back stricken with pox scars and welts. He chewed on a lump of gristle and sang himself a song. *"Cockles . . . and mussels . . . aaa-live, alive-OH!"*

The beautiful green lady whom Eliza had met levels above loitered by the King's side, draping one translucent green arm across the top of the throne. Her long apple hair frothed over his shoulder, and she stroked the rim of his hat with a glowing fingertip.

Absurdly, Eliza burned to punch her in the face. She was too pretty. Too familiar with him. *He's mine, bitch. Get your whore's tricks away from him.*

"Have you forgotten the rules?" The King of Rats tapped his cane on the floor to punctuate, *clack-clack! clack-clack!* "Don't follow me. Don't peek into my affairs. It doesn't take a genius. Yet here you stand."

What a marvel, she nearly added, with a madwoman's unseemly glee. If the Philosopher himself should suddenly crawl from the crowd and genuflect to the King, surprise would have seemed inappropriate.

The ogre woman growled and loomed menacingly, thumping a spiked club in one thick hand.

Eliza's throat crisped. "Sir, I assure you—"

"But what the hell, eh?" A beastly grin split his face. "Fuck it. Always did enjoy a wayward lass. Get up, then," he added impatiently. "I'm not Jesus bleeding Christ. A simple how-do will suffice."

Numbly, Eliza stumbled up, and dipped a shaky nod. "Er . . . how do you do?"

"I'm fucking fantastic." That grin suited him, an expression of unbridled enjoyment. Made him young, roguish, and handsome. The kind of dissolute man a woman could fall for at her peril.

"She's skinny, Eddie." The green lady's delicate nose wrinkled, and her perfume clung to the air, cloying, like sugar left too long. "All bone and no meat." She covered her mouth with green-lit fingers and snickered, *ti-hih-hih!*

"Bite your serpent tongue, woman. She's beautiful." That note of pride. "And I see you're not alone, my sweet."

Eliza nodded cautiously. "She's here."

"Let me talk to her, then."

Lizzie wriggled, eager to be free. Carefully, Eliza let out a breath, relaxed . . .

And out I come, *poppety-pop!* like a bubble in the sun.

Ahh. It's like a lungful of fresh air, so it is. Only our dress is too damn tight again, Jesus, I'm stuffed as a can of fish in here, and her spectacles make me blink like an eel. She's not far under, she can feel me breathing. It's as if we're both here, only for the moment it's me doing the talking.

I like it. It's nice to be together.

And that surprises me, when nothing else in this crazy

dungeon has raised my eyebrow. What I told Marcellus? It's true. Eliza is mine to protect.

Without that? Why, I'm disposable. Unwanted. Just one of those *accidents that happen.*

I tip my imaginary hat to the King. "Your Majesty. How do?"

"Lizzie, m'dear." Angry, but satisfied. "We meet at last. Took you long enough."

"Yeah, well, it ain't polite just to come blurting out like a fart."

Eddie laughs, rich yet dangerous, edgy. "I like your color, girl. We should talk more often."

My heart overflows, and damn it if that burning in my eyes ain't tears. I like it here. The Rats' Castle, den of the dissolute, tavern of the troubled, refuge for the royally wrecked. Can't we stay here, in this world tailor-made for freaks? I want to dive into the carousing crowd and let it swallow me. I *belong* here.

Lady Green-Tits scowls at me like I stole her ice cream and caresses the nape of his neck possessively. She's wearing long lacy gloves with the fingers cut off, and a pig on a leash snorts at her skirt hem.

I cock a saucy eyebrow back at her. "Who's she supposed to be, the Queen of Tarts?"

Eddie Rat-King lets out a bark of amusement. "Can't you tell? This is Camelot, I'm King Arthur, and she's my Guinevere."

I give meself a mental slap over the ear. A.R. Arthur is King. Savior of the people. So far as riddles go, it ain't exactly Sphinx material. "So who does that make me? Sir Galahad?"

"Darlin', meet Eliza Jekyll and Lizzie Hyde. My daughters."

Green-Tits glares down her pointy nose at me and says something, but I don't hear.

Not *Henry's daughters.*

And after all these years, in a starlit flash of *stupid* that staggers me cold, I get it.

———◦•◦———

Eliza reeled, her vision blurring. *Lizzie, where are you? I need you. Come back!*

But Lizzie just laughed and sang, a caged lunatic. *Cockles and mussels, a-live, alive-OOH!*

"We are, aren't we?" Eliza's voice croaked like rusted iron, crumbling and useless. "You and Madeleine were . . . We're your child. Not Henry's."

"Henry's gone," Edward Hyde said flatly. "Dissolved. E-*vap*-orated. There's only me, his shadow."

"But my father died," she protested, sick. All these years, she'd believed . . . "How can you even exist? I attended the funeral, there's a tomb . . ."

"An empty hole. Fine show, though, weren't it? All those smart black horses with feathered plumes. Henry would've approved, I'm certain, if he'd been there." A snort of glee. "Which he was. Sort of. Ha!"

"You forged his testament." The realization rinsed her wits thin. "'My friend and benefactor.' You wrote that."

"A good ruse, eh? 'Twas Marcellus's idea. What was I supposed to do, leave you an orphan? You're my blood." He winked, devilish. "Didn't you figure it out, my sweet? Never wonder where Lizzie came from?"

"The elixir." Her innocent trust seemed so foolish now. "You created her when you gave me the elixir."

"I gave you the elixir because you were already splitting in two." The ghost of anger long suppressed flitted dark wings over his face. "Don't you remember? She was fighting to get out. You were mad with it. I didn't break you. I *saved* you." Light as a grotesque fairy, Mr. Hyde hopped to his feet, made an elegant if crooked gentleman's bow, and tossed his dented hat into the crowd. "Shall we dance?"

And he stole her unresisting hands and whirled her into his embrace.

The maudlin carousel organ erupted into a mad circus waltz. He was short, his chin on a level with hers. Dizzy, she clutched at him, ready to stumble . . . but as if by magic, her clumsy feet found the steps. The crowd parted to give them space, a drunken parody of the dance at a wedding breakfast.

He danced gracefully, despite his hunched back. His arm was strong about her waist, his scent—leather, tobacco, a whiff of sweet alchemy—redolent with memory. A little girl's memory, the gruff-voiced shadow behind the curtain. An adolescent's memory, a whirlwind of exhilaration and danger, the first taste of that dark and bitter drink. A woman's memory, cautious, eager to please, yet . . .

He touched his forehead to hers, oddly fond. Not lascivious. Rather, affectionate. "Told you we'd waltz by candlelight," he murmured. "You're very pretty, Eliza."

I can't abide ugliness, whispered Mr. Todd in her memory.

She blinked, the scents and lights making her woozy. "Are you my angel of ruin, then? You and my mother . . ."

"I *loved* your mother." Hyde's grip clenched tighter. "I'd have given anything for her. I wanted her to live, but she died. Oh, how she *died,* that woman. A proper damn tragedy."

"But—"

He laughed and buried his nose in her hair to inhale. "Christ, you smell just like her. In love with my own wife. Pathetic." He grunted, embarrassed. "Love hurts, when you're like us. Remember that. It's raw and it's ugly and it bleeds."

Let me show you. Her head swam, feverish. *Let me show you how I love you . . .*

"But she didn't love me," Hyde added brutally. "Not for long. She was young, she longed for adventure and excitement and wild nights of pleasure, but . . . I frightened her. In the end, she wanted *him*. After all I'd shown her, all we'd done together. And you, my beautiful girls."

Eliza fought to catch her breath as he twirled her faster. "Did she know?"

"That you were mine? In her heart. It was Henry who refused to admit it. Afraid you'd inherit his . . . *affliction*." A rough grunt of disgust. "That's what he called me. God-rotted hypocrite is what he was. Wanted to share in the fun without getting his hands dirty. Spend the night drinking and whoring and worse, then turn up next morning at Harley Street fresh as a daisy, with nary a wrinkle on his conscience." Their lilting steps quickened, her skirts fanning out. "Doesn't work like that. I'm no one's plaything. Not Eddie Hyde."

"And the night Madeleine died?" She hardly dared ask. "Do you know . . . ?"

"She broke my heart." A growl, rough on Eliza's cheek. "Accidents happen. Let that be a warning."

Icy claws tore into her chest.

We had the devil's own trouble . . .

An accident, Henry. Happens all the time . . .

Shadow doesn't always behave . . .

Why does everyone assume it's the husband?

"You killed her." She fought, but he crushed her tightly, whirled her faster, the music galloping wilder, more frantic. "You killed her, and Henry and Marcellus covered it up. And then you killed Henry . . ."

"Henry killed *himself.*" He twirled her at arm's length, then pulled her close. She was breathing hard against his chest. He seemed to relish it. "With *aqua vitae,* my sweet," he whispered in her ear, and a smile licked his voice with glee. "He tried to get rid of me. They all tried. Here endeth the lesson."

"Let me go." She wriggled, but he was too strong. Her head throbbed, organ notes pounding her skull in discord. She'd made a life out of seeking justice for murdered women, trying to save a mother who could never be saved. And now her own father—God help her—her *real* father had turned out to be the enemy.

"Henry and I could've lived together, Eliza. We could've shared her. But no, he had to have everything *his* way." At last, the music crescendoed and Mr. Hyde bowed to her, coat skirts brushing the floor. The crowd cheered, raucous.

He kissed her hands, one after the other. "I took care of you, daughter." His words nearly escaped her in the din. "I made you respectable. Don't forget that."

"Then why?" Her throat ached, stubborn. "If you don't

want this for me, then why have Marcellus spoil my remedy? Why let me suffer?"

Someone threw Hyde his hat, and he jammed it on and tweaked the brim. "Because you need to realize that you can share, too. Lizzie loves you, in her way. Don't shut her out." His gaze blackened, thundery. Such an evilly handsome man. Such corruption. "Don't make my mistakes, Eliza. Mine and Henry's. It'll only end in blood."

Eliza's eyes stung, and she yanked her hand away and fled.

———❖———

Now that she was out of the King's sight—beyond his strange, invisible aura—the crowd closed in, careless. Eliza fought her way through, barely noticing the elbows and knees and sharp fingers that jabbed at her body. Her hair hung in knots, torn loose by the *change*. She didn't care.

Raw emotion clogged her throat, blinded her, filled her ears with screaming. Justice be damned. She burned for revenge. To make him scream and burn and suffer for what he'd done.

Her life was built on a lie. Her scientific rigor, the murders she'd solved . . . none of it meant anything. And it was all his fault.

Don't shut her out. Hyde's words rang an ugly carillon. She despaired. What was she supposed to do? Set Lizzie free whenever the mood struck? Let her do whatever she pleased?

Things like stalk Billy Beane. Attack anyone who threatened her. Frighten the tripe out of Marcellus Finch, who for all his lies had stood by Eliza when she'd had no one else in the world.

And as for the other thing . . . Her cheeks burned, even though no one watched. Lizzie was a flirtatious, worldly woman. Never even mind her friends in Seven Dials—could Eliza be Lafayette's lover? His mistress? Tempt an evil fate in some rust-ringed dungeon—or a bloody one at the mercy of a wolf?

Stop it, Lizzie hissed. *That's mine. He's mine.*

Eliza's head throbbed inside, bruised. As if Lizzie punched and kicked, a struggling animal trapped in a sack, clawing, bleeding . . .

Dazed, Eliza shook her head, but it wouldn't clear. Lafayette was a mistake, a moment of weakness. One of those accidents that happen . . .

Or had she secretly wanted it all along? Had she sought it out, tempted like Henry to enjoy dark pleasures without consequences? Did *we* seek it out, hell, *I* sought it out, yes, *me, us-I-her-we-me,* and if I do it again, who's gonna stop me, Eliza? You?

She fights me, but I swipe her aside. I rake out the rest of my hair, and her twisted pins drop to the floor, lost. Could you stop me, sister? Do you even want to, sweet girl?

Because in truth, we don't give a rat's arse what they all think, neither of us. Eliza with her funny gadgets and doctor's bag. Me and my cherry skirts and saucy grin.

And you know what? Remy Lafayette might be a strange one—a dangerous one, for all his manners—but he don't judge us for being different. He accepts us.

I like you just the way you are . . . A shiver spills through me, warm yet chilly, the spidery kiss of absent crimson hair . . .

Christ. And *I'm* supposed to be the depraved one? But I can't think about romance tonight. Not after finally meeting my father. My FATHER, God rot his blackened hunchbacked soul, who threw his wife down the stairs when she wouldn't have him and then cried over her corpse. Who gave Eliza a reason to live, but with the same careless hands snatched it away.

The rage bubbles inside me, a boiling volcano ready to explode. I want to rip his lying throat out and bathe in his BLOOD. I want to run laughing beside him under blazing stars, live as he lives, do as he does. I want to fall weeping at his feet and beg him to love me, just for an hour, the way he loves *her*.

Jesus on a purple-arsed donkey. Where the hell's the gin in this madhouse? That's what I'd like to know.

Behind me, the carousel organ has broken into a fierce fairy reel that makes me shudder and hurry on. I've heard the stories. Is this Rats' Castle that kind of place? Don't drink the wine, don't eat the fair folk's enchanted food, or you'll be stuck here for years at some uppity fairy bitch's whim like Tam friggin' Lin. Dance to their magical melody, and you'll dance forever.

I push through the jabbering masses to what looks like a bar, a ragged wooden bench lashed between two poles. Behind it, barrels and vats, bottles of liquid pink and green and gold, bales of strange gear. A fat leprechaun teeters on a stool, solemnly poking his fingers into a yellow-faced bloke's long droopy ears. A scaly snake-faced girl licks my shoulder with her forked tongue, and I shove her away . . .

Wild black hair, mismatched dark eyes.

Johnny pushes a cup of gin towards me. "Never thought to see you here."

I can't help but stare. The strange fey light gloats over him, lights up his *weird* with an eerie radiance, and I'm damned if I know how anyone ever thinks this man is ordinary. His hair's shredded velvet, his skin shines like pearls, and between his long fingers, shadows whisper and dance. He's luminous. Magical.

"You neither." I finger the cup, odd reluctance circling like hungry sharks in my head. I ache. I'm weary, and I long for a friend. I want to open my soul, tell him everything, lean on his warm sweet shoulder and say, my father's a murderer and I'm going right the same way, let's drink ourselves stupid and love each other to black-scarred oblivion.

But all of a moment, I'm twitchy. He's cagey, silent. Not so charming as usual. Something ain't right.

His cock-eyed gaze rolls away, just for a second. And I know.

"Oh, hell." My mouth parches with a thirst so deep I want to scream, and there's a ragged black hole where a moment ago my heart used to be. I shove the cup aside, and it spills, dark on the wooden bench like blood.

"Lizzie—"

"All this time, you knew." My eyes burn, acid-bright, and something inside my head *squeezes*. I grit my teeth. "Why didn't you *tell* me?"

"I wanted to!" He rakes at his hair, his bone-china jaw tight. "He bade me protect you. The King's the King. Ain't no defying him."

He never could convince me with a lie. I believe him, and I love him for it. But the devil take me, I hate him, too. And Lizzie don't never forgive.

"So what, you been spying on me, is that it? All these years."

Johnny don't answer.

I know it ain't fair, but my hair crackles with spite, and I say it anyway. "And what about fucking me? Did he bid you do that, too?"

His black gaze melts. "It weren't like that—"

Smack! I've hit him. Like a girl, right across his delicate fey cheek.

He don't hit me back. He just stares, shadows and pain. Already, an angry red splotch blooms on his skin.

And I walk away.

I don't much care where I'm going. I shove bodies aside, not fussed where they fall. Down, down, along rickety galleries and twisting corridors into the stinking bowels of this place, where it reeks of dead breath and even the light is weak and frightened. There's dirt on the floor here, tunnels carved from the very earth, centuries of civilization piled upon itself and crushed to death in the mud.

Eliza yells, hammering at the inside of my head. Go away, sweet girl. You won't like it here.

Water splashes under my feet. I duck under a moldy wooden lintel. A cavern, where a fire burns in an ironclad hole. Acrid smoke drifts at eye level. In the shadows, figures mutter and stretch, the dark shapes of men . . . and *things*. Someone's groaning. I glimpse misshapen limbs, a distorted face, the fleshy stumps of wings.

A green-faced man with a beak for a nose and mouth passes me a long-stemmed brass pipe. I suck on it, the smoke bitter in my mouth. My senses spin. I suck again and wobble on my feet.

"Good stuff." My voice zooms into the distance. My legs feel muddy, their strength washed away.

"Like it, cherry pie?" Beakface grins. He's wearing a coat of lank gray feathers. "More where that came from."

Someone thrusts a drink into my hand. Gritty black liquid sloshes over my wrist and stings my skin. What the fuck is this? I don't care. I raise it to the ceiling. "Hail to the King," says I, and I gulp it down.

Warm languor crawls from my stomach along my limbs. Oh, my. Which way's up? I'm floating, miles above the earth where the sky is black and silent, where stars and planets whirl in cosmic waltz. Dance, and you'll dance forever.

Somehow, that don't seem so bad any more.

Thunk! My head hits the floor. I'm on my back, someone's tugging at my hair, my dress, snapping the hooks on my bodice. Greasy fingers fold over my wrist. Something warm and wet's on my fingers, pulling. Sucking. Trying to consume. A tongue wrapping my knuckles, teeth nibbling at the skin between thumb and forefinger. The pain is muted, distant. I can barely feel it. I can't even move.

My breasts were cold, but now they're warm, slick, so tender. Something bites my nipple. A creature's crawling under my skirt. Some hot, wet thing slithers up between my legs, hunting for an opening. A mouth nibbles on my thigh. Teeth sink in. I try to yell, but all that comes out is a groan. The same noise that mutilated thing in the corner was making. Jesus fucking Christ, are they *eating* him? Are they eating *me*?

Beakface leans over me, grinning. His tiny jagged teeth gleam, and his mildewed feathers stink and crawl with fleas. "Easy, now. Relax. It'll take a while."

I try to grab him, fight back, bite his ugly face off, but my muscles are water, so heavy. So very heavy. I try to scream, but my throat is clogged with woolly goo, and something grabs my jaw and forces itself into my mouth. Fur, cold and bitter, choking me, working itself deeper down my throat . . .

Suddenly, I can breathe again. I'm free. Someone—Beakface?—screams, and cartilage pops, a horrid *crack!* Warm arms lift me, the familiar scent of flowers, his rough coat on my cheek. He carries me, light as the wind, up to where it's bright and the air is dry and warm, and now that I can taste what I've drunk, bile burns my mouth and I spew gritty black hell.

He lays me on something soft, so blessedly soft, like a cloud. I sink into it, deeper, warmer. His fingers trace my forehead, my cheekbone, my bruised lips. I struggle to focus, but his mismatched eyes guide me, lure me to safety—or is it ruin?—and I try to whisper his name, but darkness ambushes me. A rough-edged voice curses fit to strip paint, not Johnny but someone else, and I try to stay afloat but I can't and the last thing I see before I fall is my father's twisted face.

Moonlight slants silvery ghosts onto the darkened landing, and dust motes dance. It's long past little Eliza's bedtime, but she can't sleep. She keeps hearing noises. Scuffles in the dark, sobbing, the ominous creak of floorboards . . . and other, stranger sounds. The ones monsters make.

She knows about monsters. She's seen them, late at night, leering shadows on the wall of Father's laboratory. They cackle. They caper. They howl.

Maybe she was dreaming. She should go back to bed. She should call for Mother.

Anything but keep walking into the dark.

Her white linen nightdress is still warm from bed, but the old house's floor is chilly under her feet. She hugs herself, shivering. Ahead, candlelight leaks from a half-open door. Voices within, muffled, frantic. Someone is pacing, nervous, back and forth, back and forth.

Compelled, she pads up to the door and peers in.

A candlestick burns on the bedside table. Light licks the rich red carpet, the hem of the bed's white drapes. The door is in the way, she can't see the bed entire, but she can see one corner post, and the edge of the lace curtain is dipped in wet, dripping darkness.

Dangling beside the bedpost is a lady's pale arm. Limp, motionless fingers, beseeching the uncaring floor.

"No." Father's voice, his beloved scent of cigars and laboratory alcohol. "No, it wasn't the way you think. He's . . . oh, dear God." A heavy sigh. "I have to wake Gabriel, tell him—"

"Henry." A second voice interrupts, low and persuasive. "Henry, old bean, listen to me. Gabriel will go directly to the magistrate. Pretty society wife tumbles down the stairs?

In her condition? They'll never believe you, don't you see? Let me take care of it."

Father's voice drops to an angry whisper. "What do you mean, 'take care of it'?"

A rustle, maybe a shrug. "A dark street, a few strategic wounds. An accident, Henry. Poor pretty lady, a victim of senseless violence. These tragedies happen all the time—"

"I swear to God, sir, you will not violate my wife."

The strike of a match, the smell of tobacco smoke. "Who said anything about violation? A simple robbery scenario will suffice. Won't even need to crease her skirts." A sigh. "I did warn you to keep her out of it."

A fragment of harsh laughter. "You told me so, is that it? We've both been in this from the beginning—"

"Which is why we can't give up now, not after all we've worked for." A deep exhale. "One way, you'll hang. The other way, you'll burn. My way? We fix this, and we carry on. What's it to be?"

Silence, broken only by pacing footsteps and the inexorable drip-drop-drip of that dark stain.

"Very well." Father's voice trembles. "Very well, damn you. But we are proceeding with formula twenty-seven right away. I'll countenance nothing else."

"Very well. I'll return presently. Burn the sheets. And Henry . . ."

"What?"

"You know who we can talk to about this."

"Take care." Steely threat.

"Victor's ready. But we have to be quick. Before the decay sets in—"

Scuffle! Thump! *Someone falls and takes furniture with him.* "Never speak of that," Father says grimly. "Never, hear me? Not for her."

"Of course, old bean." *Indistinct, wet.* "Merely a suggestion, say what? No need for violence. Carrying on." *Light footsteps approach the door, a tune hummed under his breath.* "And her ghost wheels her barrow . . . through streets broad and narrow . . . crying, 'cockles and mussels, alive, alive-oh . . .'"

Little Eliza flees. Back to her cold bed, where she yanks the quilt over her head and curls into a tiny weeping ball, her hand stuffed into her mouth . . .

ACTUS NON FACIT REUM

. • .

ELIZA WOKE TO THE RATTLE OF LITTLE BRASS FEET. Her head pounded, swelling with each thud. Damp all over, cloth sticking to her limbs. Why so hot in here? Morning sunlight scorched her face, and she groaned sickly and rolled over.

Her cheek hit cool sheets. Her own bed. Someone had brought her home.

Our father, whispered Lizzie hoarsely. *King Eddie Hyde. Daughter of rats, that's what we is. The bad half of a bad half . . .*

For once, she hadn't the heart to tell Lizzie to shut up. The truth of it ached, deep in her soul where she'd always known something was amiss . . .

Cogs whirred, and the sheet tugged away under her cheek. "Urgency required," trumpeted a little metallic voice. "Sleep inappropriate."

She muffled her eyes with the pillow. Her stomach was scraped raw. "Go 'way."

Hippocrates pulled the sheet again. "Telegraph. Urgency required. Make greater—"

"Uhh." She fought to lift her head, which had suddenly

filled with lead, and cracked one eye open. The room swirled, underwater. "Wha'?"

"Telegraph, eight o'clock. Current time, half past nine." Hipp jigged, blinking his blue light, and his cogs grated anxiously, *rrrk! rrrk! rrrk!*

"Half past nine?" She stumbled out of bed, tangling in sweaty sheets. Her guts boiled, vengeful. "Oh, dear . . . Out of the way, Hipp." She staggered for the washstand and emptied her stomach contents into the jug. Ugh. Her eyes streamed, burning. Vile black grit swam in the mess, and she wiped her mouth and averted her gaze.

Her damp skin felt chilled, and she realized she was naked. She winced, imagining the efforts of those who'd carried her home. Wonderful. Had Mrs. Poole seen? Molly? The neighbors?

Lizzie snorted. *You think Mr. H can't deal with a few nosy servants? He'll have their eyes clawed out before they whisper a word. And Johnny might be a lying dog, but he ain't stupid.*

Mr. Hyde was a murderer. He must be brought to justice. She could call the police. She could set the Philosopher on him. She could march on down to the Rats' Castle and wring his scrawny neck . . .

Hipp bounced impatiently at her feet. "Telegraph."

She wiped her face on a towel. "What is it, Hipp? Show me."

He flashed his *happy* light and spurted out a length of ticker tape.

She tore it off and fumbled for her spectacles. Blinked at the printed letters . . . and the bottom fell out of her guts all over again.

———◄•►———

An hour later, she shoved along a crowded Strand, south of Covent Garden. Malicious sunshine glared, seeking out her eyes and making them sting. The very air seemed oppressive this morning, closing in around her, creeping cool hands up her skirts. Even Hippocrates slunk along hunched over, his little brass legs poised to scuttle beneath her petticoats.

An evil glint graced every eye. No doubt, pickpockets threaded through the crowd, taking what they pleased from unsuspecting pedestrians. That group of gentlemen by the fence were probably robbers, planning their next heist. Urchins gathered in the alleyways, envy brooding in their gazes, peering out at the world they could never belong to, only infiltrate, undermine, poison. Probably they were monsters in disguise.

A newsboy yelled and waved his paper. "Human heads in the Thames! Gruesome discovery! Moorfields Monster claims more victims!" Beside a butcher's shop, a dog growled at her, guarding a discarded pile of offal. Hipp buzzed angrily, and the urge possessed her to growl back, to kick that dog until it howled. She hurried on, turning left up Southampton Street. The church there was abandoned, the door boarded up, and the sun flashed on dusty broken glass, sharpening the edges into fiery weapons.

Above the crowd bobbed the stovepipe hats of policemen. The too-familiar sight of a barrier of bedsheets hove into view, covering the entrance to the churchyard alleyway.

She peered between a tiny gap in the sheets. A dirty bodice, the edge of a green sleeve, a neatly severed wrist . . .

Inspector Reeve grunted. "Go away," he said, puffing cigar smoke. "You're not needed here."

"Am I not?" she asked brightly. "Your case still open and shut, is it?"

Reeve bristled. "Madam, kindly escort yourself from the scene, or I'll—"

"Or you'll what?" Captain Lafayette strode up, and speared Reeve on his sharpest glare. "Dr. Jekyll's expertise seems to me just what you require. How fortuitous that she should be passing by."

Reeve looked him up and down—scarlet coat, polished arc-pistol, silvery Royal Society badge—and chewed angrily on his cigar. "The girl's a pest," he said finally. "I can't have her interfering with my investigation—"

"I'm the Royal Society, Inspector," cut in Lafayette breezily. "I'll interfere wherever I please. Come along, Doctor, no time to waste." And he lifted the sheet aside and ushered her through.

Inside the barrier, Eliza managed a cautious smile. "I received your telegraph. I confess, you surprise me."

Lafayette shrugged. "Thought you'd be interested. You're the expert, after all. Besides, I knew you'd be dying to see me."

"Naturally. I breathe again." She hesitated. "Thank you for returning my optical. It's precious to me. I shan't forget your trouble."

"Don't mention it." He tugged at a stray chestnut curl and grimaced, looking oddly boyish. "Actually, do mention it. Was that an invitation to truce?"

Unwillingly, she recalled how cold she'd been to him, that night in the rain. At least now, she knew he wasn't the murderer. "Would you like it to be?"

"I'd like it to be unconditional forgiveness." A steady stare, darkened to ocean blue. "For whatever you believe I've done."

Lizzie smiled, melting. *Oh, we know what you did, Remy. We know how you play, warm and wicked and splashed with moonlight . . .*

Eliza flushed. "Is that your idea of an apology?"

"It's my idea of a 'not guilty' plea."

"Perhaps you should retain a lawyer." She adjusted her bag over her shoulder. "But it'll do for the moment. Shall we?"

The bedsheets protected several yards of the alleyway, stretching from the church wall to the opposite building. At least Reeve had managed that much. A pair of constables squatted, picking through piles of refuse for evidence. The dead woman lay on her back, a pool of clotted blood seeping from each severed wrist.

"And we revert to type," murmured Lafayette. "Female, drugged, hands sliced off. What are the odds it's the same weapon?"

Eliza examined one thin wrist, then the other. "Same edge on the bone, same angle of slice."

Lafayette poked the dead woman's apple-green skirt hem aside—a fine lady's dress, but well-worn, second-hand—to reveal booted feet, still attached. "Was he interrupted?"

"Or perhaps . . . already fully stocked with feet? He already has Miss Maskelyne's and Miss Pavlova's."

"Are you imagining a larder?" He wrinkled his nose. "Charming."

"With three victims and counting, plus Beane? I'm not

sure what to imagine." The woman's faded brown hair spilled across her face. With one finger, Eliza pushed it back.

Empty eye sockets, caked with gore.

Oh, my. Eliza rocked back on her heels. The ruined face was horror enough. But she knew this green dress, that pinched chin, the pox scars covered up with greasepaint . . .

"Good God." Lafayette leaned over. "He's taken her eyeballs. What on earth is that about?"

"Eyeballs." Hipp jittered on unhappy feet. "Harvest conspicuous. Incompatible with speedy escape. Does not compute."

"Sally Fingers." Eliza's voice cracked. She rose, automatically smoothing her skirts, but her hands trembled.

"What's that?"

"I know this woman. Sally Fingers, she's a pickpocket from Seven Dials. A witness in the murder of Billy Beane." Eliza licked salty lips, her stomach roiling all over again.

Ophelia Maskelyne's hands, broken and therefore discarded . . . and now another pair, taken in their place. A substitute victim.

Someone had led the Chopper from Irina Pavlova to Billy Beane. And now, it seemed, from Ophelia to Sally Fingers.

Lafayette's eyebrow arched. He didn't speak. He didn't have to.

He was right. She was the connection. The killer was following her.

Both of her.

Briskly, she dusted her hands. "Well, Captain, thank you for indulging my interest. I really must be going."

Lafayette touched her arm, and her body bristled with threat. "Look. About what I said before. Have I offended you? I didn't mean—"

"It's of no consequence. I shan't mention it again. Good day." And she scooped Hipp into her bag and hurried away.

———◦∙◦———

Lafayette called after her. She didn't turn. Just kept walking, her breath squeezing tight. Her head swam, and her sickness returned full force.

The murderer had followed her. How else could he have picked Sally Fingers as a victim? It was too much a coincidence.

But Lizzie, not Eliza, had questioned Sally.

Which meant that the killer knew that she and Lizzie were the same person. Had watched her change, even.

Mr. Hyde knew, obviously. Marcellus Finch. Neither seemed likely. What profit in this slaughter for them? If Hyde wanted her out of the way, he'd have done it before now.

Of course, there was one other.

A shadow passed in front of the sun. Could it be Mr. Todd? Using this strange teleportation machine to leave the asylum and track down fresh victims?

No. It made no sense. If Todd could escape Bethlem, he'd never return. And hacking off a victim's hands—drugging her—killing in such a dogged, determined pattern? Not Mr. Todd's style.

There was no elegance in it. No art.

She turned the corner, onto a darker street, not really caring where she was going but *away*. In her bag, Hippocrates wriggled and clicked, and absently she petted him through the canvas.

Inside, something *crackled*.

She stuffed her fingers in and found a crisp roll of paper.

She'd left no notes in here. Curious, she halted and flattened the paper.

A garish penny pamphlet, printed in black ink. WALKING DEATH!! trumpeted the title, above a lithograph of what looked like an Egyptian mummy stalking a London street, stony-eyed and arms outstretched. Terrified townsfolk fled in its path. HORROR AT WATERLOO! it said underneath. NONE CAN ESCAPE THE MONSTER!

Flicking through, she skimmed what appeared to be the story of a lunatic escaped from a private hospital, at last found dead in a park, badly injured and blue with cold. She turned to the back cover. In the margin of the printed advertising— HYDE'S WART PILLS! YOU WON'T KNOW YOUR OWN FACE!—was handwriting, inked in blue.

> *Eliza,*
> *You're in danger*
> *Come to me at the Churchyard,*
> <u>*before*</u> *the moon shines*
> > *Your friend,*
> > *M*

Her mind zeroed in, swiftly discarding *Molly* and *Marcellus* and even *Malachi*. Surely, inked on such a palimpsest, "M" was for the Doyen of Dreadful himself: Matthew Temple.

She recalled Lizzie's shining rage when Reeve threw her out of Bow Street. Storming down the station steps, crashing into Temple. His bottle-green waistcoat an eyesore, that ridiculous autumn-leaf hair stuffed under his cap. They'd collided—*urgent, must speak with you about your murder case*—and Temple had grabbed at her bag. And now, this note was in it.

The same Temple who'd threatened her at the Crystal Palace. Insinuated he knew something about her and Lafayette. Watched Dr. Percival's electrical demonstration with sharp-eyed interest. Threatened in jest to send her a copy of his latest sensational crime pamphlet.

The same Matthew Temple who'd trailed after her like a choleric miasma all week. Who'd turned up outside the police station, at her omnibus, at the Crystal Palace. Even left his footprint in the shadowy cells at Bethlem, where keeper and lunatic both pored over his publications.

Who'd faithfully attended—at the very least, reported on with garish delight—every crime scene.

His cover drawings flitted through her mind, a lurid slide show. THE DYING DANCER. SLAUGHTER AT THE EGYPTIAN. THE BLOODY DEATH OF BILLY BEANE. All gory. All sensational. All described in loving, meticulous detail.

Like a wash of dark watercolor, the world changed hue, and Mr. Todd's sly suggestion—was it only five days ago?—took on a new and sinister aspect. *Your budding artist isn't angry or vengeful, heavens no . . .*

". . . he's hopelessly in love," she finished aloud, in the middle of the street. "Oh, my."

Around her, the crowd hustled on, oblivious. Her sweaty fingers clenched around the pamphlet, and she glanced again at the handwritten note, where it said

You're in danger

and

Your friend,

M

. . . and like a candle flame in a storm, the light of her courage wavered.

If she wanted the truth, she'd have to meet Temple. Tonight, at his office in St. Paul's churchyard. Alone.

THE BUSINESS OF BURNING
DOWN CHURCHES

• • •

BEFORE THE MIGHTY DOOR OF ST. PAUL'S CATHE-
dral, a yelling crowd had gathered.

And so had the Enforcers. It was execution day.

A cordon of clockwork men circled the cathedral. Hulking
brass brutes, seven feet high, white face masks impassive,
massive mechanical frames blocking out the sun. And in
their skeletal brass hands, they clutched pistols, purple coils
buzzing bright. Belligerent. Daring anyone to question them.

But at least, in this crowd, Eliza felt relatively safe. Not
alone. She'd hurried home and left Hippocrates with strict
instructions to telegraph Mr. Finch in three hours if she
didn't return. Poor precautions, perhaps. But without Griffin,
going to the police was problematic, to say the least. *Excuse
me, Inspector Reeve, would you mind terribly accompanying
me while I track down a murder suspect? The man followed me
while I was someone else, you see, and there's a lunatic razor
murderer locked in Bedlam who insists this fellow is the culprit.
Thank you, just let me fetch my hat.*

Giggles erupted in her belly. This was ridiculous. A trap. Walking into a murderer's lair yet again? Would she never learn this lesson? Apprehending criminals was not her job. She should report Temple to the Met, go home, and forget about it.

But inside her, shadows roiled, not ghostly but flesh and angry blood, and in her skirt pocket, Lizzie's stiletto hummed a madwoman's dirge of vengeance. *Don't be a fool*, Lizzie snarled. *Temple knows you're onto him. And guess what? You're next. We're next. What are you going to do about it?*

"Perhaps not get myself killed? What's our plan, Lizzie? Talk him out of it?"

Who else can you turn to, Eliza? All your friends have deserted you. You've no one but me. So deal with it, or I will.

Her thigh muscles jerked tight, and of their own accord, her legs started to move.

Eliza stumbled to keep up. "All right! Stop it. I'm going."

She pierced the crowd, dodging waving arms and people jumping up and down to see. Angry men cursed. Children jeered. She saw one fellow bend to pick up a stone. The air tingled with tension and the scent of approaching rain clouds. Over the horizon, a storm was building.

In the square, a pyre had been built, and Enforcers were strapping a woman to a stake. The lady had been stripped of her gown and wore only the remnants of a dirty chemise. The rising wind whipped dark hair from her face. She could barely stand on her own, and her bare shoulders were marked with red welts. "Go on, burn me, you metal bastards!" she jeered. "I'm not done yet. Toast me and turn me over!"

Clara Morton.

Oh, my. Eliza's heart chilled. What had Clara done? Finally spoken out once too often, her strange experiments too visible? Her unorthodox papers discovered? Worse: had Eliza inadvertently exposed her? Sickly, she wracked her brain for something she'd said, something she'd done . . .

I'll burn you alive. The Philosopher's cruel words bounced back, bitter with fresh meaning. *Alongside every misbegotten wretch who's ever had the ill fortune to be your friend . . .*

This was a threat. A warning. And Clara would die for it.

"Clara!" she yelled, but her voice was smothered by the howling crowd. Desperately, she tried to push through. The Enforcers surrounding the pyre didn't speak. They just went about their business, indefatigable, and one leveled his electric pistol at the kindling and fired.

A bright blue flash. *Crack!* Flames leapt. Smoke billowed, the groaning wind fanning the fire. The crowd jeered and whistled. A man ran for one of the Enforcers, brandishing a lump of wood, which he swung with all his might.

Clang! It bounced off the Enforcer's metal carcass. The thing didn't even stagger. It just grabbed the man by his collar and hurled him back into the crowd.

Silence fell like a fog, broken only by the wind's rising moan. The crowd held its collective breath.

Inside her Lizzie snarled wordless rage, and fresh as the pyre, Eliza's blood ignited. She sucked in a lungful of stormy air, and screamed. "God save the Queen!"

And the mob erupted into madness.

They surged forwards, a furious tide. Pistol shots sizzled with the smoke and tart stink of burned aether. Rocks and punches flew. Knives slashed. Waving arms, flapping coats, fists, kicks. In the fire, Miss Morton screamed, and men climbed the pyre to hack her free.

"Ha-ha! Take that, you brainless lackeys!" Was that her voice, or Lizzie's?

"Eliza!" A man's yell. "Eliza, wait!"

She didn't pause. Just ducked her head and kept fighting, until after what seemed like hours, she burst from the ragged edges of the crowd.

At the far end of the churchyard, along the transept, the day's usual business had halted. Storekeepers ran into the street and fixed shutters tightly over their windows, and stall owners covered their wares with tarpaulins or dragged them hastily out of sight. Costermongers still yelled gaily, offering roasted chestnuts and strawberries and salted fish. Dirty children ducked and weaved, stealing handkerchiefs and pocketbooks. In a coffee house, patrons sat back with their drinks and watched the fight.

Matthew Temple's fine publishing emporium—such as it was—was tucked by the entrance to a side street on Paternoster Row, a narrow wooden building that lurched alarmingly to one side, propped up only by its neighbor and the statistical unlikelihood of it toppling at the very moment she stood beneath. His shop front was pasted with copies of his cover drawings, murders and beheadings and gruesome crimes of all ilks.

Nice, whispered Lizzie. *The cove's got an unnatural interest, for sure,* and Eliza couldn't help but agree.

Light leaked from cracks in the shutters. She pushed on the door. Locked.

"Mr. Temple?" she called.

No answer.

Then, someone inside yelled. A rough, ragged, blood-chilling yell.

"Oh, Jesus." Frantically, Eliza rattled the handle. It wouldn't budge. Again, with all her strength.

Stand aside, snarled Lizzie, and I

(*she*)

I thrash, and force my way to the surface. *Splash!* My head breaks water, and I suck in a hungry breath full of color and light, and I take three good steps backwards and hurl meself at the door.

Crack! The wood gives way, and I hurtle in.

I hit the floor, a sick *thud!* that rattles my skull. Loose pages fly, a shower of printed words. I stagger up.

The place is a riot. Shelves overturned, books and newsprint scattered around the overturned printing press like dead leaves. THE DYING DANCER. HORROR AT WATERLOO. A cabinet's doors are torn off, the files inside tossed every which way. Copies of books in French and Russian spill out, along with reams and reams of leaflets entitled *A Meeting to Debate Parliamentary Concerns.*

I poke through them with my toe, incredulous. The Thistlewood Club. Is this what Temple's bloodthirsty crime pamphlets pay for? Holy seditious libel, friends. There's enough here to hang him a dozen times over. Further into the lamp-lit dark, broken bottles lie skewiff, oil and ink pissing out in dark pools, and . . . sweet baby Jesus, there's Matthew Temple, on the floor in a mess of crimson death.

He's choking, pawing at the blood that pumps red rhythm from his opened throat. And as the blood glows redder, brighter—as his life seeps away—it's as if the rest of the

world fades to sepia. It's lurid, shocking. A lunatic's oil painting of beauty.

In the corner crouches a growling yellow beast.

Head too big for its body, twisted limbs, deformed spine
ridged with bumps. Fur in damp clumps, narrow jaws dripping with saliva. Around one paw, it wears a bolted metal
contraption, like a clunky manacle wrapped with crackling
copper wire. Its hackles bristle with coarse golden hair, and it
rakes the floor with ugly claws, splinters cracking. Amber
eyes, shiny with hunger, fix on mine

(hers)

and something in 'em recognizes us, because it *howls* with
rage fit to curdle my mouth . . . and leaps.

I lurch out of the way, graceless. The beast slams into my
shoulder. I tumble, and my skull cracks the floor again, hard.
Thump! I'm dizzy, I'm fumbling for my weapon, screw these
skirts, where is that pocket? My sweet steel sister is singing,
don't let her go hungry . . .

The creature twists to all fours and advances. Spit drools
in strings from its jaws. It stinks of wet fur and blood. Its flat
eyes gleam, inhuman. I scrabble away on my back like a crab,
desperate. I can't escape, it's poising to spring . . .

Crack! Blinding blue light melts my eyeballs. Aether zings,
fire and thunder.

And the beast yowls in pain and blurs across the room into
the dark.

"After it!" Captain Lafayette sprints into the dim backwa-
ters of the office, and *boom!* Another aether explosion, loud
enough to shake the room and shower me in plaster dust.

Only this time, it ain't his pistol.

Dazed, I chase after him through the dust cloud. The back office is dim, narrow, cluttered with lithograph frames and stacks of movable type. No windows. No doors. No exits.

Just a smoking hole in the wooden wall, six inches wide, charred at the edges. And the monster is gone.

I catch my breath, try to rein in my heartbeat. Lafayette holsters his pistol, dust drifting from his hair. If I were a lesser woman, he'd be my bleedin' hero.

"You missed," I accuse.

A flash of glorious smile. "You moved."

Bumps tingle my arms, and something sweet and tempting melts like warm chocolate over my heart. Fact is, for all his damned annoying attitude, the world's brighter and less ugly with him in it. He's sunshine through my rain clouds. A light on my black-crusted soul.

Curse him. I wipe my dusty face. "So what was that? Your ugly little brother?"

"I told you I was a hunter. That's the thing I'm hunting. Seems you and I are on the same trail." He turns those heaven-blue eyes on me, and it isn't the raw, bleeding look he gave me that night in Seven Dials. It isn't even the dark, fiery look of desire. It's bruised, bewildered, a little bit awestruck.

It's the look he gives *her*.

He called to her outside. Saw her enter this building. Now no one's here but me.

Oh, shit.

A wet gurgle breaks the mood. Temple's still alive. I dive to my knees, press my palm to his throat, try to stop the blood, but I'm not Jesus fucking Christ. I'm not even Eliza Jekyll. "God's innards. It's everywhere."

A shadow flits across Lafayette's face. As if he's seen death before and knows the bastard's ugly face. He pokes at something on the floor with his toe. "Knife," he reports softly. "Stabbed in the throat, just like Billy Beane. Good God."

I grip Temple's hand, despairing. "Hush, now. You're not alone." The best I can do. Damn it, it's all I can do. Poor bastard. How we've underestimated you.

Temple stares up at me, pleading. He's trying to speak, but bright red froth spurts from his mouth. Red like his waistcoat. His hair's soaked with it, that stupid autumn-leaf tuft of his, and stupidly I wipe it back from his cheek, but it just keeps dripping.

I scream, but it comes out as a gurgling mess. I've never felt so helpless. His face slackens, and the blood goes from a spurt to a trickle.

"I'm sorry," I whisper. "Don't die. Please, don't die."

But he does. His breath rattles, and the sparkle in his eyes winks out.

God fucking damn it. My skirts—*her* skirts—are soaked with warm gore. My hands run with it, it's soaking my sleeve to the elbow. I don't even bother to wipe clean.

Because I killed him. Never mind that bristly-haired monster that just zapped out of here with the portable half of Clara's teleportation machine bolted around its paw. Temple tried to help us, and we treated him like scum. *You're in danger,* he'd scribbled. He knew the killer were after us. He tried to tell us—put himself in harm's way, for God's sake—and this is what he gets.

The man was more than we gave him credit for. But we *assumed.*

It don't matter that we were Eliza at the time. I'm not some drug-addled fantasy of hers brought to life. We're two halves of the same damn person. And I can't pretend anymore that what she does—what she wants and fears and longs for—is naught to do with me.

Lafayette watches me. "I'm sorry. He was your friend."

"No. But he should've been."

He offers me his hand. I haul myself up. Blood gums our fingers together. It seems right, somehow. My cheeks burn, and I close my eyes.

It hurts. It's marvelous. A strange satisfaction, not having to hide anymore.

"So." I open my eyes again. "I'm her. She's me. And now you know."

His gaze is steady, unafraid. "I think I always knew. Since that night in Seven Dials, anyway."

"How's that?"

"You saw me, in the moonlight. You saw what I would become, and you didn't run."

I edge closer, restless. He smells of aether and steel. "And what if I like what you become?"

He lets my hand go. "Lizzie, you shouldn't. I'm dangerous."

"But—"

"When I'm that *creature*"—a spit of distaste—"I want to kill you. I want to tear your flesh to scraps and have my way with your bleeding remains. The curse is that powerful."

His poetic description makes me squirm. But it's dark, compelling, like my nightmares. Such wild, uncontrollable impulses . . .

"So," says I, after a moment. "How did you, er . . . ?"

"How did I become this way?" A little laugh. "A beast attacked me in the Kashmiri jungle. I barely escaped alive. The
wound festered, and then it healed. I felt stronger and health-
ier than I'd felt in my life. I imagined I'd dodged a bullet, so
to speak. Then the moon waxed. I thought it was a nightmare, until I saw what I'd done."

I ache for his sorrow. At least Eliza had Marcellus to guide
her, that first time. To explain what was happening. Lafayette
had no one. "It happens at the full moon?"

"And other times. I can't change at will, at least not so far.
Certain circumstances set it off. I, er . . . haven't quite figured
out the rules yet." He bites his lip. Sweet lord, that's a sight. I
want to taste the little bruise he's made. Kiss his flushed
mouth, forget who and where and *what* we are . . .

"So why return to England? India's the perfect place to put
yourself in lavender."

"I killed someone it was my job to protect." He's strangely
detached, as if once the wound in his heart bled freely and he
screamed curses at the sky, only now it don't hurt so much
anymore. "The air howled with my guilt. I needed to escape."

I understand exactly what he means. "And now you're a
monster-hunter for the Royal, eh? Nice twist."

"It isn't for the reason they think. There's safety in it, so
long as no one finds out. I was hoping this other fellow might
help me."

"The 'Moorfields Monster,' eh?"

"Apparently." He shrugs, rueful. "Same reason I sought
you out, and Mr. Finch. I've tried all kinds of remedies, as you
see"—he fingers that odd bracelet he wears, the silver one
with the seal, and I wonder what kind of charlatan spellwork

resides there—"but nothing works. I'd heard rumors of Henry Jekyll's experiments. I thought if the elixir could split a man in two . . ."

". . . then it might be able to put you back together." My stomach swells with salt like a drowned woman's. I feel as if I'm being forced to eat a pudding the size of a house.

A cure. As if I'm a plague, a foul disease to be eradicated. The fleas in Eliza's hair, the dirt under her nails. Unwanted.

I want to jump up and down, yell like a thwarted child. *He's mine, bitch. Not yours. Mine . . .*

I find my voice, a stab of fake bravado. "So you know me, and I know you. What now? You gonna arrest me to shut me up?"

"That depends."

"On what?"

He turns my hand over, studies my smeared nails. Is he afraid to look at me? "Can I trust you, Miss Hyde?"

Daring, I take his hand and press his palm over my racing heart, where my flesh is soft and warm. "What do you think?"

He hesitates.

Just an instant of indecision, but it's enough for me.

"Fine." I turn away and laugh as if I don't care. But like a gutted fish I'm torn gritty and ragged inside. "Guess you always did like her better."

He catches my shoulder, pulls me back around. "Look, I'm sorry that—"

"She won't have you, you know." Bitterness scorches my guts, fiery like rotgut gin. "Not Eliza. She's in love with someone else. What a fucking pity you had to lower yourself to my level."

"Lizzie, that's ridiculous—"

"You know what? Forget it." It hurts, deep inside, a tumor I can't never cut out. "You don't trust me? Fine. Maybe I'll call on that crusty old bastard in the Tower after all and tell him what his precious investigator really is—"

Boots thud on bricks, and a gang of men burst in.

We jump apart, as if we're doing something indecent. Already I miss his warmth, his scent, the touch of his hand. In this moment, I'm certain as death that I'll never know them again.

Coppers. Two constables, stovepipe hats and polished buttons. And then that fat inspector with the cigar waddles in.

Eliza's anger chimes, low and resonant like the bottom end of a piano.

Crap. I can't run now. I can't *change,* not in front of Reeve. Will he recognize Eliza's dove-gray gown? Ask my name? Equate me with his famous lady in red?

Curse my weak woman's heart. My jealousy seems so stupid now. Will Lafayette drop us both in it? He's every reason to want us gone. Apart from Finch—whom he can blackmail in an instant—we're the only ones who know Remy's secret. And as for what happened that night in the cage, well, I don't flatter myself that he can't get it elsewhere in a heartbeat.

I'm replaceable. Just another girl. Just another whore to look away from.

If we were *her* right now, would he act the same?

"What the hell's going on here, then?" Reeve plants his stocky legs apart. "Lovers' tiff?"

Eliza bristles, and I open my mouth to say *fuck off, you smarmy little weasel.*

But Lafayette cuts in. "Naturally," says he. "I was just wooing this lady over a man's bleeding corpse when you blundered in. That's Matthew Temple, the resident publisher, if you hadn't figured it out. I don't think it was suicide, do you?"

Reeve eyes Lafayette sourly. "A riot's going on out there. Isn't that more like your business, Royal Society?"

"Funny. I was about to ask the same of you. Isn't controlling an affray a police matter?" Lafayette fires me a blue-eyed warning shot. *Be quiet, Lizzie. Don't make a fuss . . .* but it's Eliza he ought to be glaring at.

Eliza, who's seething just beneath my skin. Who loathes this self-important, woman-hating squeezer with every muscle. It's men like him who keep her down. Who obstruct her at every turn, who think she's stupid and useless for everything but needlework and pushing out babes.

"Where's your pet doctor? Swap her already for this saucy bit of skirt?" Reeve gives a gruesome leer. "Can't say I blame you. What's your name, dolly?"

Mist. That's what's buzzing in front of my eyes. Boiling mist, the color of Temple's waistcoat. Eliza's furious. *I'm* furious. At Reeve, at Temple for dying on me, at everyone who ever looked at us and *assumed,* the way we assumed Temple was a shallow idiot with no conscience or politics just because he wrote lurid crime stories for a living.

I grin my best shit-eating grin. "Fuck you, copper. *That's* my name."

Reeve points his cigar at me. "Arrest that woman."

"Bastards, get your hands off me!" I struggle, but the constables are already grabbing me, pinning my sticky wrists together behind my back. "What you charging me with?"

"Foul language, disturbing the peace. Being a mouthy twat." Reeve brandishes his cigar. "Oh, and standing at a murder scene covered in blood, when you're already a suspect. Constables, I've reason to believe this woman's a murderess. Take her away."

I fight and kick and scream bloody rage, but there's two constables and only one me and I can't break free. "Remy, tell 'em it weren't me," I plead. "I didn't mean what I said. Make 'em let me go."

But Lafayette's gaze slides away, blue as aether flame with guilt, and he don't speak a word.

SHOPPED

• • •

THE BOW STREET CELLS STINK A LOT WORSE FROM the inside.

The crushers heave me in and slam the iron-barred door. I land on my chest, *splosh!* Mud and shit splatter my face. I crawl to my knees and let the curses blister off my tongue and roll after 'em up the stairs.

A bunch of greasy blokes is crammed into the cell next to me. We're separated only by bars, there's no wall, and I hear snoring, farting, the mutters and complaints of bored and thirsty men. That Geordie kid ain't here. Probably off somewhere getting the tripe beaten out of him.

I wipe muddy hands. "Baby Jesus," I mutter, "you lot stink like a sewer."

"Shut up, you moldy snatch." Sullen, from the rear of my murky cell. Great. I'm not alone.

"Piss off, Limpdick." My throat burns, swollen, as if a poisonous toad is buried in there. That final image of Lafayette—stripped of his courage, suspicion like a beacon on his face—rips me raw. I told him I'd betray his furry little secret to the Royal, and he *believed* me. My eyes ache for tears, but I won't weep.

I won't.

I clang my head against the bars, frustrated. The rust-coated iron is unbreakable in my fists. Luckily for me, no one's in this cell but me and Mr. Limpdick. They've emptied my pockets, taken my stiletto. Even pulled the pins from my hair, and it flops stinking onto my face. The light in here . . . well, there really ain't no light in here. Just a few queasy leaks, from cracks in the floorboards above. The stench of ordure, sweat, and bad breath makes me want to rake out my mouth with a brush.

I am, as they say at the Metropolitan Board of Works, knee-deep in shit.

I can't stay here. I'm weary, and already, Eliza mutters and wriggles beneath my skin. My bruised heart clenches for her. She won't never survive in here, with her stiff manners and nice ideas about fairness and equality. This dank, filthy place is Miss Lizzie's world, and I'm damned if I'll make Eliza suffer it just because I can't solve my own problems.

Solving problems, after all, is what I'm here for.

I grip the bars and bellow at the copper on duty at the top of the stairs. "Oi! You there! Mr. Crusher, sir!"

He don't answer. Probably used to prisoners hollering.

"Ain't no place for a lady down here, is it?"

The bloke in my corner guffaws. "Good thing you ain't no lady."

He's old, maybe forty, mud caked on his coat and at least a week of bristly gray beard. In here on his own. Hmm, thinks

Miss Lizzie. Could it be because them other blokes might tear strips off him? A snout, maybe, what stirs up radicals and then betrays them to the brass? Some corrupt putter-up what entraps good honest villains and sings like a canary? Or just some filthy sod like Billy Beane, whose crimes they despise?

I spit in his direction. "Oh, aye? A limp dick, that's your problem," I yell out again. "Constable, never mind. I were a-fearing for my poor woman's virtue, but there weren't no cause. This bloke's dick is just as limp as can be." And I kick mud at him, splashing his face with piss. "Couldn't raise a stand for the fanciest whore in London—"

He comes for me. I dance aside and slam his head into the bars. *Clang!* A fine noise he makes, too. "Ha ha! Beaten by a girl. What do you say to that, gents?"

The blokes in the next cell jeer and make ruckus. Any entertainment's good down here. I bang Limpdick's head again and knee him in the guts a few times. "Constable!" I holler. "Damsel in distress down here. You gonna be a hero?"

At last, the copper's coming down, boots splashing on the steps.

What's my plan now? No idea. I just hurl Limpdick aside—*splat!*—and get ready to run.

The policeman lifts his lamp to peer into my face, and the halo of light swings, crazy-like. It's Mr. Avid Reader, from the corridor outside the morgue. Blond boy, daft eyes. "What's going on here?"

"He attacked me," I announce. "What a beastly fellow. Let me out of 'ere, guvnor, or I declare I shan't last the night." The clowns in the next cell are laughing. Behind me in the mud,

Limpdick groans and bleeds, and hastily I kick him quiet and fan out my wet skirts to hide him.

The copper peers in, befuddled.

God spare me from idiots. I lean closer, show off the ripe female flesh at the top of my bodice. Ain't quite the same effect without the cherry satin, but a girl makes do. "I'd be ever so grateful, sir," I purr. "Maybe there's somewhere we can go. Y'know, private-like."

Sorry, sweet Eliza, but my life's at stake. *Our* life is at stake. If we have to suck and swallow our way outta here, we will. Just close your eyes and think of Chelsea.

The circus act over there hoot and call out crude suggestions. "Give it to her!" "Stuff her face with it!" "See if her arse is as smart as her mouth!" O-ho-ho, my sides are splitting.

The copper glances at me. Down at my chest. Back to me. Down at Limpdick, who's moaning and rolling about like a leper. Back to me. Pulls out his iron key ring and unlocks the door.

Yes. I simper and sashay out into the corridor. "Righto, let's get it over with—ugh!"

He just grabs my elbow and drags me off. Not towards the stairs. Further down into the dark, where stinking oily water drips down the walls and rats writhe in the mud, and there's a cell with no one in it.

Clunk! Now, *I'm* in it. Alone.

I grab the bars and hurl curses, but the copper just hooks his keys back onto his belt and stamps away, towards the far-distant mist of light.

Shit.

I yell a bit more, but no one takes notice, and eventually I give up. I can barely see my fingers in front of my nose. Rats nibble at my boots, and I kick 'em away. I'm weak, exhausted. This dank blackness chills me to the core. But I won't let despair overtake me, never mind that cold bitter crunch in my mouth and the roiling in my stomach that whispers *you're screwed, Miss Lizzie, so you are, screwed right to the wall, and how'd you like* them *apples?*

I won't.

But there ain't no escape, not from the Bow Street house of fun. I've naught to pick the keyhole with, and even if I could, there's a station full of crushers to worry about.

I'm here until they decide to come get me. And that could be a very long time.

I'm tired. My eyelids can barely stay apart. I swallow on cold slimy fear. Bear with me, Eliza. We've got each other. I'll hold on, just as long as I can. I promise.

But I'm so very tired.

And I fold my muddy skirts, and sit on my haunches in the corner, and stare stubbornly into chilly dark.

PRIMUM NON NOCERE

· • ·

L AMPLIGHT SHOCKED ELIZA AWAKE.

Doiiing! Her forehead clanged against the bars. She blinked gritty eyes. It was freezing, her clammy limbs chilled in the mud. The fetid cell's stench made her ill. Her mouth was parched, and hunger stirred in her stomach.

Lizzie must have fallen asleep. For how long? What was that light? Was Inspector Reeve coming to interrogate his prisoner?

"Lizzie!" she whispered fiercely. "Come back. I need you!"

And Lizzie struggled and kicked and pawed, but like a drowning woman, she couldn't break the surface.

Eliza almost chewed her tongue in frustration. It was the same with the elixir. Eventually, Lizzie exhausted herself. Like anyone, she needed sleep, time to recuperate.

Time Eliza didn't have.

The light brightened. Booted feet sloshed in the mud. Prisoners at the far end grumbled and swore. "Fuck off and let us sleep, you nosy swine," called one. Eliza scrambled up, wet skirts slopping around her ankles, and rats scattered.

First, a constable, holding a lantern aloft in the bluish light. Not the same man, but someone Eliza didn't know. At least that was something . . .

"Open up," ordered Captain Lafayette, halting before her cell. The light fractured in his eyes, cold like broken glass. "This woman's under investigation by the Royal. Give her to me."

Eliza gripped the bars urgently. "Captain, I must—"

"Silence," he snapped. Not angry. Disinterested. Bored, almost. As if he really didn't care. All in a day's interrogations. He glanced at her muddy skirts and ruined bodice, and it didn't even raise a flicker.

The constable unlocked the door, and before she could protest, Lafayette dropped a bag over her head.

She squealed, the sound amplified inside the rough linen. "What are you doing? Let me go!"

But she knew what he was doing.

Strong hands grabbed her elbows, bound her wrists efficiently with wire that bit into her soft skin, and escorted her firmly from the cell.

Up the steps, splashing through the mud, the musty smell of the bag stifling. At least this time, there was no cherry-blossom drug. The corridor above was silent. Perhaps the hour was very late.

Outside, where an icy breeze dragged at her hair, and down the steps. Her shins cracked into something sharp—a step?—and instinctively she climbed. Her rear hit a hard wooden bench, and a door clacked shut with a rattle of glass panes. A carriage.

"I'll take it from here, Constable." Lafayette's effortless authority sliced like sharpened steel, and the policeman muttered something and shuffled away.

Wheels and brassy feet clattered, and the carriage jerked forwards. Eliza's head swam with hunger and fatigue, and she fought to sit straight. Her wet skirts stank of grime even through the canvas bag. The wire on her wrists cut in too tight. Her fingers ached and puffed up, the circulation blocked.

She reached out with her feet, but met only empty air. The rumble of metal wheels on flagstones drowned out her ragged breathing. "Captain? What's going on?"

No answer. No hint of movement. But she couldn't help feeling that he was sitting only inches away. Watching her. Staring at her and saying nothing.

"Remy, please, we can talk about this like civilized people . . ." Her voice crisped, scraped away by despair. They'd gone far beyond civilized. She recalled her vision of Lafayette as a torturer—how *wrong* it had seemed—and crazy, high-pitched laughter choked her.

Wrong, indeed. Lafayette hadn't needed to stoop to torture, not with foolish Eliza. He already knew all her secrets, and he'd extracted them efficiently, callously, without a single scream or one solitary drop of blood. And now she'd burn, like Clara Morton, on a pyre in St. Paul's churchyard, only she'd be surrounded by a jeering death-hungry crowd.

What an accomplished, abominable man.

After a few minutes—an hour? who could tell?—the carriage lurched to a halt. The street was strangely quiet, as those same steely hands dragged her from the carriage, over a gutter, her wet skirts slapping against stone. Wind groaned, and the air sparkled with the fresh sensation of distant rain, prelude to a storm. A door creaked open. He pushed her into a close, threateningly warm room. Her heartbeat ran wild, and instinctively, she stumbled, desperate to delay whatever was about to happen.

The door tinkled shut, and he tore the bag away.

Apothecary's counter, rows upon rows of drawers, gleaming golden in warm firelight. The smell of herbs and alchemy, welcome after the bag. The blinds were drawn, and outside, it was dark. Distant thunder crashed, and the air stung with latent power.

Marcellus Finch blinked at her, his white hair sticking up like a bleached porcupine. He wore a purple velvet smoking jacket and a yellow scarf. "I say, young man, is this necessary?"

Dumbly, she stared back. The hairs on her arms crackled.

Lafayette cut the wire that bound her wrists—*snip!*—and eased it free. "Worked, didn't it?"

"But look at the poor girl. She's . . . *soiled.*"

Lafayette emerged into her view and shrugged sheepishly. "Sorry about that, Doctor. All the killer's teleportations have been to open spaces. I figured the cells were the safest place for you while I figured things out."

Eliza spat out the breath she'd been holding. Her heart still hammered, her limbs reluctant to obey her. Good thing, because she burned to hit him. Longed for violence with a ferocity that would have stunned Lizzie herself. She didn't know which was more infuriating: that he'd left her out of his plans or her absurd gratitude and relief that he hadn't betrayed her after all. Not to the police. Not to the Royal. Not to anyone.

Her eyes burned. Furious, she shoved Lafayette in the chest. "Safe? Is that what you call it?"

"I didn't know what else to do—"

"You let the police *arrest* me," she accused. "They threw me into a filthy cell riddled with rats and maggots and lice and God knows what else, not to mention killers and thieves. I'm freezing. I stink. Everything hurts. Just what, pray, have you been 'figuring out' that necessitated that?"

The Philosopher's portrait frowned down at her from the wall, and she wanted to tear it down and stamp on it. Lafayette didn't retaliate. It just made her itch harder. Punch him. Claw his face. Grab his pistol and fire. "Tell me what's going on," she demanded, "or so help me, I'll break your neck with my bare hands."

Lafayette only nodded towards Marcellus. "Mr. Finch has news."

"Hmm?" Finch blinked, befuddled. "Oh, yes. Your famous drug. Ha-ha! I've completed my analysis. Tricky little animal, too."

Eliza glared at Lafayette, but curiosity got the better of her. "Well?"

"It's a psycho-active alchemical preparation," supplied Finch. "Fire and mercury, a little wormwood, some other things. A poison, yes. In sufficient dosage, it stupefies in seconds."

"And in insufficient dosage?"

Finch beamed. "That's the best part, dear girl. An automaton effect! The mind is dissociated, but the body functions normally. When the patient awakens, they suffer drowsiness, confusion, memory loss. They don't remember what their body did without them."

"Like Lizzie . . ." She swallowed. "Like me, the night Billy was murdered."

"Excellent, say what?" Happily, Finch scratched his head, raising more tangles.

"And where would our killer obtain such a substance?"

"Well, either he's an alchemist . . ."

"Makes it himself?" Lafayette wrinkled his nose. "Busy chap, isn't he? Talented, too."

". . . or he ordered it from one." Finch yanked his fingers from a nest of knots and peered at the white strands caught under his nails. "Thing is, you see, the method is obsolete."

Eliza frowned. "So?"

"It's clumsy technique. That's why the effects are so alarming if it's overdosed. No one's done transformation this way for thirty years or more. If they had, I'd know about it. We alchemists have principles, you know. *Primum non nocere*— first do no harm, all that."

"So what, the killer's had it in storage for thirty years?"

"More or less." Finch gave a rueful shrug. "It's even possible . . . well, it could have been I who made it, by accident, back in the day. I wasn't always so careful."

"And who," cut in Lafayette, "would have stockpiled this drug, so long ago?"

"See, that's the thing." Finch picked at his fingernails, scowling at a broken one. "It's a very specialized psycho-active substance. Alters higher cognitive function. Used for targeted narco-analysis, on delusional or recalcitrant subjects."

Eliza blinked, baffled. "Narco-analysis? But—"

"Interrogation by hypnotic suggestion," explained Lafayette coolly. "We have such things at the Royal. Recalcitrant subjects being our speciality. What he means to say is: it's a truth drug."

"Just so." Finch grinned. "Brilliant, say what? A tool for torturers. And—"

"Mad-doctors," cut in Eliza suddenly, her bones rattling cold. "Delusional subjects. Hypnotic suggestion. Oh, my."

"What?" Lafayette and Finch spoke together.

"Mr. Fairfax's new experimental regime at Bethlem." A torrent of broken thoughts rushed out. "Electroshock, sensory stimulation, mind-altering substances. It's like my remedy, see? *Lux ex tenebris,* 'light from darkness.' Only my remedy *suppresses* the truth, whereas *this* drug . . ." Mr. Todd wired to the wall, drugged, hypnotized, plied with questions about blood and razors and exactly how long it takes a mutilated body to die . . .

"It doesn't matter," she cut herself off impatiently. Outside, lightning erupted, a brilliant triple flash. "Mr. Fairfax has supplies of this drug. He uses it to pierce his patients' delusional state and get at the truth. He's been interrogating the criminal lunatics, don't you see? Discovering the best method to kill!" She finished, breathless, but her blood stung, acid poison staining her heart.

If you want instruction, all you have to do is ask.

What a fool she'd been. Mr. Todd, who knew so much about the murderer. Because Mr. Todd knew exactly who the murderer was. And craftily he'd guided her to the solution, for sick and secret reasons of his own. It was all just a game.

Then again, Todd loathed Fairfax. What if . . .

Marcellus Finch stared, bewildered. "Oh, Jedediah. For shame. I thought we'd been through this with Victor."

Lafayette's eyebrow cocked. "Fairfax? But—"

"That's where I got the book about the teleporter," she explained. "His secret library at Bethlem."

A flintlock flash of vintage Lafayette smile. "Secret library? Do tell."

"Never mind," she said hastily. "He has the means to build the machine. He has access to the drug. What more?"

Lafayette considered. "You know what we saw at Temple's," he said at last. "Do you mean to say Fairfax is a—"

"What other explanation is there?" Eliza thought of Fairfax's mild eyes, his careful smile, and shuddered. He covered the monster inside well. "Perhaps he caught it from a patient. Maybe he even infected himself with the disease. You never could fault his experimental rigor."

"But what about the missing body parts?" asked Lafayette reasonably. "Fairfax is a surgeon. He can get all the cadavers he wants from medical schools, not to mention the dead from Bethlem itself. Why go to such dangerous lengths to collect these pieces?"

"Why, indeed?" murmured Finch.

Eliza's thoughts collided, fighting for an explanation that made sense. "Because they're special," she offered at last, desperate. "Because the parts themselves mean something. A ballerina's feet, a pickpocket's hands and eyes . . ."

Her throat corked. *He's making them perfect,* she'd told Mr. Todd. But it wasn't the victims who were being perfected. The victims were leftovers. Discarded. Their admirable parts removed and stored, and anything broken or unfit for the killer's purpose thrown aside . . .

Images jumbled and coalesced, like puzzle pieces clicking into place.

The cover of a crumpled pamphlet, a stiff-limbed figure in mummy wrappings stalking Waterloo. WALKING DEATH!! NONE CAN ESCAPE THE MONSTER!

A cadaver riddled with wires, striding jerkily across the amphitheater floor at the Crystal Palace. Matthew Temple's blithe grin. *The fellow's dead, isn't he? Can't bring him back to life with a spark up his arse.*

Mr. Todd's sly whispers, electric light glistening in his hair. *Your killer isn't angry or vengeful. He's hopelessly in love.*

That pale, wrinkled human brain, floating in the jar on Fairfax's desk.

Victor's ready. But we have to be quick. Before the decay sets in.

And the portrait of dead Lady Fairfax, edged in black . . .

Oh, my.

"Marcellus," she cut in, "who's Victor, and what's he ready for?"

"Say what?"

"'I thought we'd been through this with Victor,' you said, just a moment ago. Been through what?"

Lafayette touched her arm. "Am I missing something?"

"Victor," she insisted. "Enough secrets, Marcellus. Tell me."

Reluctantly, Finch sighed. "Well, it was a long time ago. I don't suppose it matters now." And he opened a drawer and plucked out a faded sepia photograph.

The same photograph that hung on the wall at Bethlem. A dusty laboratory, her father's associates, stiff in starched suits and cravats, pausing impatiently for the camera, as if they'd better things to do.

Finch laid the image on the counter and pointed to each figure in turn. "Here's me. Goodness, I'm a mere child, eh? This one with his nose in the air is Fairfax. The rest are all dead now. Henry, of course. The bright-faced fellow in the pale suit is Mr. Faraday, rest his tactless soul, and God rot the fools who burned him . . . present company excepted," he added hastily.

Lafayette managed a twist of smile. "Before my time, Mr. Finch. No offense taken."

"This older fellow here by the name of Davy, a friend of Faraday's. Fairfax electrocuted him once," Finch added moodily. "Set his hair on fire. Never saw much of him after that. And . . . yes. Here, on the end. Tall fellow in a top hat, looks like a foreigner."

Lightning flashed, illuminating the photograph. A thin man of middle age, pointed beard, dark hair curled in the European fashion. His wide eyes held a fanatical glow. He stood apart from the others, as if he wasn't quite part of the group. As if they feared him.

Finch tapped the man's face. "That's Victor. Not an Englishman, you know, the most frightful Teutonic accent. Spent years in Bavaria as a student. Family seat some crumbling stone pile outside Geneva. I heard he died abroad . . . let's see . . . twenty years ago?" He gave a sickly grin. "Well, there you go. Old memories, eh? Nothing else to see." He began to return the picture to the drawer.

Eliza grabbed Finch's arm, desperate. "No. I read his diary. The one with the electrical teleporter in it."

"Don't know what you're on about, dear girl. I say, is that the time?"

"In German, to be sure," she persisted, "so mostly I looked at the pictures. Title page torn out, half the book missing? Locked in a secret cell at Bethlem? Ringing any bells?"

Finch ruffled his hair, sheepish. "Oh, dear. I told Fairfax to get rid of that when Henry passed. Jedediah, I said to him, Jedediah, you foolish old fox, are you mad? We can't keep this now, not after what we've done—"

"And what exactly did you do, Marcellus?" She felt sick. Bells clanged in her skull, as if she were locked in the belfry while a frenzied mob pulled the ropes. "Don't lie to me anymore. I know the pair of you covered up my mother's death. What did you do that drove Henry to . . . be consumed?" *His death,* she'd been about to say.

Finch's gaze slid away, sullen. "Ask Eddie. He was heartbroken. It was his idea."

Mr. Hyde's words razored into her memory, ripping flesh from bone. *Oh, how she died, that woman.*

Emphasis on the *died*. Oh, how she *died,* and *died,* and *died . . .*

"The diary's back half was torn out," she stammered. "Wh—what was in it?"

Finch didn't reply.

"It was a different kind of electrical machine, wasn't it?" she accused. "Animal electricity, like Dr. Percival's. The kind that animates flesh. Tell me!"

"You really don't want to know—"

"I was there, Marcellus!" Her voice rose, frantic, and Lafayette put a hand on her arm. She shook him off. Sucked in a breath she had no room for. "I was outside Mother's bedroom that night. I heard everything."

"Ah." Finch pursed his lips. "I see."

"You mentioned Victor's name, and Henry hit you. 'Never,' he said, 'not for her.'"

Finch rubbed his jaw, as if in rueful memory. "Fellow was upset. Recently bereaved. Not himself. You know how it is."

"But you did it anyway, didn't you?" Crazy laughter hurt her throat, but it was distant, echoing pain. As if it wasn't really her throat. "You and Victor and Eddie Hyde. You brought Madeleine back to life. And Henry had to kill her all over again."

"Victor did it anyway," retorted Finch. "Eddie was brutal with grief. Homicidal. A difficult man to deny. And Victor was a scientist, not a coward. He didn't give up on his experiments just because things went wrong—"

"Wrong?" Eliza tugged poor Mr. Temple's pamphlet from her bodice—WALKING DEATH!! NONE CAN ESCAPE THE MONSTER!—and shook it before Finch's nose. "He was resurrecting the dead! Making them into . . . *things!* What on earth isn't 'wrong' about that?"

Lafayette blinked, as he'd woken from an incomprehensible dream. "I'm sorry, can someone please explain what just happened?"

Eliza folded her arms and stared at Finch, merciless. "Mr. Fairfax is building his dead wife's brain a new body. A body made from the best parts of other women. He always did esteem her above all others, didn't he, Marcellus?"

Finch snorted. "Esteem? Worshipped the floor she crossed. His third wife, you know. The others barely caught his attention, but this one . . ." He shook his head. "Wept over her body for weeks when she passed. Smell was terrible."

"Because he couldn't make Victor's machine work, could he? He couldn't resurrect her in time."

"There was no machine," explained Finch, "not anymore. Henry destroyed it, after Madeleine. In any case, it requires quite astounding voltages. Victor's technology was before its time. The batteries Fairfax had just weren't up to it. And Victor and Faraday couldn't help him, you see. Victor had escaped to the Continent. Ended up in the Arctic, so I heard, on some wild chase or other. Mr. Faraday wasn't so lucky."

"So Fairfax has had to build another, all by himself," mused Eliza. "And he's been testing it out on cadavers from Bethlem. Hence the 'Walking Death'!"

She looked again at the lurid cover drawing and bit her lip. She could still feel Temple's blood, gushing hot over her wrists. "For once, he wasn't making things up," she murmured. "Poor Matthew."

Lafayette tugged at a curl over his ear. "So Temple found out, and Fairfax got rid of him?"

"It appears so."

"Then what about Billy Beane? What's Fairfax's interest there?"

"I should very much like to ask him." She glanced at the covered window, where lightning erupted, the thunder boiling ever closer. The storm was about to break. A foul night, indeed. She stuffed the paper back into her bodice. "No time like the present. Are you coming, Captain?"

"To Bethlem? On a night like this? Voltage exploding everywhere, thunder bellowing, lunatics going doubly off their heads?" Lafayette's eyes glinted eagerly. "Do you really want to see what Fairfax is up to tonight?"

Her blood thrilled, a cocktail of excitement and dread. "Resurrecting a stitched-up corpse with his wife's brain inside? Absolutely I do. It's potentially the ground-breaking experiment of our age."

"Well, when you put it like that . . ."

"The end of mystical superstition and irrational fear of death," she added. "If you care about that sort of thing. Oh, and the chance to bring a ruthless murderer to justice. Wouldn't miss it for the world."

"How inappropriately fascinating."

"Thank you."

Lafayette grinned. "Telling, that you should think it worthy praise."

"For shame, Captain," she scolded lightly. "I fancy it's the highest praise of all."

WHOM THE GODS WOULD DESTROY

•••

OUTSIDE, THE BOILING SKY TORE ASUNDER. Blinding light flashed on windows, and street-lights popped dark. Thunder crashed, so close that the current zinged Eliza's tongue and her ears throbbed. Wind howled down New Bond Street, dragging leaves and hats and other refuse in its wake. The few brave folk who were out scuttled for cover.

A pair of horses bucked, snapping their traces with no one to calm them. A parked electric carriage crackled bright with over-voltage, and *bang!* the coil exploded, blue current arcing over its metal frame. Above distant rooftops, forked lightning struck the new clock tower on the Palace of Westminster, setting it alight.

The aether-bright wind sharpened Eliza's senses like a drug, burning her sinuses clear. She struggled to hold down windblown skirts. Lafayette grabbed her elbow. "I don't fancy getting fried," he yelled. "Let's ride."

Next to them, a bay mare tossed her head and rolled her black eyes. She'd already halfway broken her harness, the wooden shafts cracked to splinters. Lafayette drew his saber and sliced through the leather lines, *swick! swock!* He sheathed the blade and vaulted onto the mare's back. The horse wheeled and kicked in protest, but he held on with hands and thighs. A bizarre feat of balance and skill.

"Show-off," she muttered, but the sound was ripped away by the wind.

He wrapped the broken reins around one hand and reached down to her as the horse snorted and curvetted. "Madam," he yelled.

Eliza gripped his wrist, and he hauled her up in front of him, catching her around the waist. *Smack!* Her backside banged painfully on a harness buckle. The horse squealed and bucked, threatening to tip them both off.

"Hold on, if you don't mind terribly," called Lafayette shortly, as the world rocked and he fought to bring the horse under control. "I believe I'll need both hands."

She obeyed, wrapping her arms around him. Beneath her, his thighs strained to keep him in his seat. His heartbeat was swift and even. His breathing was controlled but exhilarated. He was warm, strong, talented, confident to the point of easy recklessness. Everything that terrified her.

And everything Lizzie longed for.

The revelation struck her momentarily dumb. "Uh," she said lamely, struggling to recover her wits. "Are you sure this is a good idea?"

Lightning lit his grin devilish, and the wolf glimmered in his eyes. "Madam, I charged the field at Samarkand, outnumbered ten to one beneath a barrage of enemy guns. I can surely cope with a blushing embrace from you." And he wheeled the mare around to run.

Clattering hooves, swirling wind, crashing thunder. Roof tiles and thatching blew free. Carriages lay overturned or abandoned, debris tumbling along deserted streets. The air whipped taut and angry, ready to crack. Eliza's hair prickled with static, and her nose stung with the sparkling scent of ultimate power.

Her belly ached, and she realized she was laughing. It was good laughter, from deep inside. The way Lizzie laughed.

By the Houses of Parliament, rioters' barricades lay deserted. The black Thames raged, whipped to froth. As they hurtled across an eerily empty Westminster Bridge, she risked an upwards glance. The storm illuminated Lafayette's visage with a weird, almost fey radiance. Sweat and raindrops glittered like tiny gemstones in his hair. He spared a moment to catch her eye, and his lips formed a word she couldn't hear. "Madwoman."

"Headed to the right place, then," she called back, as they dashed off the bridge and plunged into darkened Lambeth. The streets were eerie, howling, trees swaying and groaning. Lightning sheeted above domed Bethlem, licking the wicked spikes on the wall with fire.

The gate lay ajar, unattended. Lafayette skidded the horse to a halt in the windswept courtyard. The whinnying mare's hooves clattered, but she kept her feet. Eliza jumped down, and he jumped down behind her. The horse snorted and sidestepped, unsure what to do.

Briskly, Eliza tugged her skirts into place. "How invigorating," she said coolly, but she knew her eyes were bright, her cheeks flushed.

"Thank you. Ah," he added, forestalling her protest with a grin. "Allow me my shining moment, if you please. There's no chance you can pretend that wasn't a compliment."

"I was referring to the horse, but by all means—"

Lightning lashed again, closer, and the air strung taut on a human scream that echoed on after the thunder. Eliza and Lafayette looked at each other and sprinted for the door.

Inside, a zoo raged. The lights had gone out, and howls and screeches pierced the dark. Someone sobbed. A woman whooped in a high-pitched witch's laugh. Glass shattered, metal screeched, wood banged and split.

Through the archway, beneath the leering naked statues of Mania and Dementia with their contorted marble muscles. Their dead eyes followed her, splashed in stormlight. Eliza took the stairs three at a time, grabbing her damp skirts, heedless of bared ankles. The place seemed deserted, filled only with noise that shrank her skin cold. On a night like this, the keepers had likely fled for their homes. Left the lunatics to their madness. They'd clear away the mess in the morning. Easier than listening to these insane, godforsaken sounds. Stand here too long, and you'd go mad, too.

If she wasn't already.

Eliza and Lafayette reached the first landing, where the wards peeled off left and right. On the men's side, a malformed man banged his bulbous head into the floor, grunting with each bloody smack of bone. On the women's side, Annie the pig girl clawed at the bars, weeping. Blood dripped from her snout. "It weren't me!" she howled. "Not this time. I never."

At her feet lay pretty Miss Lucy's severed head.

"Good God." Lafayette's expression was grim. "What is Fairfax doing to these people?"

"Upstairs," yelled Eliza. "His new laboratory, where he performs the treatments."

"Lead on."

Ahead, a single gaslight still flickered, a cruel will-o'-the-wisp, leading the way to treasure or ruin. Another flight of stone steps. That scream again, ragged like torn silk; the echo of rough-edged laughter. On the second floor, a long corridor stretched, lit only by stray lightning and the eerie bruised aura of storm clouds.

Ahead, the door to Fairfax's laboratory loomed, a double edifice of steel-banded wood. Light glimmered under the door.

Lafayette flexed his fingers, eager. "Sword or pistol?"

"Excuse me?"

He drew his weapons, one in each hand, *slice-snap!* "On second thought, don't answer that. This is more your size." And he tossed her the pistol.

She caught it. It fit smoothly in her palm, pleasantly heavy. She tested the spring lock, *click-clack!* and the purple coil made a satisfying *buzz*. "Are you certain I won't shoot *you*?"

"I'll take my chances."

"Brave of you."

"Yes, well. I'm a cursed ex-army monster-hunter moonlighting as a Royal Society investigator, not an ornament." He flexed his fingers around his saber's grip. "Shall we?"

Eliza edged up to the door. Pushed on it. It wasn't barred. Softly, she gripped the cold iron-ringed handle and turned.

Inside, a dim anteroom stretched into the gloom. Wild laughter—or was it screaming?—echoed. Somewhere, a rat scuttled.

Cupboards and shelves lined the walls, stacked neatly with bottles of chemicals, pipettes and retorts, apparatuses for operations and blood transfusions, a case of surgical instruments, a whetstone for sharpening knives. Drugs in glass ampoules, buckled leather garments, hoods and shackles, hoop sticks and whips and electric stingers. Metal rattles, whistles, a set of bongo drums, a gleaming silver trumpet, all designed to make noises a patient in restraints could not escape.

Lafayette made a disgusted face and mimed smashing the lot of it. Eliza shuddered in agreement and crept on. At the end, a doorway led into the laboratory proper. Her nose tingled with acid, phosphorus, sulphur, the tang of aether.

Softly, she padded up and peered inside. Gaslights gleamed on broken plastered walls and exposed pipes. As if the room was not yet renovated. The ceiling vanished into cobwebbed darkness. Opaque shutters were fitted tightly over the windows. In one corner hunkered an empty whirling chair: a wooden seat pinned to an apparatus that forced it to spin at the turn of a wheeled handle. A square porcelain bath lay sunken deep into the floor, a single dark plughole in the bottom. An ice bath, empty for now.

Ice, thought Eliza distantly. *He has an ice machine. That's how he's preserving the parts.*

In the center, partially hidden by a black rubber screen, an angular aetheric generator hulked on a wheeled trolley. Beside it, a wooden bed frame. Curly wires hung suspended between them. Electricity crackled and popped, and she could smell singed skin . . .

In front of the generator capered the tall, sticklike figure of Mr. Fairfax. Fiddling with levers and dials, steel-gray hair swept back, immaculate white collar and charcoal tie. His shirtsleeves were neatly rolled up, and dark wire-rimmed spectacles protected his eyes from aether flash. He rubbed his hands and twirled a dial meticulously, peering close to ensure accuracy.

On the bed frame, laughing like a demon, squirmed Mr. Todd.

Eliza halted, chilled yet burning. Cruel wire bound his bleeding wrists to the frame. He wore the same clothes—like a photograph, forever trapped in what he'd worn that night in Chelsea—and his shirt was even filthier now, stained with bloodied sweat. A broad leather band wrapped his temples, flattening his wild crimson hair. Fine filaments of wire protruded from the leather. As Eliza watched, Fairfax tightened a screw where the electrodes pierced the leather, then flipped a lever on his console.

Blue fire crackled along the wires. Mr. Todd's body arched, bound at wrists and ankles, a grotesque puppet with the strings yanked tight. Every muscle contracted, strained beyond endurance, for surely no one could endure this for long. Not even Mr. Todd, a man more used to strangeness and pain than anyone she'd ever met.

Fairfax flicked his switch again, and Todd collapsed, gasping bloody laughter.

Eliza reeled, momentarily blind. *Drowning Ophelia, floating in black water. A sliced wisp of her own hair, drifting to her shoulder. A whisper burning her ear, smooth steel glittering in her palm. Let me show you . . .*

"Hurt him again and I'll melt your face off."

Her own voice shocked her to consciousness. Six feet from Fairfax, pistol aimed at his head. The pistol's coil buzzed alight, primed, the trigger snug in the curl of her finger.

Lizzie? She was breathing hard, barely in control. The rage charring her soul felt all too real. *What are we doing? You awake?*

Never me, returned Lizzie stoutly. *But you go right ahead. Hang the felons, burn 'em, let the surgeons chop 'em up. That's different. I don't care what your Mr. Todd's done, he don't deserve this. No one does.*

Fairfax tugged off his dark glasses and smiled that fragile smile. "Dr. Jekyll, how surprising. Is there a problem?"

"Step away from the machine." Her voice was steady, in control. "Now, Mr. Fairfax. Or so help me, I'll shoot you where you stand." More like something Lizzie would say. But she didn't need Lizzie, not now.

Not when Mr. Todd lay bleeding.

Todd coughed. He couldn't turn his head, not in that evil leather contraption, but he was laughing again. Shrill, wheezing laughter that grated. "How about it, Fairfax?" he rasped. "A duel to the death? I know where I'd wager."

Eliza circled, keeping Fairfax in her sights. "Move," she ordered again, gesturing with the weapon. Something didn't seem right. She couldn't see any other apparatus, body parts, Victor's horrid machine. But she didn't dare look away.

Fairfax edged away from the controls. Outside, lightning crashed, and lunatics howled in far corridors like beasts.

"Capital," announced Todd. He spat out another mouthful of blood and smacked his lips. "Most excellent. Now, if someone could kindly unwire me—"

"Not so fast." Lafayette tickled Todd's throat with his sword point and winked. "Nice shackles. Do they hurt?"

Todd glared up at him, cross-eyed. "You again. Honestly, Eliza, the company you keep. Strangely enough, lapdog, no, they don't. Forgive me if I'm a whisker more concerned about the wires he's jabbed into my brain. Now, if you don't mind—"

"Todd, be silent," snapped Fairfax. Sweat beaded on his impeccable forehead. "Put the pistol down, Eliza. What's this about?"

"You know what it's about." She steadied her shaking grip, but indignation scorched her blood. How she longed to fire, watch him burn and scream and suffer for what he'd done. "Where is she?"

"Who?"

"Lady Fairfax."

His face darkened. "How dare you?"

"Brain in a jar. Severed body parts. Where's the machine?"

The storm raged, glimmering brightly in the crack between the shutters. The anteroom door clattered, and William Sinclair burst in, carrying a load of glass pots and rubber tubes. His hair was damp, his dark coat spotted with rain. "I say, Mr. Fairfax, this transfusion kit is not the one we . . ." He halted, nonplussed. "Good God. Eliza, what on earth is going on?"

"Will, stay back," Eliza warned. "Put that down, whatever it is."

Will obeyed. His equipment clattered into a pile on the floor.

Lafayette backed away from Todd, sword leveled. "It's getting awfully crowded in here, Doctor. Make it fast."

Fairfax frowned. "Eliza, are you quite well? You look fevered. What's this machine you're speaking of?"

"Victor's animal electricity machine," she insisted. "The one that brought Madeleine Jekyll back to life."

Mr. Todd giggled. "Well done, my sweet. I knew you'd see the light. Do you recognize that scent, lapdog? Very like your own, eh?"

"Shut up," ordered Lafayette, but his voice was oddly strained.

Fairfax cleared his throat. "Madam," he said mildly, as if calming a violent patient, "such a vile contraption no longer exists. Your father's experiments are over. I know this is hard for you to accept, and heaven knows that idiot Finch isn't helping matters—"

"Show her the machine, Mr. Fairfax."

The sound of Will's voice snapped Eliza's head around.

He was walking towards Fairfax. Calm, unthreatening, one hand forward. "Come, sir, no point carrying on. She knows. Show her the machine."

Fairfax laughed. Hollow laughter, like a man who'd lost his way. "Sinclair, have you finally gone out of your mind? The only machines I possess are right here. You know that. Electroshock and sensory pressure. Look." And he pointed at the rack of aetheric cells, so lately Mr. Todd's torment.

"The machine, Sir Jedediah," Will repeated, hypnotic. He moved another step closer, stormlight tarnishing his hair with copper. "In the secret laboratory, hidden in the dome where the lightning will strike. Where the bodies are on ice, and everything's prepared."

Fairfax's face drained like death.

Lightning sheeted, directly overhead. Current enlivened the air, sharp like metal on Eliza's tongue. "It's ended, Mr. Fairfax," she called. "No one else need be hurt."

Wildly, Fairfax turned from Eliza to William and back. He stuttered, at a loss. His mouth opened and closed. "Eliza—"

"Don't dissemble, Fairfax. You know what she's talking about." Lightning flung Will's face into sharp relief, an eerie sketch of shadows and light. And then, he grinned, ghastly. "Oh, wait. That's right. *You don't.*"

And he swept a burning arc-pistol from his pocket and shot Fairfax in the face.

THEY FIRST MAKE MAD

• •

ZZAP! THE SHOT FLARED, DAZZLING. FAIRFAX'S limbs jerked in the throes of electric fit, and his hair caught fire. His cheeks melted and bubbled. Smoke hissed from his burning clothes, bringing the sweet smell of scorched flesh. He opened his mouth to scream, but before he hit the floor, he was dead.

Blue static crackled over his corpse, and wisps of smoke curled upwards.

Eliza froze. Mr. Todd grinned. Lafayette lunged for Will, saber a-flash.

"Not so fast," said Will calmly, and fired.

But the shot fizzled, only a faint flash. The pistol hadn't had time to recharge. The weak electric fireball hit Lafayette in the chest and he fell, jerking, unconscious. A lick of flame crept into his hair and blew out.

And Will turned to her.

Eliza fought for her wits. *Lizzie, come back. Where are you?*

Well, hell, said Lizzie dryly. *Will Sinclair. Never can pick 'em. Shoot the little squeezer.*

Eliza fired.

Zzzp-crack! But her hand was numb, and the shot missed Will by inches and crackled into the wall behind him. Damn. She clenched her grip tighter. "Get back."

"Do you really want to shoot me, Eliza?" Will's own pistol glowed brighter by the second, recharging. "After all we've shared? That upsets me. Truly."

"Good question, William!" called Mr. Todd from his bed frame. "Straight to the point."

"Shut up!" yelled Will. He paced, up and down, yanking his hair in one fist. Lightning crashed again, and his eyes flared, unnaturally golden. "Do you know what it's like, Eliza? To have that *person* in your head? Whispering in your *ear*? Giving you *ideas*? Gnawing at your *brain,* every day, with his *questions* and his *temptations* and never a moment's *peace*?" He kicked at the equipment on the floor, scattering it with an un-William-like curse.

"Typical," muttered Todd. "Blame me for everything. 'Mr. Todd made me do it!' Honestly, you'd think me the Devil himself." But his crafty grin spoke otherwise.

Eliza searched frantically for courage. No time to waste. Whose pistol would recharge first? "Give up," she said desperately. "It's over. Whatever you've done, we can . . ."

"Oh, I don't think it's over." Will smiled, his same old boyish smile, but now it glittered, unhinged. To think she'd ever thought him pleasant-looking. "I've only just begun. And I am *so* pleased you're here at last. I've been waiting for you."

"Why?" she spat. "Am I the last piece of your abomination? Which part of me will you chop off? Or will you just light up my corpse with electrical fluid and see what happens?"

Will gaped, incredulous. "Don't be ridiculous. Self-improvement, Eliza. I want you to be the best you can be. I have all the parts ready. I collected the last one just tonight. This is all for you, my darling."

A hissing serpent coiled cold in her belly.

A ballerina's legs, talented where Eliza was clumsy. A pickpocket's skilled hands—and her eyes, too, sharp where Eliza's were weak.

"No." The world telescoped, sucking to a tiny vanishing point. Her voice echoed, faint and far away. "No, you can't."

"*Eliza . . .*" Mr. Todd, speaking her name, *sotto voce*. She didn't turn. Couldn't move.

"*Eliza, look at me.*"

"Fairfax had it all wrong, you see." William scratched his hair, which was sprouting longer in patches, a coarse yellow mat. "Completely removing the brain is a mistake. Vital connections are severed. So that's why I'll need your entire head. I hope you don't mind," he added. "I could have found you a new face, but . . . well, I'm rather fond of the old one." He blushed. "You'll be so beautiful at our wedding, my love."

"Wedding?" she repeated stupidly.

"*Eliza.*" Todd again, calm, insistent. The voice of sanity.

"We needn't accept your failings anymore," said Will earnestly. "You can change. You can be a new person! And I'm going to help you. Now"—he kicked up the fallen saber on the toe of his boot, flicked it into his hand, and jabbed the point into unconscious Lafayette's throat—"will I drop my pistol, do you think? Or should you?"

Lizzie cursed, and Eliza fought to steady her aim. "Let him go, or I swear—"

"You know what happens if you fire. My muscles contract. *Boiing!*" Mockingly, Will faked a spasm, twisting the sword point. Blood trickled down Lafayette's neck.

Lizzie yowled, an angry cat. *Get away from him, you ugly circus freak!* Eliza stumbled a step forwards.

Will laughed. And when he laughed, the beast sprang alive. His pupils flared, and sharp wolfish teeth glinted at the corners of his mouth. "He'll be dead before I fall. I had to kill Matthew when he discovered my secret, and Matthew was my *friend*. Don't imagine I'll hesitate now. Or, you can come quietly. Your choice."

The impassive, rational part of Eliza whispered deadly sense. This was her chance to be rid of Lafayette. The monster who knew her secret. Who'd seduced Lizzie, made her weak. Not as if it'd be murder. Just let him die, and she'd be safe forever . . .

Lizzie growled, furious. *Don't you frickin' dare . . .* Eliza shook herself, mortified. Lafayette had lied for her more than once. Put his own life at risk. She couldn't betray him now.

"*Eliza.*" At last, Mr. Todd's voice broke through Eliza's trance. Wildly, she glanced around.

Todd jerked his chin minutely towards Will, and his red lips mouthed two words.

Trust me.

Her thoughts knotted, wet and woolly. Trust him to do what?

Stiffly, she uncocked her pistol, *hiss-flick*. The purple glimmer faded. She tossed it aside. It bounced away.

Will grinned and dropped the saber. "Knew you'd see it my way."

He stuffed his pistol into his pocket and plucked a brown leather garment from the floor. Evidently, the restraining coat Mr. Todd had worn on his way to the lab. Will bundled Lafayette into it, efficiently binding the captain's limp arms to his sides and buckling the garment at the back.

Lafayette stirred groggily. Will tested his handiwork with a few experienced tugs. "Very good."

Lafayette snarled, wolflike, so baleful that his blue eyes caught fire, and sharp teeth glinted at the corners of his mouth. "You'd better hope so."

"I say, lapdog," called Todd, "that jacket's mine. I shall want that back clean. William, don't say you'll leave me here. I want to watch."

Will shot him a cunning glance. "Oh, you'll be watching, Mr. Todd. Wouldn't want you to miss a thing." He tossed Eliza a pair of wire cutters. "If you please."

Mr. Todd winked up at her. His hair was singed, blood-stained where the twin electrodes pierced his temples. Dimly, she recalled lectures on brain anatomy. Frontal lobes. Impulse control. Just perfect.

His soft hair tickled her fingertips. She eased one wire free. *Schlllp!* Two inches deep, almost too fine to see, coated in bloody fluid. The second electrode, opposite side, just the same.

Her stomach lurched. She wanted to vomit. She wanted to blot the blood from his temples, bathe him clean . . . Quickly, she tugged off the leather strap around his head and hurled it away as if it were a dead thing. Disgusting.

"You're very kind." Mr. Todd's murmur tingled her spine. She didn't dare catch his eye.

Snip! Snap! Snick! His wire restraints parted in her clippers. Todd sat up, rubbing his bleeding wrists, and swiftly Will pulled his arms behind his back and clapped him into a pair of steel manacles with a sturdy lock attached.

Will ran his finger inside one steel cuff. "Not too tight, Mr. Todd?"

"Perfectly fine, William." Todd clambered off the bed frame and popped his neck bones with a *crunch!* Wriggled his bloodstained clothes into place. Puffed a singed crimson strand away from his eyes, and grinned at no one in particular. "Capital. Shall we be off? I do so love a wedding, don't you?"

LUX EX TENEBRIS

• • •

WITH EFFICIENCY BORN FROM YEARS OF TENDING the unruly, William herded them all up the final stairway, a narrow one that twisted beneath rafters and around hidden corners. Mr. Todd first, humming a little ditty under his breath. Then Lafayette, stumbling. Will prodded his pistol into the small of Eliza's back. "Up, my lady. It isn't far."

Eliza's mind scrambled for a plan. Cut and run? Even if she could overpower Will and his pistol . . .

Lizzie snarled like a beast. *We ain't leaving Remy behind with these crazy folk. You're the clever one. Think of sommat else.*

"Will, listen," Eliza began desperately, "we don't have to do this. We can—"

"You never talked nonsense before." Will's tone sharpened. "Please don't spoil things now."

He pushed her through a small wooden door at the top of the stairs. A large area of attic floorboards had been cleared beneath the dome's inner structure, wooden beams and rafters exposed.

A vast door in the dome had been dragged aside by pulleys, and wind groaned and whistled through the gaps. At the top, a copper lightning rod stabbed to the sky, attached to a web of grounding wires. A massive aetheric generator sat bolted to the floor, and blue-white current crackled between copper points in the smell of ozone. Stinging raindrops swirled, mixed with flying leaves and grit. Lightning splashed like paint thrown at a wall. The air shook with thunder. And still the storm grew fiercer.

Will laughed, exulting in the weather's power. His eyes shone yellow, luminous in the stormlight. Where had he caught his curse? Attacked, like Lafayette? A diseased cadaver at medical school? Or from a patient, some hybrid mutation of the hunger that infected poor Miss Lucy? Maybe she'd never know.

"Perfect!" Will yelled over the wind. "Mr. Todd, sit over there, if you please. Take that stinking dog with you. I'll deal with him when I'm done."

"Try it, puppy," growled Lafayette. "I'll tear your skin off and eat it in strips. Seems I'm not a pack animal."

"Oh, calm down, lapdog." Todd took a seat on a bench and hooked his foot around Lafayette's ankle to make him follow suit. "Sit, there's a good boy. Have a chocolate drop."

Above, an intricate network of ropes and pulleys had been strung. Wires, cables, chains, and counterweights, all connected to a contraption hidden beneath a vast tent of white sheets. Will ran across the room—or rather, shambled, half-man, half-beast, wriggling his misshapen shoulders, his wolfen knee joints popping inside his trousers—and hauled on a rope. The sheets dragged upwards and blew aside.

An oblong metal frame hung from four chains, one at each corner. It held the naked, headless body of a woman. She was starved, ribs standing out, but Eliza could tell she'd once been voluptuous, with curving hips and breasts . . .

Miss Lucy. Poor, hungry, headless Lucy, who'd lusted after Will's blood. She'd made an easy target, in the end.

A line of stitching—a surgeon's sutures, neat and clean, no madman's frenzied effort at sewing—circled each forearm. Another line around each thigh. Blood oozed from the junctions of flesh. The feet—Miss Pavlova's feet—were scarred and unlovely, tortured by years of effort. Sally's hands were thin, the nails broken but meticulously cleaned.

Lucy's body—*the creature*—was clamped to the frame by iron straps that wrapped the chest and thighs. From a metal node above, dozens of wires hung like a bed's canopy, feeding into the corpse, via copper clamps and spikes that pierced her flesh. A helmeted mask of buckled leather sat ready on a table. Countless hair-fine electrodes sprang from it in a bright steel flower.

Beside the creature lay a full-length operating table, empty. Shining steel, a gutter down each side to catch the blood. Suturing tools—thread, curved needles, scissors—were laid out meticulously. Surgical instruments, too. Scalpels, clamps and tourniquets, a bone saw, a long-bladed knife. Swabs for blood were piled neatly. On the floor sat a bucket half-filled with sand.

Instruments for amputation.

In a jar of preserving fluid floated a pair of bloodied eyeballs. Ragged red nerves dangled. The irises were green, pale, startled. Mortified. As if their owner's last thoughts were fixed there forever.

All the creature needed was a head.

Transfixed, Will stroked the creature's pale thigh. "Isn't she lovely? It took me a few practice pieces to get the stitching just right. Oh, you needn't worry," he added, seeing Eliza's expression. "About our marriage bed, I mean. I've tested it most scientifically. This body and I have a certain . . . affinity. I'm confident it'll be the same with your head on."

Unwelcome images flooded, of Will and Lucy, doing sordid things in the filthy darkness of the asylum. Bared flesh, juddering teeth, grunts . . . "You horrid boy," she burst out. "You're supposed to be taking *care* of them."

Will wrenched her elbow cruelly. "Don't test me," he hissed, spit flecking from his growing teeth. "This is all for you. I loathe ingratitude."

Red rage boiled over her eyes. Her shadow swelled like a monster, bursting out, *I* burst out, juddering and fuming and growling alive and fuck me, I've had enough of this rotten little weasel's attitude.

"Oh, aye?" says I. "Well, I loathe dirty murdering squeezers who screw sick girls for a thrill. How'd you like *them* apples?"

"Oh, no, you don't." Sinclair's face twists, and his nose pulls longer, into a snout. "I killed Billy Beane for her sake, not yours. Bring her back."

I cackle, just to enrage him more. "Eliza don't want you, idiot. Never did, never will."

He shakes me, growling, his hair sprouting wild. "Bring her *back,* whore."

"Look at them two. Go on, look." I jerk my chin at Athos and d'Artagnan over there on the bench. "More wit and grace in their spit than in the whole of your weedy little idiot's body. Jesus in a gin palace, do you really think *you* could win a woman like her? Don't make me heave."

"I want Eliza. Bring her back!" He drags me towards the operating table. Damn, he's stronger than he looks. I kick and lose my footing, but he just wraps a fist in my hair and keeps right on dragging. Grabs a bottle of golden liquid, uncorks it with his teeth. Slops some onto a swab and forces it over my mouth.

My blood howls. It's the drug. The knock-out medicine. I snarl and spit and shake my head like an angry lion, but he smothers my nose and jams his knee into my guts.

Uhhh! My lungs cramp, and I can't help but take a fat. gulp . . .

But it ain't cherry blossoms.

It's bitter, like Eliza's remedy. Like the stuff she gives to the lunatics to keep them calm. To banish their shadow. *Lux ex tenebris.*

Oh hell.

I fight. I really do. But no matter how much I cough and spit, I can't stop the drug seeping into my blood. My vision pinwheels. I can't breathe. I'm shrinking, the shadow is writhing and screaming, smaller and smaller, and like a black rubber ball it squeezes unbearably tight . . .

And *pop!* Eliza's eyes snapped open.

She wriggled furiously in Will's grip. *Lizzie!*

But Lizzie was gone. Eliza was on her own.

Will grinned, ghoulish. "Better. Your Mr. Finch truly is a genius. It's fleeting, unfortunately, with painful side effects. But it's amazing stuff." He helped her stand and smoothed her skirts for her. "Come, it's time. This won't take long. I've practiced over and over, you know. I can take off a head in two minutes."

Human heads in the Thames! recalled Eliza dully. The Moorfields Monster. He'd been practicing, all right.

"Trickier when the patient's alive," added Will, "but still, one adapts and overcomes." And he ushered her towards dead Lucy and the glistening operating table.

"Let go!" She struggled. No use. This beast-Will had a grip like a brass Enforcer. Lightning erupted, brain-rattling, and blue current crackled around the dome's rim. The floor quaked. Will paid no heed. When he reached the table, he bent to lift her . . .

Eliza rammed her knee into his groin.

He retched and staggered. She whirled and ran.

And collided with a tough-muscled body.

Mr. Todd trapped her in front of him, one warm arm around her waist. "Let's re-evaluate, shall we, William?"

Shock trickled ice water into her blood. Her heart pounded. How had he gotten free? Lafayette still struggled on the bench in his leather casing, but a wry smile turned his lips. A few feet away on the floor, next to Mr. Todd's unlocked shackles, lay a twisted sliver of dark metal.

A hair pin.

Her skin tingled with reluctant, black admiration. That lamp-lit book room, his fingers brushing her waist, the spidery walk of his breath across her loosened hair . . .

He'd wanted the pin. The rest of that tragic little scene? Academic. A tease. A lie.

Behind her, she felt him smile. She didn't need to see. She just knew.

She'd never get out of here alive.

Will coughed, sucking in his breath at last. His yellow eyes burned in jealous rage. "Give her back. Eliza, my love, come to me."

"Oh, I think not," remarked Todd carelessly. His grip on her waist shifted, and a metallic chill sparkled against her throat.

It warmed rapidly with her body heat. With a sinking stomach, she risked a glance at the plate of surgical instruments. One was missing. Not the scalpel. The long-bladed knife.

Irony choked her. *One makes do,* after all. *Trust me,* he'd said.

How she'd wanted to believe him.

"Here we are at last." Todd licked his lips, that tiny provocative sound. His scent—so many velvet memories—made her shiver and burn. "I confess, I've often dreamed about this. Since you kindly turned me over to your energetic friends at the Met, that is. And just when we were getting on *so* well."

Her primeval brain screeched nonsense. *Run! Scream! Fight! Roll over!* But none of it would save her. Not from him.

Or from herself.

But her breath hurt her chest, and she swallowed. She wasn't ready to die. "I had no choice."

Todd inhaled delicately, smelling her storm-damp hair. "Mmm. That's not true. You said unkind things about me, Eliza. A lesser man might want revenge."

"No!" Will's eyes glistened with tears, and he fumbled for his pistol. Long claws juddered from his thumbs, curling around the iron grip. His voice dived in pitch, a lisping growl. "It isn't fair. You can't have her. Not after all this. You promised. Give her back!"

"Don't be needy, William," scolded Todd. "It only makes you ugly and irritating. Come, we all know you won't shoot me. Especially not while I'm holding such a valuable shield."

Will cursed and clutched the pistol tighter. Sweat poured into patches of fur on his face. His nose had distorted into an inhuman snout with teeth curving up like tusks. "Don't make me angry, Mr. Todd," he snarled, a rain of spit flying. "Don't make me become this *thing*. Please, I just want her back. Give her to me."

Todd clicked his tongue, pretending to consider. "Seems high-handed, don't you think? I can't abide bad manners. What say . . . we leave it up to the lady?"

Eliza swallowed, a warm sting of steel. "That won't be necessary—"

"I'm afraid I must insist you choose." Todd laughed, as black and empty a sound as she'd ever heard. "You had your chance to end me, Eliza. You wasted it. Now, either you go with Will, and live a long and dismal life as that cold undead thing over there. Or, you stay with me"—he traced the knife lightly under her chin, a tiny electric shock—"and I carve your pretty flesh into a warm and lovely work of art."

———◆◆———

So it comes to this.

Shock didn't seem appropriate. Nor fear, nor despair. Ever since that warm velvet night in Chelsea, she'd known he'd be her death. No point crying about it now.

She choked on stupid laughter. That was something Lizzie might say. *You're screwed right and proper, missy, screwed to the wall, and you might as well just accept it.*

Whatever her fate, Lizzie would share it. It wasn't fair. What would Lizzie choose? Life at any cost? Or a swift end?

Overhead, lightning crashed, blinding. Current crackled along the dome's metal-studded struts. Behind her, Lafayette growled, a wolfish curse. Was he *changing,* in the storm's flashing fire, with wind whirling and thunder dragging madness from his blood? She felt half-mad herself, crazed, reckless.

Life as an undead monster? Or a quick death?

Will shook his ragged yellow hair, sweat flying on the wind. His face—that young, earnest face she'd been so fond of—had become but half a man's . . . yet still not fully warped by the beast inside. "Only you can save me, Eliza," he pleaded. "Without you, I can't control it. I can't make it stop. Be my perfect wife. Please."

And in a glassy flash of unreason, she knew what she must do.

She closed her eyes. Inhaled the stormy air once more, the tingle of power along her skin, the knife's sweet sting on her throat. Basked in Mr. Todd's strange-scented fever, imagined one more time trailing her lips over his silken hair. Listened to a few more beats of his secret heart.

Will screamed, coarse fur sprouting on his cheeks. "Stop it. Don't make me change. I don't like it. Don't . . ."

Heedless of the sharp knife, she twisted in Mr. Todd's embrace. Gazed up into his bloodshot green eyes, drank in his wild crimson locks, his sharp nose, the delicate lines of his chin. A stubborn knot in her heart dissolved—*melted,* a flood of breathless release—and if it was her common sense, or her will to resist, or just long months of pretending that died, she couldn't say.

She knew only that it felt right.

"Kill me." The whisper slipped out, gentle as her first sighing breath and as perfect.

Mr. Todd tightened his embrace, a secret space for them alone. Outside this magical bubble, the storm no doubt still raged, but Eliza heard nothing and no one.

"Thank you." His whisper brushed her cheekbone, alive like spelldust. He dipped his forehead to hers, a childlike gesture of surrender, and traced his blade point in sparkles down the vein in her throat. Her pulse swelled, searching, pleading, and entranced in a fairy-lit dream, she tilted her chin up . . .

Lightning slashed the sky, a hellish boom of thunder. The moment shattered, a magic mirror in shards. And Will howled, *aah-OOOH!* like a moonstruck fiend, and lost control.

His body strained and shuddered, fury upon stormlight upon hungry curse. His fangs crunched, spit dripping from mottled jaws. His arms erupted in muscle and fur, tearing his shirtsleeves to shreds. His hands contorted, his thumb joints popped backwards into *toes* . . . and the glittering pistol dropped from his grip.

And swift as a striking cobra, Mr. Todd hurled Eliza at him.

Crunch! She and Will collided, knocking her breath away. Will skidded backwards . . . and fell onto the metal frame atop Miss Lucy.

The frame swung under his weight, and he scrambled to climb off. But a snarling pile of fur and claws hurtled through the air and landed on top of Will, pinning him down. Lafayette, wolf-turned, his leather restraints burst apart.

The two beasts roared and dived for each other. Fangs clashed, and blood splattered in arcs.

Eliza dived for Will's fallen pistol. But Mr. Todd was quicker. With a snap of his wrist, he hurled his knife. It flew in a spinning steel arc and sliced a taut rope in half.

Twang! Whizz! A counterweight whistled downwards. And the metal frame hurtled skywards, taking Will and Lafayette with it.

Chains rattled, *zingg!!* Webs of ropes and wires snapped. The weight crashed into the floor, splinters flying. And the frame clanged into the iron-studded rafters and stuck there. The wolf-things snapped and clawed, drawing blood.

Crack! Lightning struck the dome. Bethlem quaked to its foundations. Blue fire crackled along the lightning rod and raced earthwards. Wolf-Lafayette roared and leapt into space, brandishing wicked claws.

He hit the grounding cable, and *ping!* it snapped. And blue electricity speared down the broken wire and stabbed Wolf-Will in the heart.

He screamed, his fur alight. Skin melting, muscles lique-fying, bones popping in extreme heat. The stink of burning flesh fell like rain, and Will and headless Miss Lucy roasted together into a black husk of charred meat.

Lafayette landed on all fours, *thud!* He arched his back to howl at the storm, and the triumphant storm howled back.

Dazed, Eliza backed off. The pistol slipped in her sweaty palms. Now what?

But Lafayette—always somehow "he," never "it"—just growled softly, tongue lolling. He paced a few steps, back and forth like a caged lion, his lean golden body rippling. His tail bristled and twitched, unsettled. One restless forepaw clawed the floor. His gaze never left hers all the while . . . but it shone clear, intelligent, impossibly blue.

And with a groan of cosmic surrender, the clouds broke and rain fell. Cold, diamond raindrops, pelting onto her up-turned face. The burning dome hissed, and static crackled, lighting the falling raindrops like a web of fairy lanterns.

Only then did Eliza jerk to her senses and glance around, her treacherous heart skipping all over again.

But the talented Mr. Todd was gone.

FIAT JUSTITIA RUAT CAELUM

•••

LATE AFTERNOON SUNLIGHT PEERED THROUGH THE window of Eliza's study, inquisitive. Pen stand and clock threw long, reddish shadows onto her desk. The fire had burned dim, and the tea Mrs. Poole had fetched sat cold on the tray, untouched.

The report on which she was working was lengthy and detailed, and she was finished at last. She signed her name— *Eliza Jekyll, M.D.*—blotted, and addressed an envelope: *Commissioner, Metropolitan Police, Great Scotland Yard.* Tucked the report inside. Sealed it and put down her inky fountain pen with a sigh.

In the end, she'd confined the report to pure forensic evidence. Never mind bothering Harley with the details. He had enough to deal with.

She'd attended Mrs. Griffin's funeral with a heavy heart. Another woman in a coffin, dead too soon. Harley was gutted, going through the motions, a corpse brought woodenly to life. Eliza had vowed she'd not let Inspector Reeve take the credit for his work. But the funeral had left her in a dark place, a shadowy tomb inhabited by the ghosts of dead women. Miss Lucy, Lady Fairfax, Irina Pavlova, Ophelia Maskelyne, Sally Fingers, Madeleine Jekyll. She knew they'd haunt her for a long time.

Death was death. You couldn't defeat it. You couldn't come back. Not without . . . *spoiling* something.

But the Commissioner would have her report in the morning, and it left no room for argument. The Chopper was dead. Case closed. End of story.

End of story, hell, whispered Lizzie dismissively. *You know this ain't over.*

Eliza shivered, though the room was over-warm. Will Sinclair had proved true to his word about one thing, at least. The drug he'd given her was temporary, and once it wore off, Lizzie had woken, bad-tempered and sore but intact.

But they'd searched the asylum up and down, high and low, in every gallery and twisting staircase and hidden corridor, under every sodden bush in the garden. Mr. Todd was gone. Skipped out into the storm and vanished, a stain of breath on glass. And next morning, when she'd awoken late, exhausted and bleary-eyed after that mind-bending night, she'd almost tumbled from her bed in shock.

On her pillow lay a single, perfect, long-stemmed rose. Crimson, the exact shade of Mr. Todd's hair. And beside it, on the pristine white linen, a single, perfect teardrop of blood.

That was a week ago.

She was still jumping at the tiniest sound, her pulse skipping at shadows, flickering lamps, unexpected chilly breezes. She'd barely slept. And in those moments when exhaustion did claim her, she dreamed. Sprinting along endless midnight streets, a nightmare city drenched in blood and fire. A monster breathing on the back of her neck, heartbeat in rhythm with hers, limbs moving in step, its distorted shadow hulking on the wall. Fingertips brushing her shoulder, a soft kiss on her cheek, the sweet scent of blood and starlight and wild red hair . . .

Rat-a-tat! A doorknock snapped her awake. She caught her breath. "Come."

Mrs. Poole strode in. "What kind of visiting hours do you call this?"

Eliza smiled weakly. "Quite. Could we start from the beginning?"

Mrs. Poole busied herself clearing the untouched tea tray. "There's a gentleman to call on you. Some presumptuous fellow. Shall I get rid of him?"

Her heart squeezed tight. "Who is it? Did he leave a card?"

"He left a pair of dazzling blue eyes and a grin fit to stun a horse. Is that enough?"

Faint bitterness stung her mouth. *Disappointed?* whispered Lizzie slyly. And Eliza had no answer.

She and Lafayette hadn't spoken since that night at Bethlem. What did he want? And from whom?

Her gaze fell once more upon her desk, where a second, unfinished letter sat. She'd addressed it simply to *The Philosopher, Royal Society, Tower of London.*

Sir,

With respect to your kind offer of 21st instant

That was all she had so far.

She chewed her lip, troubled. Mr. Hyde had killed Madeleine. Twice. Killed Henry, too, though proving *that* in a court of law would be a first. And he'd threatened her with the same fate. He deserved to be brought to justice. Protecting him would cost Eliza her career, and probably her life.

But he was her father. He'd cared for her and Lizzie all these years, asking nothing in return but to be left alone. In his twisted way, he loved her—both of her. Was it justice to condemn him for his sins, when she knew too well the dark temptations of her own shadow side?

Lizzie snorted derisively. *Whatever you say. You gonna let that mean old walking skeleton order us about? Screw him, and his brass-brained lackeys too.*

Resolved, Eliza picked up her pen once more.

With respect to your kind offer of 21st instant, I must make further investigation. Expect to hear from me in due course.

Yours, &c.
Dr. Eliza Jekyll

That would buy her some time. No matter her father's crimes, she couldn't betray him to save her own skin. Not to the Royal. Not to anyone. She'd just have to deal with the Philosopher when the time came. In the meantime, she'd conduct investigations of her own into what the King of Rats was up to. If he truly was plotting against the Royal, she'd discover it. And she had Lizzie to help her. It wasn't finished between Eliza Jekyll and Edward Hyde. Not by a long shot.

Eliza smoothed her hair and reluctantly headed downstairs. The delicious smell of warm pork pie drifted from the kitchen, but her appetite had long since withered.

The fire in her consulting room wasn't lit. Sun slanted through the blinds. On the mantel, in a narrow glass vase, Mr. Todd's rose still bloomed, unwilted. A solitary green thorn curled from the stem. The crimson petals were startling, incriminating. Passionate. Not a color associated with chaste courtship.

Lafayette stood tall, hands behind his back. Weapons polished, Royal Society badge bright on the breast of his scarlet tailcoat. He'd cut his hair, she noticed, but his curls already crept too long, and with a start she realized why. It must be difficult, staying presentable.

Her stomach parched, sick. He was intelligent. Amusing. Handsome. Had a refreshing lack of respect for propriety. Everything that made his acquaintance desirable, or at least acceptable. And at the sight of him, Lizzie's smile shone, filling her heart with liquid sunshine.

But it only made Eliza's guts twist tighter.

She nodded stiffly. "Captain, how good of you to call."

"Doctor." He wasn't fidgeting, not exactly—nothing so insecure—but did his gaze slip, just a fraction?

"Still with the Royal, I see." Had she expected him to quit? Things seemed different. But . . .

A gunflash smile. "I've lied to them this long. I confess I rather enjoy it."

"Still monsters to hunt?"

"Always."

"The world is alive with strangeness, Captain. May there be mythical foes aplenty in your future." She waited. "Well, if—"

"I could use a good crime scene investigator," he remarked, gazing out the window. "From time to time. Off the books, of course. The Royal doesn't take kindly to your flavor of meddling, madam. But in your case, I can make an exception."

Despite her misgivings, the prospect tantalized. The stranger the case, the better . . . "Are you offering me a job?"

A little grin. "For shame. Nothing so mundane. What I'm offering is a few hours of subterfuge, cutting-edge science, and deadly peril in your otherwise excruciatingly dull days of ham-fisted bludgeonings and idiots with arsenic. Sounds more outrageous that way."

"In that case," she said brightly, "how could a respectable lady refuse?"

"A respectable lady *would* refuse, madam. That's the point." His grin faded. "How is Griffin, by the way? I was sorry to hear. He's a decent fellow."

"He's . . . having a hard time. You know, I think he'd appreciate your call."

"Really?" A bashful shrug. "I had the idea I annoyed him."

She twisted her hands. "I'm sorry for what happened. That Will Sinclair was killed, I mean, before you had the chance to question him. I know you were counting on him for help."

"For a cure, you mean." This time, he looked directly at her. "It's different for me. We don't all cope as brilliantly as you."

She squirmed. She felt too much of what Lizzie felt. She didn't feel enough of it. "Listen, I know that Lizzie—"

"I didn't come to see Lizzie. I came to see you."

"Captain . . ." She saw his expression and broke off with a sigh. "Remy . . . I'm afraid this isn't going to work. Whatever you and she might . . ." She flushed. "We're not the same person, do you see? I mean, we are, but . . ."

"I understand that," said Lafayette softly. "Truly, I do. I won't embarrass you by asking what you remember. I only hope you can accept my apology. I am so desperately sorry, Eliza, that things happened this way."

How she longed to vanish. Fall into a suddenly yawning crevasse. Combust spontaneously. "Then what else is there to say?"

"Please, just hear me out. First a confession, then a promise. Finally, a request. If you don't like any of the three, I swear I'll never speak of it again. Fair?"

Numbly, she sat on the sofa and waved him to a chair.

Lafayette didn't sit. Didn't pace or fidget. Just stood straight, square, fearless. "You once asked me why I fled India for England. I told you I killed someone." He swallowed. "The person I killed was my wife."

Eliza stared. She should feel disgust, or horror, or fear. But all she could feel was a pale reflection of the pain he must have suffered. She knew what it was like, to want to tear your own insides out. And Lizzie knew the same.

For the time being, she and Lizzie were reconciled. But what in the future? They wanted different things. Adventure. Safety. Independence. Love. What would Eliza do when . . . ?

"I couldn't control what I'd become," admitted Lafayette, "and I destroyed what I should have treasured most of all. I vowed with her blood on my hands that I would learn to control it or die trying. And I make you that promise now. I won't ever hurt you, Eliza. I cannot. I'll die first. And that goes for Lizzie, too."

"I see." She licked dry lips, seasick. That was heartfelt. Romantic, even.

"You think you're speechless now." A wry grin. "I haven't finished."

"Do your worst, sir. I warn you, I don't shock easily."

"I've noticed." He took a steadying breath. "We can help each other, you and I. You can help me find a cure while we hunt monsters and miscreants. I can protect you from the Royal, and from any other idiot who decides to meddle in your affairs. And I don't mean to be crude, but there's also the matter of a sizable pile of money, which I have and you could surely put to use."

Oh, no. Eliza's brain froze. *No no no . . .*

"I understand that you don't appreciate interference," he added. No flicker in his courage, no glimmer of doubt. "And I'd be the last man to intrude where I'm not wanted. But alone, you and I are oddities. We attract unwelcome attention. Together, we're respectable. Untouchable, even. And curse me for a self-punishing fool, but I rather enjoy your company."

All Eliza's instincts implored her to speak, say anything, stop him before he said more. He was rational. Mathematical. He made perfect, terrifying sense.

But on the mantel, Mr. Todd's crimson rose bloomed. Vibrant, fresh, its passion undimmed.

Lizzie held a warning breath.

And for once in her life, Eliza couldn't find a single thing to say.

IN UMBRIS POTESTAS EST

...

AFTER SUNSET, NEW OXFORD STREET SPRINGS alive. Shoppers, thieves, clockwork carriages and clattering hooves. Along the sidewalk, fine ladies and their gentlemen promenade in expensive suits and silken skirts, crinolines and stoles of every shade.

Alone, the crowd parting around him out of some primitive collective instinct, strolls Mr. Todd.

Inhaling the scents, tasting the sky. His scars are healing quickly, and already his time in the asylum has faded, washed thin like an inked sketch abandoned in the rain. The air is fresh now, after the stormy weather, and the clean smells of stone and rain are miraculous. The city's chattering melodies shed welcome ease on his music-starved ears. He wears a new suit—black, all the better to blend in—and the crispness of the fine wool and linen pleases him.

But most of all, he's *watching*.

After so many months in hueless squalor, the colors make him weep. Mr. Todd lives in a world of rainbows, and to deprive him of color is crueler torture than any electroshock. Innumerable shades breathe on his skin, tingling, stimulating.

A glaring chartreuse skirt; a pile of cerise roses on a cart; a young lady's eyes, so ultramarine, his mouth waters. He can stare for hours at a single subtle shift in shade. Some might call that insane.

Bethlem hasn't tarnished his manners. He touches his hat to the girl and smiles. She flushes, avoiding his gaze.

Decent people—self-appointed, naturally—look away from Mr. Todd because his red hair is threatening and he thinks bright thoughts and smiles just so. As if by existing, he's somehow scandalous. Briefly, he imagines this girl sliced and bleeding, her warm wet breath on his cheek, the slick soft-ness of her lips as she dies . . . But it's all wrong, a pointless brushstroke that must be erased before the paint sets. He walks on.

A courtesan dressed as a lady slants her painted lashes at him. His glance slides over her and on. The idea of her hurts, faintly, like prodding an old bruise. Across the street, a pair of clockwork Enforcers strut along in line. There are more of them now than before. The way the light strikes their brass chassis offends him, and he looks away.

Into the darker parts of town, now, where the smells of decay reign amidst dirt and pain. Black is thicker here, true black, the absence of light, in hovels and fireless tenements, down stinking alleys where no sunlight ever shines. He enjoys a dark frisson of delight. Mr. Shadow likes stark contrasts, black and vermilion and blinding white, and Mr. Todd and Mr. Shadow have partnered in the dance so long, he barely recalls what it's like to walk alone.

In a doorway, a dog snarls. Children wail like vermin. A woman staggers, drunk, her skirts flapping with mud. A public house shines from the gloom, firelight leaking beneath the shabby door.

Inside, drinkers carouse, and Mr. Todd threads through to a quiet area at the back. The man he's come to see slouches on a bench, a tankard of beer at ease in his hand. His suit is burnt umber, his hat the color of coal dust. In the corner slouches his sidekick, a handsome black-haired fellow in a hyacinth-blue coat, to whom Mr. Shadow takes an instinctive dislike. The fellow tastes odd. Hostile, his crooked eyes dark with challenge. An enemy.

Neatly, Mr. Todd sits. "Mr. H."

Mr. H grins, his bent nose twisting. "Malachi Todd, my boy. Heard you were back in the land of the living." His voice abrades the skin like sandpaper, unsettling.

Todd just smiles thinly. He has reason to be careful here.

"Drink?" Mr. H offers absinthe and cognac, as always. Its mottled hue fascinates, swirling emerald and burnt sunset gold, hypnotic . . . and then the substances mix and the subtlety is lost.

Mr. Todd drinks. Liquid fire, the flavor of guilt and sorrow. The memory is startling.

The other man's stormy eyes miss nothing. "Work to be done, sunshine. There be restless days ahead. In the meantime, I've got a thing for you."

"I expected as much." But his pulse quickens. Despite the drink, his mouth is dry. Just a taste, he'd had, in that aether-bright laboratory with sweet Eliza in his arms. That surgical knife was blunted, coarse, ugly. Not the real thing. Not the truth.

Mr. H places *it* on the table.

Breathless, Todd reaches for it. The polished silver steel is light, cool in his palm. He lets it slip to his fingertips and flicks it open. *Ping!* Firelight kisses the whetted edge. His eyelids flutter, and he recalls with utter clarity a single drop of Eliza's blood. How it glistened. How it tasted . . .

"Have fun. I'll be in touch." Mr. H doesn't lay hands on him, but his voice holds Mr. Todd in place as stiffly as any rusted shackle. "One thing more, sunshine."

"Say on." Todd lets his tone glimmer. He doesn't like threats. And it isn't what Mr. H thinks.

Mr. H's eyes glint, beastly. "Stay away from my daughter. She's not for you."

Secretively, Todd smiles. He flicks the razor closed—how he's missed that perfect, melodic chord—and makes it disappear into the sleeve of his new coat. His dull, unremarkable coat. The one that makes him look exactly like everyone else.

But Eliza will know him. Eliza sees him when no one else does. And Mr. Todd plans to show her just how exquisitely— just how painfully—he loves her.

Because when you're special—when you lurk as a shadow in a world filled with rainbows—love aches. And screams. And bleeds.

"Edward, I assure you," says Mr. Todd, tipping his hat with one fingertip, "nothing could be further from my mind."

· AUTHOR'S NOTE ·

A BRIEF HISTORICAL NOTE,
IN WHICH THE AUTHOR HUMBLY JUSTIFIES
HER ANACHRONISMS

As with every fantasy, the corresponding truth is at least as fantastic. Eliza and Lizzie's world was inspired by a few delightful (and a few sobering) historical curiosities:

The real Sir Isaac Newton (knighted for his modernization of the Royal Mint, and not, as is often supposed, for his staggering scientific achievement) is almost certainly dead, and never discovered *aqua vitae,* the secret of eternal life. He did, however, believe he'd discovered the Philosopher's Stone: the substance that transmutes lead into gold. Newton's subsequent realization that his meticulous alchemical methodology was flawed—that he had, after all, reduced God to Laplace's famous "unnecessary hypothesis"—pushed the greatest mind of the age around the bend, into what we'd today call a nervous breakdown. But Sir Isaac had the courage of his scientific convictions: on his deathbed, he is said to have rejected the sacrament, and died an atheist.

Eliza's world is teeming with revolutionaries, and the real world wasn't so different. It's popular to romanticize the early nineteenth century, but like much of Europe, England was a totalitarian police state. The radical Thistlewood Club is fictional, but reform clubs of this nature existed, and were forced underground by anti-radical laws passed in the wake of the French Revolution and mass demonstrations in England demanding what we'd now call human rights. Publishers like my fictional Matthew Temple were arrested. Any large meeting to discuss political reform was deemed an "overt act of treasonable conspiracy," punishable by death, and deep infiltration of government spies in radical circles created a climate of suspicion and terror.

The eponymous Mr. Thistlewood himself was hanged and beheaded (just in case?) in 1820 for his part in the Cato Street Conspiracy, a badly botched attempted revolution oddly reminiscent of the more famous Gunpowder Plot, both for its audacity in planning to blow up the entire British Cabinet and for the fact that it was masterminded in part by a government *agent provocateur*—an example of how perilous, even for a seasoned political pest like Thistlewood, it was to be radical in nineteenth-century England. By the end of the 1820s, it appears that almost every important radical leader in England was either dead, in prison, or transported to Australia—one reason why the Continental "Year of Revolution" in 1848 (which in the real world, sadly, wasn't incited by sorcerers) never took root in England, while Australia had its own working-class rebellion at the Eureka Stockade in 1854 and continues merrily to celebrate rebels and outlaws to this day.

Thought crime was an ugly reality in England. The anti-

Jacobin Treasonable and Seditious Practices Act of 1795 made it high treason even to imagine deposing the King: republican thoughts could get you hanged. Happily, republicanism is today merely punishable by life imprisonment, and it's unlikely ever to be prosecuted as treason again.

But scientific radicalism was just as provocative. Political radicals often preached iconoclastic theories such as Lamarckian evolution, which contradicted Church of England teachings. The 1859 publication of *On the Origin of Species*—the culmination after two centuries of Newton's scientific deconstruction of God—re-opened the door for Enlightenment principles that had been ridiculed as dangerous folly since Robespierre *et al.* made such an unfortunate scene. Still, so far as I know, the real Royal Society never tortured or burned anyone for scientific heresy, and Michael Faraday died of natural causes.

In Eliza's world, social reforms are long overdue. In the real world, partial reform was grudgingly passed in 1832, with England on the brink of its own Bastille. It took thirty more years and firebrand Benjamin Disraeli to push through the basic rights that the demonstrators of the 1820s had risked hanging for—votes without property, regular elections, "one vote, one value"—and Disraeli's party promptly lost the election their reform legislation demanded.

I've taken liberties with London, especially with the layout of Bethlem Hospital (popularly known as Bedlam; today the building houses the Imperial War Museum) and the streets of Seven Dials (now a trendy shopping district and not the stinking rookery made famous by Charles Dickens). Marcellus Finch's shop at 143 New Bond Street is actually the old pharmacy of Savory and Moore, of which the original façade can still be seen, albeit with a different kind of store inside. If you go to Russell Square, you can still see the town house in which Eliza might have lived.

The real Maskelyne family, those celebrated stage magicians of the Egyptian Hall whose tricks included levitation but not disappearing, never claimed anyone named Lysander or Ophelia. The electrical experiment with the murderer Forster's corpse is real; Dr. Percival's is not. A prototype pneumatic railway was indeed built in London in the 1840s, but it never caught on and Mr. Paxton (architect of the fabled Crystal Palace, which unfortunately burned to the ground at Sydenham in 1936) never built one across the Thames. Electric trains weren't used in the Underground until the 1890s, and sadly, the fabulously named "luminiferous aether" does not exist.

Likewise, crime scene science wasn't invented until the late nineteenth century; there were no recognized female medical practitioners in England until 1865; and it's unlikely that Henry Jekyll and Victor Frankenstein even lived in the same time period, let alone worked together. Such happy absurdities, as well as any genuine errors, are my own.

· ACKNOWLEDGMENTS ·

My agent, Marlene Stringer, who liked the idea, and waited. My editor, Kelly O'Connor, and the team at HarperCollins, who took a chance on Eliza and Lizzie, and wrapped them in such a saucy little package.

I could go on, but let's just round up the usual suspects and be done: all my friends who read, encourage, support, flatter, wheedle, cajole, and commiserate to make me the writer I am. I could name you all, but you'd only stutter and blush. You know who you are, and what you did.

• ABOUT THE AUTHOR •

Viola Carr was born in a strange and distant land, but wandered into darkest London one foggy October evening and never found her way out. She now devours countless history books and dictates fantastical novels by gaslight, accompanied by classical music and the snores of her slumbering cat.

2-15